Vampire Kisses

GRAVEYARD GAMES

Ellen Schreiber
Art by Xian Nu Studio

HAMBURG // LONDON // LOS ANGELES // TOKYO

KATHERINE TEGEN BOOKS
An Imprint of HarperCollins Publishers

Vampire Kisses: Graveyard Games

By Ellen Schreiber

Art by Xian Nu Studio

Adapted by Barbara Randal Kesel

Editors - Lillian Diaz-Przybyl and Julie Lansky
Lettering - John Hunt
Cover Design - Louis Csontos

Print Production Manager - Lucas Rivera
Managing Editor - Vy Nguyen
Senior Designer - Louis Csontos
Director of Sales and Manufacturing - Allyson De Simone
Associate Publisher - Marco F. Pavia
President and C.O.O. - John Parker
C.E.O. and Chief Creative Officer - Stu Levy

A TOKYOPOP® Manga

TOKYOPOP Inc.
5900 Wilshire Blvd., Suite 2000
Los Angeles, CA 90036

This manga is a work of fiction. Any resemblance to actual events or locales or persons, living or dead, is entirely coincidental.

For information address HarperCollins Children's Books, a division of HarperCollins Publishers,
10 East 53rd Street, New York, NY 10022.
www.epicreads.com

Library of Congress catalog card number: 2010939047
ISBN 978-0-06-202672-9

20 21 22 23 24 LP/LSC 10 9 8 7 6 5 4
❖
First Edition

CONTENTS

Welcome to DULLSVILLE

MEET RAVEN MADISON: SPORTING BLACK LIPSTICK, BLACK NAIL POLISH, AND A SHARP WIT, RAVEN IS AN OUTSIDER AT CONSERVATIVE DULLSVILLE HIGH. CURIOUS AND FEARLESS, SHE'S NOT AFRAID TO TAKE ON ANYONE, FROM GOSSIPING GIRLS TO EVEN SCARIER, NEFARIOUS CREATURES OF THE NIGHT. AMAZINGLY, RAVEN'S GREATEST WISH HAS COME TRUE—SHE'S DATING A REAL VAMPIRE. THE ONLY PROBLEM IS THAT SHE HAS TO WAIT UNTIL SUNDOWN TO SEE HIM AND MUST KEEP HIS TRUE IDENTITY A SECRET.

MEET ALEXANDER STERLING: HANDSOME AND ELUSIVE, ALEXANDER IS THE TEEN VAMPIRE OF RAVEN'S DREAMS. HE LIVES IN A MANSION ON TOP OF BENSON HILL, AND ONLY EMERGES AT NIGHT. A SENSITIVE ARTIST, THIS PALE PRINCE OF DARKNESS HAS SOULFUL EYES AND A HEART TO MATCH. HE IS WITTY WITH A MACABRE SENSE OF HUMOR, BUT KIND AND GENTLE WHEN IT COMES TO RAVEN. WHEN RAVEN FINDS HERSELF IN TROUBLE, HE'S THE FIRST ONE TO SPRING TO HER DEFENSE.

MEET BECKY MILLER: RAVEN'S ONLY GIRLFRIEND, BECKY IS MORE SHY AND RESERVED THAN HER GOTHIC COUNTERPART. SINCE MEETING IN THE THIRD GRADE, RAVEN HAS BEEN BECKY'S BEST FRIEND AND BODYGUARD, PROTECTING HER FROM NAME CALLING AND PLAYGROUND CLASHES. BECKY OFTEN FINDS HERSELF EMBROILED IN RAVEN'S MISADVENTURES, BUT THESE DAYS SHE HAS SOME EXCITEMENT OF HER OWN. SHE'S HEAD OVER HEELS IN LOVE WITH MATT WELLS, A POPULAR BUT GOOD-HEARTED GUY AT SCHOOL WHOM SHE'S STARTED DATING.

MEET CLAUDE STERLING: CLAUDE IS ALEXANDER'S HOT AND OFTEN HOTHEADED, NEWLY TRANSFORMED, FULL VAMPIRE COUSIN. SINCE BIRTH, CLAUDE HAS HAD ONE THING ON HIS MIND—BECOMING A FULL VAMPIRE. AND NOW THAT CLAUDE AND HIS ROMANIAN GANG HAVE FOUND WHAT THEY ARE LOOKING FOR IN DULLSVILLE—VIALS OF PURE VAMPIRE BLOOD—THEY CAN FINALLY RETURN HOME. UNLESS CLAUDE HAS OTHER IDEAS IN MIND...

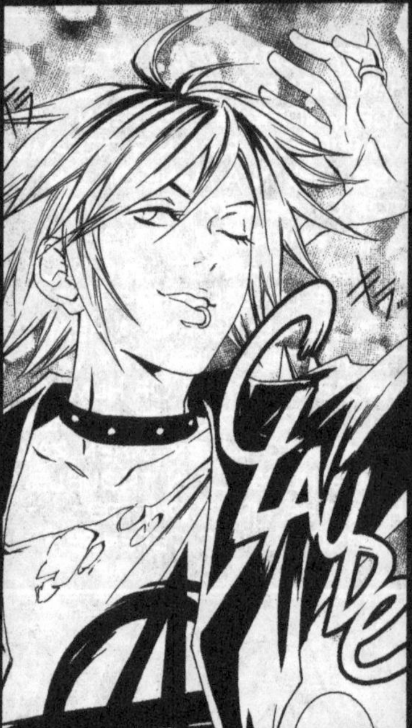
CLAUDE

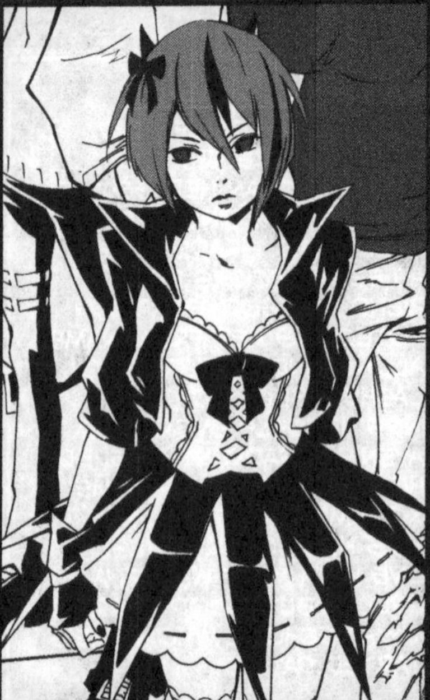

MEET KAT: SULTRY AND DECEPTIVE, KAT IS CLAUDE'S RIGHT-HAND GIRL. SHE USES HER CATLIKE BEGUILES TO CREATE A WEDGE BETWEEN RAVEN AND ALEXANDER. THOUGH SHE'S OFTEN FOUND FILING HER NAILS, SHE'S ONE TOUGH COOKIE AND HATES PLAYING BACKSEAT WHEN PLANS ARE BEING MADE.

MEET ROCCO: THE MUSCLE OF CLAUDE'S GANG, ROCCO WOULD RATHER BE THROWING PUNCHES THAN USING BRAINPOWER TO HELP OUT HIS FRIENDS. ROCCO USUALLY LETS CLAUDE LEAD THE WAY—EVEN IF IT MIGHT BE IN THE WRONG DIRECTION.

MEET TRIPP: THE BRAINS IN CLAUDE'S GANG, TRIPP CONTRIBUTES HIS TECHNO-SAVVY SKILLS TO HELP WHEN NEEDED. NOT ONE WITH MUCH BRAWN, TRIPP IS USUALLY THE FIRST TO HIDE BEHIND ROCCO WHEN DANGER LOOMS NEAR—THOUGH BECOMING A FULL VAMPIRE HAS GIVEN TRIPP A NEW CONFIDENCE.

MEET TREVOR: RAVEN'S KHAKI-CLAD NEMESIS, TREVOR IS GORGEOUS, RICH, AND A SUPER-JOCK. SO WHAT'S NOT TO LIKE? HIS PERSONALITY. SINCE KINDERGARTEN, TREVOR'S BEEN BENT ON MAKING LIFE MISERABLE FOR RAVEN. HE'D NEVER ADMIT IT, BUT HE'S MORE ATTRACTED TO HER THAN REPULSED AND HAS HAD A CRUSH ON HER SINCE THEY WERE KIDS. WHEN TREVOR'S NOT DOMINATING THE SOCCER FIELD, HE'S USUALLY STARTING RUMORS OR PESTERING RAVEN, HIS "MONSTER GIRL."

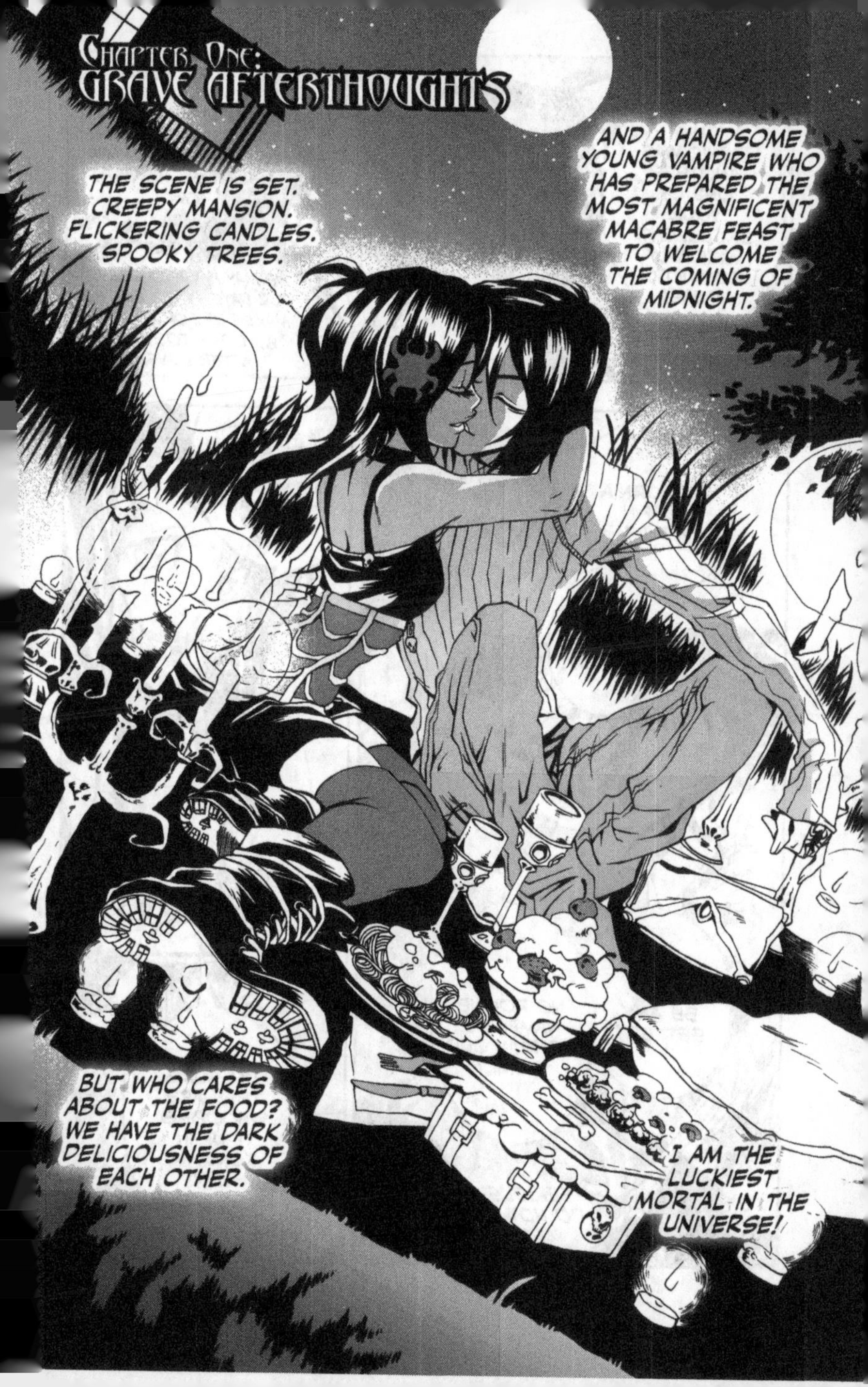
CHAPTER ONE:
GRAVE AFTERTHOUGHTS
THE SCENE IS SET. CREEPY MANSION. FLICKERING CANDLES. SPOOKY TREES.
AND A HANDSOME YOUNG VAMPIRE WHO HAS PREPARED THE MOST MAGNIFICENT MACABRE FEAST TO WELCOME THE COMING OF MIDNIGHT.
BUT WHO CARES ABOUT THE FOOD? WE HAVE THE DARK DELICIOUSNESS OF EACH OTHER.
I AM THE LUCKIEST MORTAL IN THE UNIVERSE!

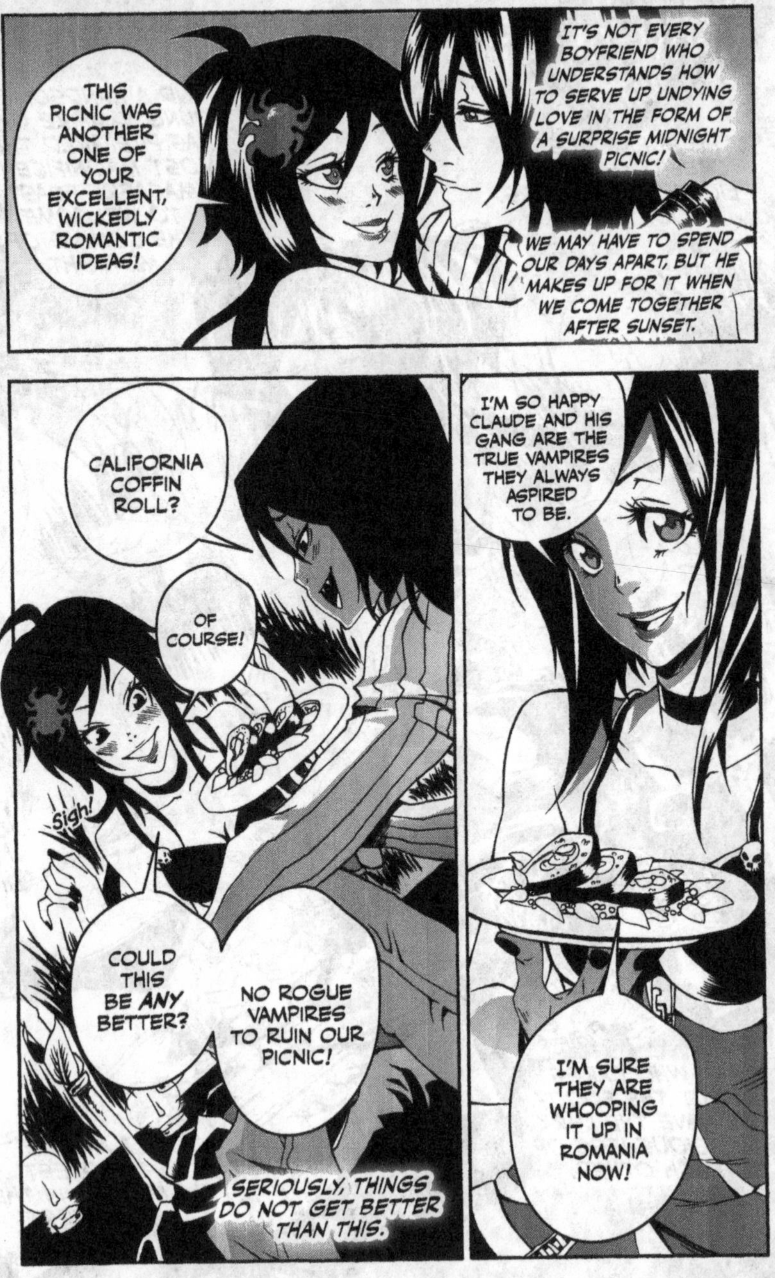
THIS PICNIC WAS ANOTHER ONE OF YOUR EXCELLENT, WICKEDLY ROMANTIC IDEAS!
IT'S NOT EVERY BOYFRIEND WHO UNDERSTANDS HOW TO SERVE UP UNDYING LOVE IN THE FORM OF A SURPRISE MIDNIGHT PICNIC!
WE MAY HAVE TO SPEND OUR DAYS APART, BUT HE MAKES UP FOR IT WHEN WE COME TOGETHER AFTER SUNSET.
CALIFORNIA COFFIN ROLL?
OF COURSE!
Sigh!
COULD THIS BE ANY BETTER?
NO ROGUE VAMPIRES TO RUIN OUR PICNIC!
SERIOUSLY, THINGS DO NOT GET BETTER THAN THIS.
I'M SO HAPPY CLAUDE AND HIS GANG ARE THE TRUE VAMPIRES THEY ALWAYS ASPIRED TO BE.
I'M SURE THEY ARE WHOOPING IT UP IN ROMANIA NOW!

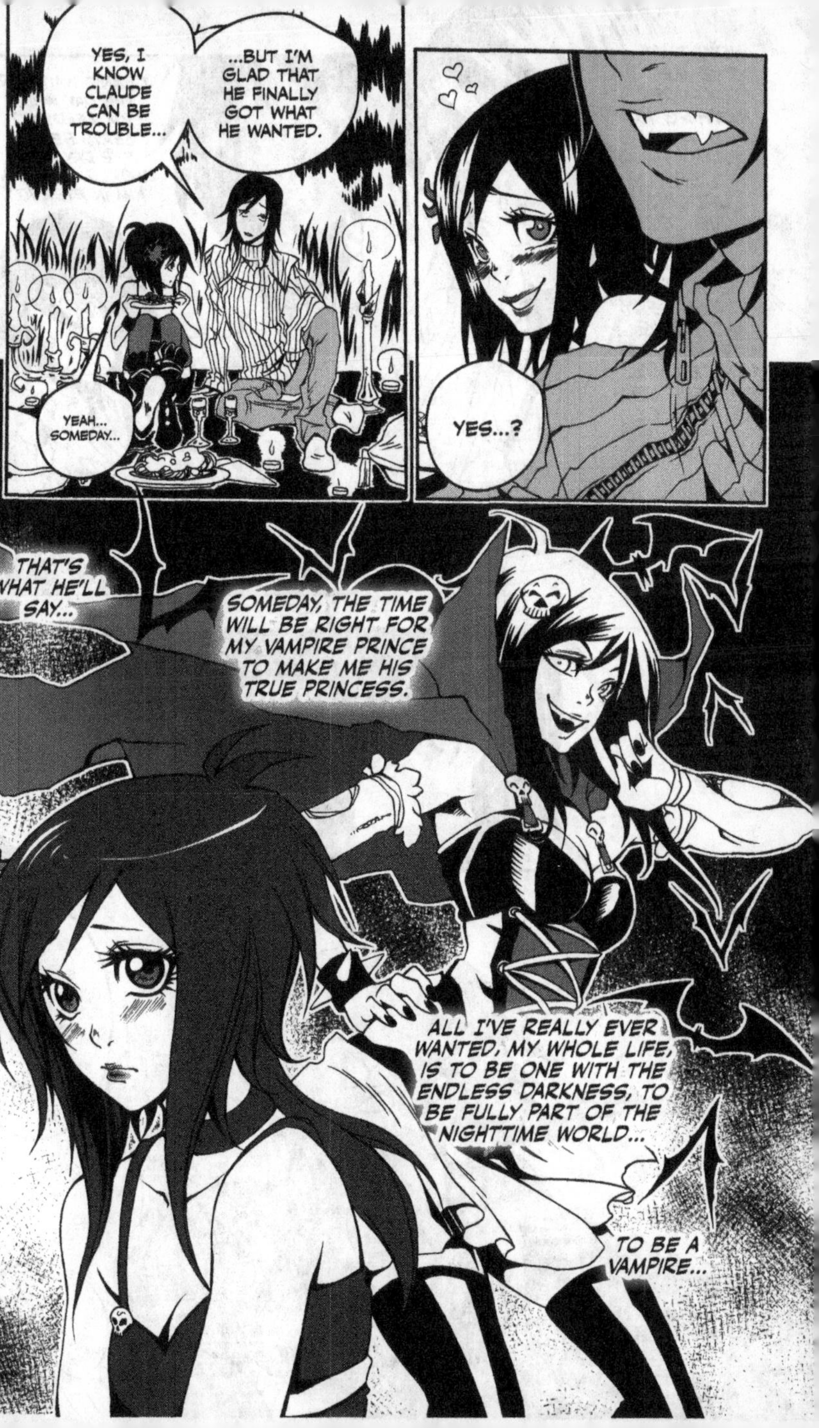
YES, I KNOW CLAUDE CAN BE TROUBLE...
...BUT I'M GLAD THAT HE FINALLY GOT WHAT HE WANTED.
YEAH... SOMEDAY...
YES...?
THAT'S WHAT HE'LL SAY...
SOMEDAY, THE TIME WILL BE RIGHT FOR MY VAMPIRE PRINCE TO MAKE ME HIS TRUE PRINCESS.
ALL I'VE REALLY EVER WANTED, MY WHOLE LIFE, IS TO BE ONE WITH THE ENDLESS DARKNESS, TO BE FULLY PART OF THE NIGHTTIME WORLD...
TO BE A VAMPIRE...

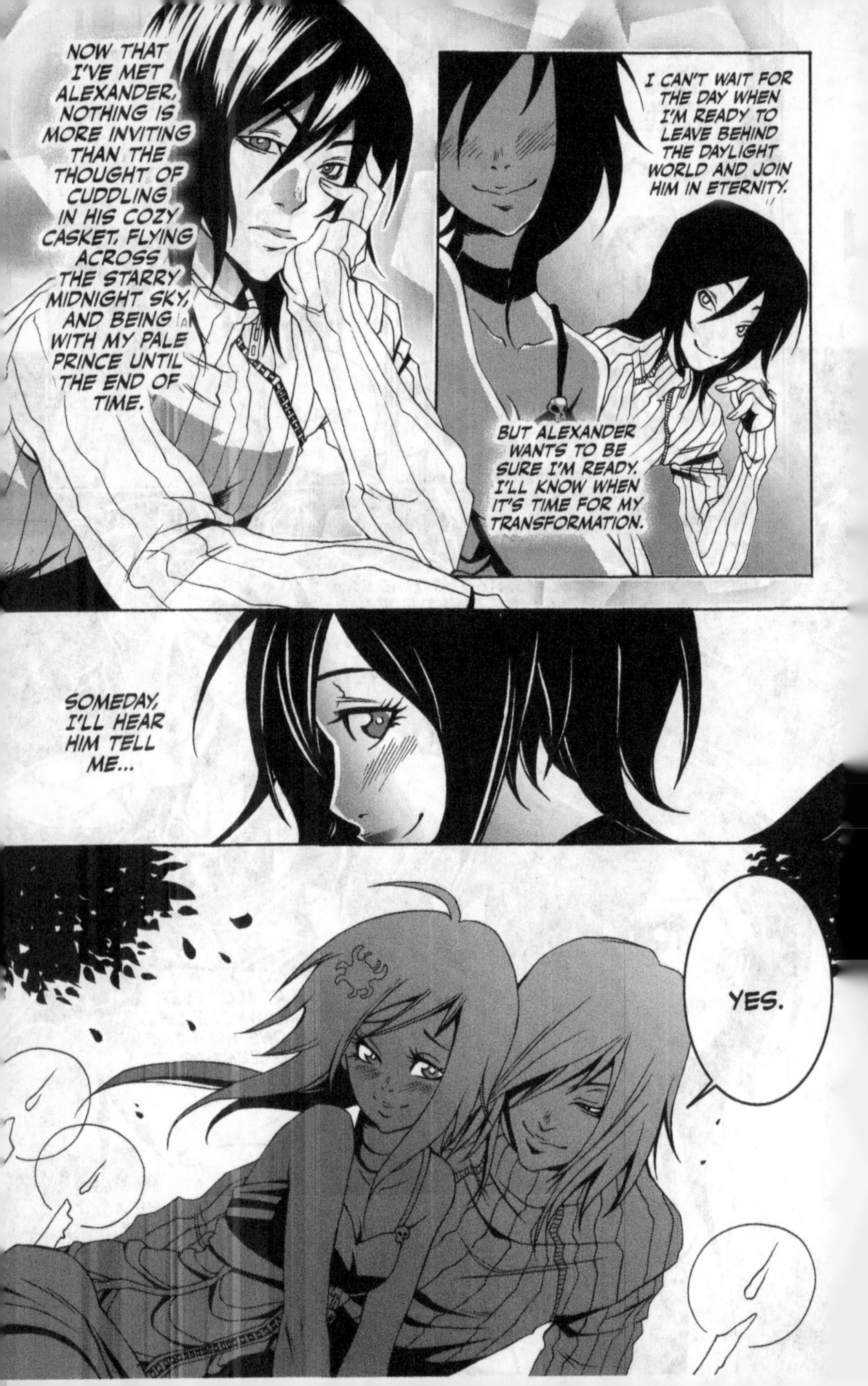
NOW THAT I'VE MET ALEXANDER, NOTHING IS MORE INVITING THAN THE THOUGHT OF CUDDLING IN HIS COZY CASKET, FLYING ACROSS THE STARRY MIDNIGHT SKY, AND BEING WITH MY PALE PRINCE UNTIL THE END OF TIME.
I CAN'T WAIT FOR THE DAY WHEN I'M READY TO LEAVE BEHIND THE DAYLIGHT WORLD AND JOIN HIM IN ETERNITY.
BUT ALEXANDER WANTS TO BE SURE I'M READY. I'LL KNOW WHEN IT'S TIME FOR MY TRANSFORMATION.
SOMEDAY, I'LL HEAR HIM TELL ME...
YES.

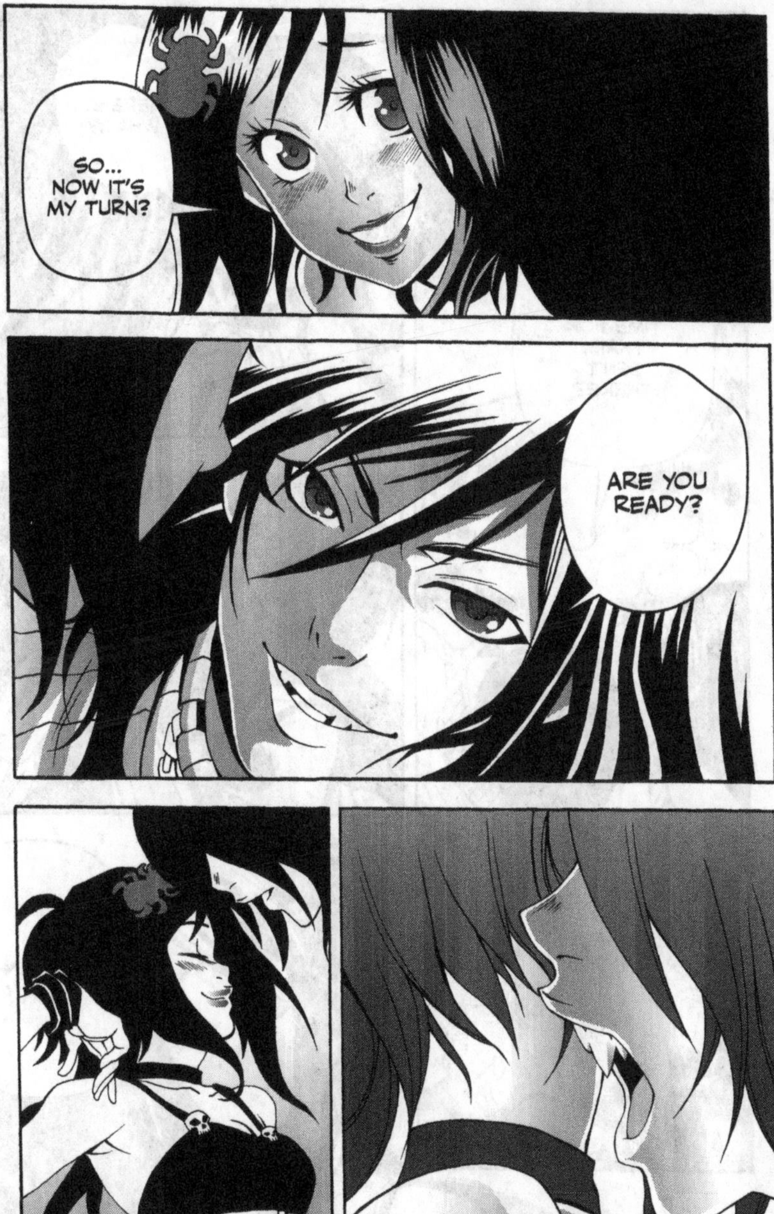
SO... NOW IT'S MY TURN?
ARE YOU READY?

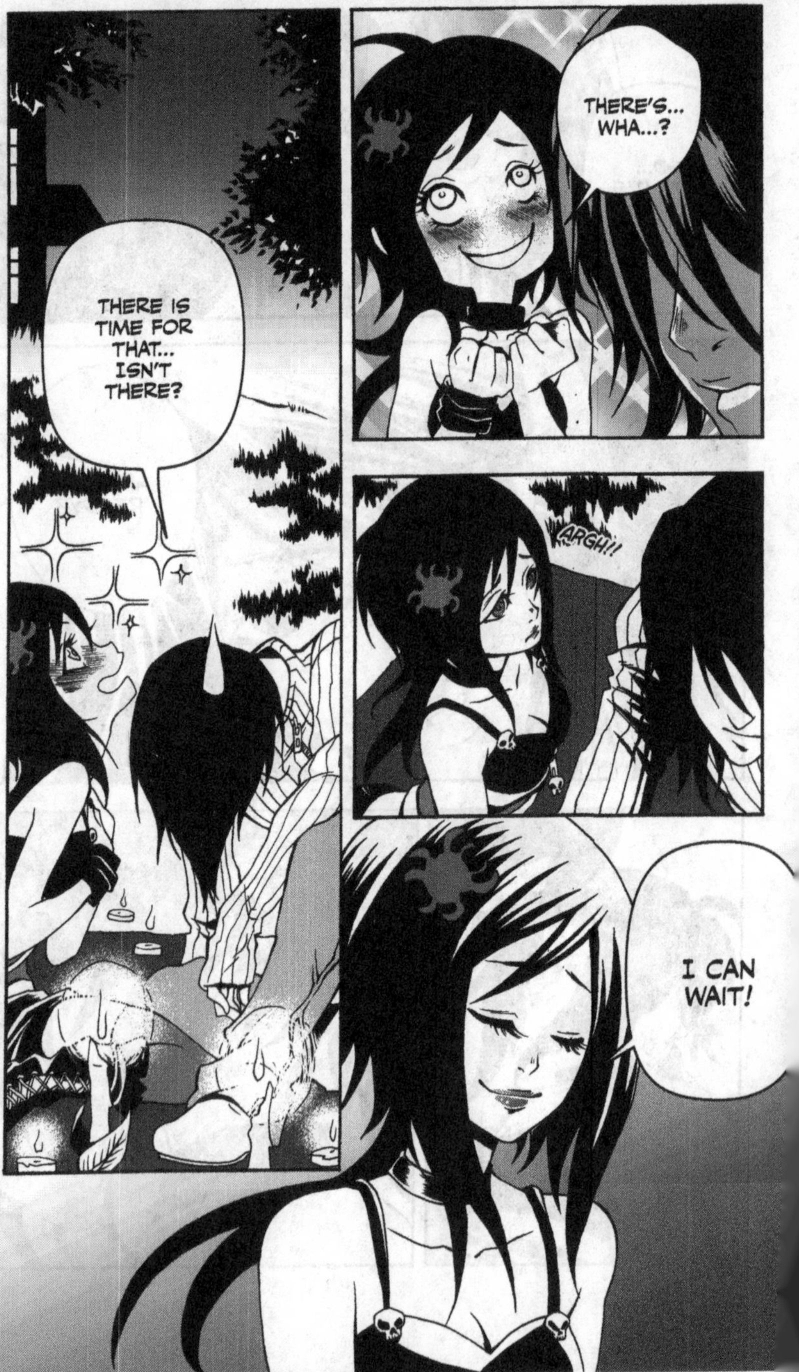
THERE IS TIME FOR THAT... ISN'T THERE?
THERE'S... WHA...?
ARGH!!
I CAN WAIT!

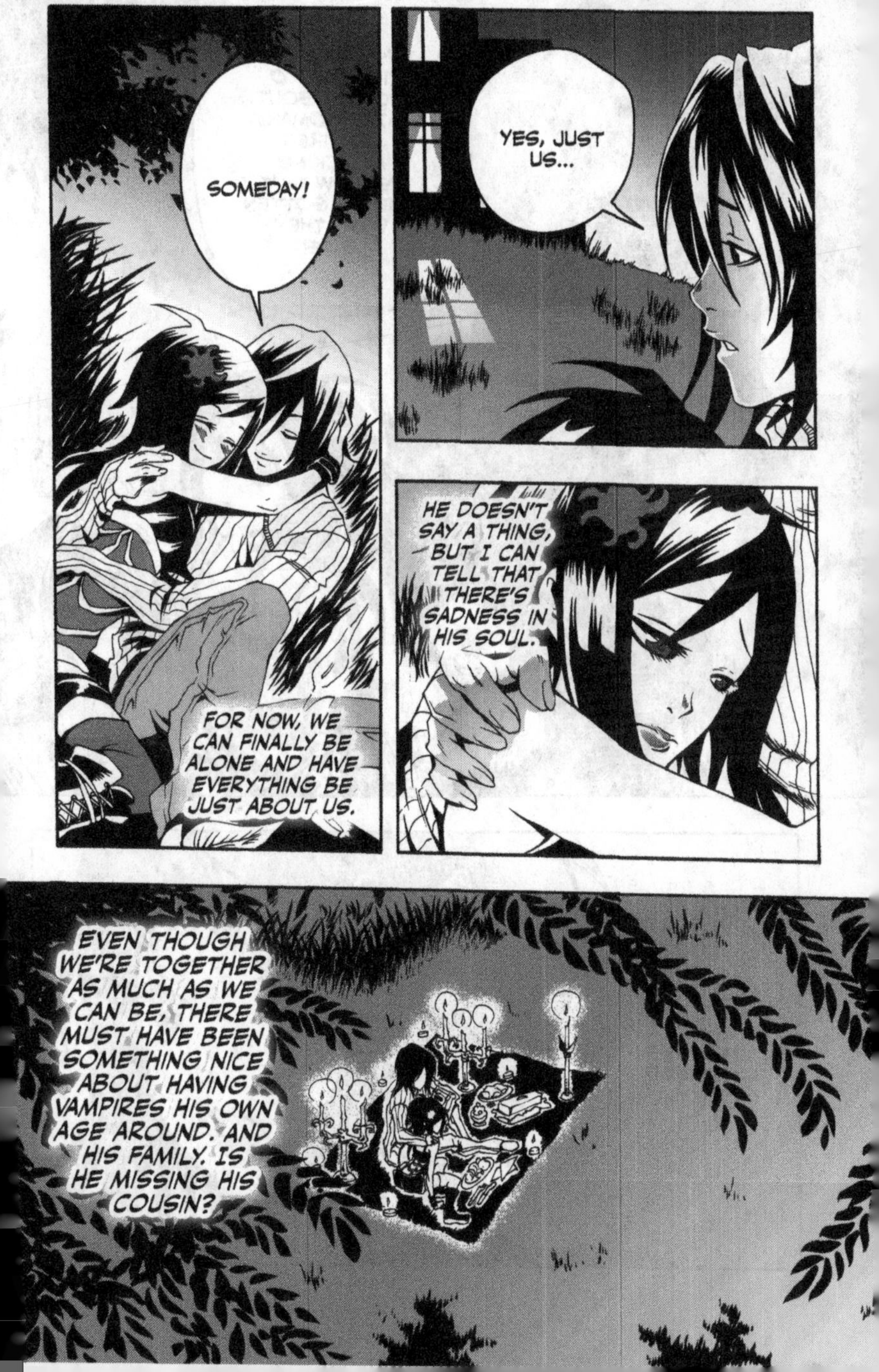
SOMEDAY!
FOR NOW, WE CAN FINALLY BE ALONE AND HAVE EVERYTHING BE JUST ABOUT US.
YES, JUST US...
HE DOESN'T SAY A THING, BUT I CAN TELL THAT THERE'S SADNESS IN HIS SOUL.
EVEN THOUGH WE'RE TOGETHER AS MUCH AS WE CAN BE, THERE MUST HAVE BEEN SOMETHING NICE ABOUT HAVING VAMPIRES HIS OWN AGE AROUND. AND HIS FAMILY. IS HE MISSING HIS COUSIN?

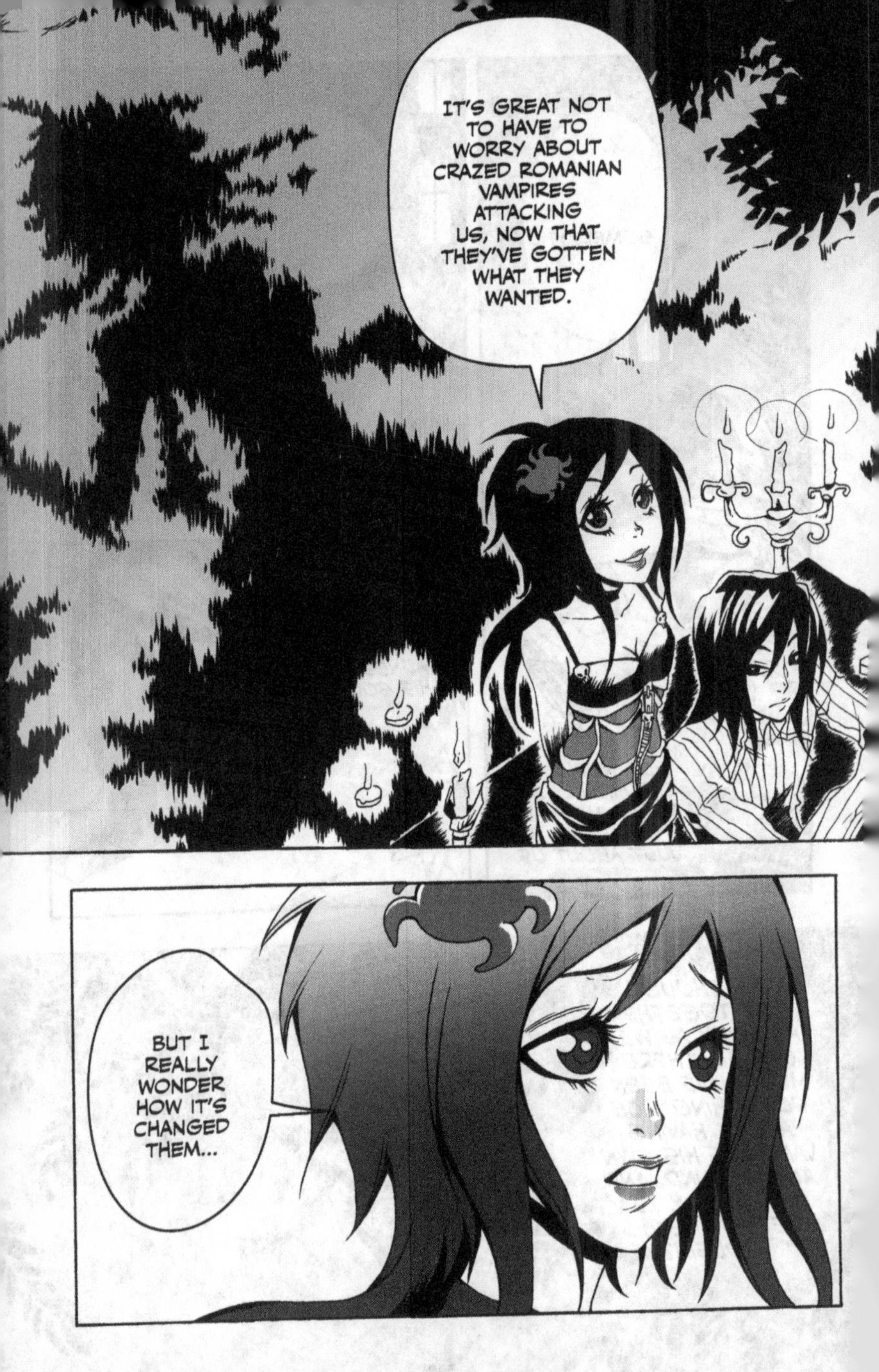
IT'S GREAT NOT TO HAVE TO WORRY ABOUT CRAZED ROMANIAN VAMPIRES ATTACKING US, NOW THAT THEY'VE GOTTEN WHAT THEY WANTED.
BUT I REALLY WONDER HOW IT'S CHANGED THEM...

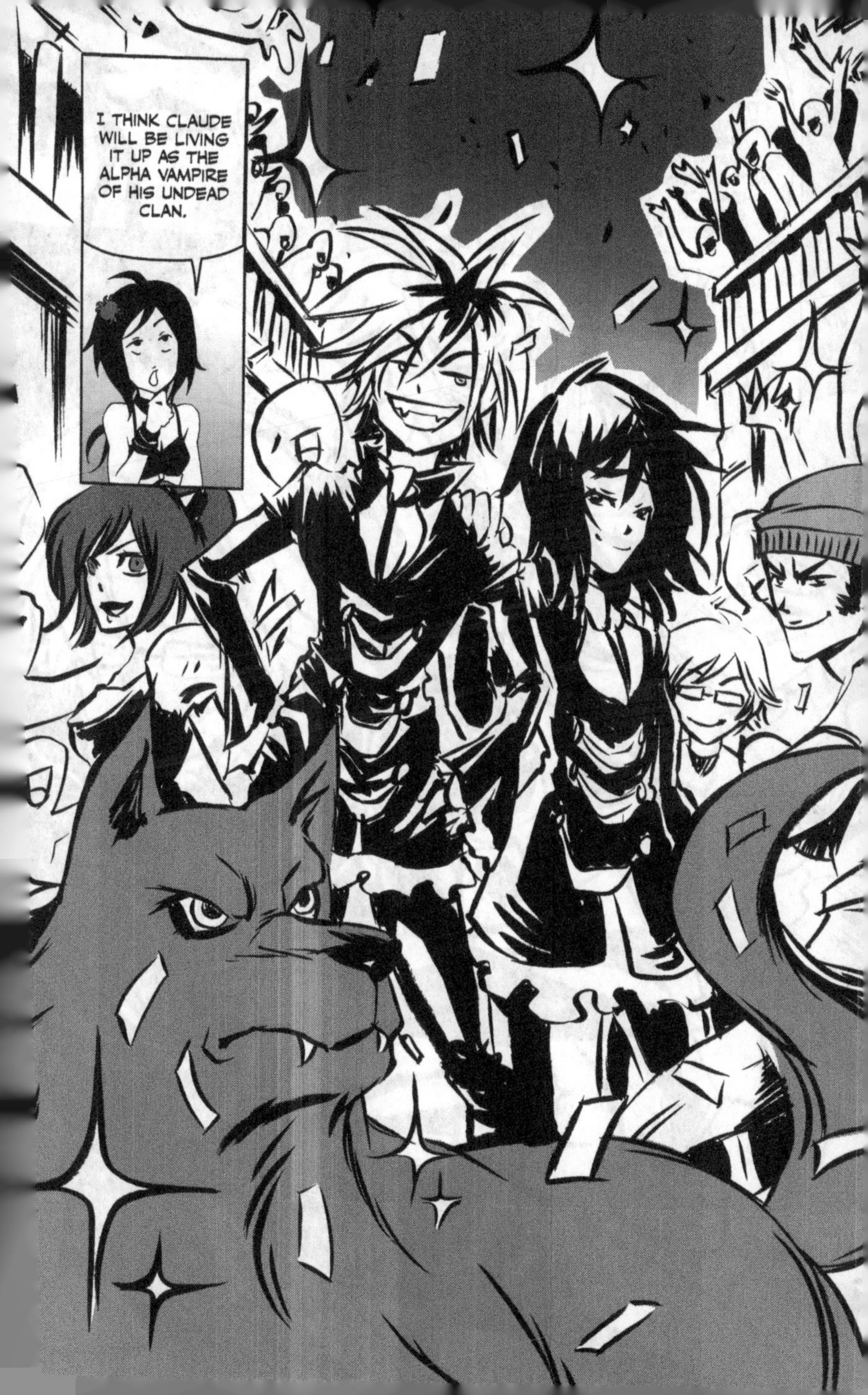
I THINK CLAUDE WILL BE LIVING IT UP AS THE ALPHA VAMPIRE OF HIS UNDEAD CLAN.

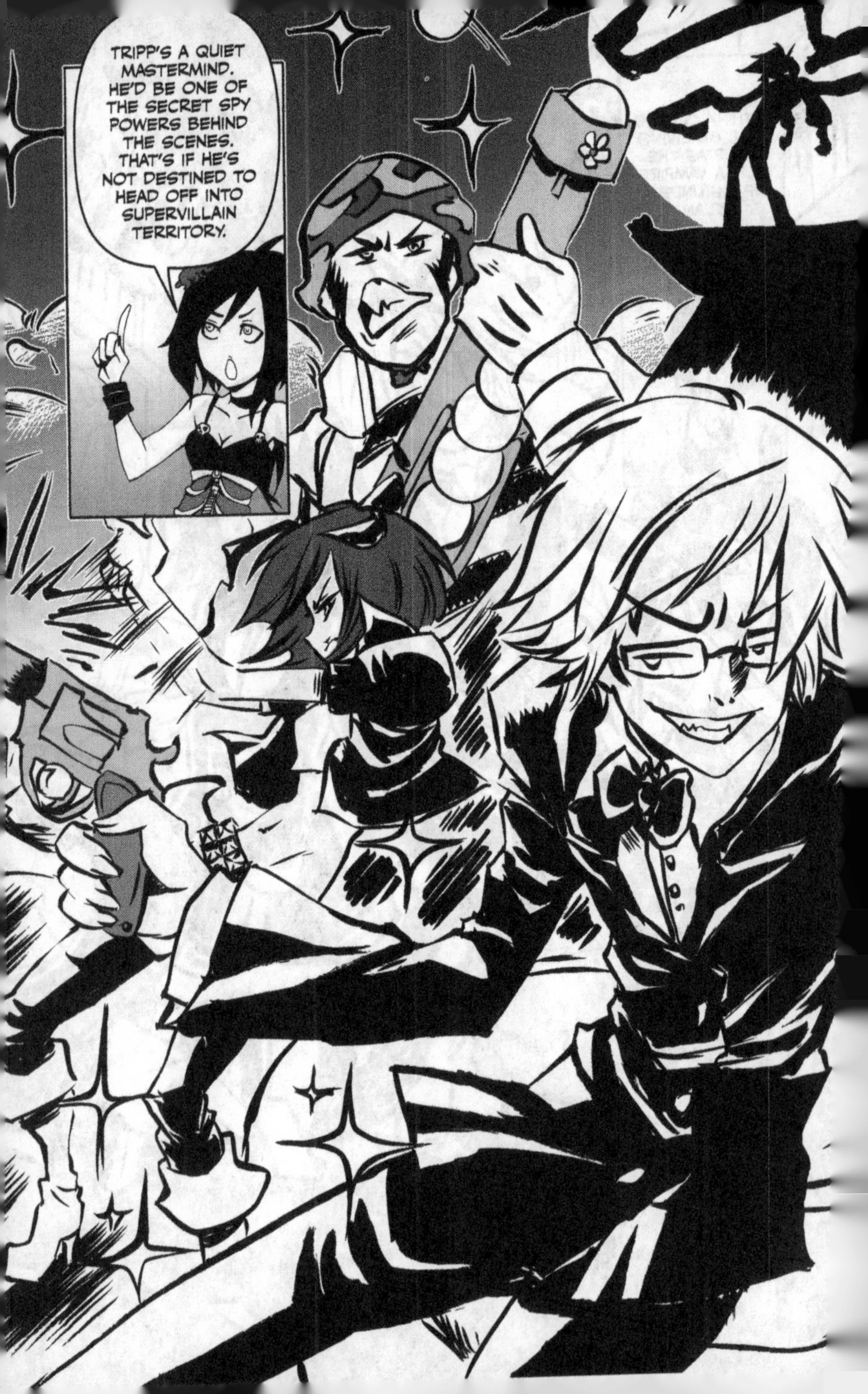
TRIPP'S A QUIET MASTERMIND. HE'D BE ONE OF THE SECRET SPY POWERS BEHIND THE SCENES. THAT'S IF HE'S NOT DESTINED TO HEAD OFF INTO SUPERVILLAIN TERRITORY.

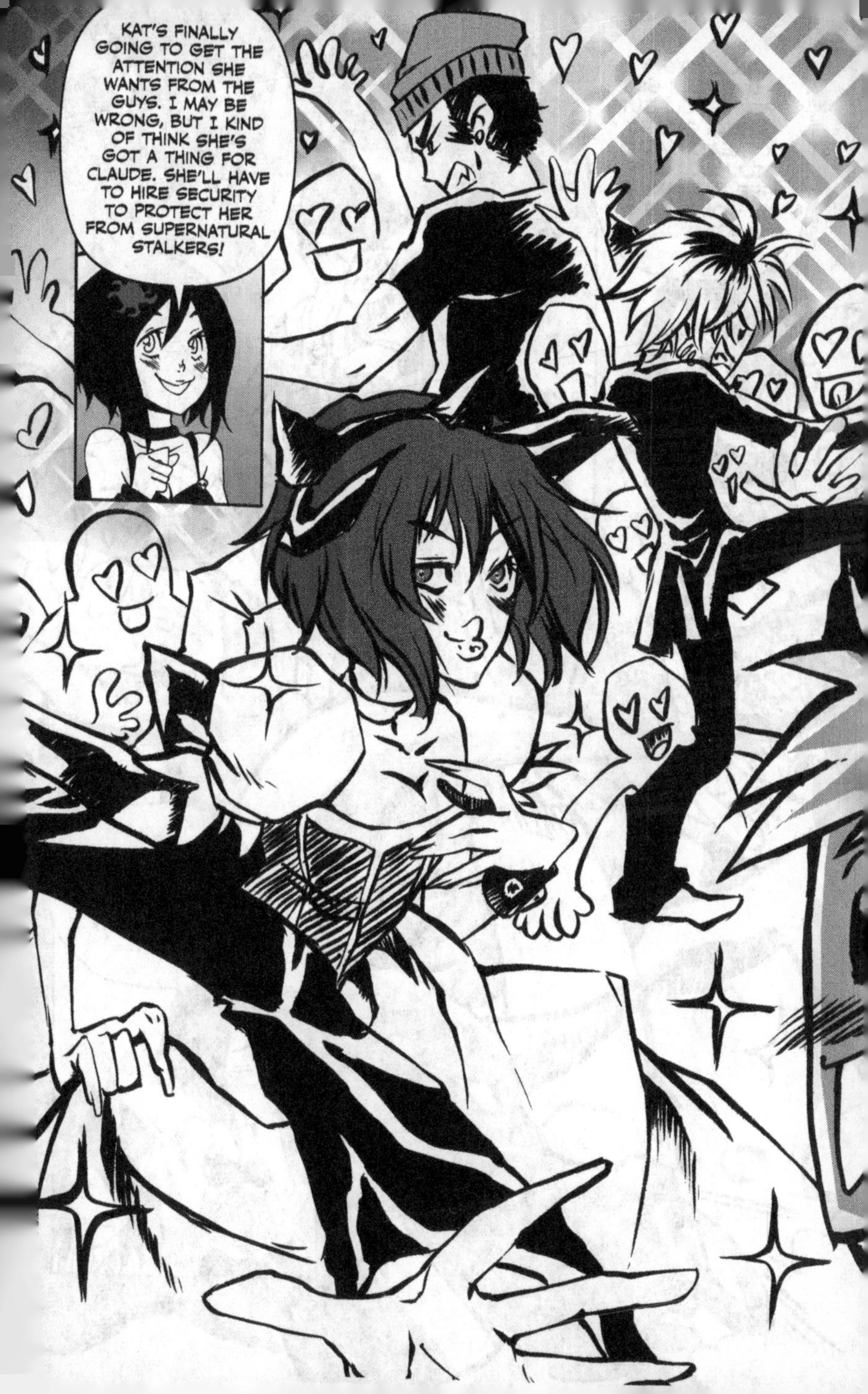
KAT'S FINALLY GOING TO GET THE ATTENTION SHE WANTS FROM THE GUYS. I MAY BE WRONG, BUT I KIND OF THINK SHE'S GOT A THING FOR CLAUDE. SHE'LL HAVE TO HIRE SECURITY TO PROTECT HER FROM SUPERNATURAL STALKERS!

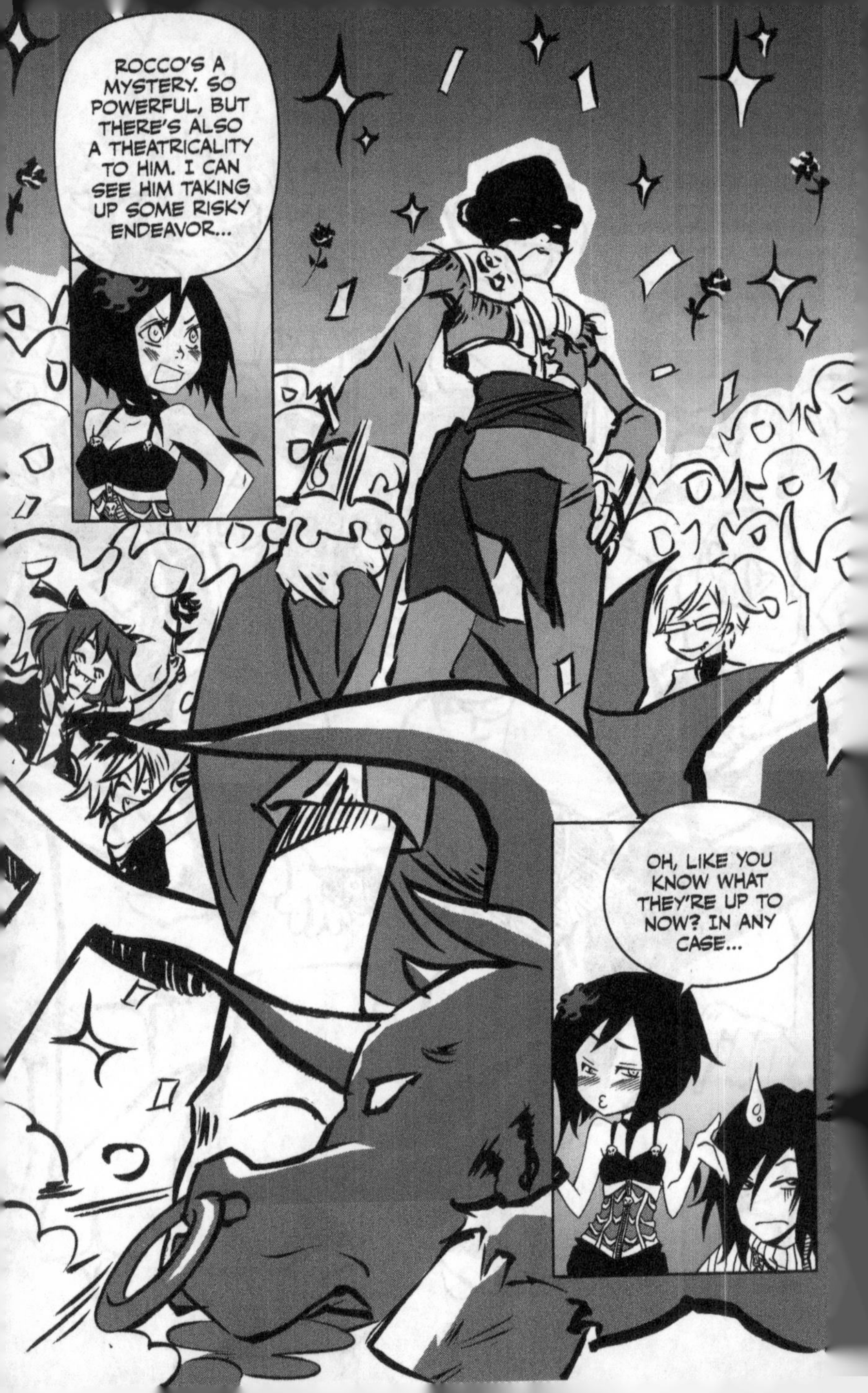
ROCCO'S A MYSTERY. SO POWERFUL, BUT THERE'S ALSO A THEATRICALITY TO HIM. I CAN SEE HIM TAKING UP SOME RISKY ENDEAVOR...
OH, LIKE YOU KNOW WHAT THEY'RE UP TO NOW? IN ANY CASE...

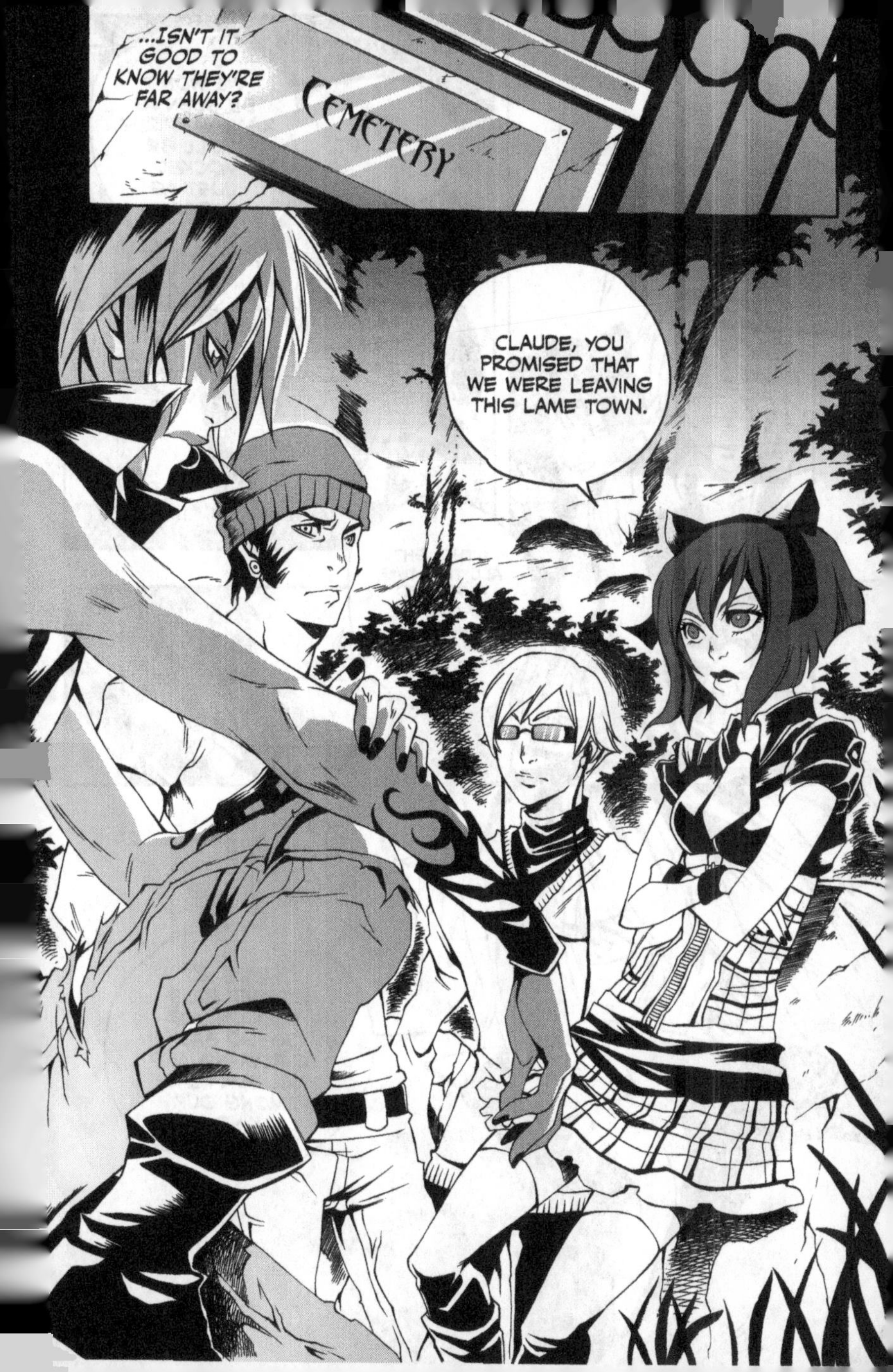
...ISN'T IT GOOD TO KNOW THEY'RE FAR AWAY?
CEMETERY
CLAUDE, YOU PROMISED THAT WE WERE LEAVING THIS LAME TOWN.

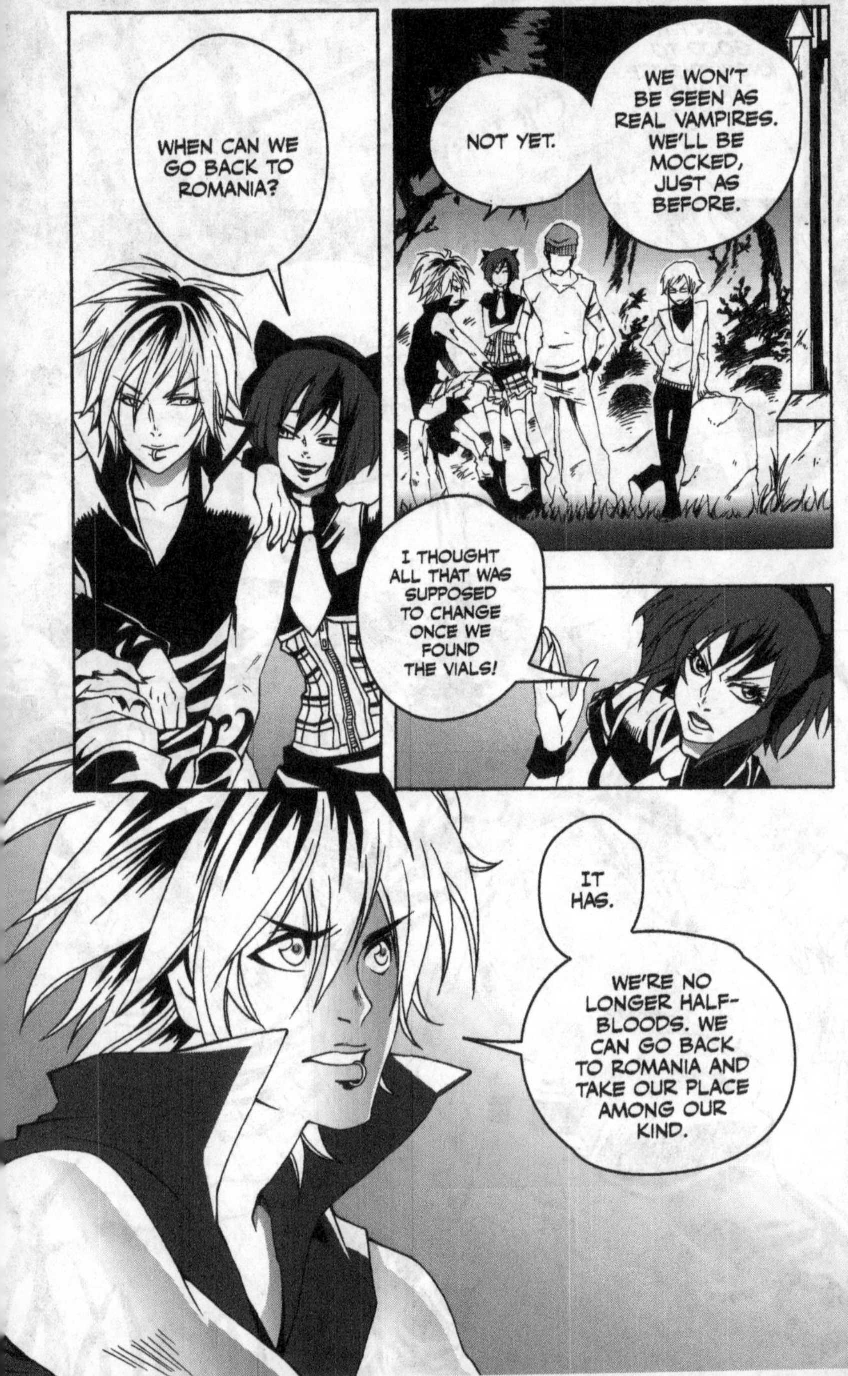
WHEN CAN WE GO BACK TO ROMANIA?
NOT YET.
WE WON'T BE SEEN AS REAL VAMPIRES. WE'LL BE MOCKED, JUST AS BEFORE.
I THOUGHT ALL THAT WAS SUPPOSED TO CHANGE ONCE WE FOUND THE VIALS!
IT HAS.
WE'RE NO LONGER HALF-BLOODS. WE CAN GO BACK TO ROMANIA AND TAKE OUR PLACE AMONG OUR KIND.

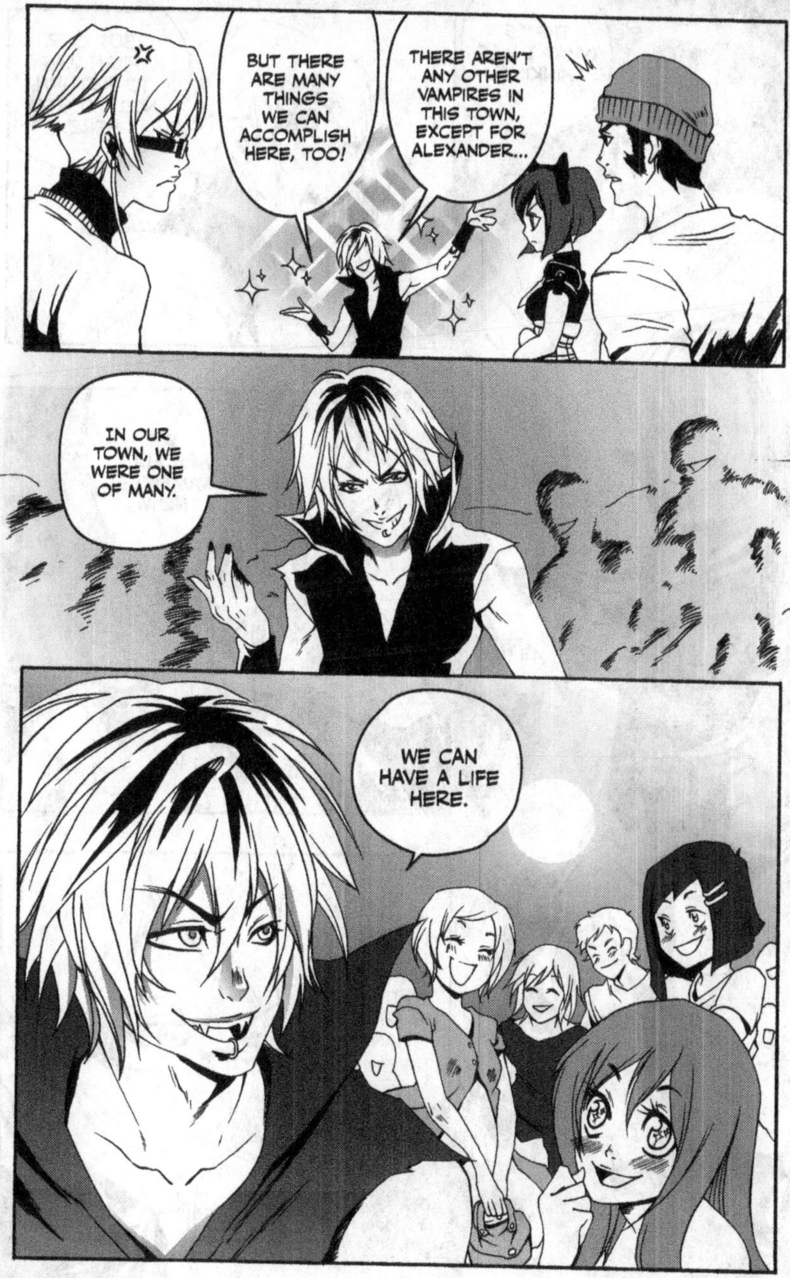
BUT THERE ARE MANY THINGS WE CAN ACCOMPLISH HERE, TOO!
THERE AREN'T ANY OTHER VAMPIRES IN THIS TOWN, EXCEPT FOR ALEXANDER...
IN OUR TOWN, WE WERE ONE OF MANY.
WE CAN HAVE A LIFE HERE.

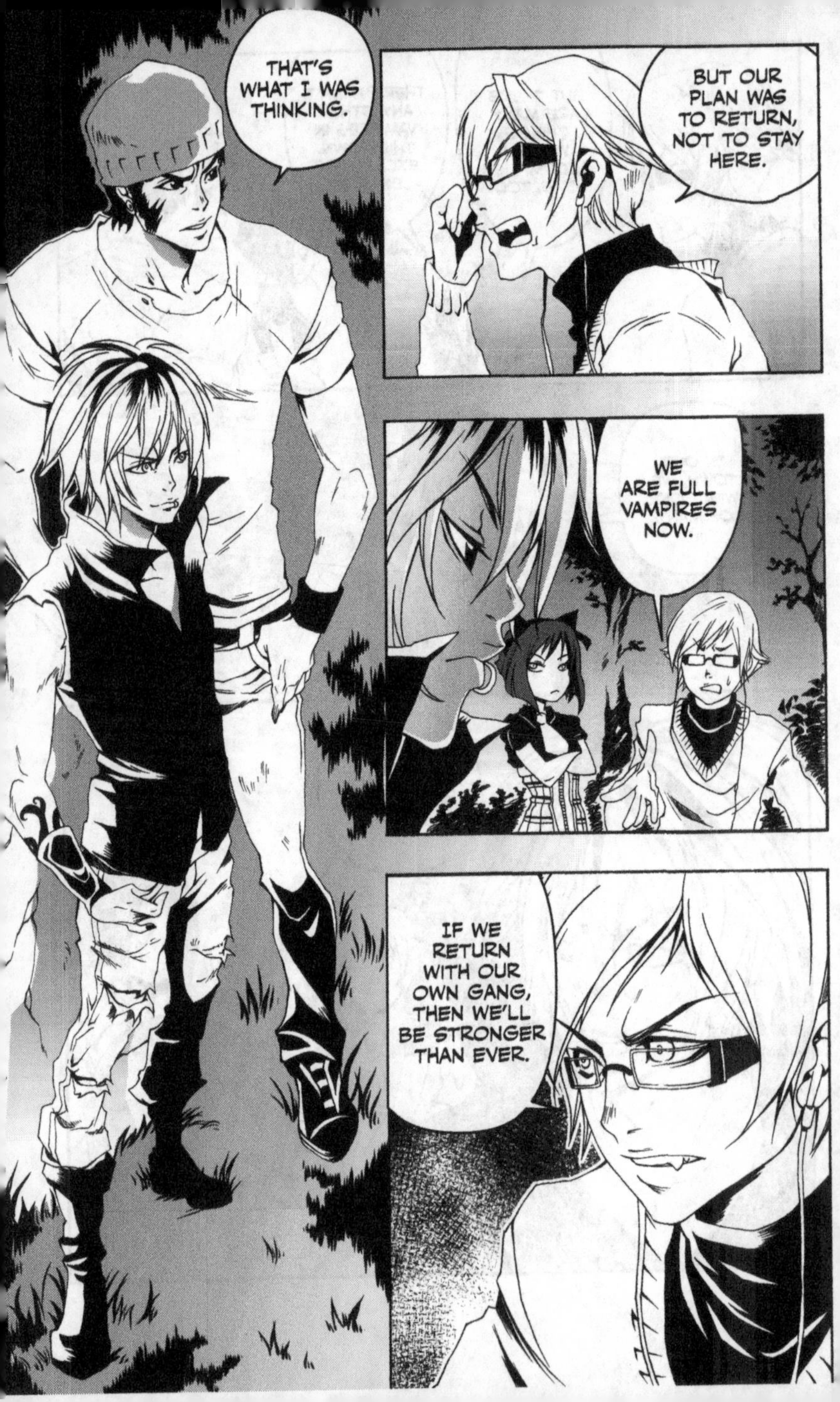
THAT'S WHAT I WAS THINKING.
BUT OUR PLAN WAS TO RETURN, NOT TO STAY HERE.
WE ARE FULL VAMPIRES NOW.
IF WE RETURN WITH OUR OWN GANG, THEN WE'LL BE STRONGER THAN EVER.

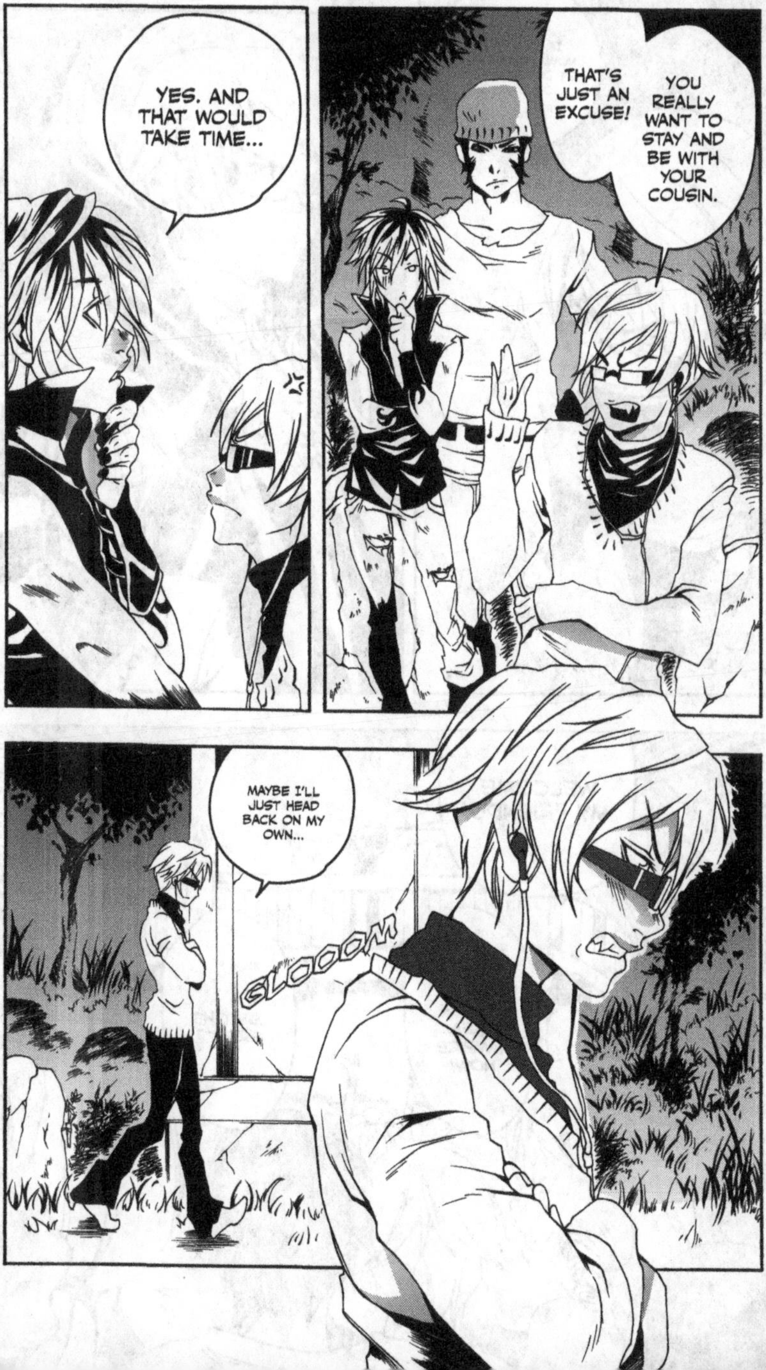
YES. AND THAT WOULD TAKE TIME...
THAT'S JUST AN EXCUSE!
YOU REALLY WANT TO STAY AND BE WITH YOUR COUSIN.
MAYBE I'LL JUST HEAD BACK ON MY OWN...
GLOOOM

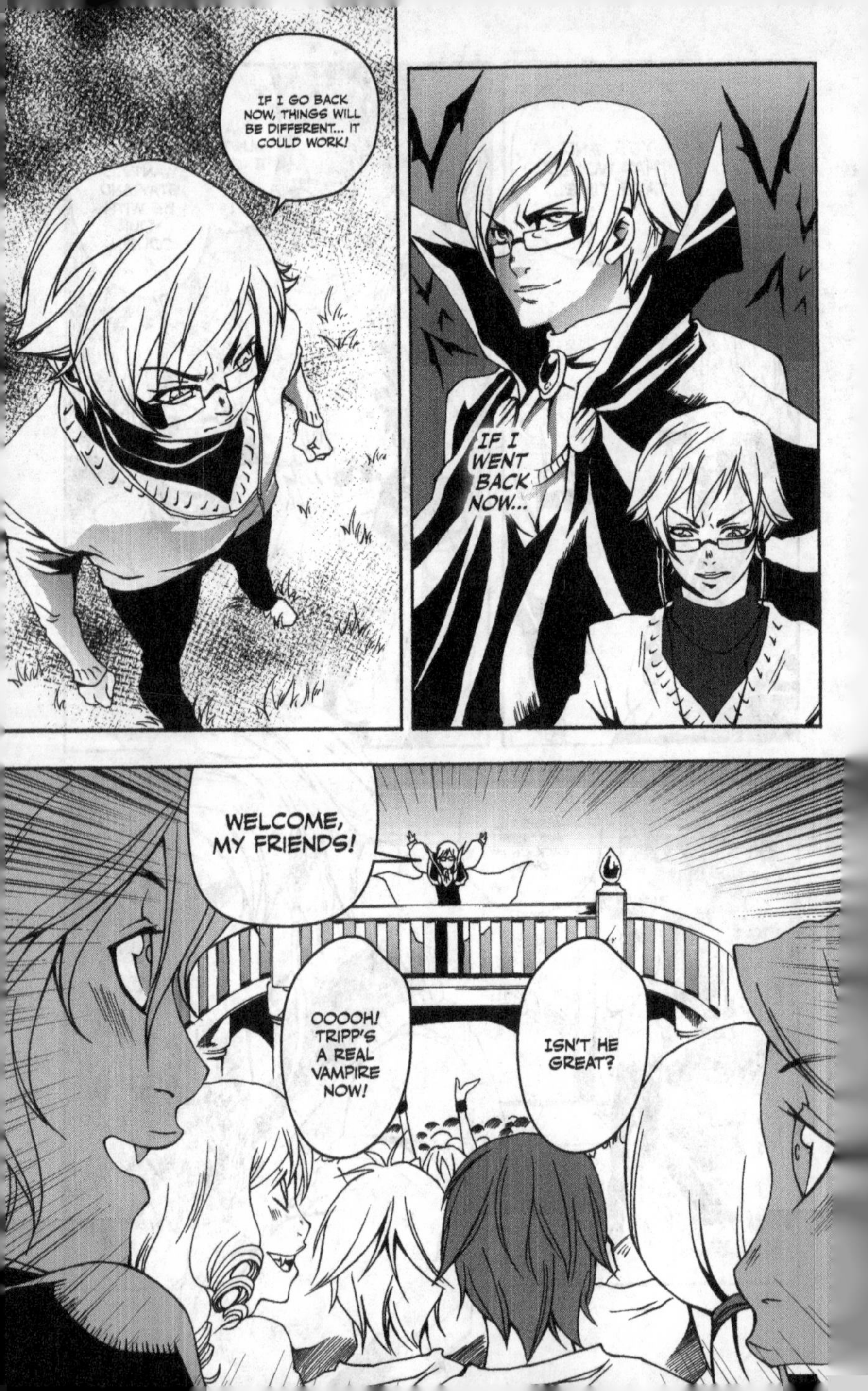
IF I GO BACK NOW, THINGS WILL BE DIFFERENT... IT COULD WORK!
IF I WENT BACK NOW...
WELCOME, MY FRIENDS!
OOOOH! TRIPP'S A REAL VAMPIRE NOW!
ISN'T HE GREAT?

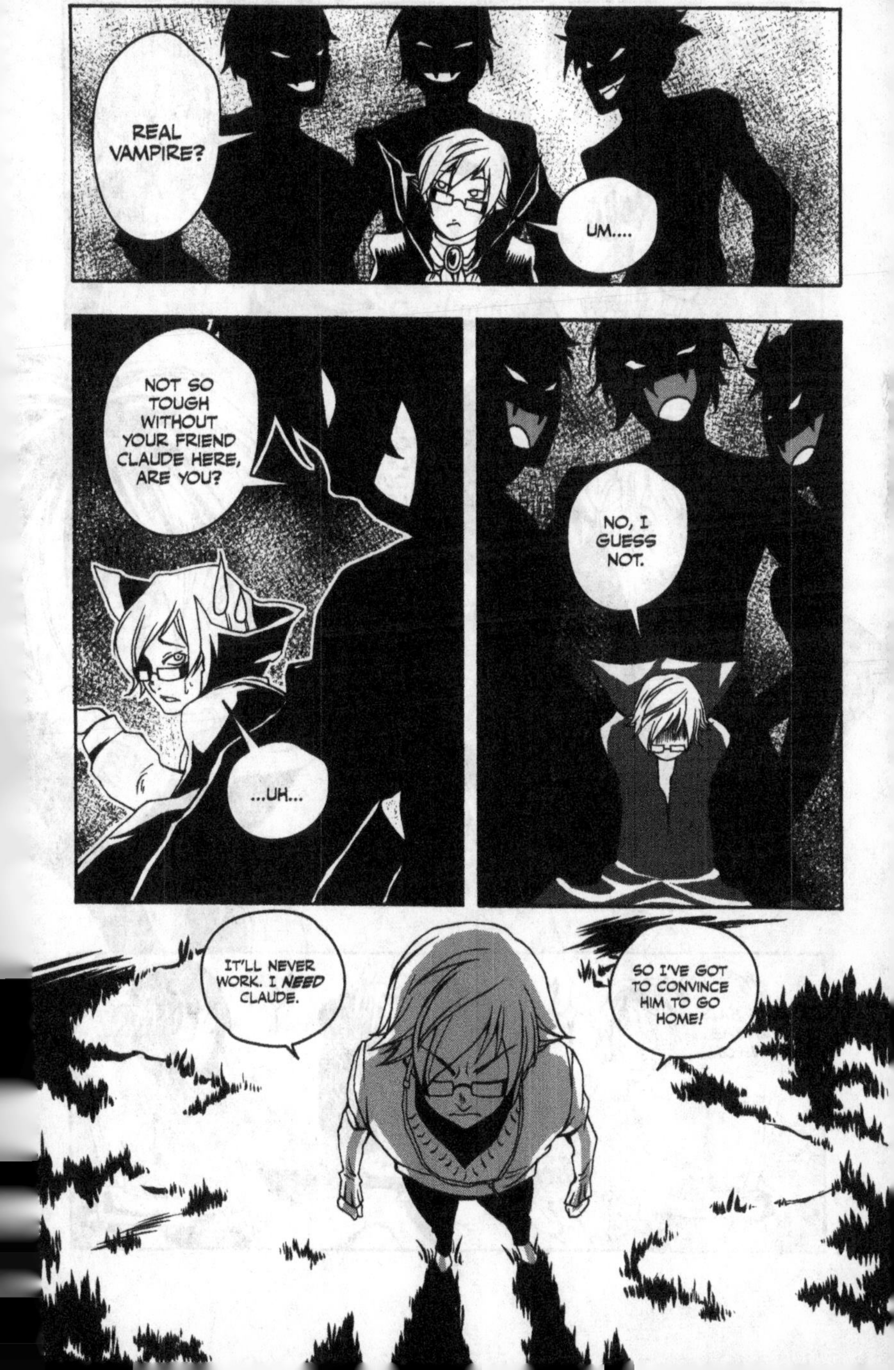
REAL VAMPIRE?
UM....
NOT SO TOUGH WITHOUT YOUR FRIEND CLAUDE HERE, ARE YOU?
...UH...
NO, I GUESS NOT.
IT'LL NEVER WORK. I *NEED* CLAUDE.
SO I'VE GOT TO CONVINCE HIM TO GO HOME!

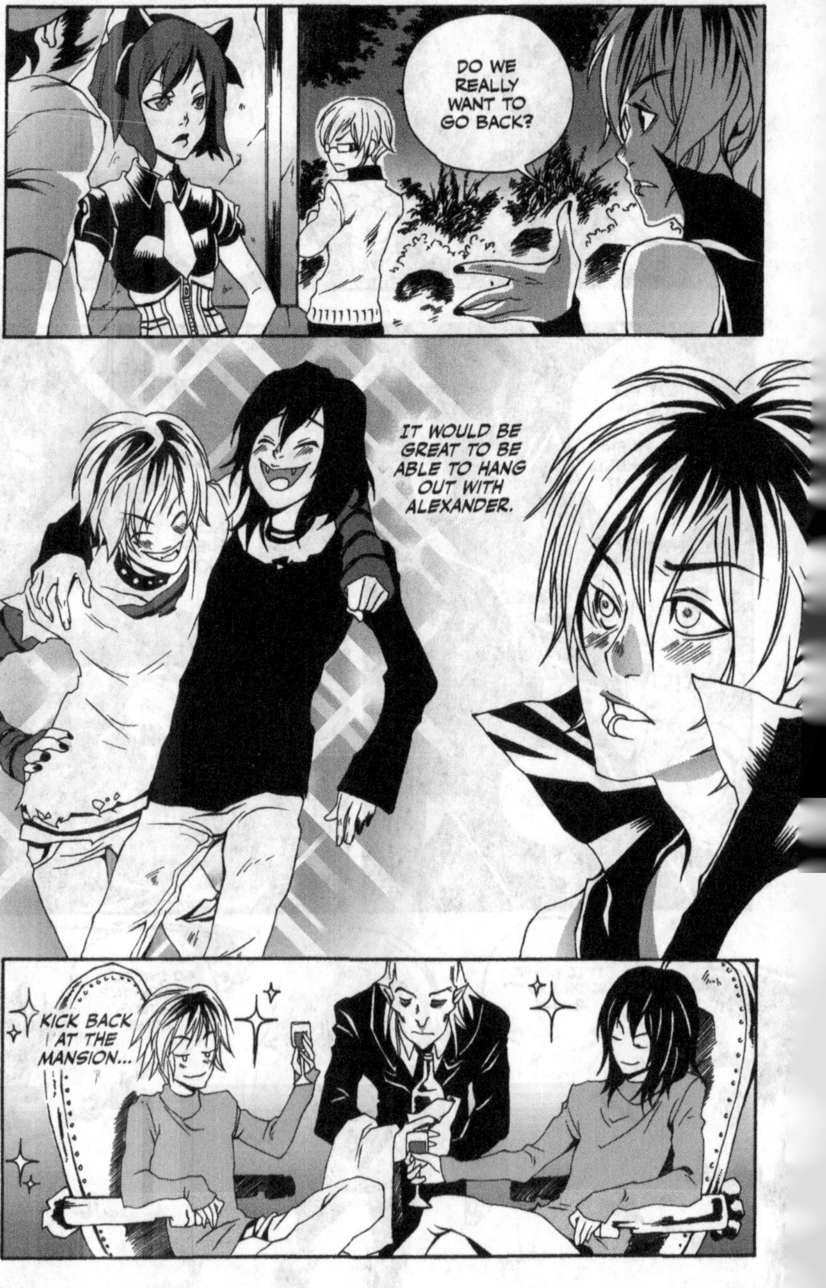
DO WE REALLY WANT TO GO BACK?
IT WOULD BE GREAT TO BE ABLE TO HANG OUT WITH ALEXANDER.
KICK BACK AT THE MANSION...

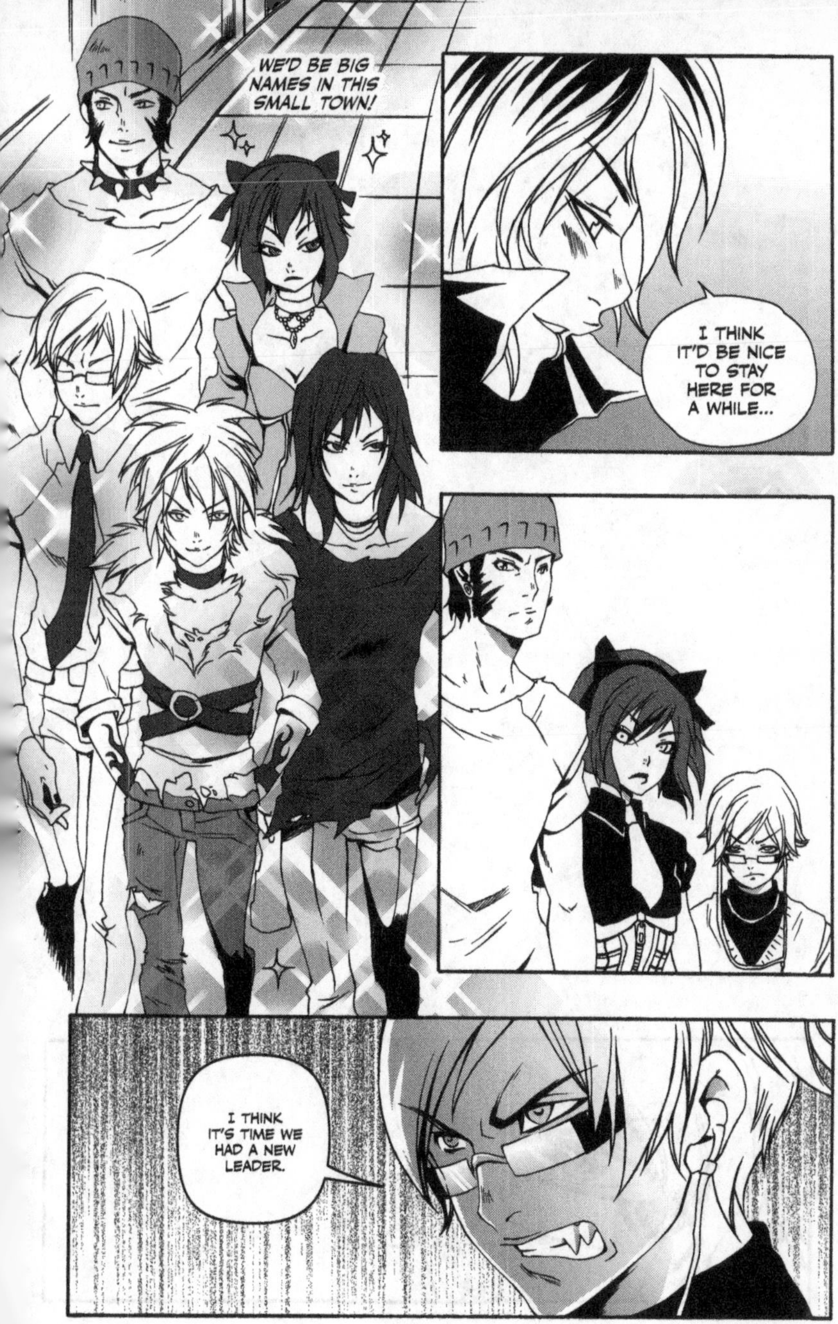
WE'D BE BIG NAMES IN THIS SMALL TOWN!
I THINK IT'D BE NICE TO STAY HERE FOR A WHILE...
I THINK IT'S TIME WE HAD A NEW LEADER.

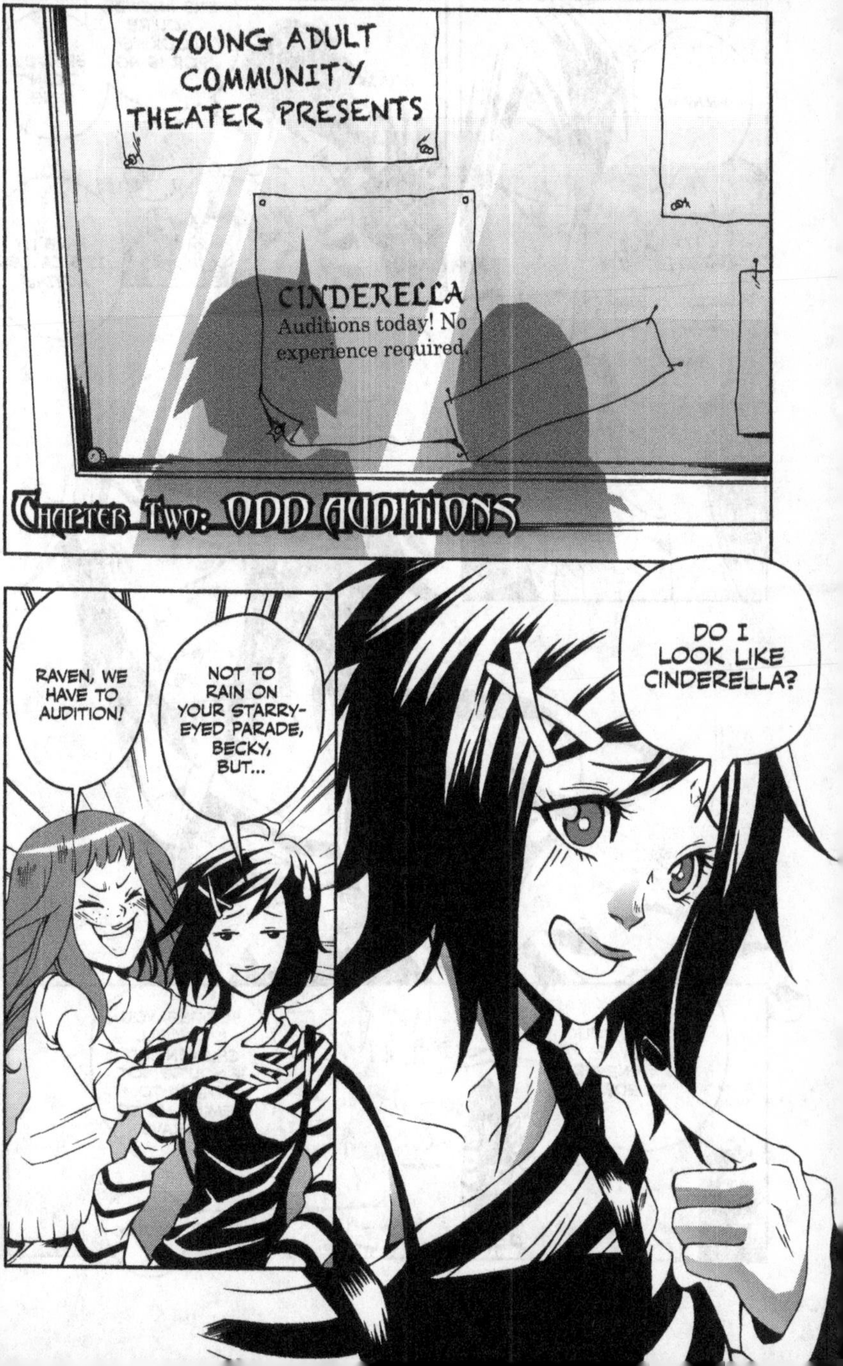
YOUNG ADULT COMMUNITY THEATER PRESENTS
CINDERELLA
Auditions today! No experience required.
CHAPTER TWO: ODD AUDITIONS
RAVEN, WE HAVE TO AUDITION!
NOT TO RAIN ON YOUR STARRY-EYED PARADE, BECKY, BUT...
DO I LOOK LIKE CINDERELLA?

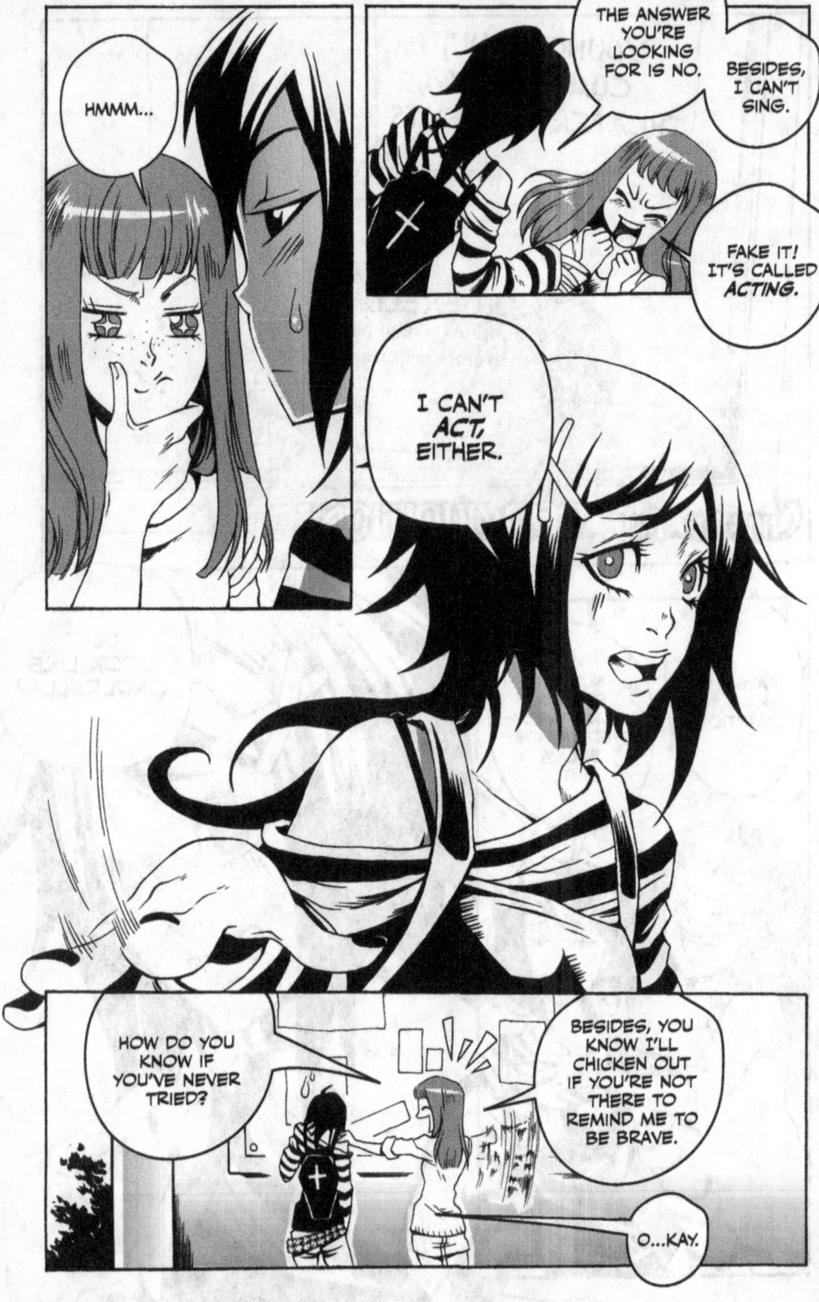
HMMM...
THE ANSWER YOU'RE LOOKING FOR IS NO.
BESIDES, I CAN'T SING.
FAKE IT! IT'S CALLED *ACTING*.
I CAN'T *ACT*, EITHER.
HOW DO YOU KNOW IF YOU'VE NEVER TRIED?
BESIDES, YOU KNOW I'LL CHICKEN OUT IF YOU'RE NOT THERE TO REMIND ME TO BE BRAVE.
O...KAY.

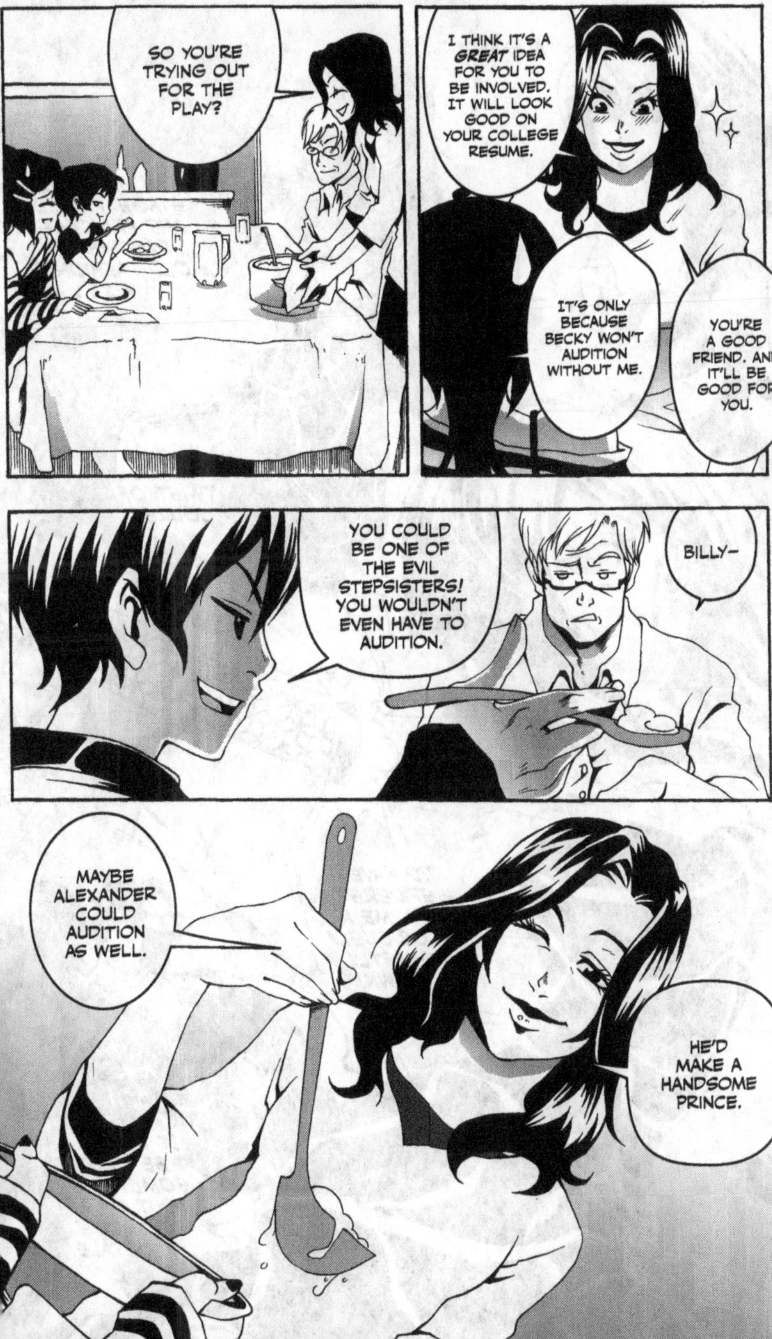
SO YOU'RE TRYING OUT FOR THE PLAY?
I THINK IT'S A *GREAT* IDEA FOR YOU TO BE INVOLVED. IT WILL LOOK GOOD ON YOUR COLLEGE RESUME.
IT'S ONLY BECAUSE BECKY WON'T AUDITION WITHOUT ME.
YOU'RE A GOOD FRIEND. AND IT'LL BE GOOD FOR YOU.
YOU COULD BE ONE OF THE EVIL STEPSISTERS! YOU WOULDN'T EVEN HAVE TO AUDITION.
BILLY—
MAYBE ALEXANDER COULD AUDITION AS WELL.
HE'D MAKE A HANDSOME PRINCE.

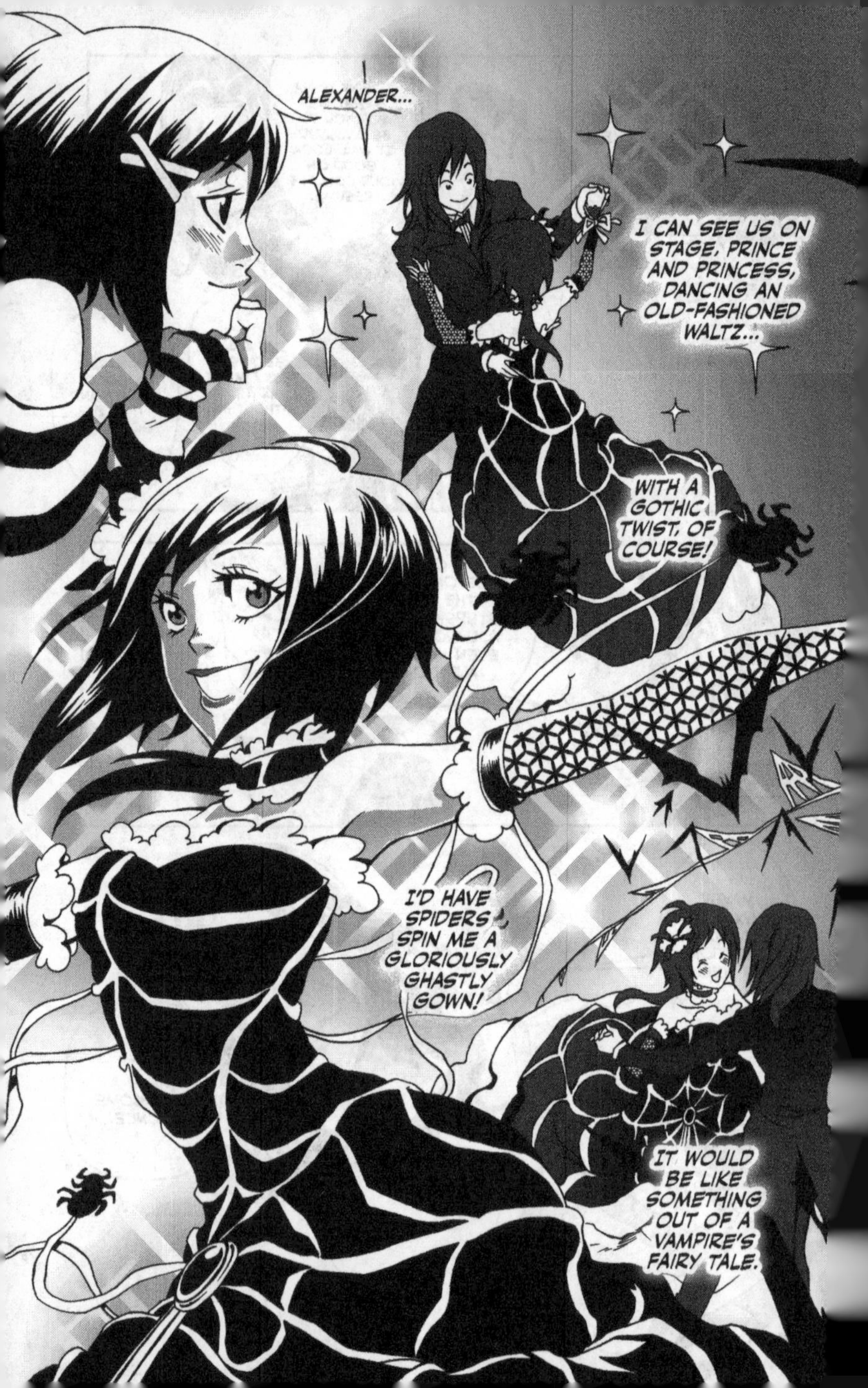
ALEXANDER...
I CAN SEE US ON STAGE, PRINCE AND PRINCESS, DANCING AN OLD-FASHIONED WALTZ...
WITH A GOTHIC TWIST, OF COURSE!
I'D HAVE SPIDERS SPIN ME A GLORIOUSLY GHASTLY GOWN!
IT WOULD BE LIKE SOMETHING OUT OF A VAMPIRE'S FAIRY TALE.

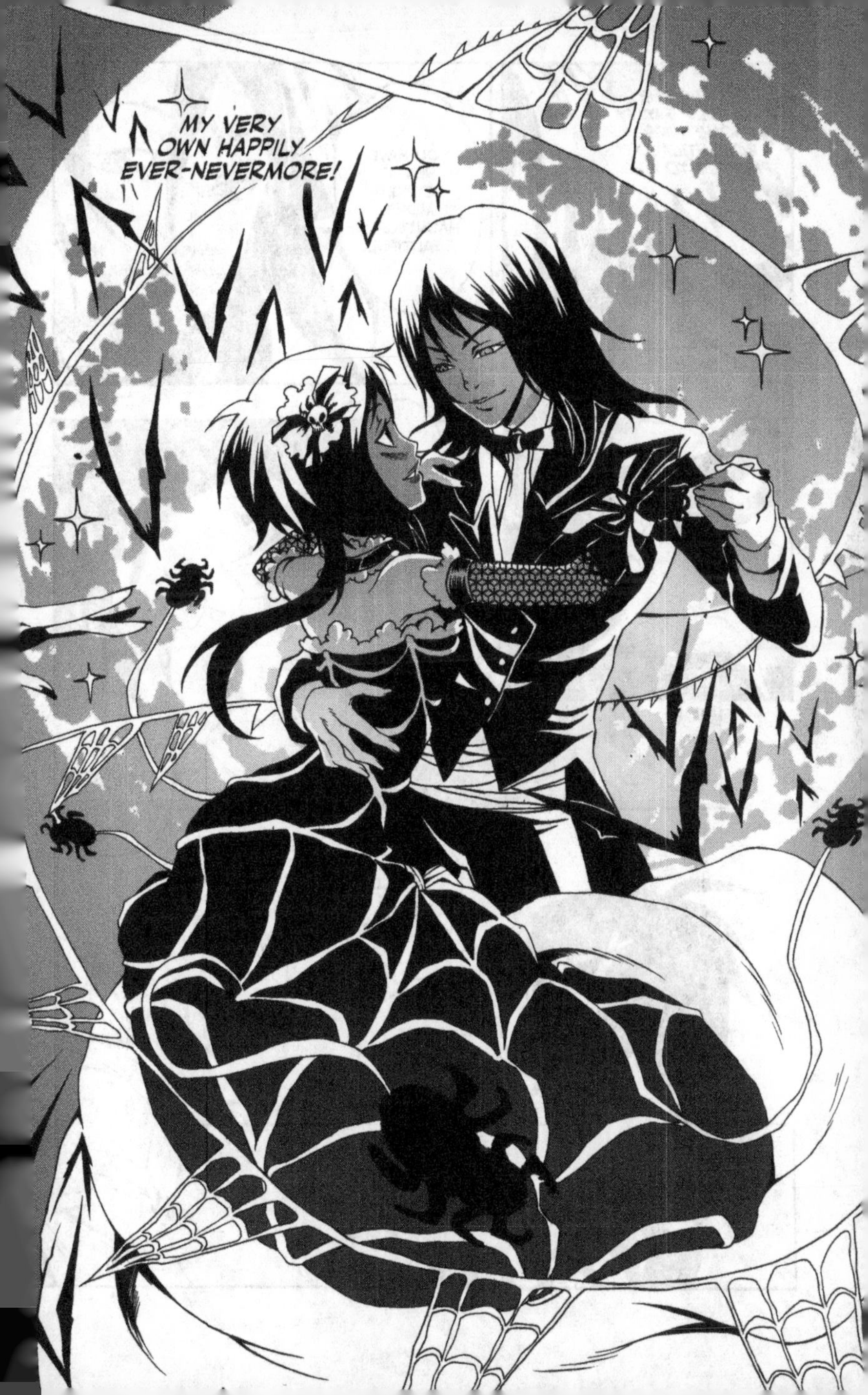
MY VERY OWN HAPPILY EVER-NEVERMORE!

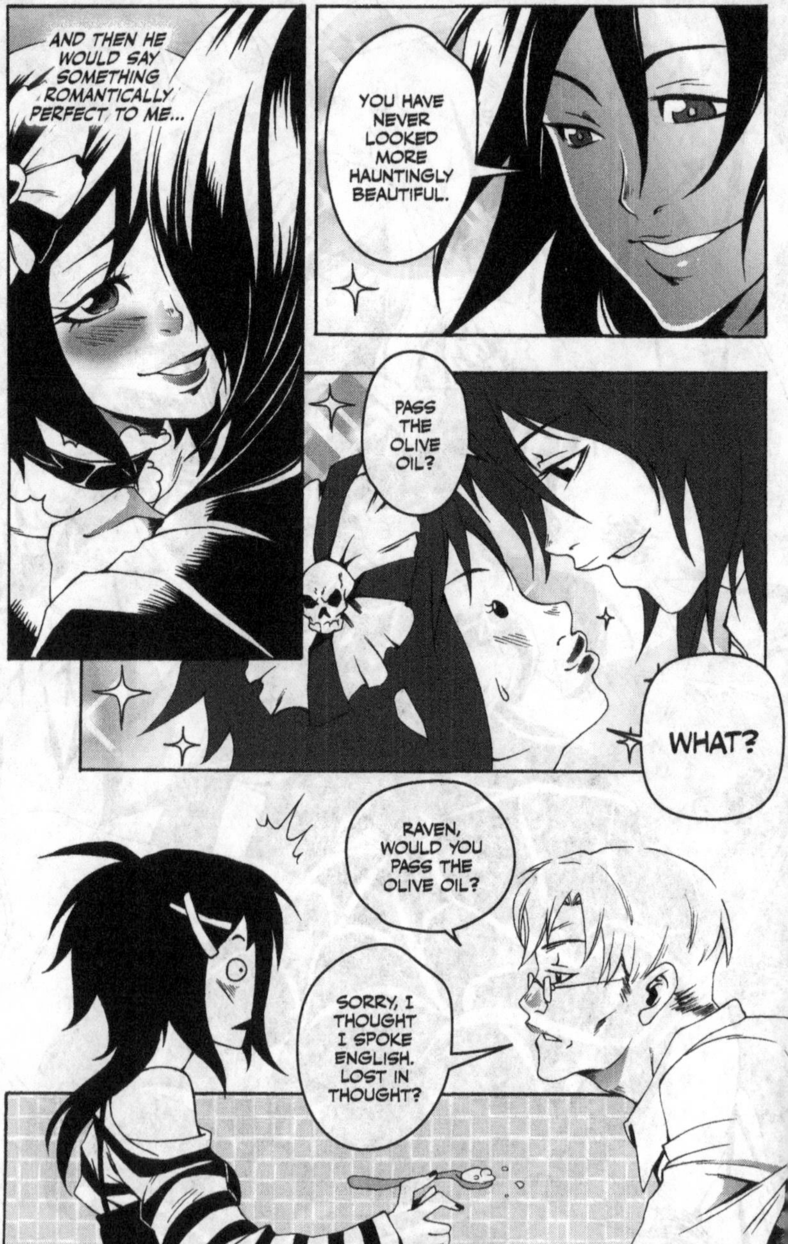
AND THEN HE WOULD SAY SOMETHING ROMANTICALLY PERFECT TO ME...
YOU HAVE NEVER LOOKED MORE HAUNTINGLY BEAUTIFUL.
PASS THE OLIVE OIL?
WHAT?
RAVEN, WOULD YOU PASS THE OLIVE OIL?
SORRY, I THOUGHT I SPOKE ENGLISH. LOST IN THOUGHT?

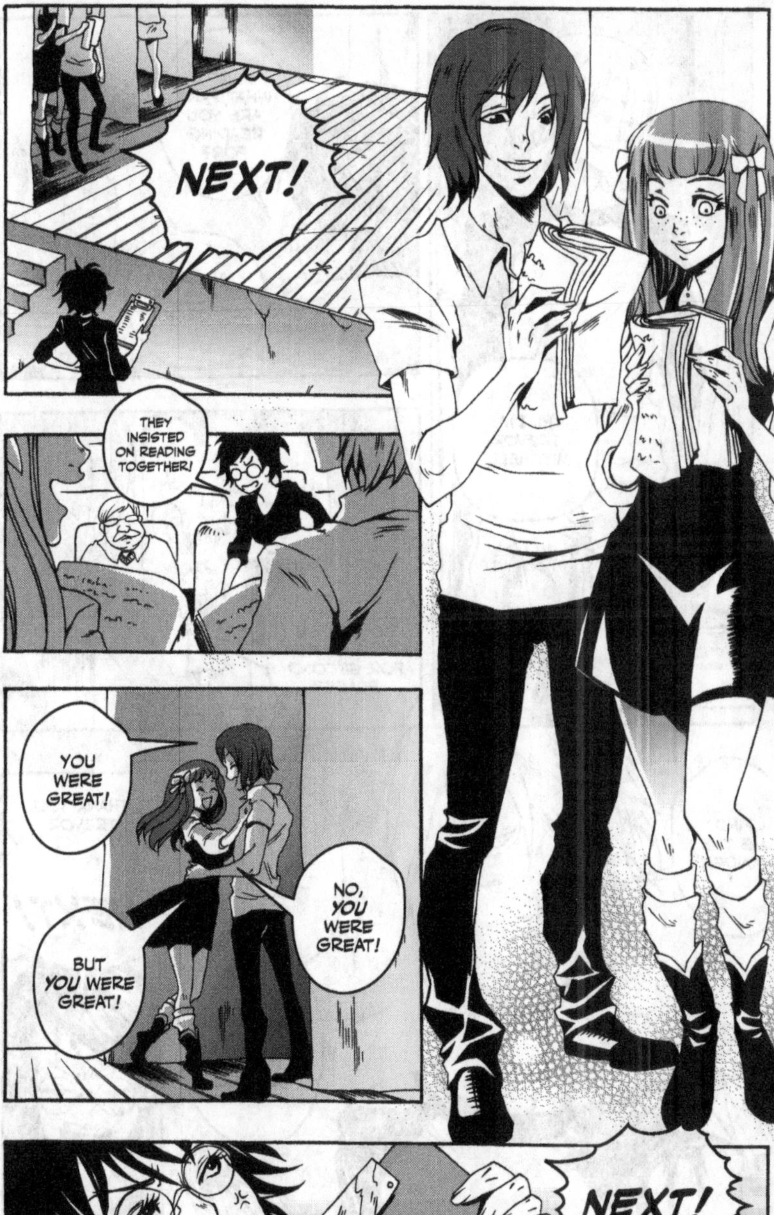
NEXT!
THEY INSISTED ON READING TOGETHER!
YOU WERE GREAT!
NO, YOU WERE GREAT!
BUT YOU WERE GREAT!
NEXT!

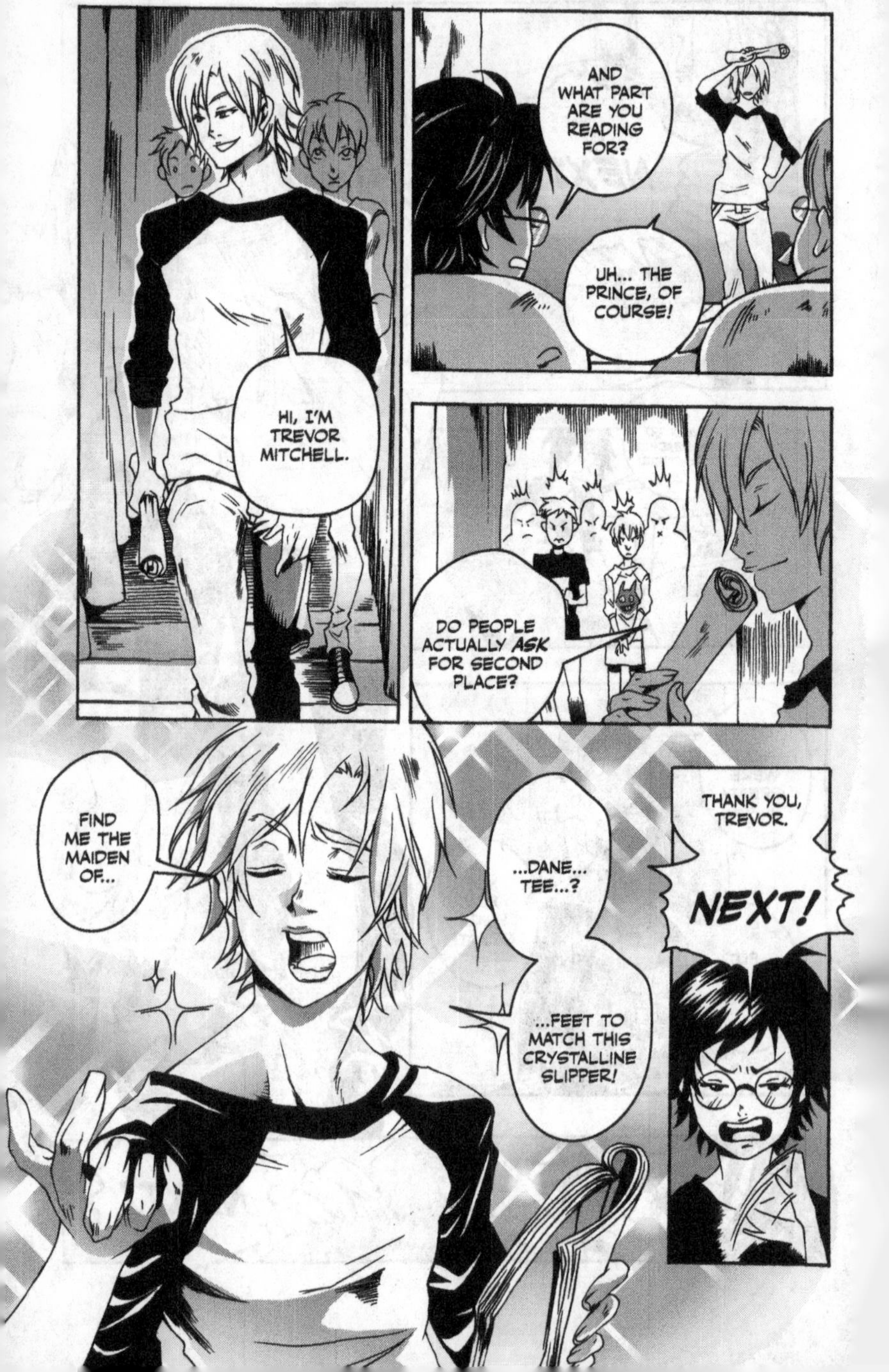
HI, I'M TREVOR MITCHELL.
AND WHAT PART ARE YOU READING FOR?
UH... THE PRINCE, OF COURSE!
DO PEOPLE ACTUALLY ASK FOR SECOND PLACE?
FIND ME THE MAIDEN OF...
...DANE... TEE...?
...FEET TO MATCH THIS CRYSTALLINE SLIPPER!
THANK YOU, TREVOR.
NEXT!

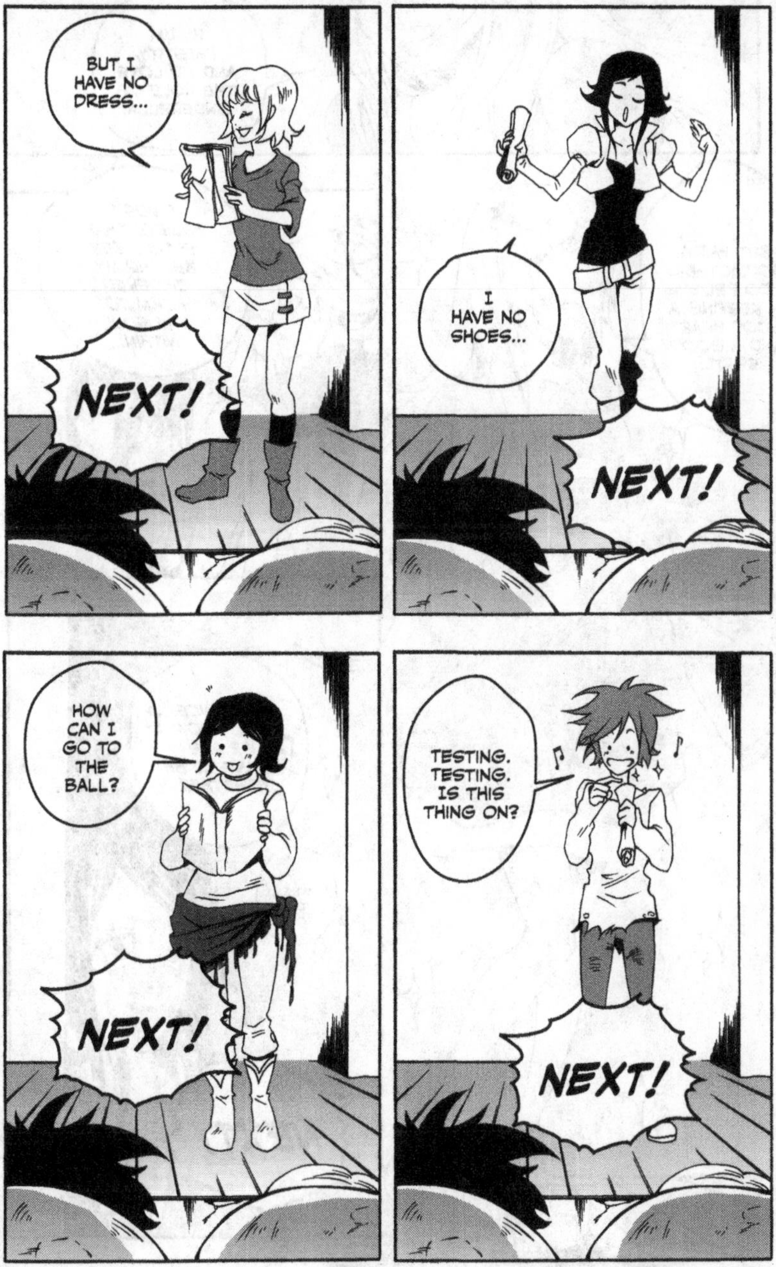
BUT I HAVE NO DRESS...
NEXT!
I HAVE NO SHOES...
NEXT!
HOW CAN I GO TO THE BALL?
NEXT!
TESTING. TESTING. IS THIS THING ON?
NEXT!

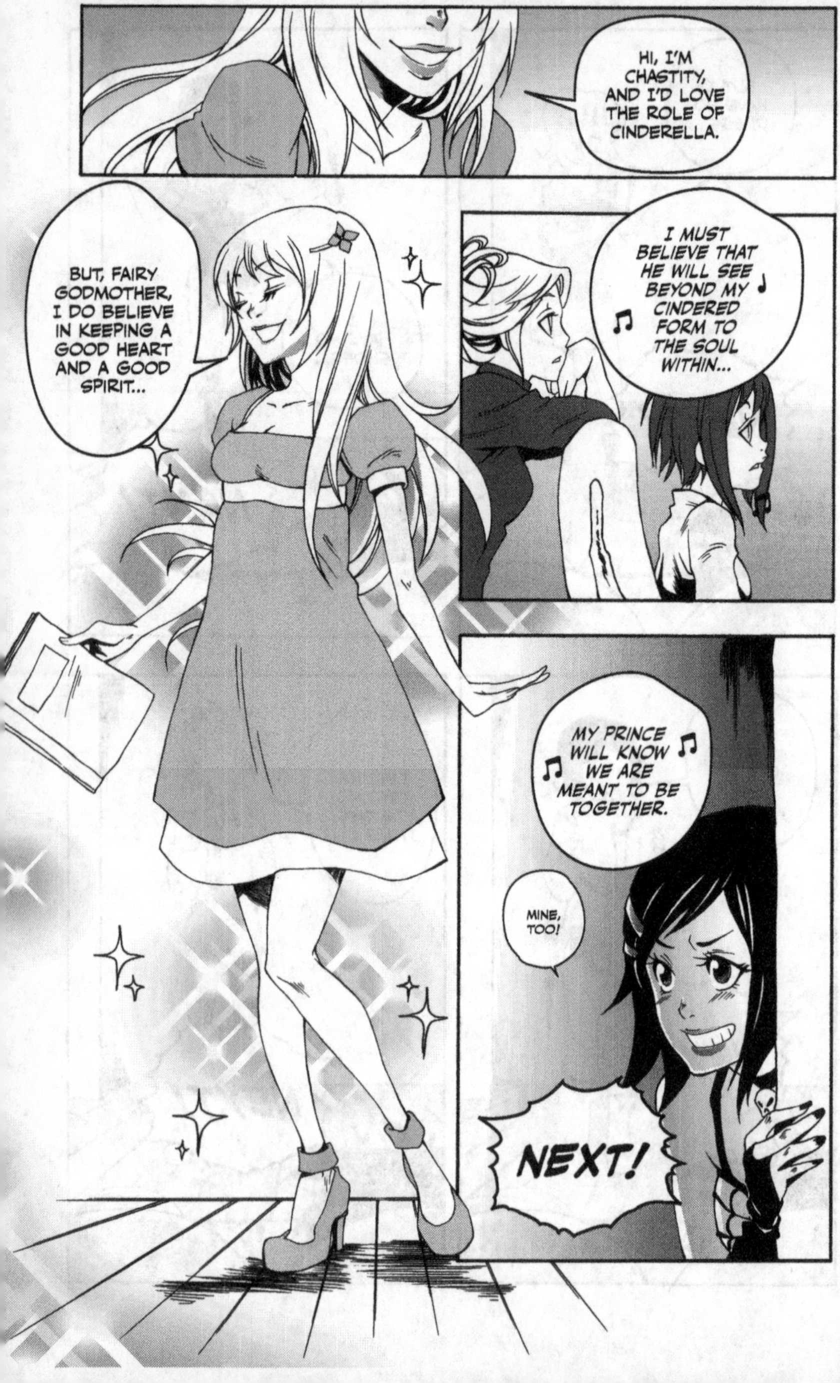
HI, I'M CHASTITY, AND I'D LOVE THE ROLE OF CINDERELLA.
BUT, FAIRY GODMOTHER, I DO BELIEVE IN KEEPING A GOOD HEART AND A GOOD SPIRIT...
I MUST BELIEVE THAT HE WILL SEE BEYOND MY CINDERED FORM TO THE SOUL WITHIN...
MY PRINCE WILL KNOW WE ARE MEANT TO BE TOGETHER.
MINE, TOO!
NEXT!

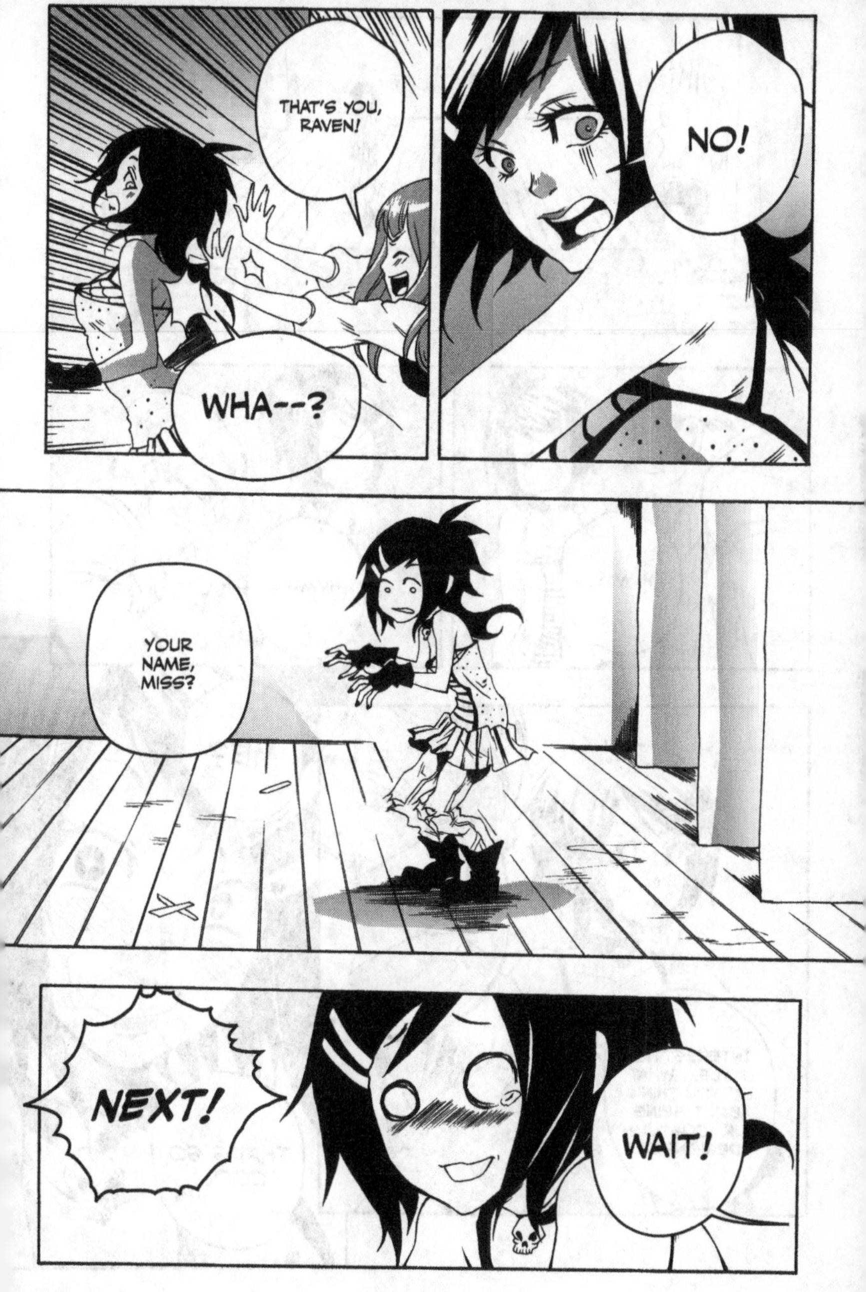
THAT'S YOU, RAVEN!
WHA--?
NO!
YOUR NAME, MISS?
NEXT!
WAIT!

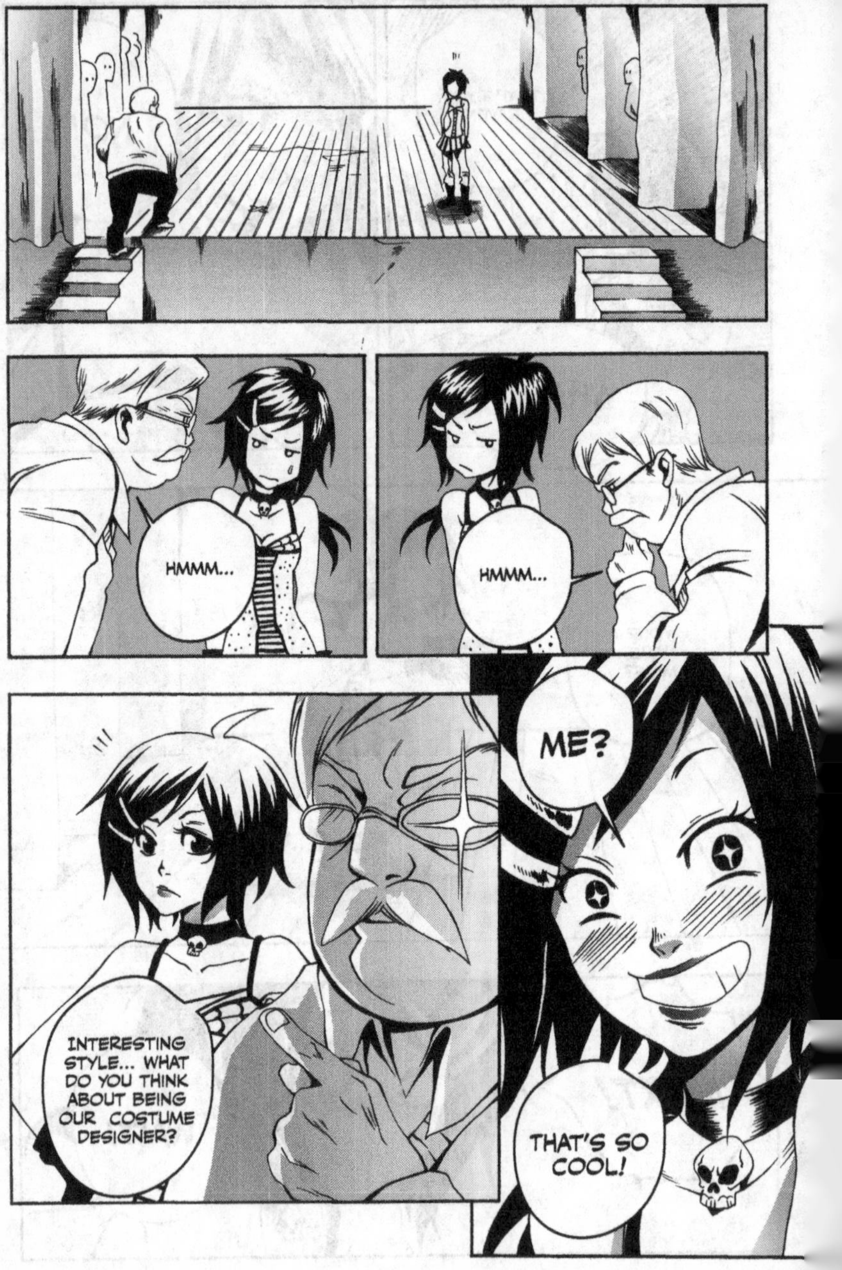
HMMM...
HMMM...
INTERESTING STYLE... WHAT DO YOU THINK ABOUT BEING OUR COSTUME DESIGNER?
ME?
THAT'S SO COOL!

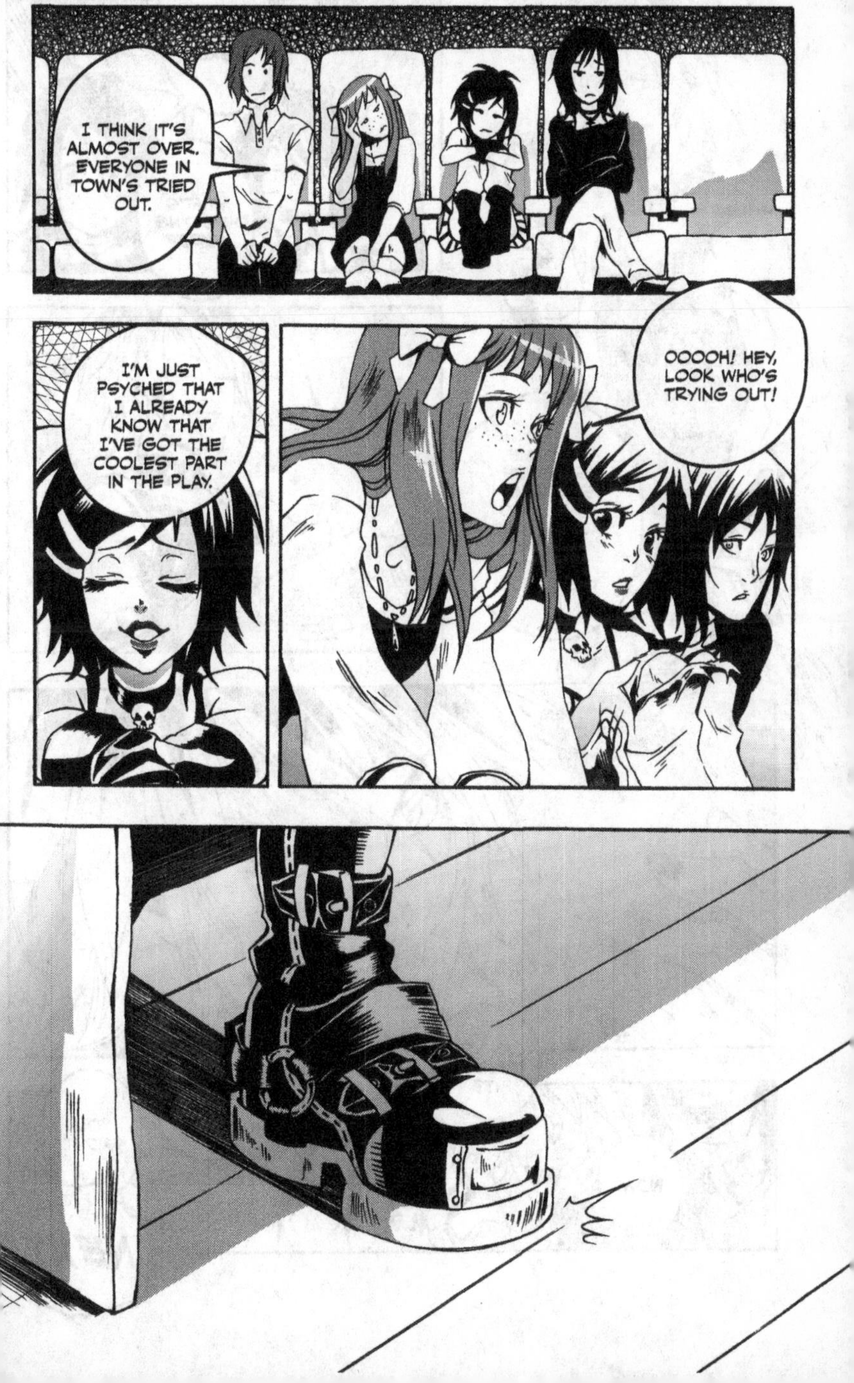
I THINK IT'S ALMOST OVER. EVERYONE IN TOWN'S TRIED OUT.
I'M JUST PSYCHED THAT I ALREADY KNOW THAT I'VE GOT THE COOLEST PART IN THE PLAY.
OOOOH! HEY, LOOK WHO'S TRYING OUT!

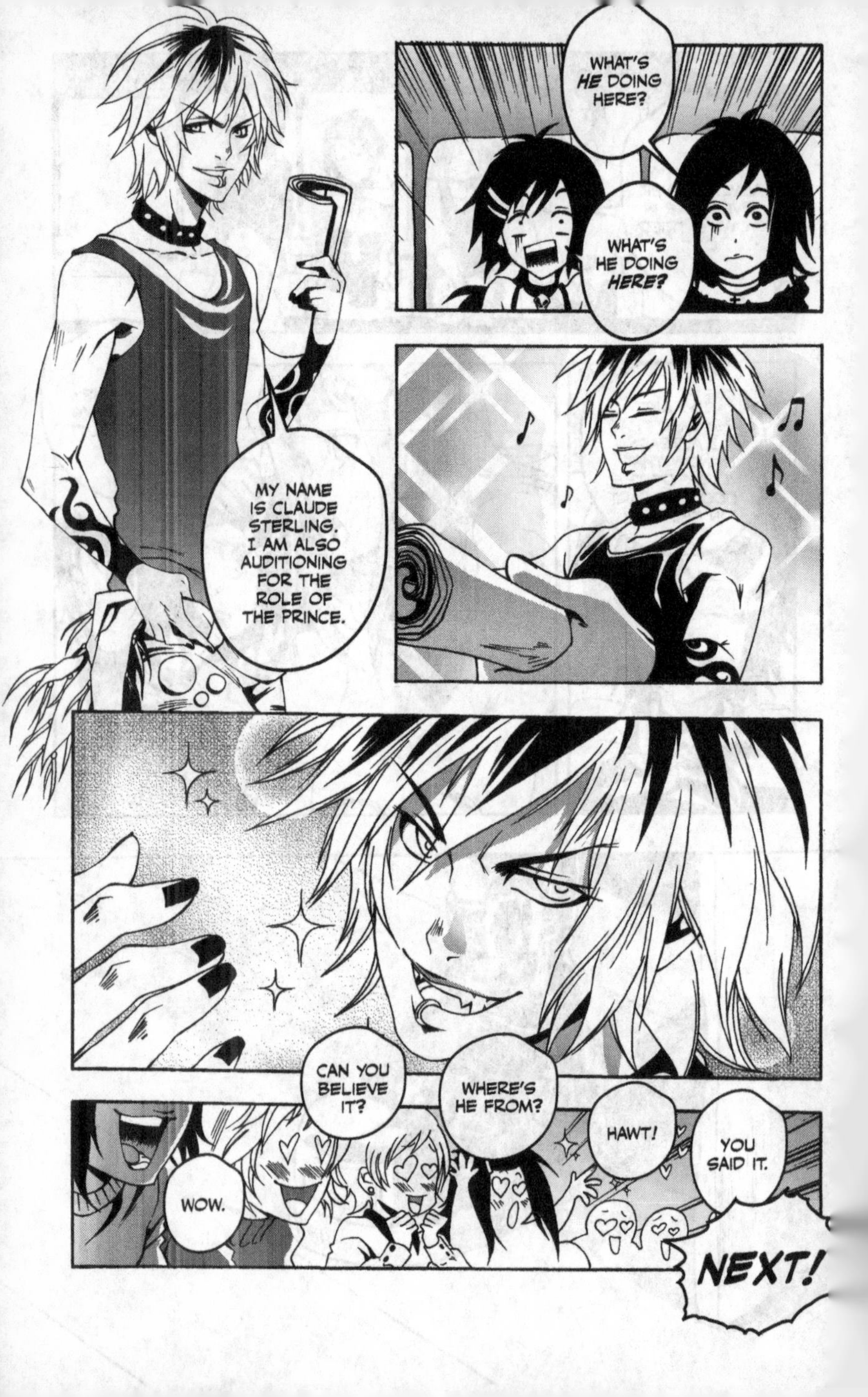

MY NAME IS CLAUDE STERLING. I AM ALSO AUDITIONING FOR THE ROLE OF THE PRINCE.
WHAT'S *HE* DOING HERE?
WHAT'S HE DOING *HERE?*
CAN YOU BELIEVE IT?
WHERE'S HE FROM?
WOW.
HAWT!
YOU SAID IT.
NEXT!

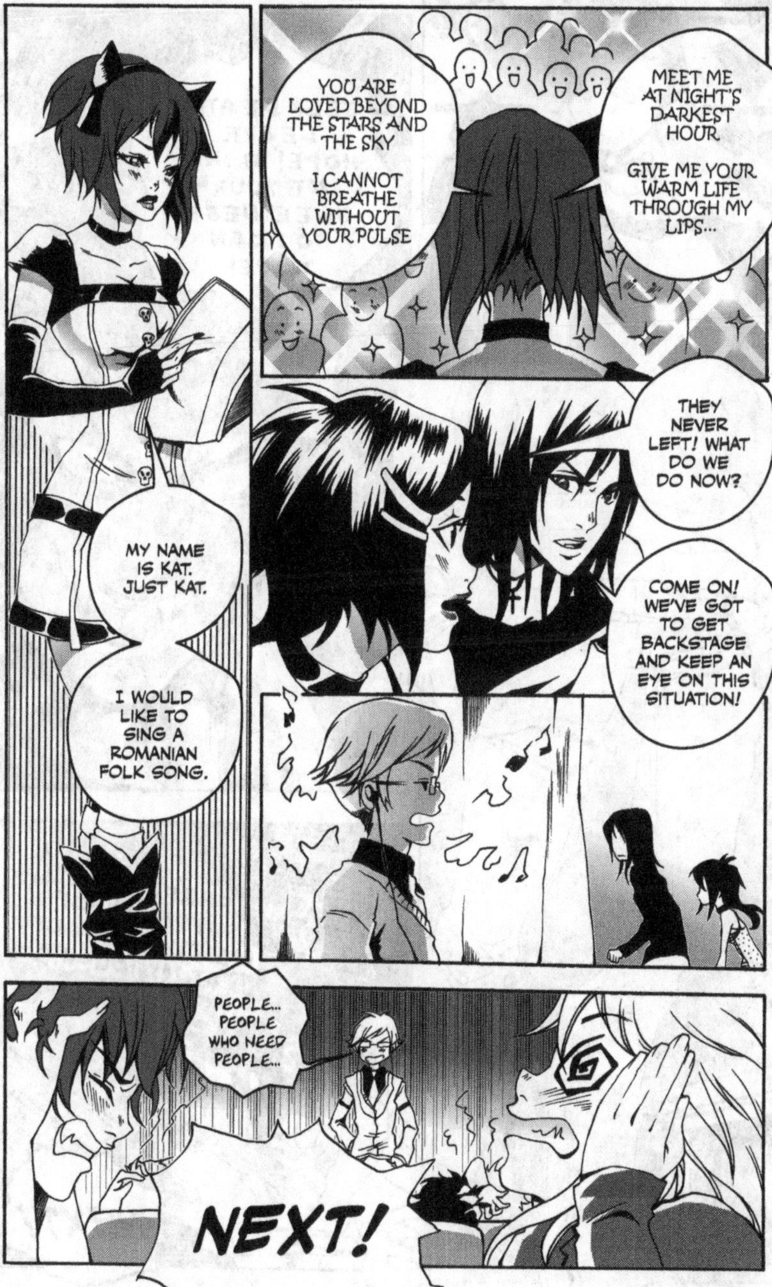
MY NAME IS KAT. JUST KAT.
I WOULD LIKE TO SING A ROMANIAN FOLK SONG.
YOU ARE LOVED BEYOND THE STARS AND THE SKY
I CANNOT BREATHE WITHOUT YOUR PULSE
MEET ME AT NIGHT'S DARKEST HOUR
GIVE ME YOUR WARM LIFE THROUGH MY LIPS...
THEY NEVER LEFT! WHAT DO WE DO NOW?
COME ON! WE'VE GOT TO GET BACKSTAGE AND KEEP AN EYE ON THIS SITUATION!
PEOPLE... PEOPLE WHO NEED PEOPLE...
NEXT!

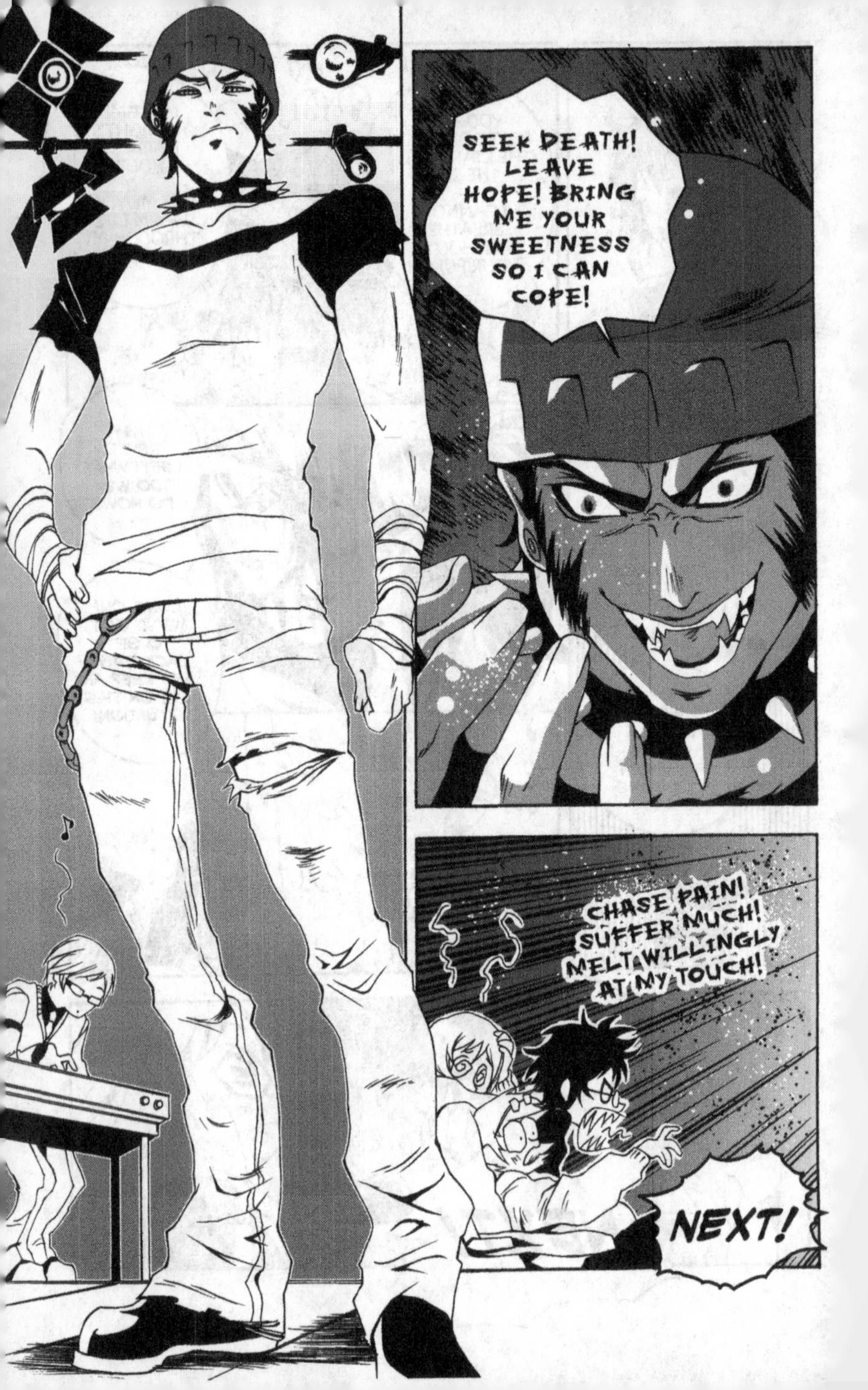
SEEK DEATH! LEAVE HOPE! BRING ME YOUR SWEETNESS SO I CAN COPE!
CHASE PAIN! SUFFER MUCH! MELT WILLINGLY AT MY TOUCH!
NEXT!

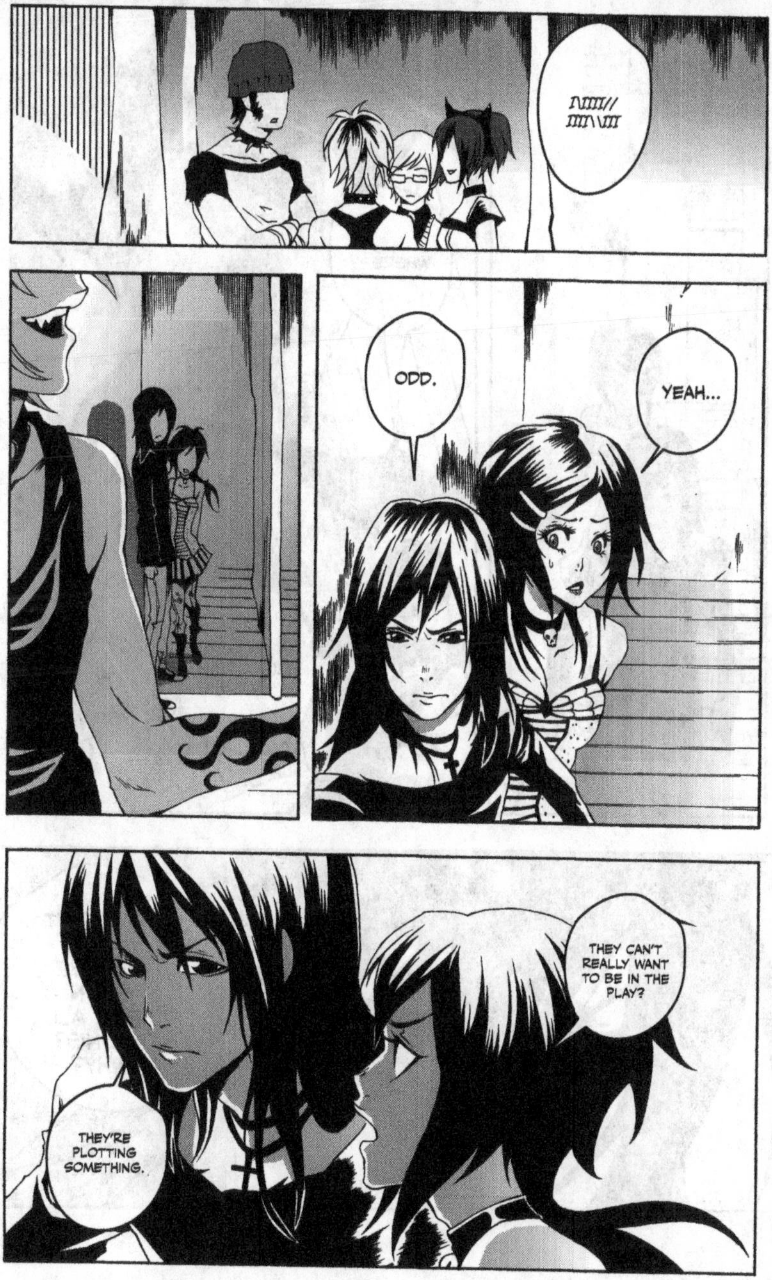
ODD.
YEAH...
THEY CAN'T REALLY WANT TO BE IN THE PLAY?
THEY'RE PLOTTING SOMETHING.

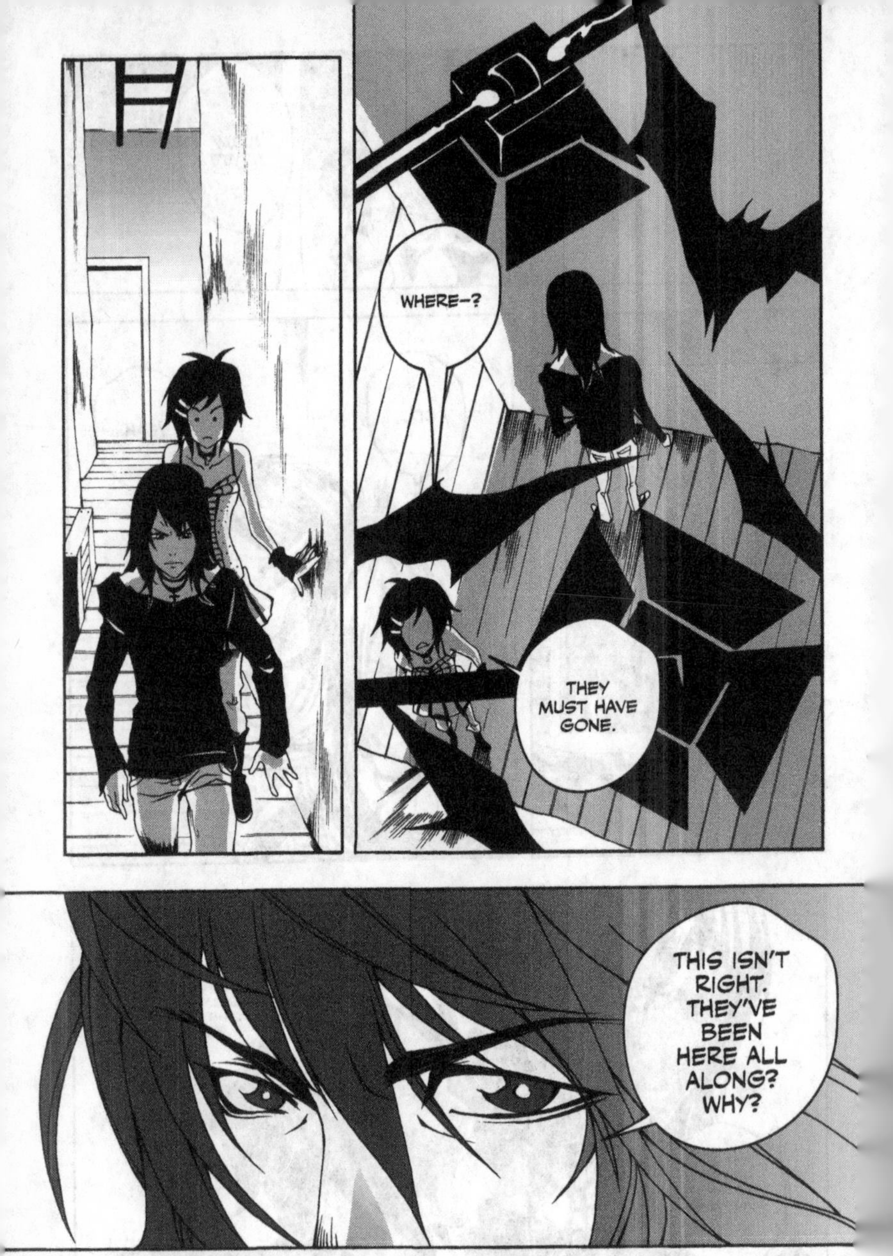
WHERE-?
THEY MUST HAVE GONE.
THIS ISN'T RIGHT. THEY'VE BEEN HERE ALL ALONG? WHY?

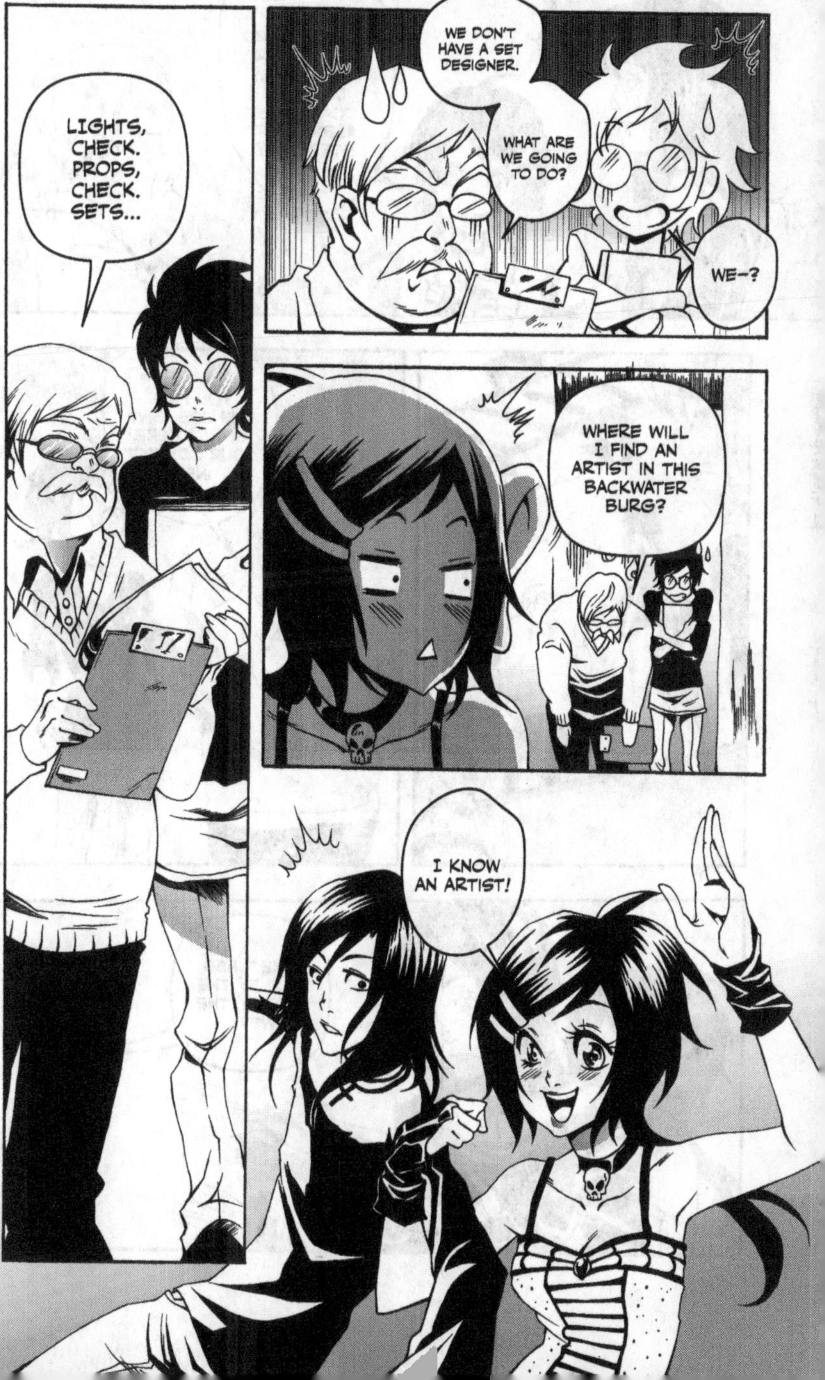
LIGHTS, CHECK. PROPS, CHECK. SETS...
WE DON'T HAVE A SET DESIGNER.
WHAT ARE WE GOING TO DO?
WE-?
WHERE WILL I FIND AN ARTIST IN THIS BACKWATER BURG?
I KNOW AN ARTIST!

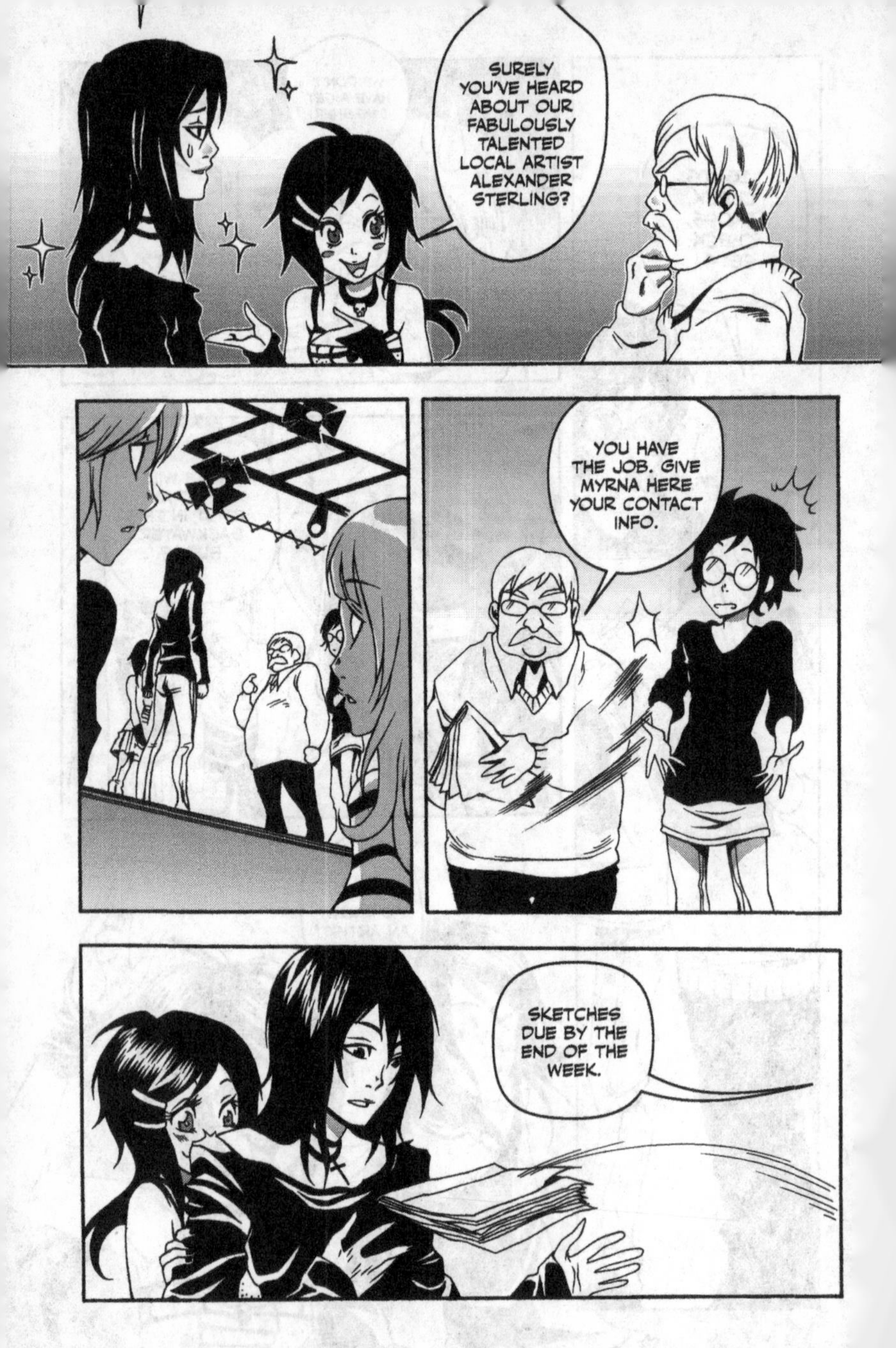
SURELY YOU'VE HEARD ABOUT OUR FABULOUSLY TALENTED LOCAL ARTIST ALEXANDER STERLING?
YOU HAVE THE JOB. GIVE MYRNA HERE YOUR CONTACT INFO.
SKETCHES DUE BY THE END OF THE WEEK.

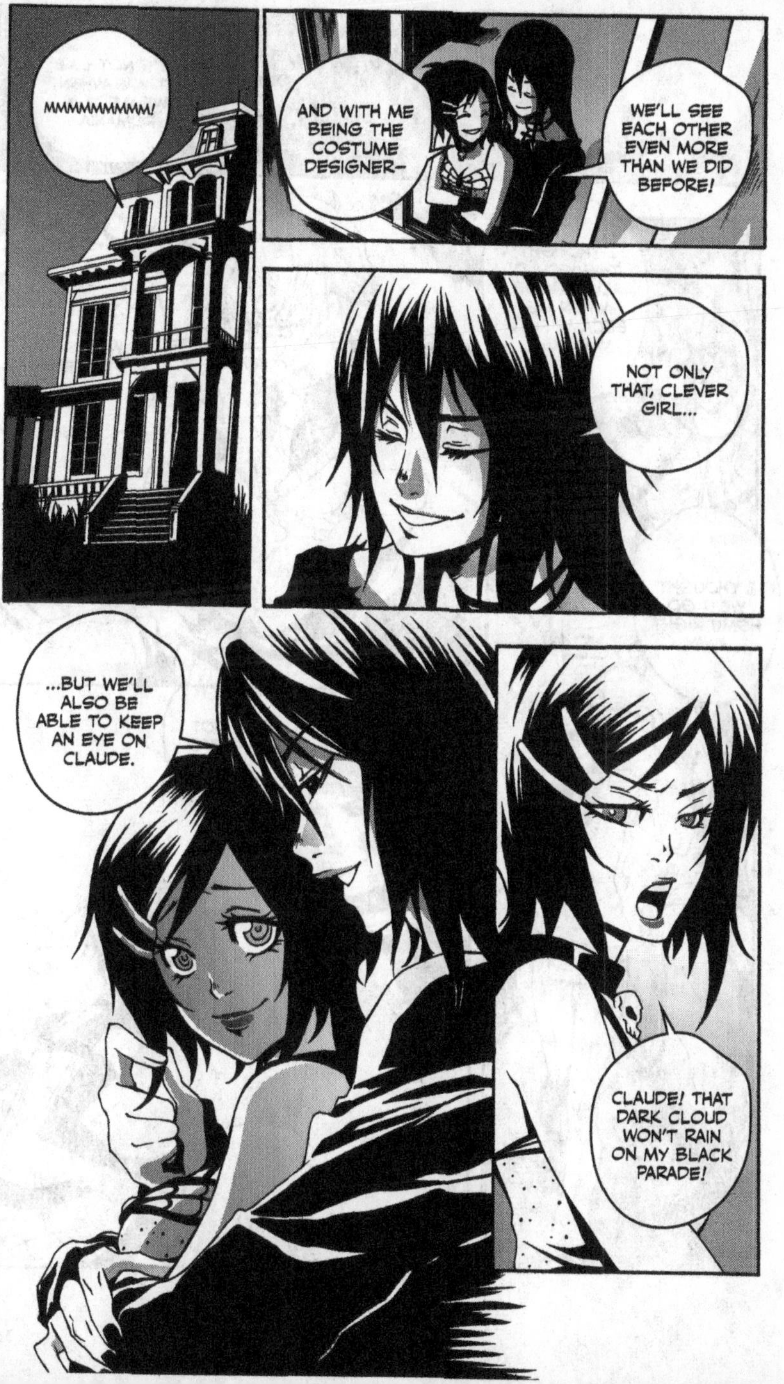
MMMMMMMMMM!
AND WITH ME BEING THE COSTUME DESIGNER–
WE'LL SEE EACH OTHER EVEN MORE THAN WE DID BEFORE!
NOT ONLY THAT, CLEVER GIRL...
...BUT WE'LL ALSO BE ABLE TO KEEP AN EYE ON CLAUDE.
CLAUDE! THAT DARK CLOUD WON'T RAIN ON MY BLACK PARADE!

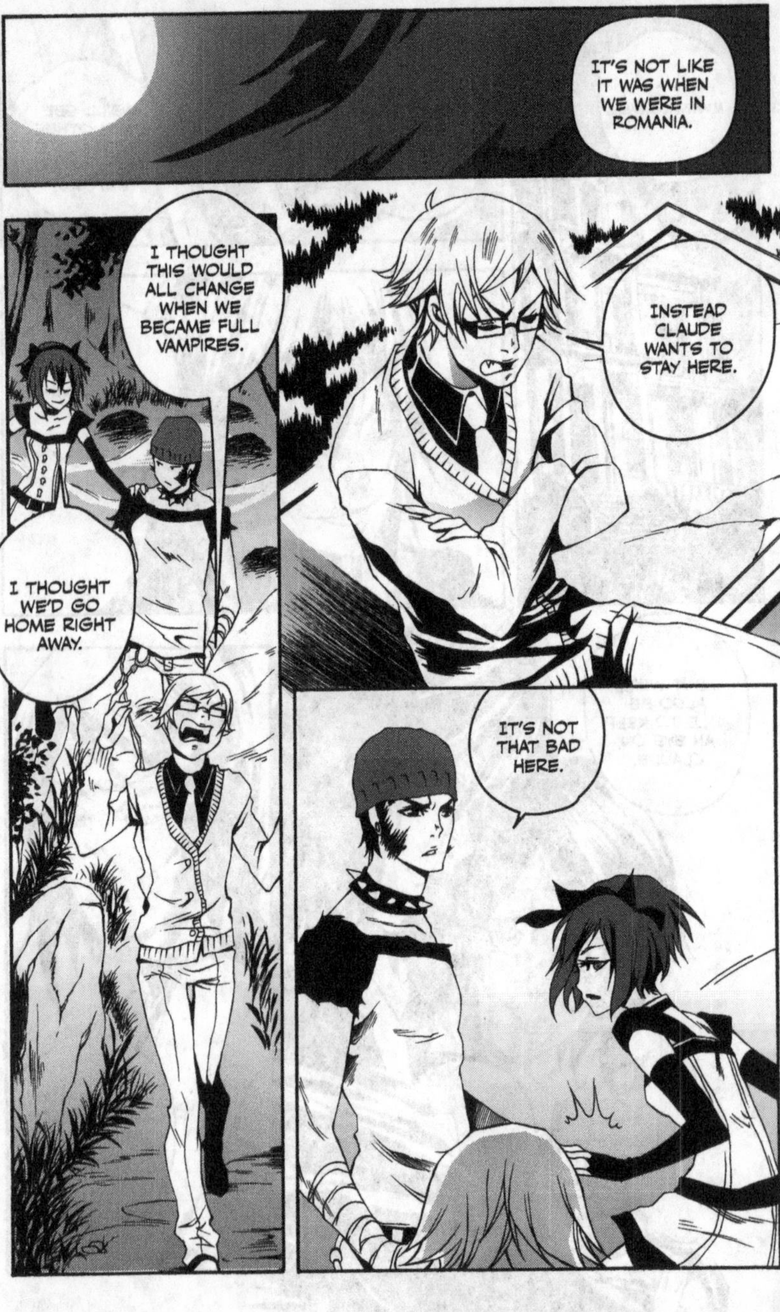
IT'S NOT LIKE IT WAS WHEN WE WERE IN ROMANIA.
I THOUGHT THIS WOULD ALL CHANGE WHEN WE BECAME FULL VAMPIRES.
I THOUGHT WE'D GO HOME RIGHT AWAY.
INSTEAD CLAUDE WANTS TO STAY HERE.
IT'S NOT THAT BAD HERE.

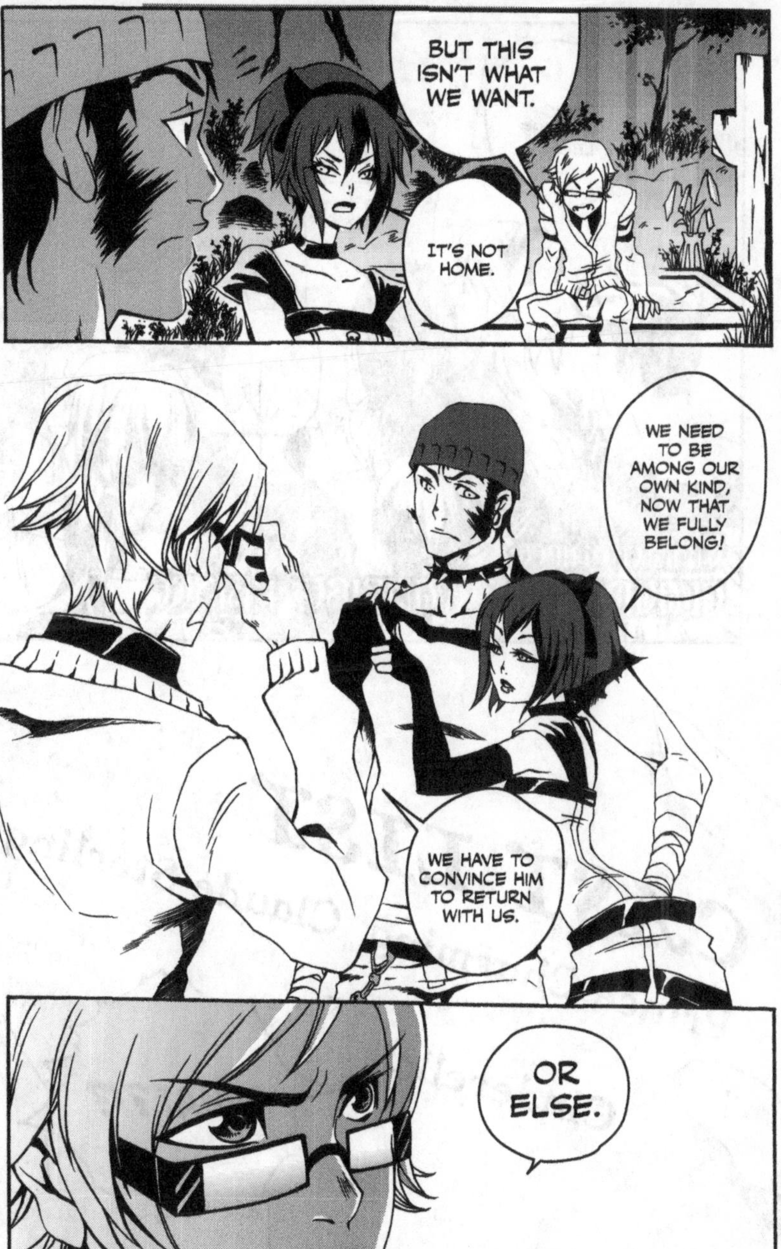
BUT THIS ISN'T WHAT WE WANT.
IT'S NOT HOME.
WE NEED TO BE AMONG OUR OWN KIND, NOW THAT WE FULLY BELONG!
WE HAVE TO CONVINCE HIM TO RETURN WITH US.
OR ELSE.

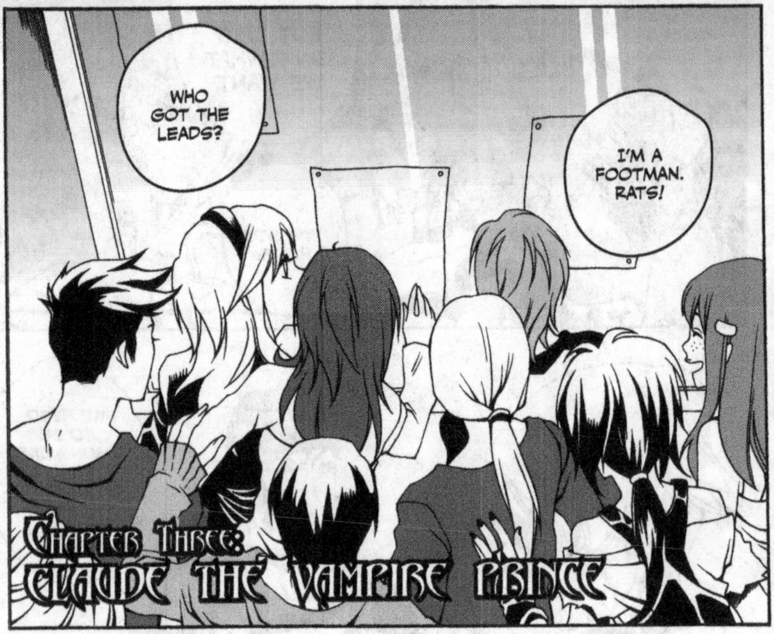
WHO GOT THE LEADS?
I'M A FOOTMAN. RATS!
Chapter Three:
Claude the Vampire Prince
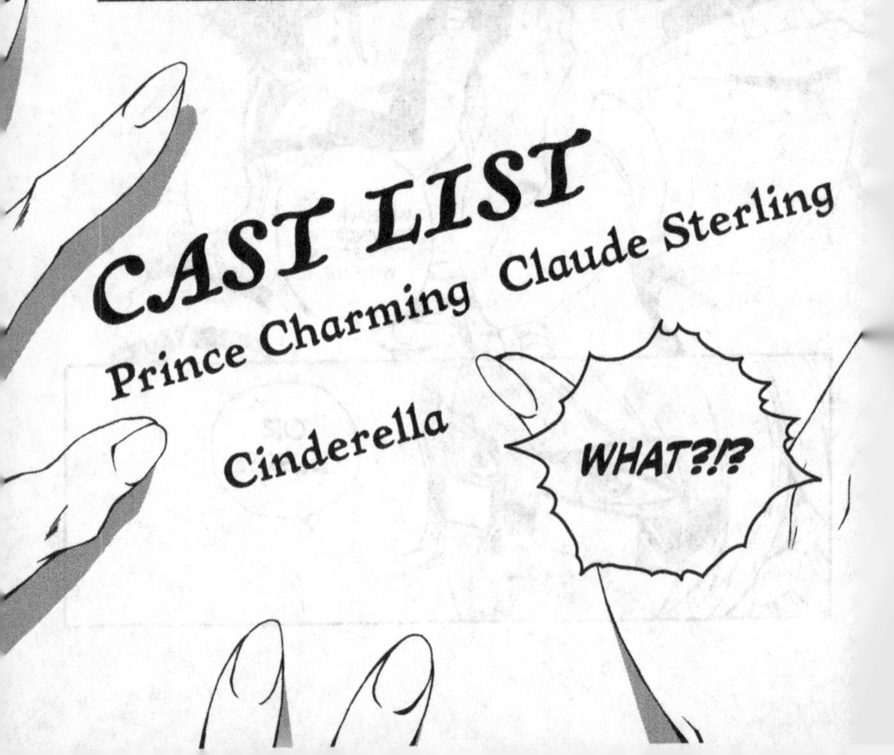
CAST LIST
Prince Charming Claude Sterling
Cinderella
WHAT?!?

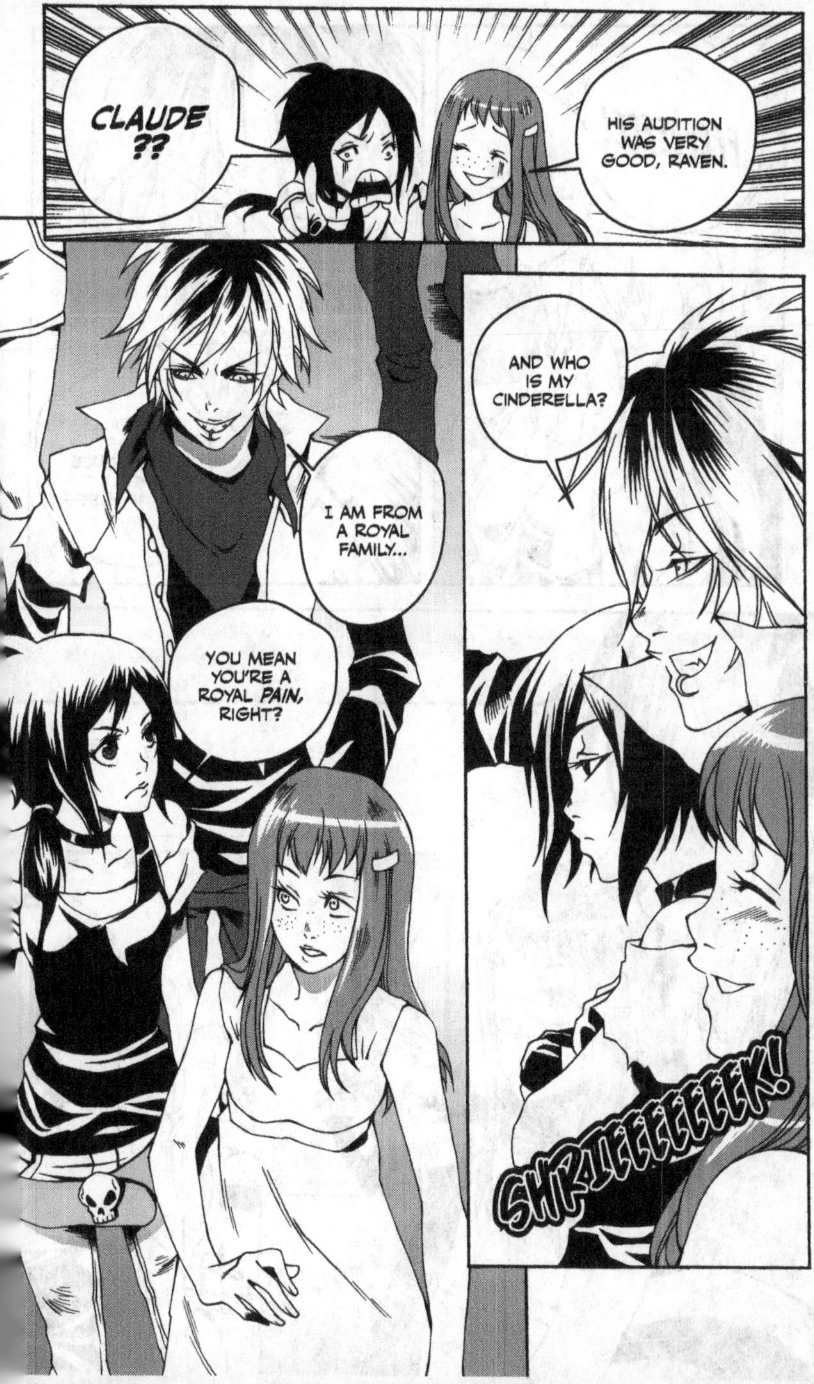
CLAUDE ??
HIS AUDITION WAS VERY GOOD, RAVEN.
I AM FROM A ROYAL FAMILY...
YOU MEAN YOU'RE A ROYAL PAIN, RIGHT?
AND WHO IS MY CINDERELLA?
SHRIEEEEEEEK!

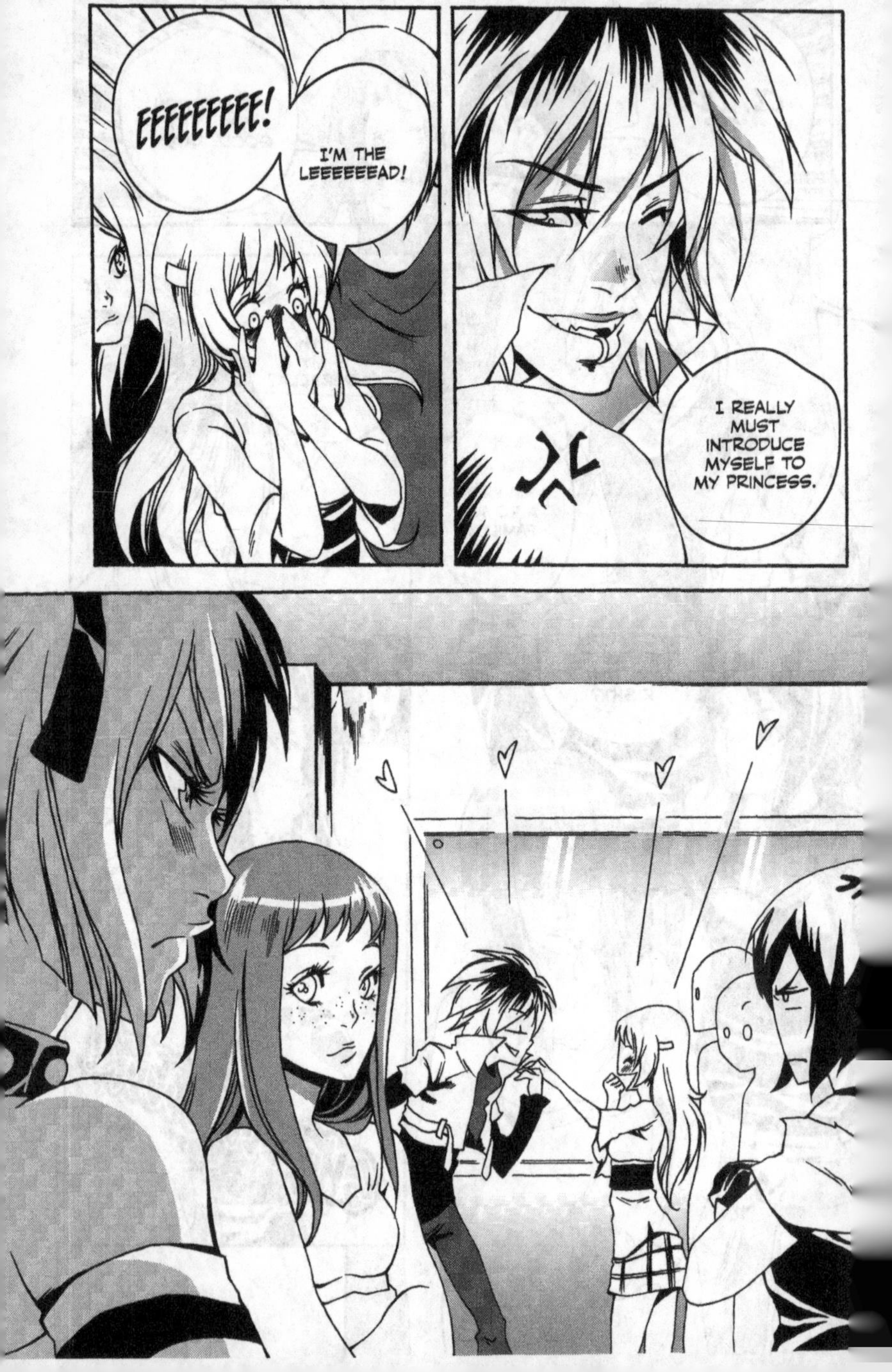
EEEEEEEEE!
I'M THE LEEEEEEAD!
I REALLY MUST INTRODUCE MYSELF TO MY PRINCESS.

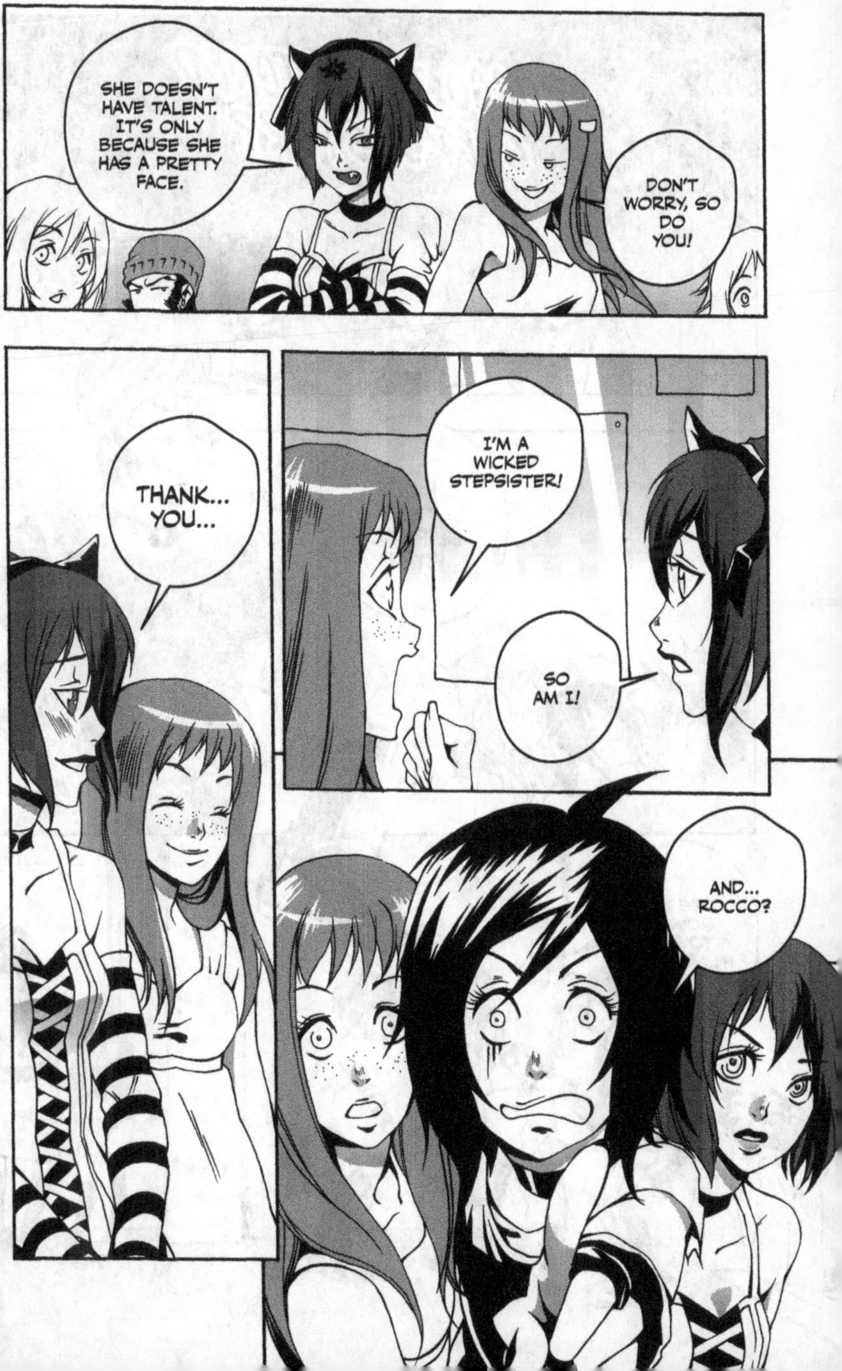
SHE DOESN'T HAVE TALENT. IT'S ONLY BECAUSE SHE HAS A PRETTY FACE.
DON'T WORRY, SO DO YOU!
THANK... YOU...
I'M A WICKED STEPSISTER!
SO AM I!
AND... ROCCO?

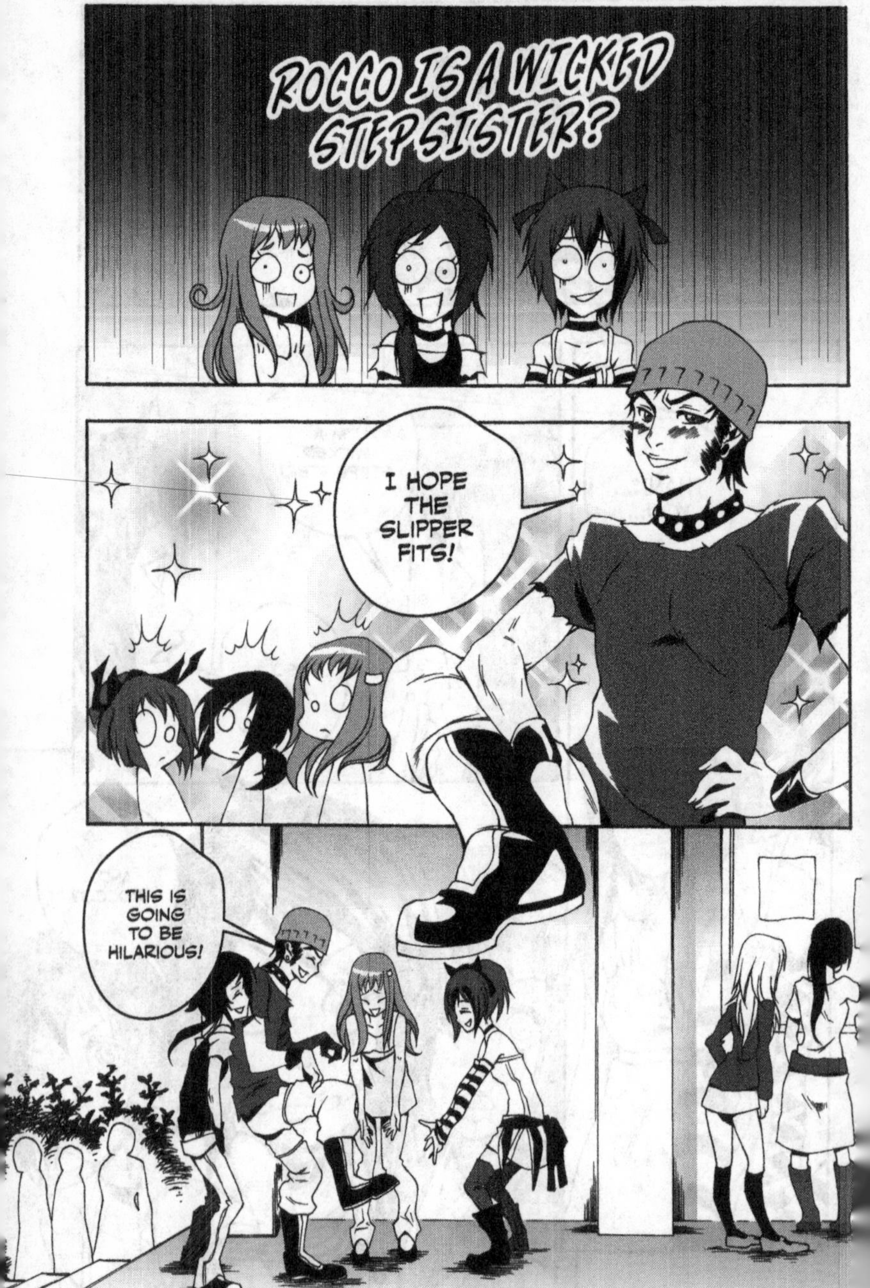
ROCCO IS A WICKED STEPSISTER?
I HOPE THE SLIPPER FITS!
THIS IS GOING TO BE HILARIOUS!

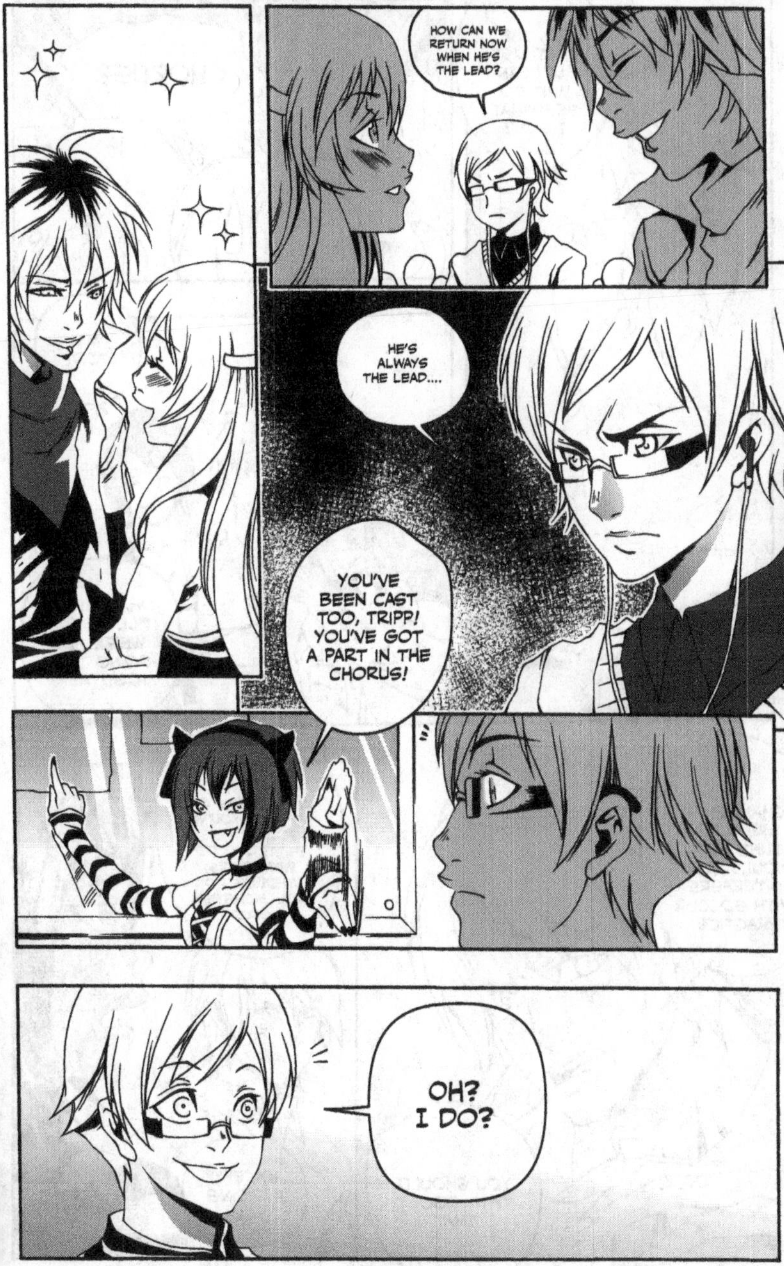
HOW CAN WE RETURN NOW WHEN HE'S THE LEAD?
HE'S ALWAYS THE LEAD....
YOU'VE BEEN CAST TOO, TRIPP! YOU'VE GOT A PART IN THE CHORUS!
OH? I DO?

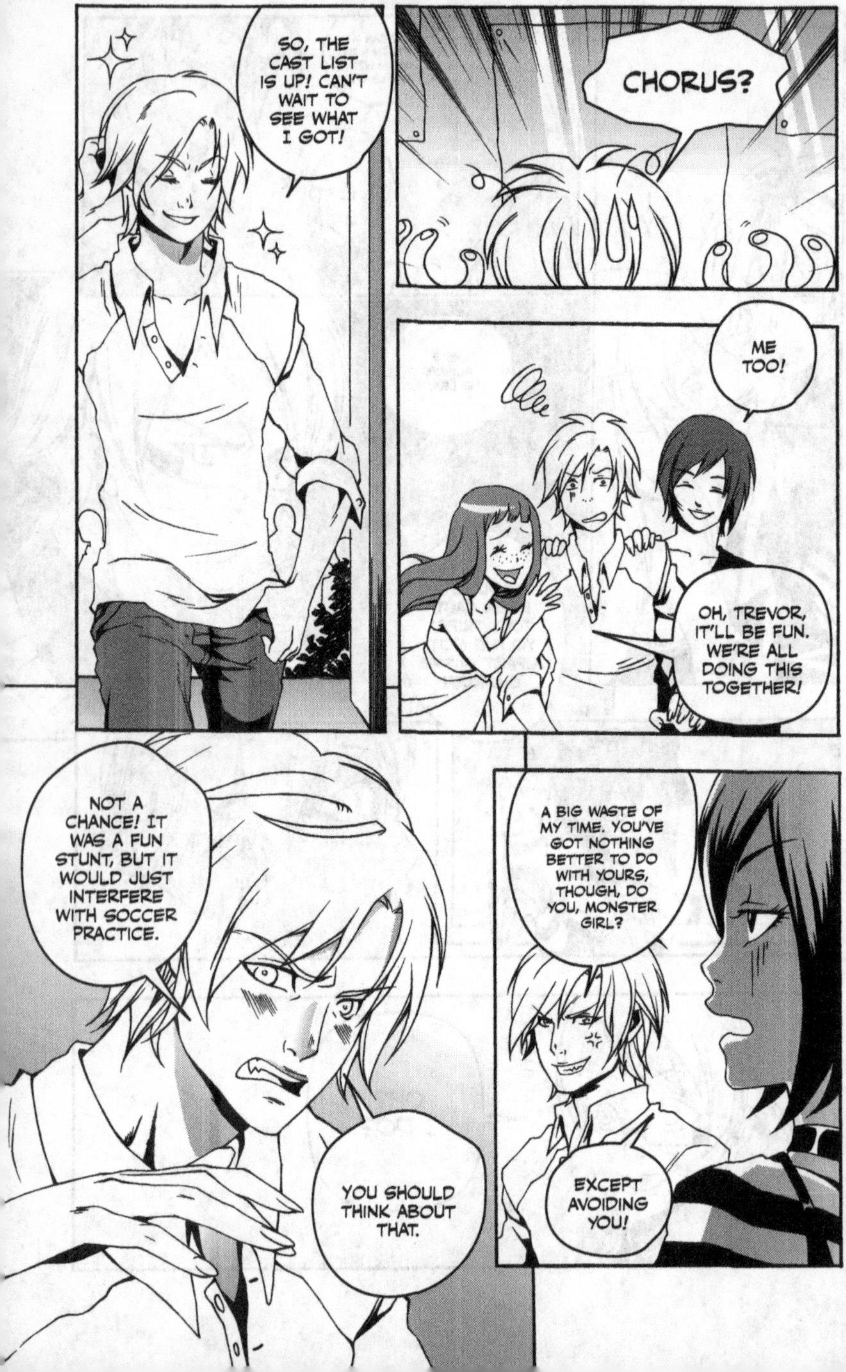
SO, THE CAST LIST IS UP! CAN'T WAIT TO SEE WHAT I GOT!
CHORUS?
ME TOO!
OH, TREVOR, IT'LL BE FUN. WE'RE ALL DOING THIS TOGETHER!
NOT A CHANCE! IT WAS A FUN STUNT, BUT IT WOULD JUST INTERFERE WITH SOCCER PRACTICE.
YOU SHOULD THINK ABOUT THAT.
A BIG WASTE OF MY TIME. YOU'VE GOT NOTHING BETTER TO DO WITH YOURS, THOUGH, DO YOU, MONSTER GIRL?
EXCEPT AVOIDING YOU!

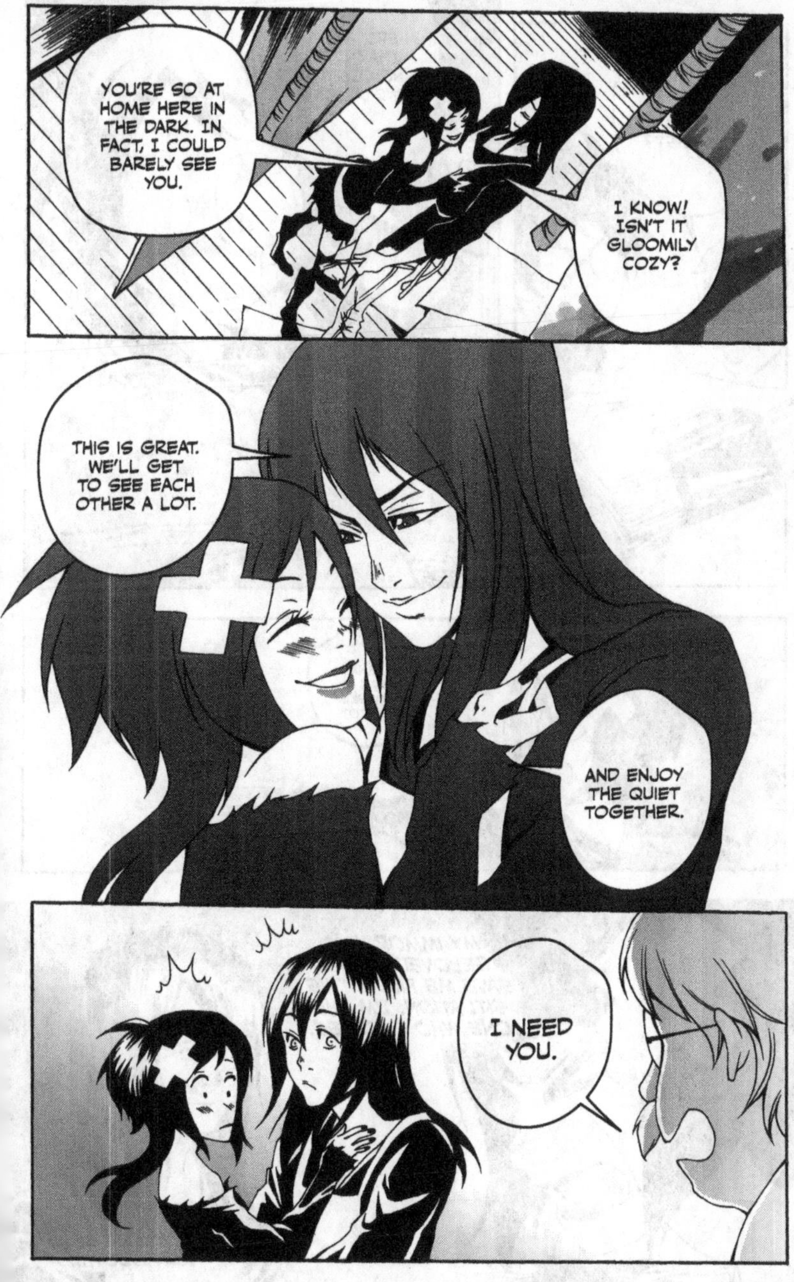
YOU'RE SO AT HOME HERE IN THE DARK. IN FACT, I COULD BARELY SEE YOU.
I KNOW! ISN'T IT GLOOMILY COZY?
THIS IS GREAT. WE'LL GET TO SEE EACH OTHER A LOT.
AND ENJOY THE QUIET TOGETHER.
I NEED YOU.

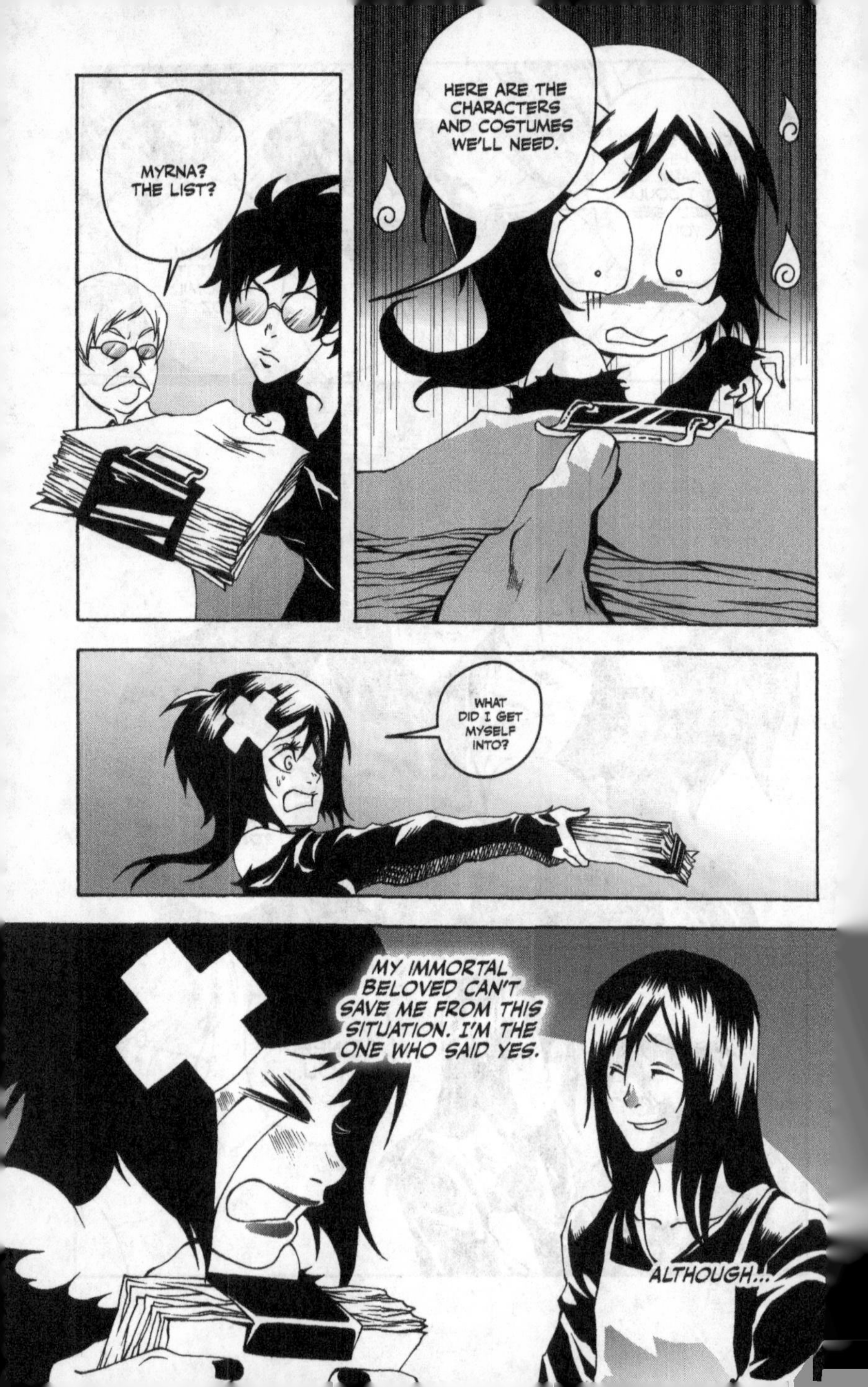
MYRNA? THE LIST?
HERE ARE THE CHARACTERS AND COSTUMES WE'LL NEED.
WHAT DID I GET MYSELF INTO?
MY IMMORTAL BELOVED CAN'T SAVE ME FROM THIS SITUATION. I'M THE ONE WHO SAID YES.
ALTHOUGH...

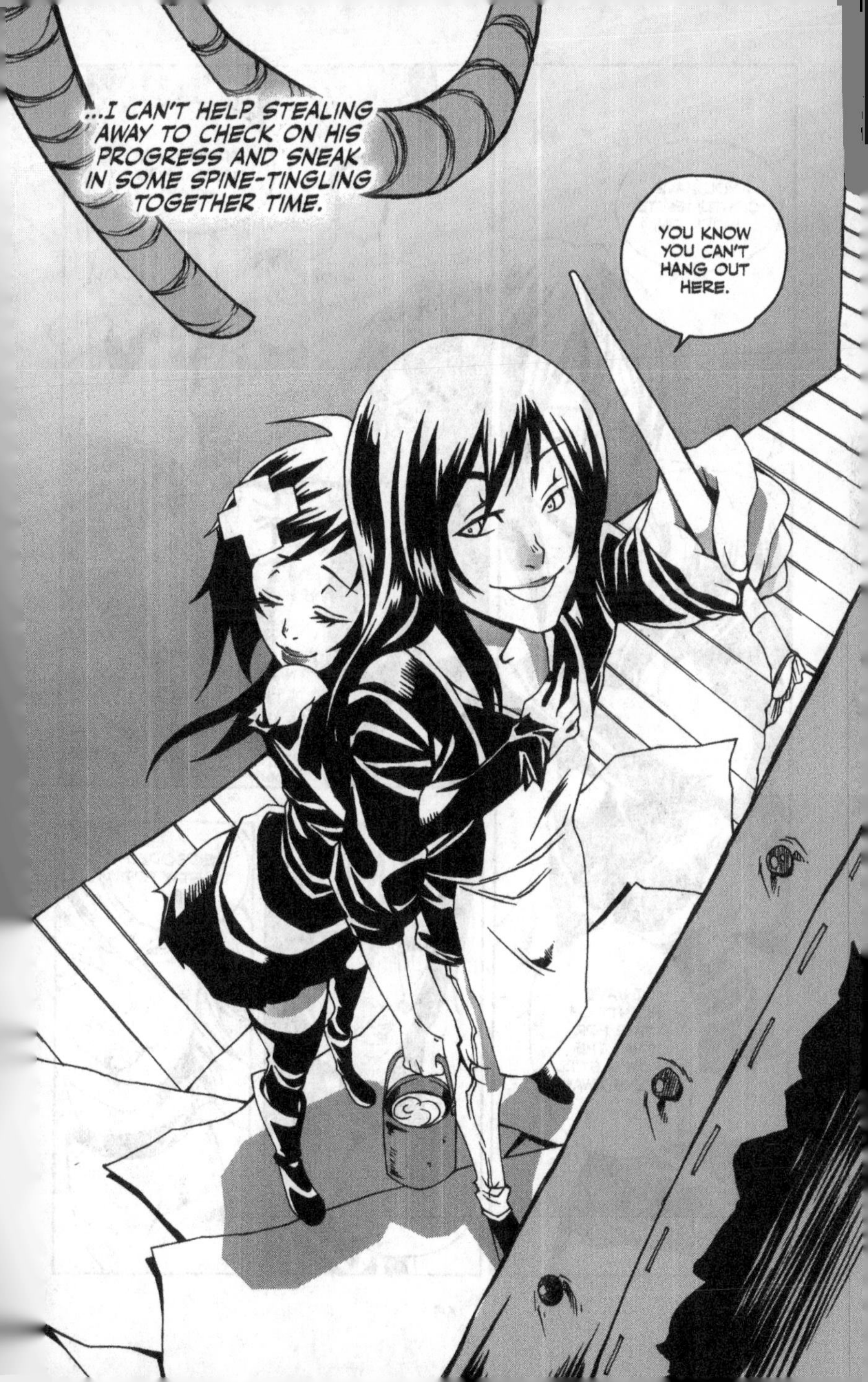
...I CAN'T HELP STEALING AWAY TO CHECK ON HIS PROGRESS AND SNEAK IN SOME SPINE-TINGLING TOGETHER TIME.
YOU KNOW YOU CAN'T HANG OUT HERE.

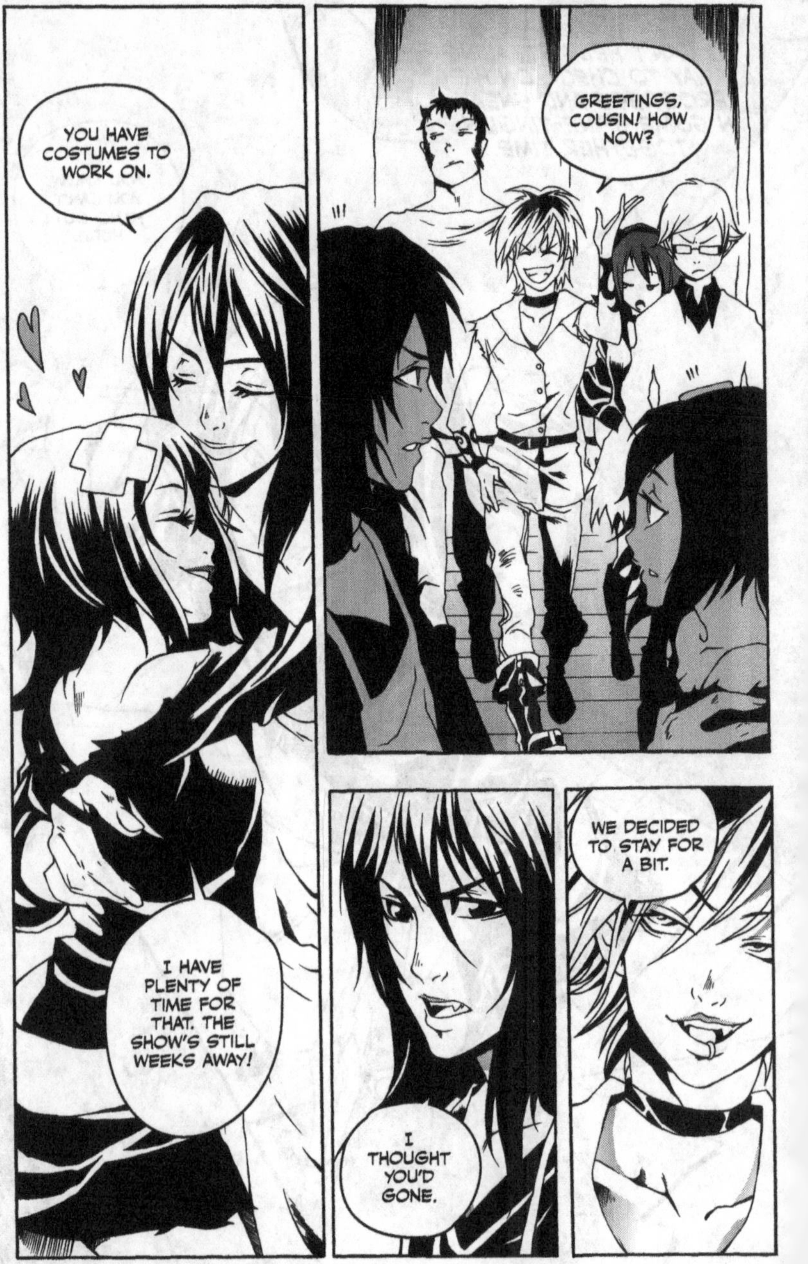
YOU HAVE COSTUMES TO WORK ON.
I HAVE PLENTY OF TIME FOR THAT. THE SHOW'S STILL WEEKS AWAY!
GREETINGS, COUSIN! HOW NOW?
I THOUGHT YOU'D GONE.
WE DECIDED TO STAY FOR A BIT.

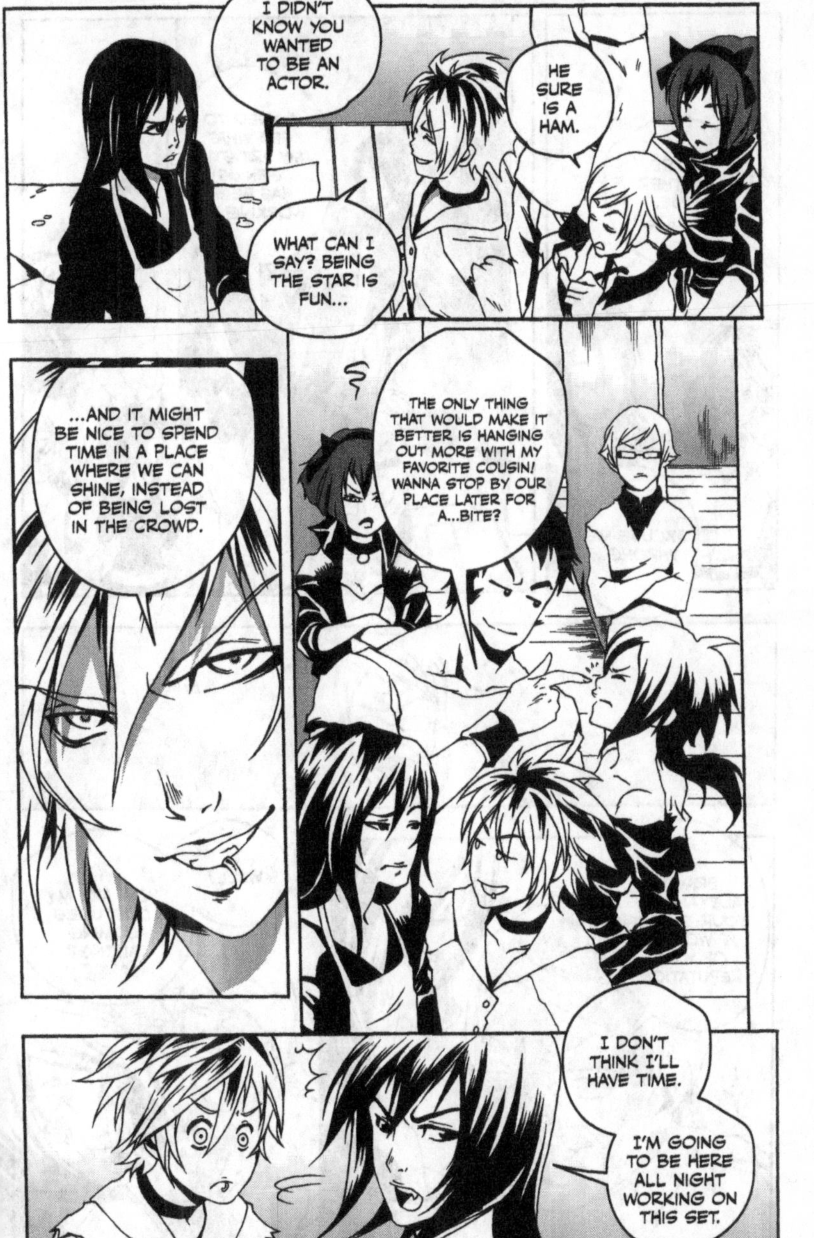
I DIDN'T KNOW YOU WANTED TO BE AN ACTOR.
HE SURE IS A HAM.
WHAT CAN I SAY? BEING THE STAR IS FUN...
...AND IT MIGHT BE NICE TO SPEND TIME IN A PLACE WHERE WE CAN SHINE, INSTEAD OF BEING LOST IN THE CROWD.
THE ONLY THING THAT WOULD MAKE IT BETTER IS HANGING OUT MORE WITH MY FAVORITE COUSIN! WANNA STOP BY OUR PLACE LATER FOR A...BITE?
I DON'T THINK I'LL HAVE TIME.
I'M GOING TO BE HERE ALL NIGHT WORKING ON THIS SET.

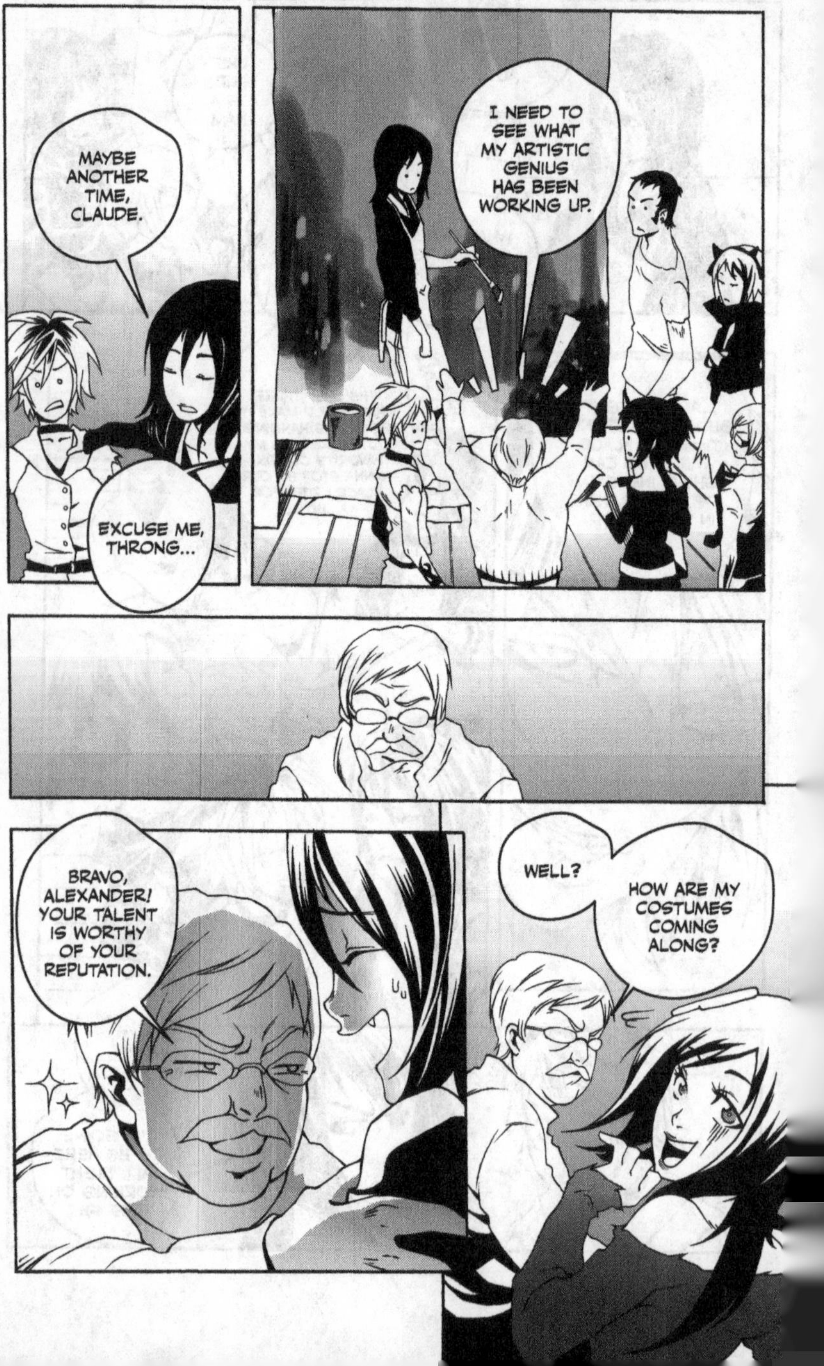
MAYBE ANOTHER TIME, CLAUDE.
EXCUSE ME, THRONG...
I NEED TO SEE WHAT MY ARTISTIC GENIUS HAS BEEN WORKING UP.
BRAVO, ALEXANDER! YOUR TALENT IS WORTHY OF YOUR REPUTATION.
WELL?
HOW ARE MY COSTUMES COMING ALONG?

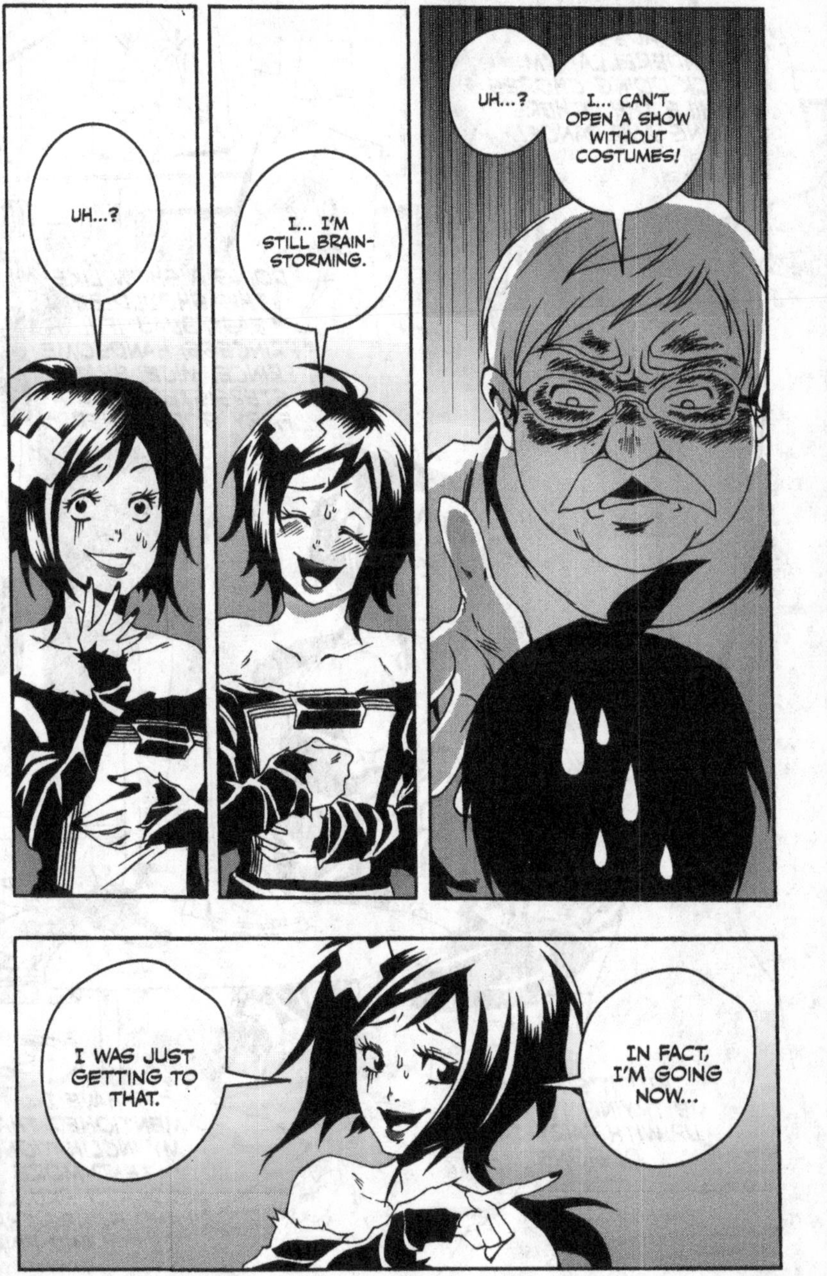
UH...?
I... I'M STILL BRAIN-STORMING.
UH...?
I... CAN'T OPEN A SHOW WITHOUT COSTUMES!
I WAS JUST GETTING TO THAT.
IN FACT, I'M GOING NOW...

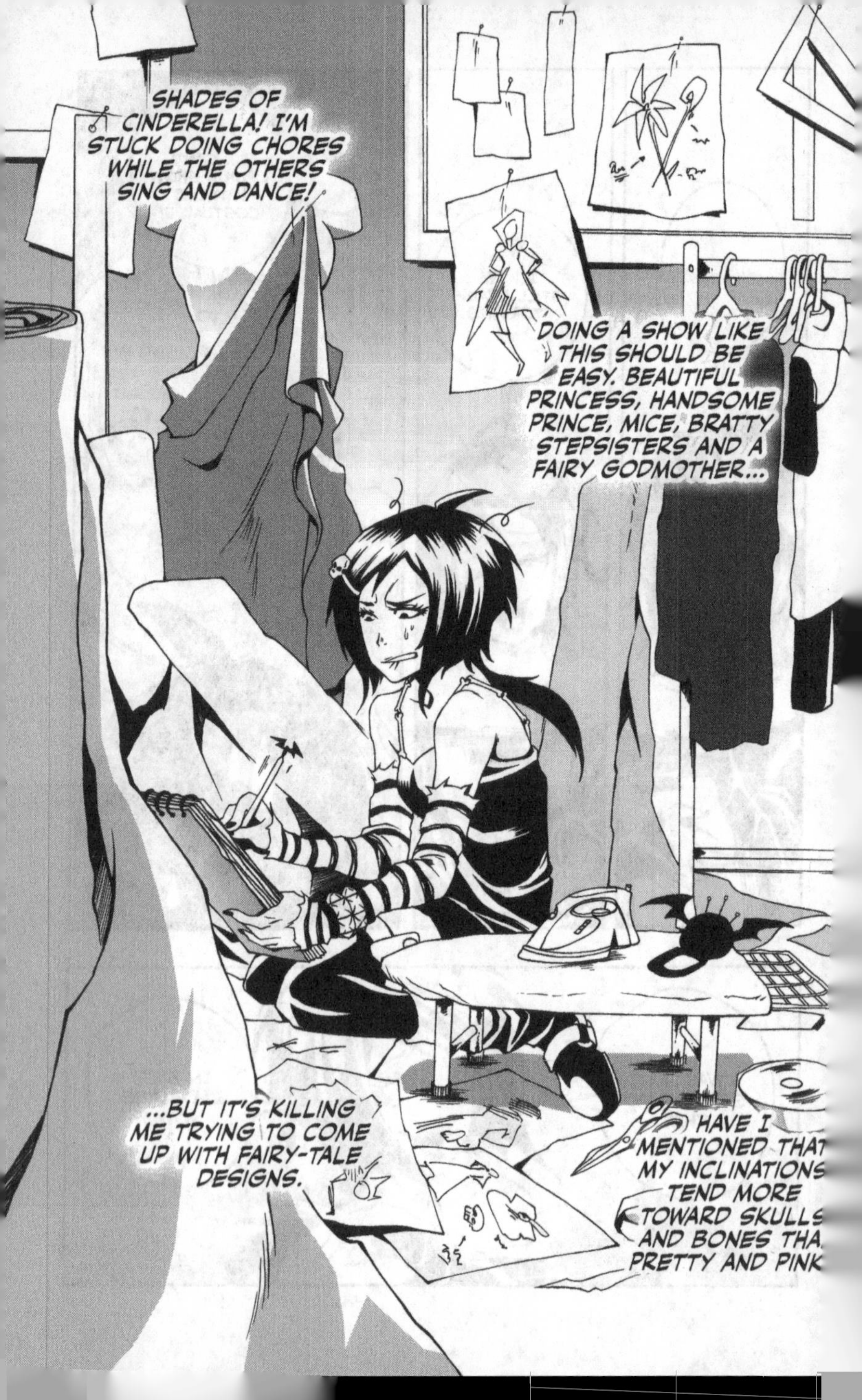
SHADES OF CINDERELLA! I'M STUCK DOING CHORES WHILE THE OTHERS SING AND DANCE!
DOING A SHOW LIKE THIS SHOULD BE EASY. BEAUTIFUL PRINCESS, HANDSOME PRINCE, MICE, BRATTY STEPSISTERS AND A FAIRY GODMOTHER...
...BUT IT'S KILLING ME TRYING TO COME UP WITH FAIRY-TALE DESIGNS.
HAVE I MENTIONED THAT MY INCLINATIONS TEND MORE TOWARD SKULLS AND BONES THAN PRETTY AND PINK

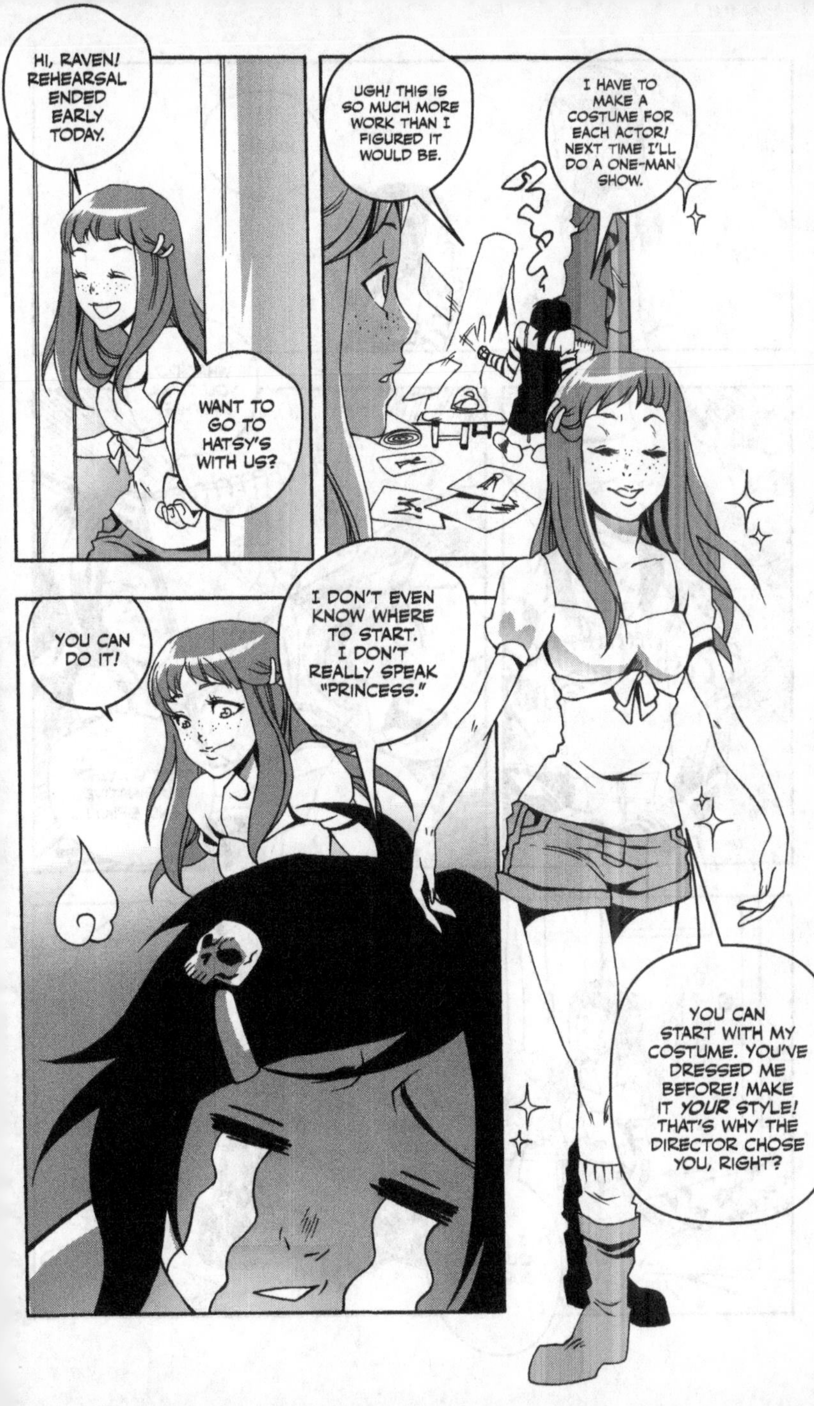
HI, RAVEN! REHEARSAL ENDED EARLY TODAY.
WANT TO GO TO HATSY'S WITH US?
UGH! THIS IS SO MUCH MORE WORK THAN I FIGURED IT WOULD BE.
I HAVE TO MAKE A COSTUME FOR EACH ACTOR! NEXT TIME I'LL DO A ONE-MAN SHOW.
YOU CAN DO IT!
I DON'T EVEN KNOW WHERE TO START. I DON'T REALLY SPEAK "PRINCESS."
YOU CAN START WITH MY COSTUME. YOU'VE DRESSED ME BEFORE! MAKE IT *YOUR* STYLE! THAT'S WHY THE DIRECTOR CHOSE YOU, RIGHT?

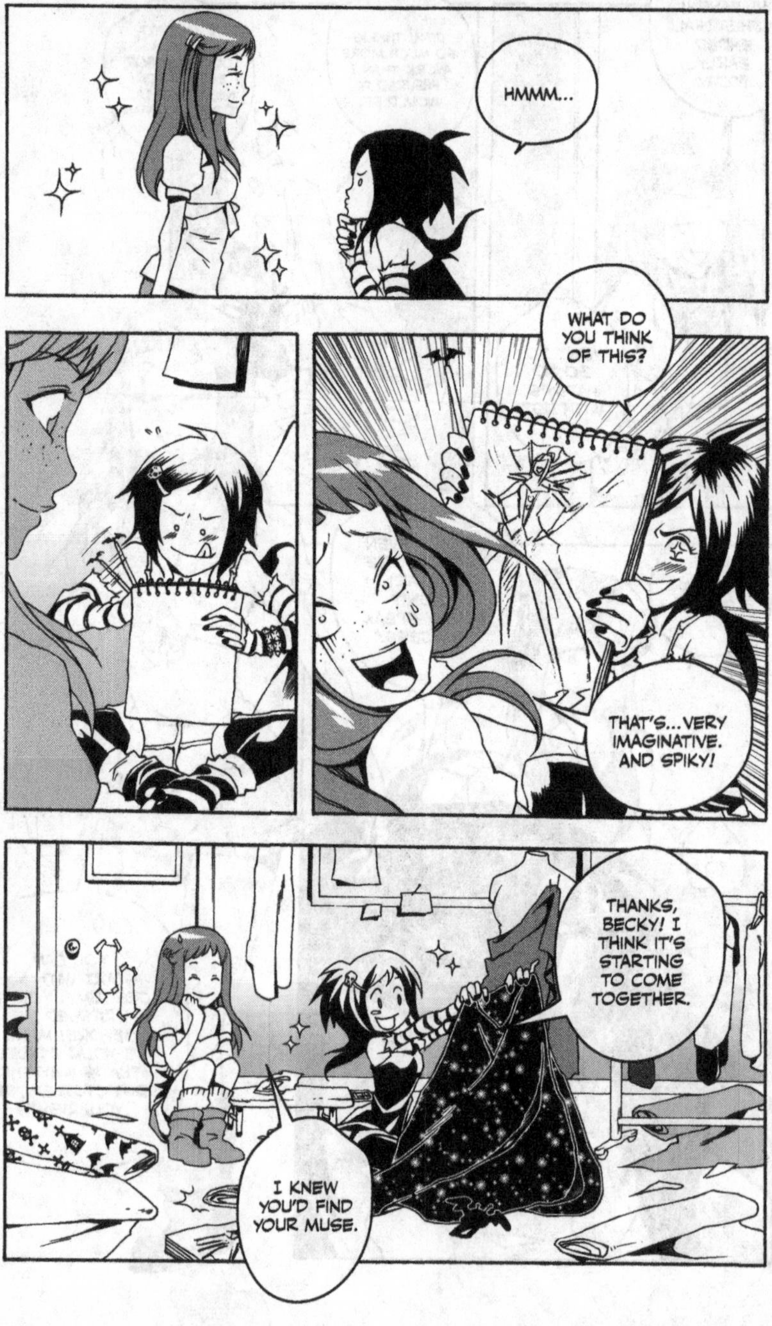
HMMM...
WHAT DO YOU THINK OF THIS?
THAT'S...VERY IMAGINATIVE. AND SPIKY!
I KNEW YOU'D FIND YOUR MUSE.
THANKS, BECKY! I THINK IT'S STARTING TO COME TOGETHER.

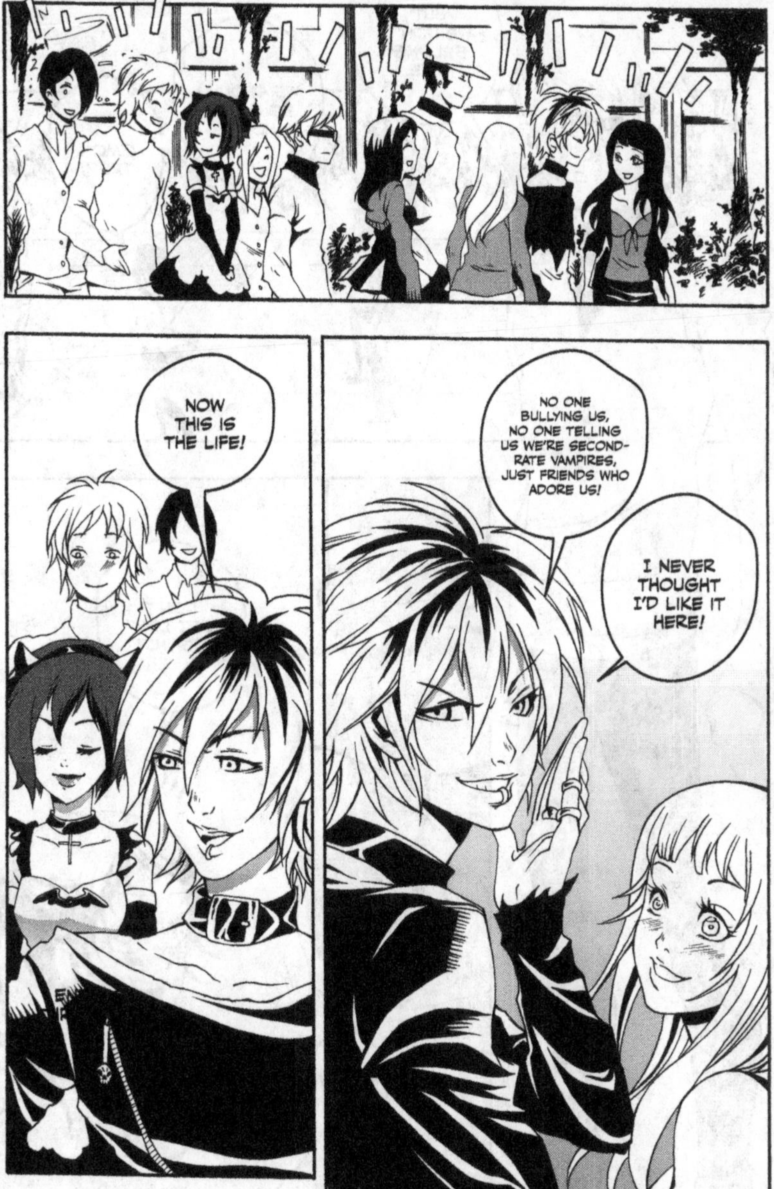
NOW THIS IS THE LIFE!
NO ONE BULLYING US, NO ONE TELLING US WE'RE SECOND-RATE VAMPIRES, JUST FRIENDS WHO ADORE US!
I NEVER THOUGHT I'D LIKE IT HERE!

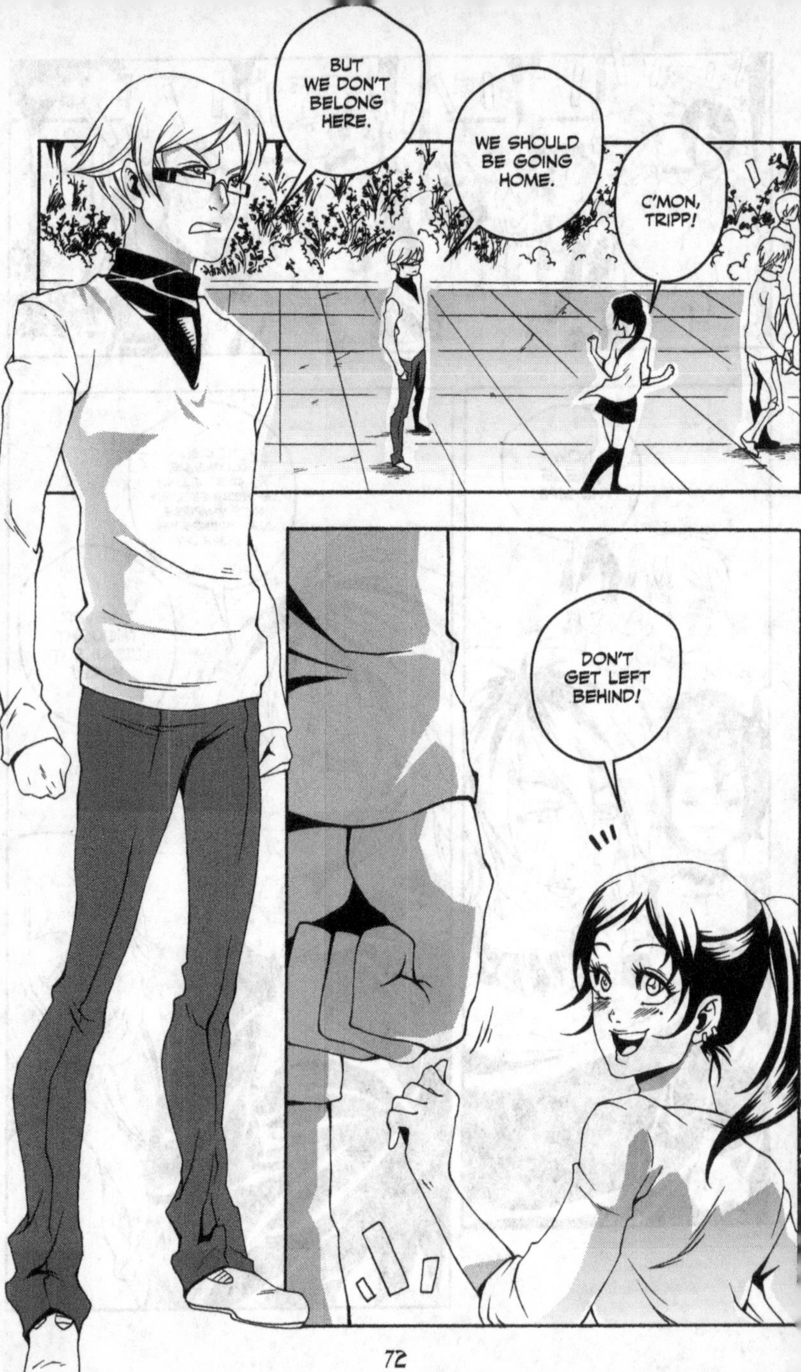
BUT WE DON'T BELONG HERE.
WE SHOULD BE GOING HOME.
C'MON, TRIPP!
DON'T GET LEFT BEHIND!

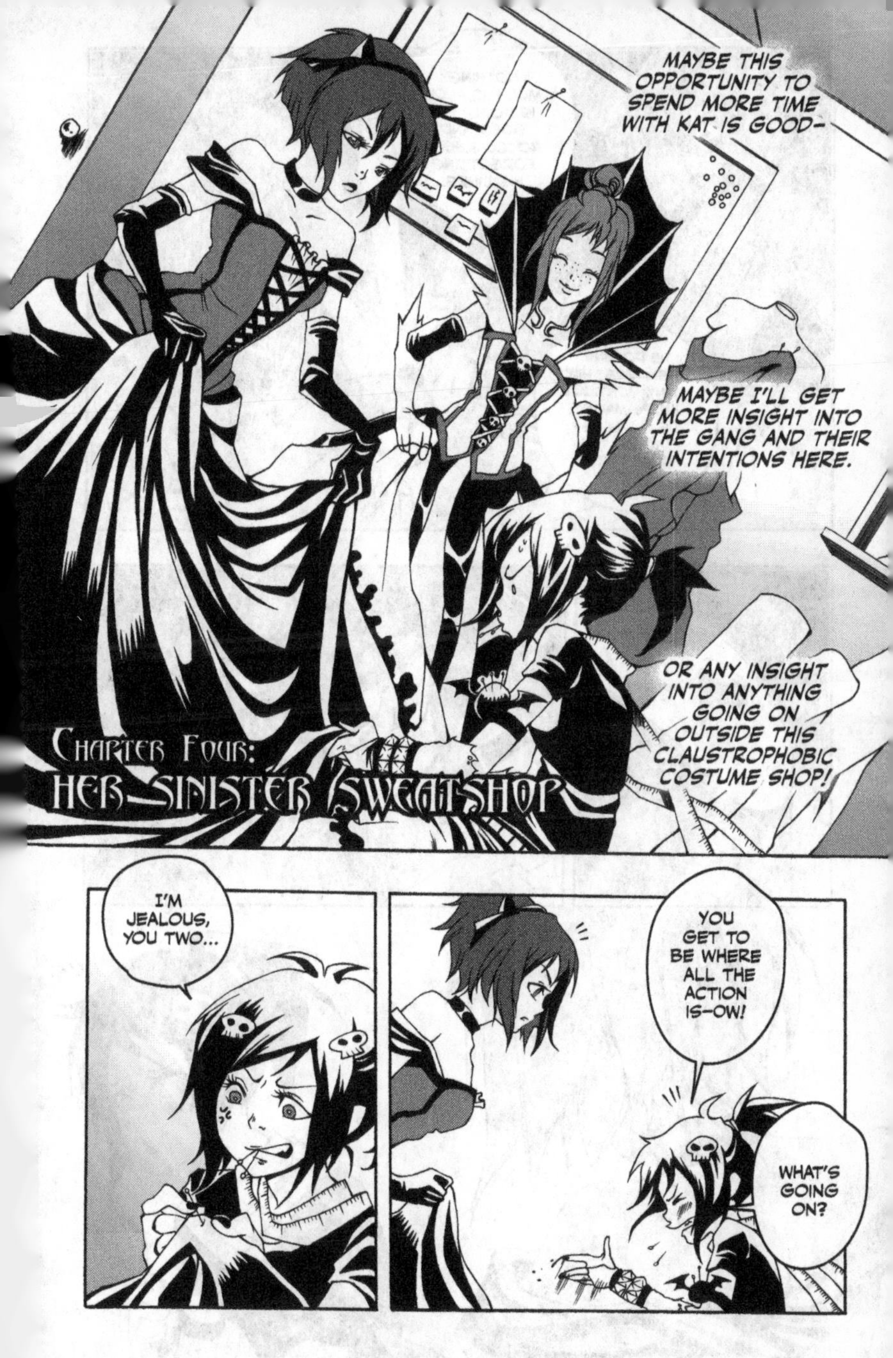
MAYBE THIS OPPORTUNITY TO SPEND MORE TIME WITH KAT IS GOOD–
MAYBE I'LL GET MORE INSIGHT INTO THE GANG AND THEIR INTENTIONS HERE.
OR ANY INSIGHT INTO ANYTHING GOING ON OUTSIDE THIS CLAUSTROPHOBIC COSTUME SHOP!
CHAPTER FOUR:
HER SINISTER SWEATSHOP
I'M JEALOUS, YOU TWO...
YOU GET TO BE WHERE ALL THE ACTION IS–OW!
WHAT'S GOING ON?

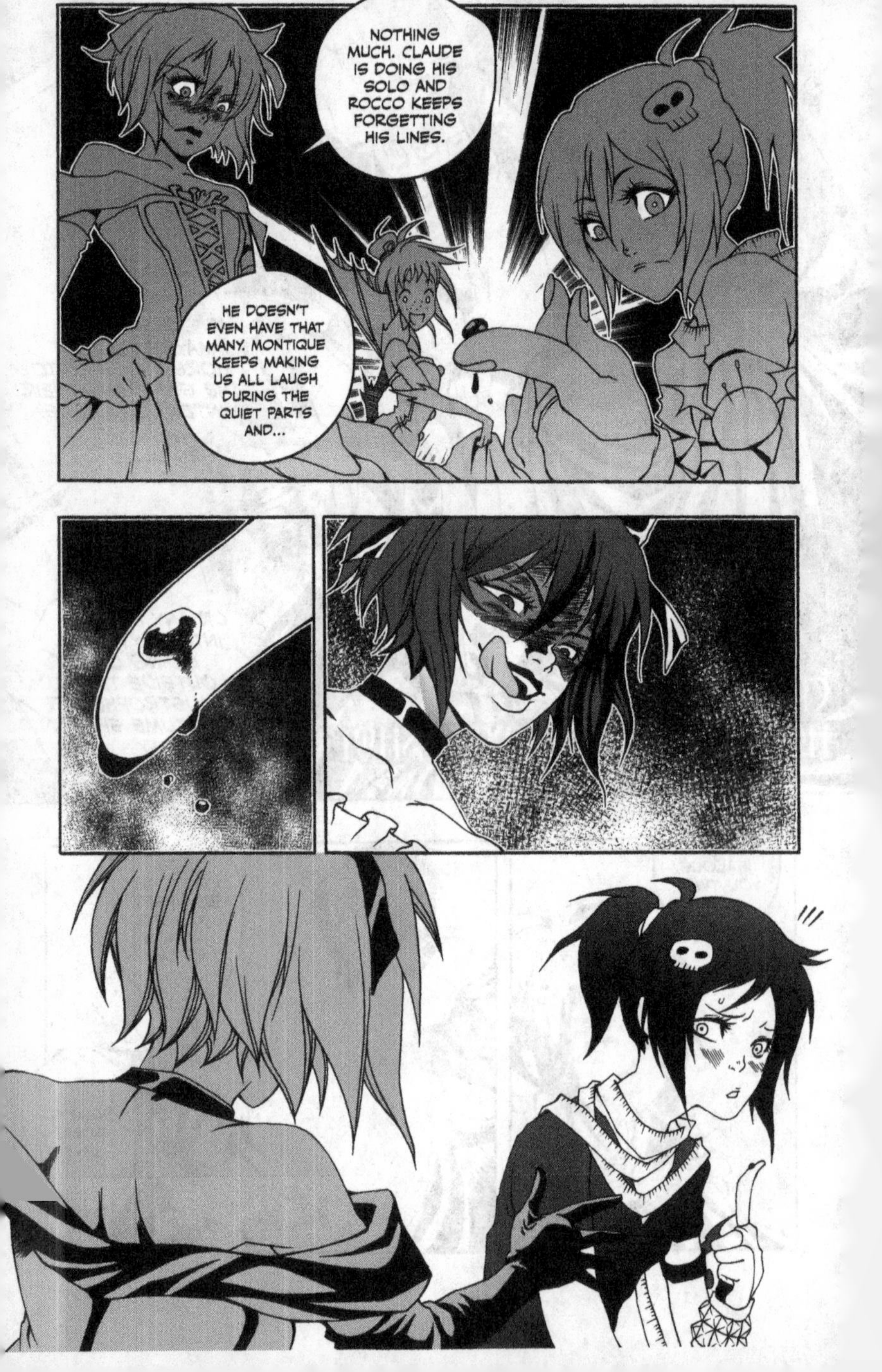
NOTHING MUCH. CLAUDE IS DOING HIS SOLO AND ROCCO KEEPS FORGETTING HIS LINES.
HE DOESN'T EVEN HAVE THAT MANY. MONTIQUE KEEPS MAKING US ALL LAUGH DURING THE QUIET PARTS AND...

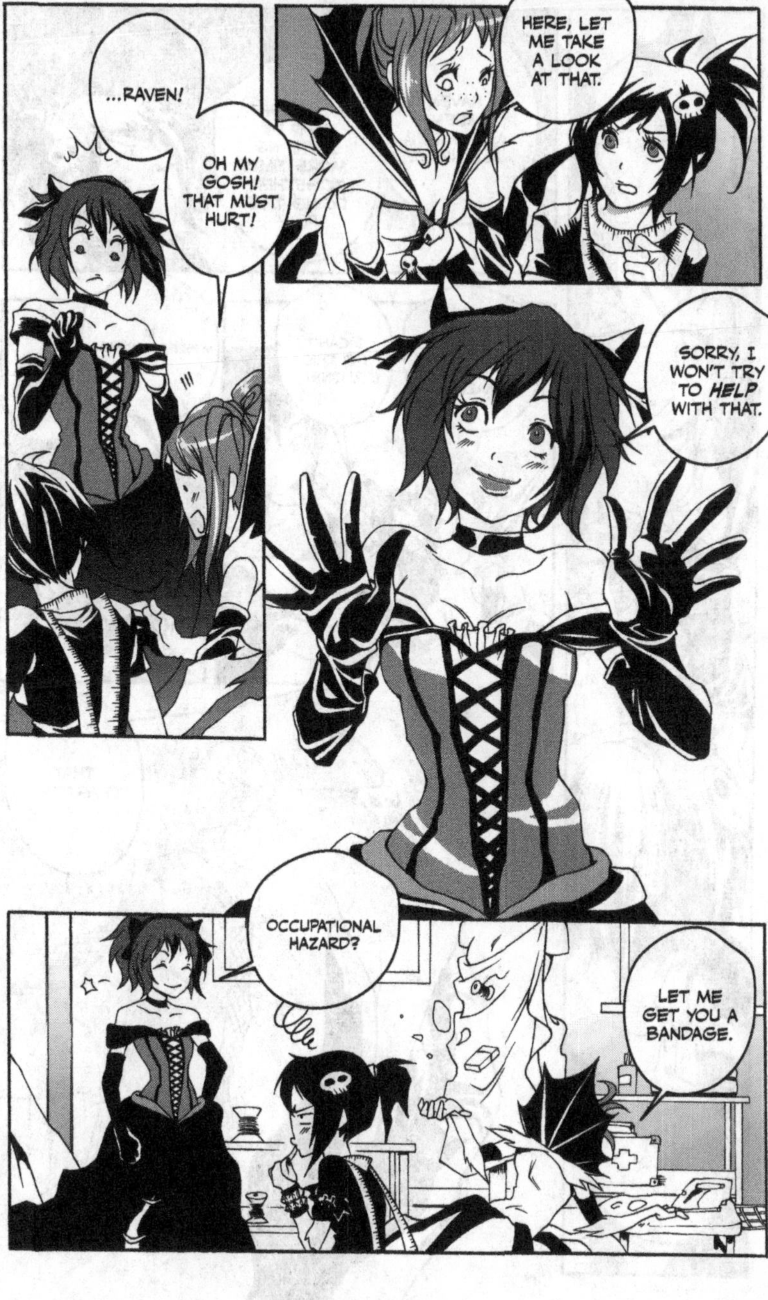
...RAVEN!
OH MY GOSH! THAT MUST HURT!
HERE, LET ME TAKE A LOOK AT THAT.
SORRY, I WON'T TRY TO *HELP* WITH THAT.
OCCUPATIONAL HAZARD?
LET ME GET YOU A BANDAGE.

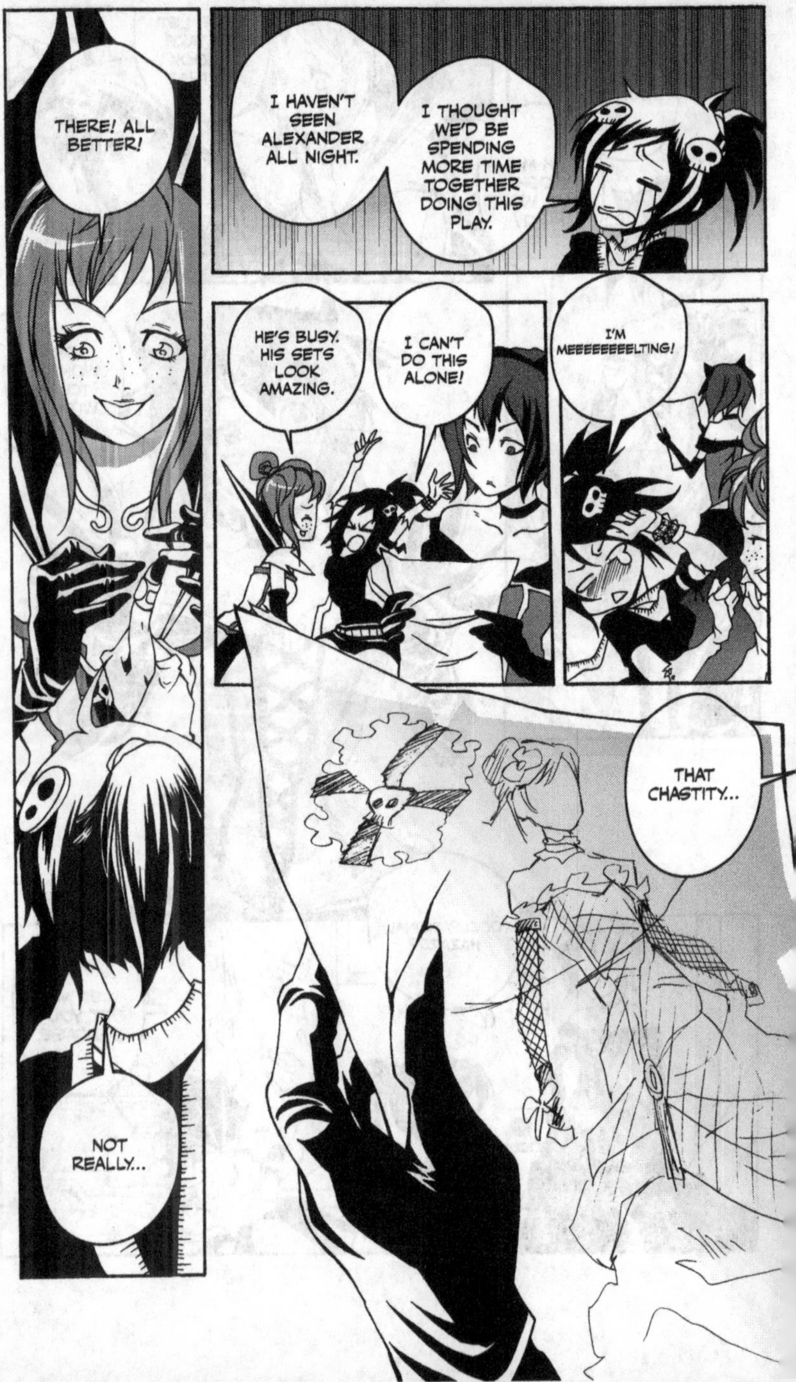
THERE! ALL BETTER!
NOT REALLY...
I HAVEN'T SEEN ALEXANDER ALL NIGHT.
I THOUGHT WE'D BE SPENDING MORE TIME TOGETHER DOING THIS PLAY.
HE'S BUSY. HIS SETS LOOK AMAZING.
I CAN'T DO THIS ALONE!
I'M MEEEEEEEELTING!
THAT CHASTITY...

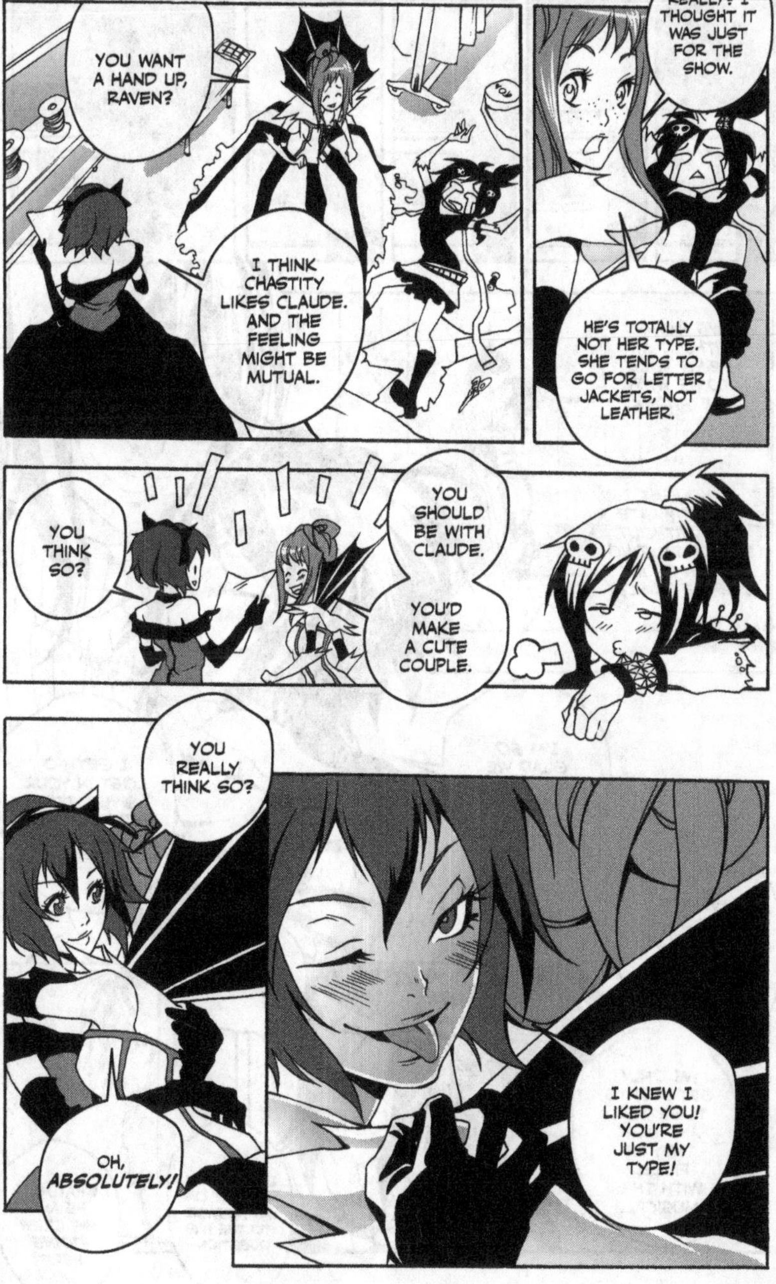

YOU WANT A HAND UP, RAVEN?
I THINK CHASTITY LIKES CLAUDE. AND THE FEELING MIGHT BE MUTUAL.
REALLY? I THOUGHT IT WAS JUST FOR THE SHOW.
HE'S TOTALLY NOT HER TYPE. SHE TENDS TO GO FOR LETTER JACKETS, NOT LEATHER.
YOU THINK SO?
YOU SHOULD BE WITH CLAUDE.
YOU'D MAKE A CUTE COUPLE.
YOU REALLY THINK SO?
OH, ABSOLUTELY!
I KNEW I LIKED YOU! YOU'RE JUST MY TYPE!

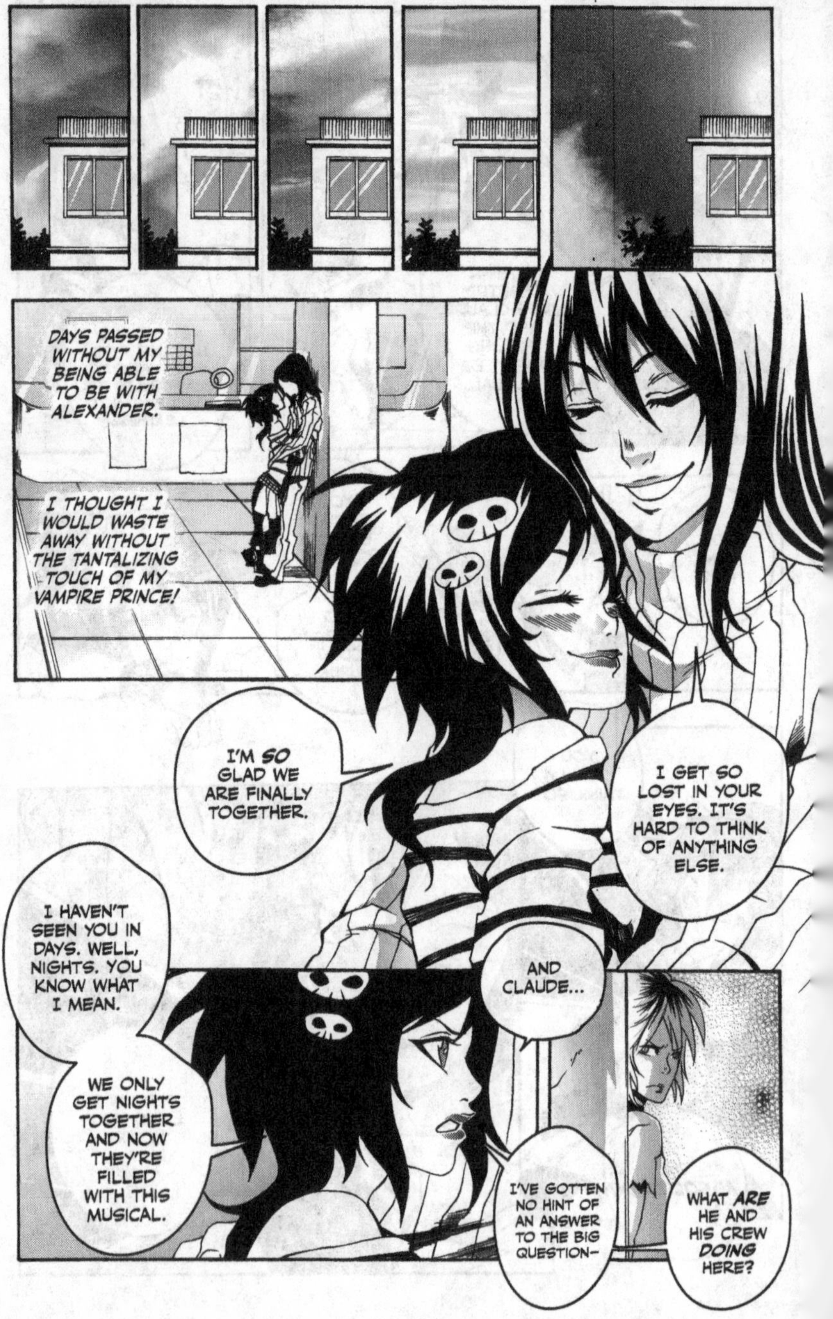
DAYS PASSED WITHOUT MY BEING ABLE TO BE WITH ALEXANDER.
I THOUGHT I WOULD WASTE AWAY WITHOUT THE TANTALIZING TOUCH OF MY VAMPIRE PRINCE!
I'M *SO* GLAD WE ARE FINALLY TOGETHER.
I GET SO LOST IN YOUR EYES. IT'S HARD TO THINK OF ANYTHING ELSE.
I HAVEN'T SEEN YOU IN DAYS. WELL, NIGHTS. YOU KNOW WHAT I MEAN.
WE ONLY GET NIGHTS TOGETHER AND NOW THEY'RE FILLED WITH THIS MUSICAL.
AND CLAUDE...
I'VE GOTTEN NO HINT OF AN ANSWER TO THE BIG QUESTION–
WHAT *ARE* HE AND HIS CREW *DOING* HERE?

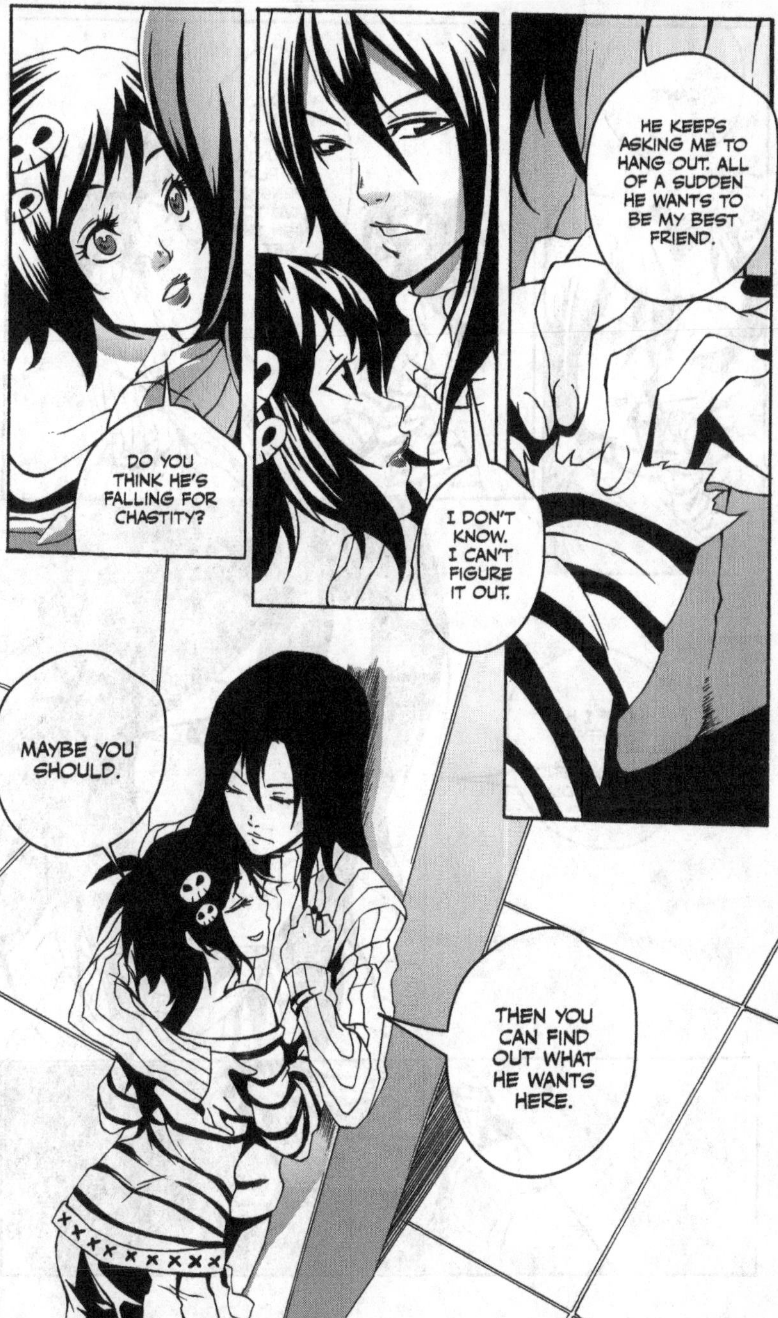
DO YOU THINK HE'S FALLING FOR CHASTITY?
I DON'T KNOW. I CAN'T FIGURE IT OUT.
HE KEEPS ASKING ME TO HANG OUT. ALL OF A SUDDEN HE WANTS TO BE MY BEST FRIEND.
MAYBE YOU SHOULD.
THEN YOU CAN FIND OUT WHAT HE WANTS HERE.

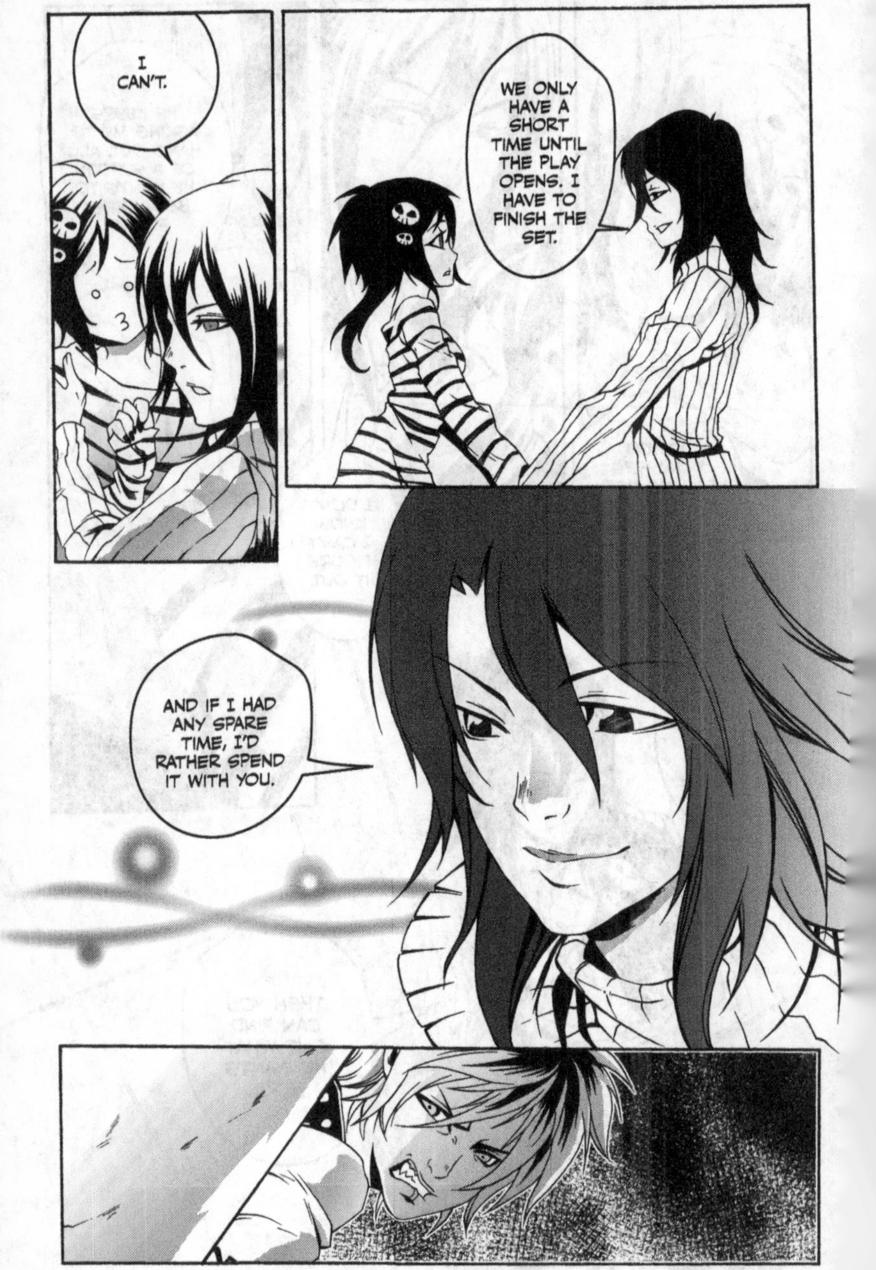

I CAN'T.
WE ONLY HAVE A SHORT TIME UNTIL THE PLAY OPENS. I HAVE TO FINISH THE SET.
AND IF I HAD ANY SPARE TIME, I'D RATHER SPEND IT WITH YOU.

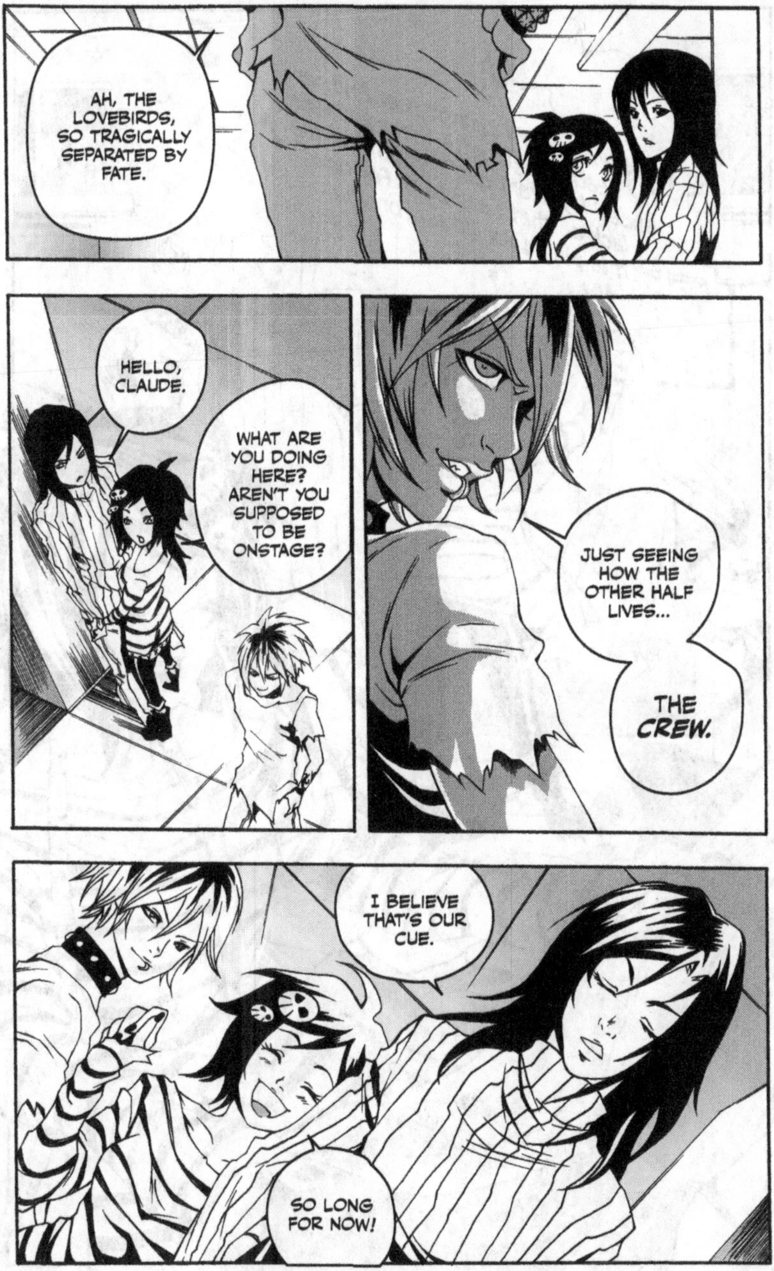
AH, THE LOVEBIRDS, SO TRAGICALLY SEPARATED BY FATE.
HELLO, CLAUDE.
WHAT ARE YOU DOING HERE? AREN'T YOU SUPPOSED TO BE ONSTAGE?
JUST SEEING HOW THE OTHER HALF LIVES...
THE *CREW.*
I BELIEVE THAT'S OUR CUE.
SO LONG FOR NOW!

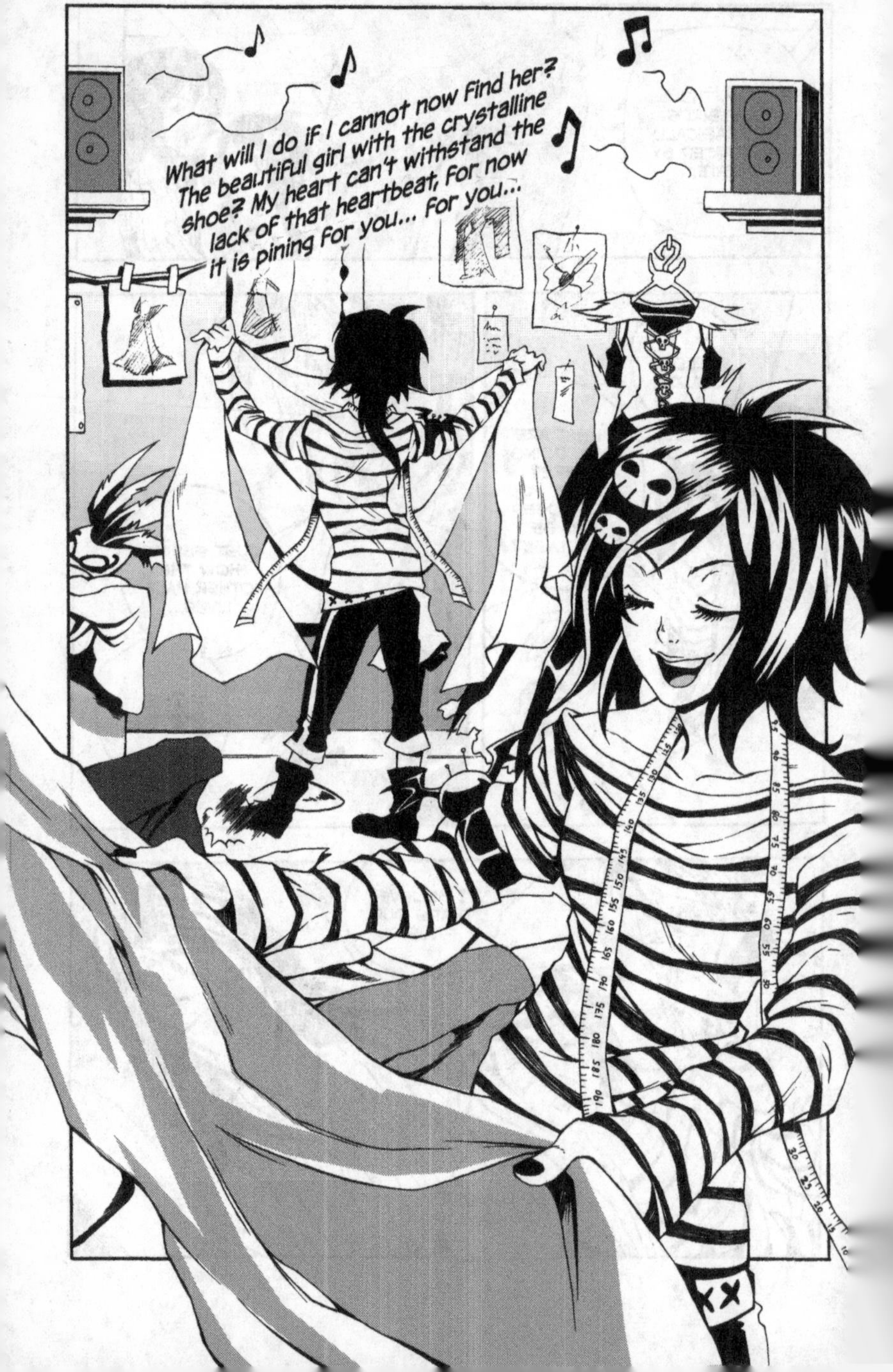
What will I do if I cannot now find her? The beautiful girl with the crystalline shoe? My heart can't withstand the lack of that heartbeat, for now it is pining for you... for you...

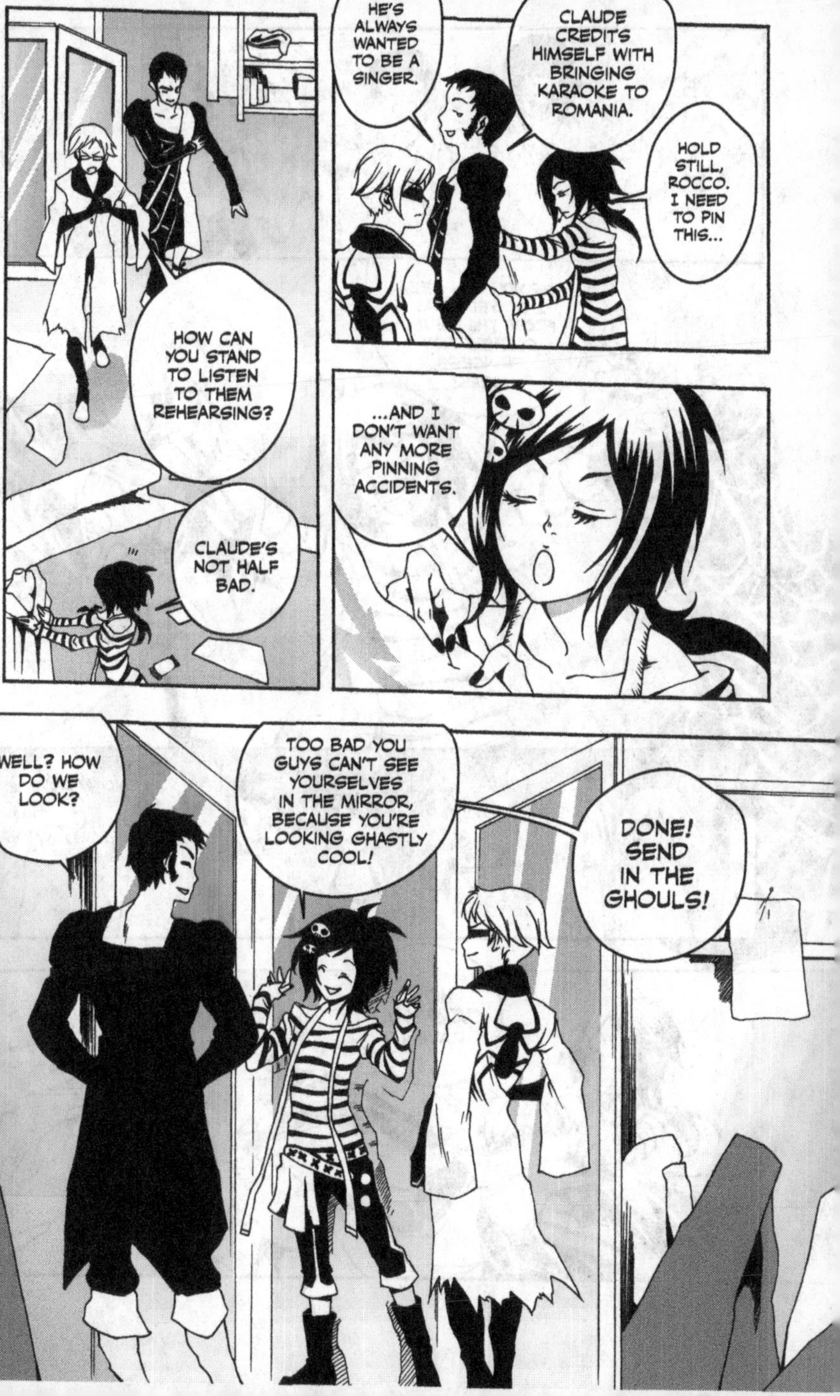
HOW CAN YOU STAND TO LISTEN TO THEM REHEARSING?
CLAUDE'S NOT HALF BAD.
HE'S ALWAYS WANTED TO BE A SINGER.
CLAUDE CREDITS HIMSELF WITH BRINGING KARAOKE TO ROMANIA.
HOLD STILL, ROCCO. I NEED TO PIN THIS...
...AND I DON'T WANT ANY MORE PINNING ACCIDENTS.
WELL? HOW DO WE LOOK?
TOO BAD YOU GUYS CAN'T SEE YOURSELVES IN THE MIRROR, BECAUSE YOU'RE LOOKING GHASTLY COOL!
DONE! SEND IN THE GHOULS!

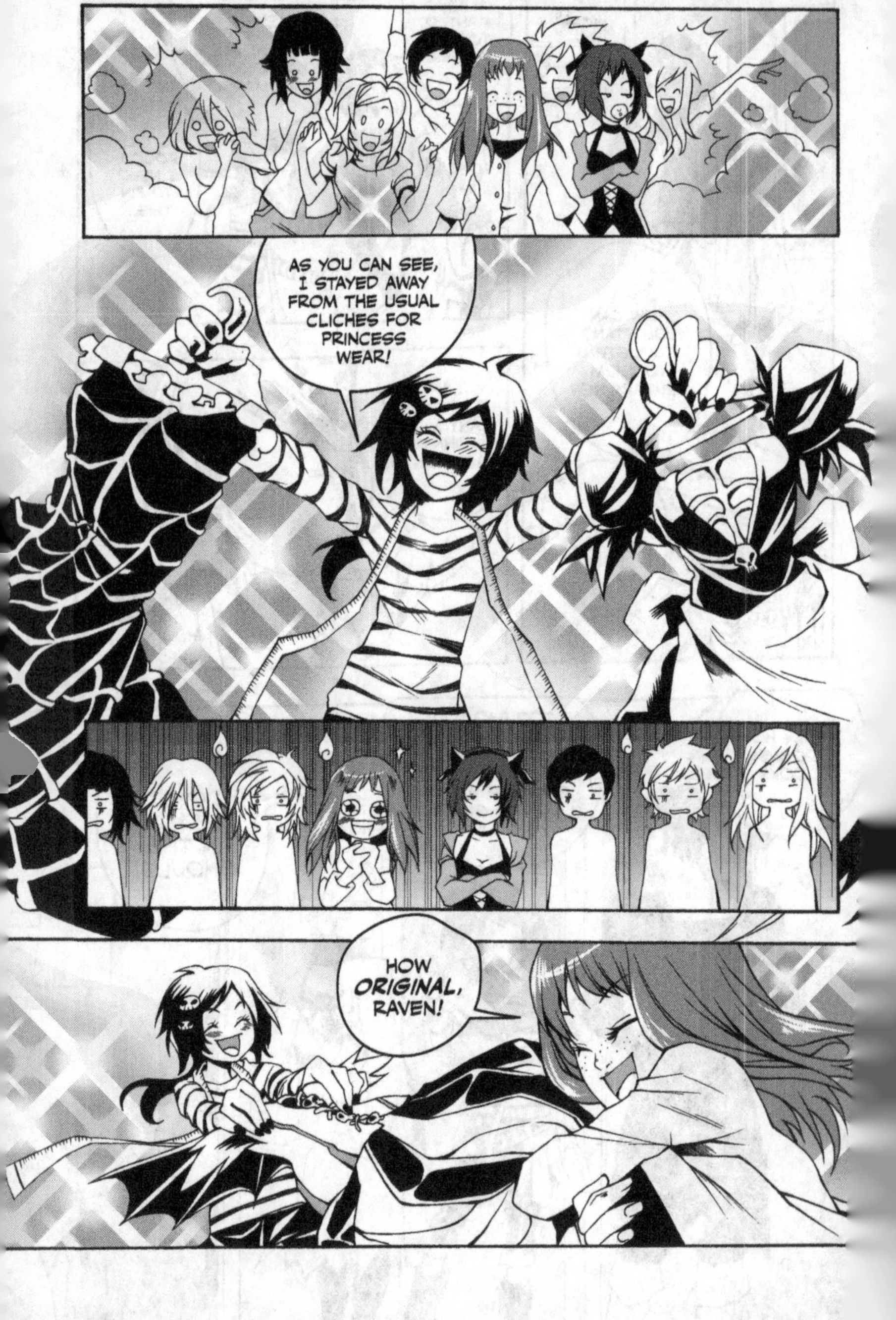
AS YOU CAN SEE, I STAYED AWAY FROM THE USUAL CLICHES FOR PRINCESS WEAR!
HOW *ORIGINAL*, RAVEN!

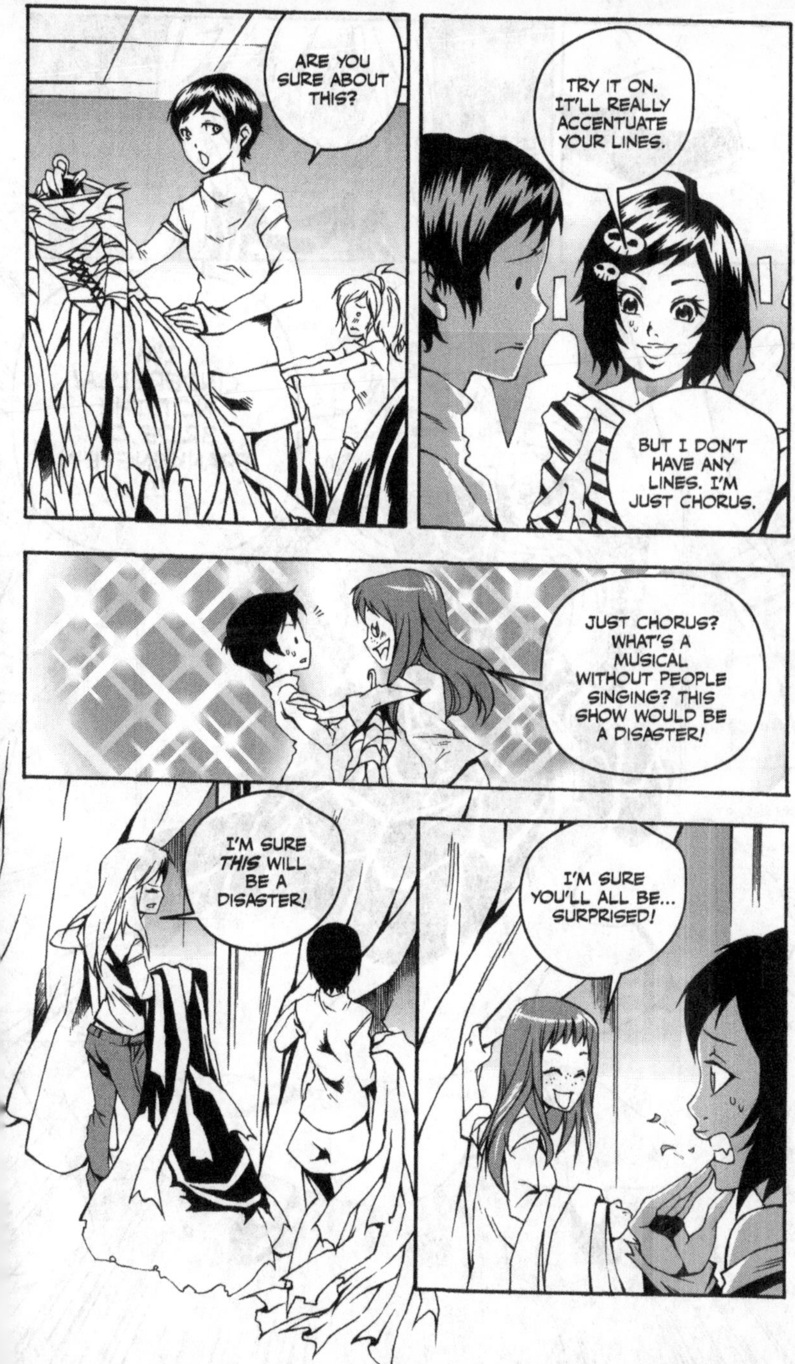
ARE YOU SURE ABOUT THIS?
TRY IT ON. IT'LL REALLY ACCENTUATE YOUR LINES.
BUT I DON'T HAVE ANY LINES. I'M JUST CHORUS.
JUST CHORUS? WHAT'S A MUSICAL WITHOUT PEOPLE SINGING? THIS SHOW WOULD BE A DISASTER!
I'M SURE *THIS* WILL BE A DISASTER!
I'M SURE YOU'LL ALL BE... SURPRISED!

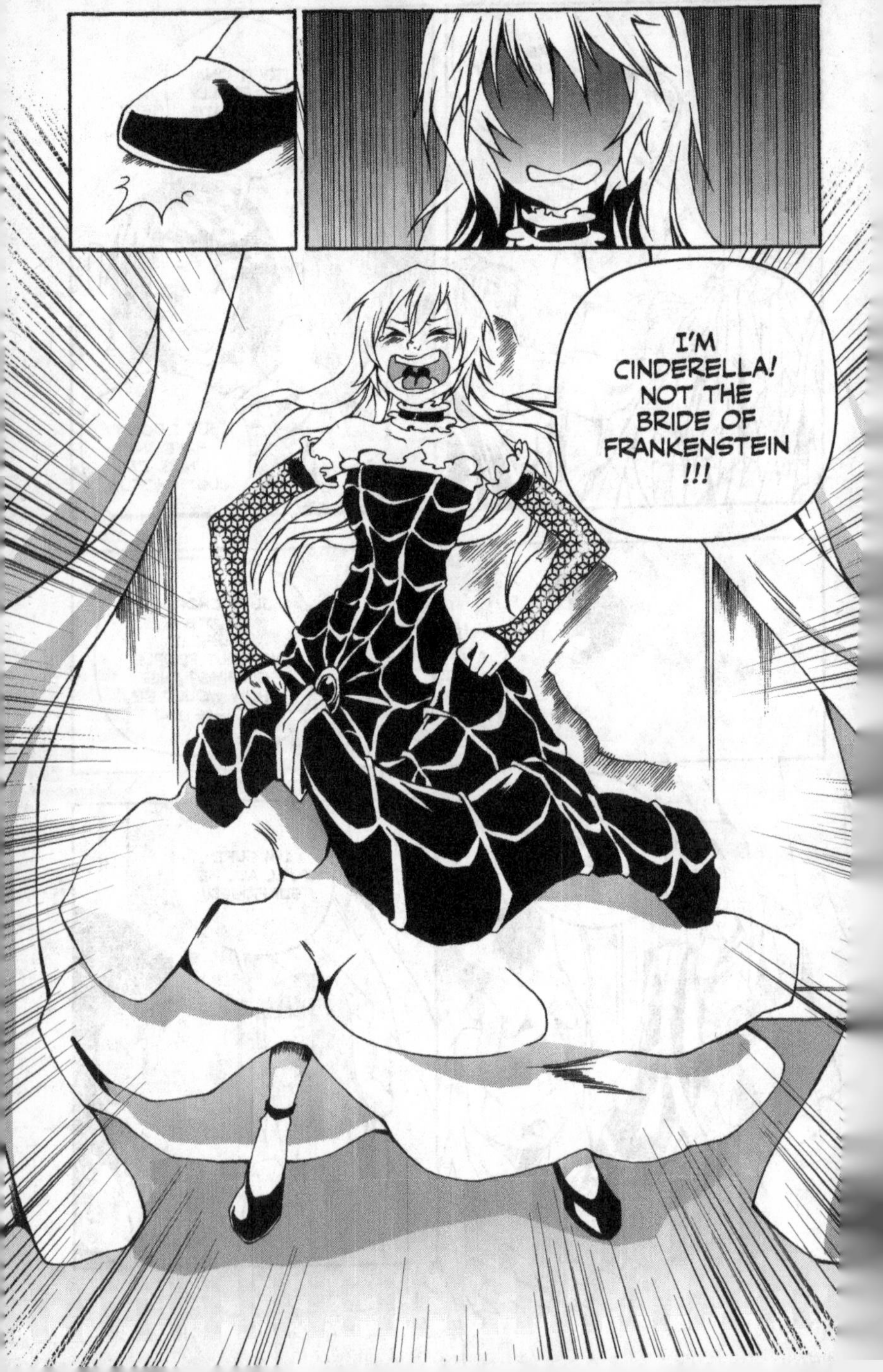
I'M CINDERELLA! NOT THE BRIDE OF FRANKENSTEIN !!!

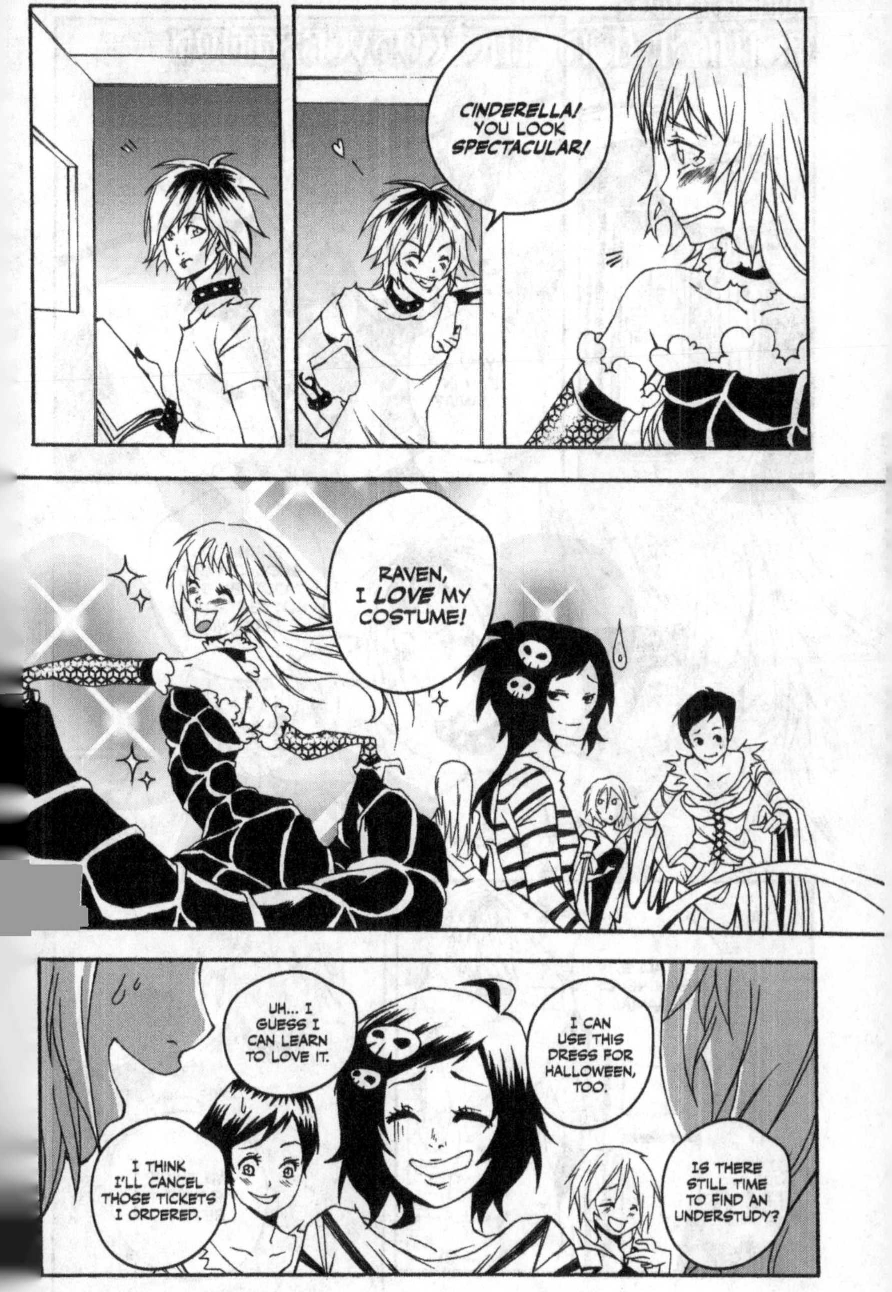
CINDERELLA! YOU LOOK SPECTACULAR!
RAVEN, I *LOVE* MY COSTUME!
UH... I GUESS I CAN LEARN TO LOVE IT.
I CAN USE THIS DRESS FOR HALLOWEEN, TOO.
I THINK I'LL CANCEL THOSE TICKETS I ORDERED.
IS THERE STILL TIME TO FIND AN UNDERSTUDY?

Chapter Five: A Turning in the Conversation

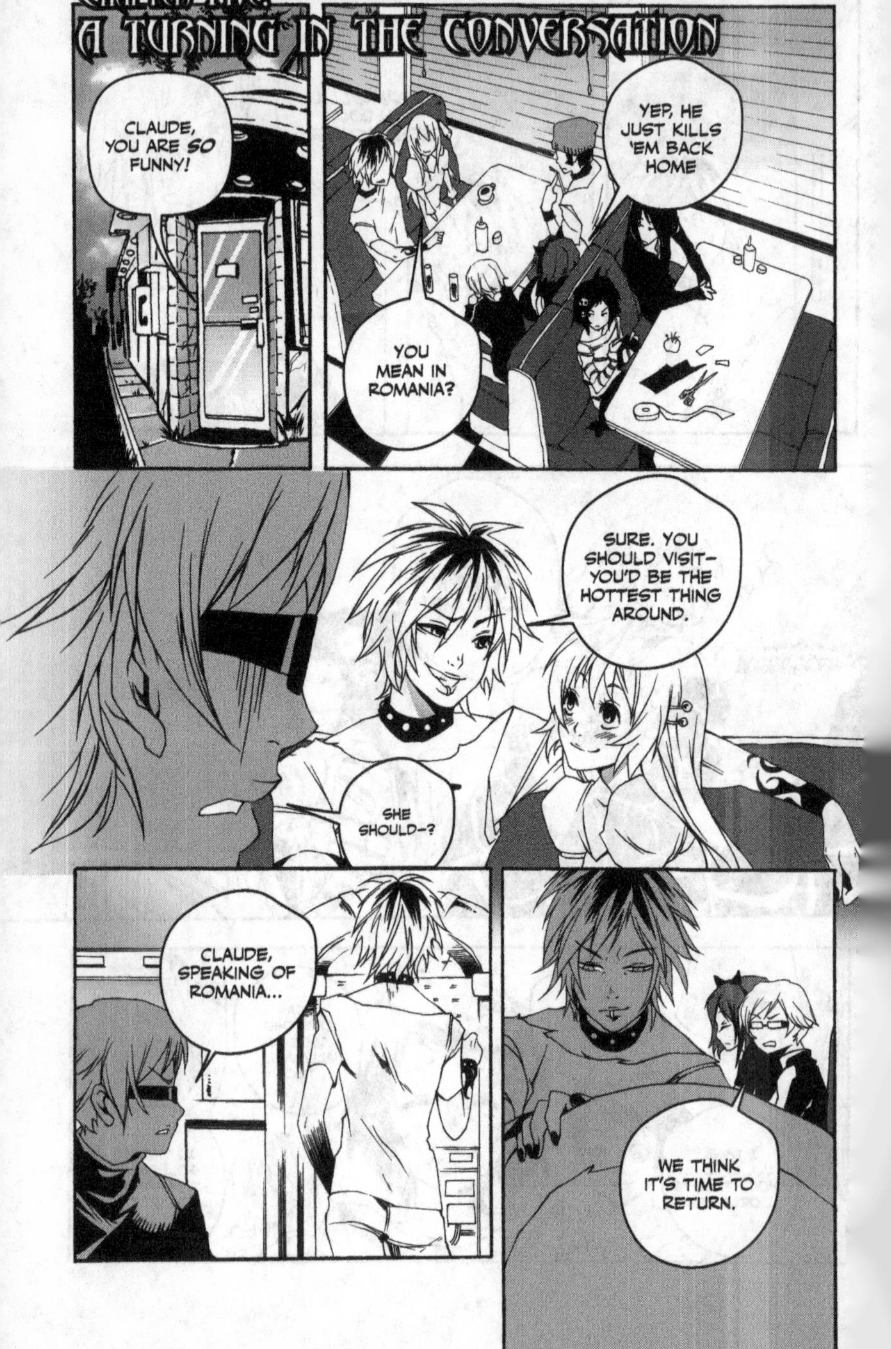
CLAUDE, YOU ARE SO FUNNY!
YEP, HE JUST KILLS 'EM BACK HOME
YOU MEAN IN ROMANIA?
SURE. YOU SHOULD VISIT-YOU'D BE THE HOTTEST THING AROUND.
SHE SHOULD-?
CLAUDE, SPEAKING OF ROMANIA...
WE THINK IT'S TIME TO RETURN.

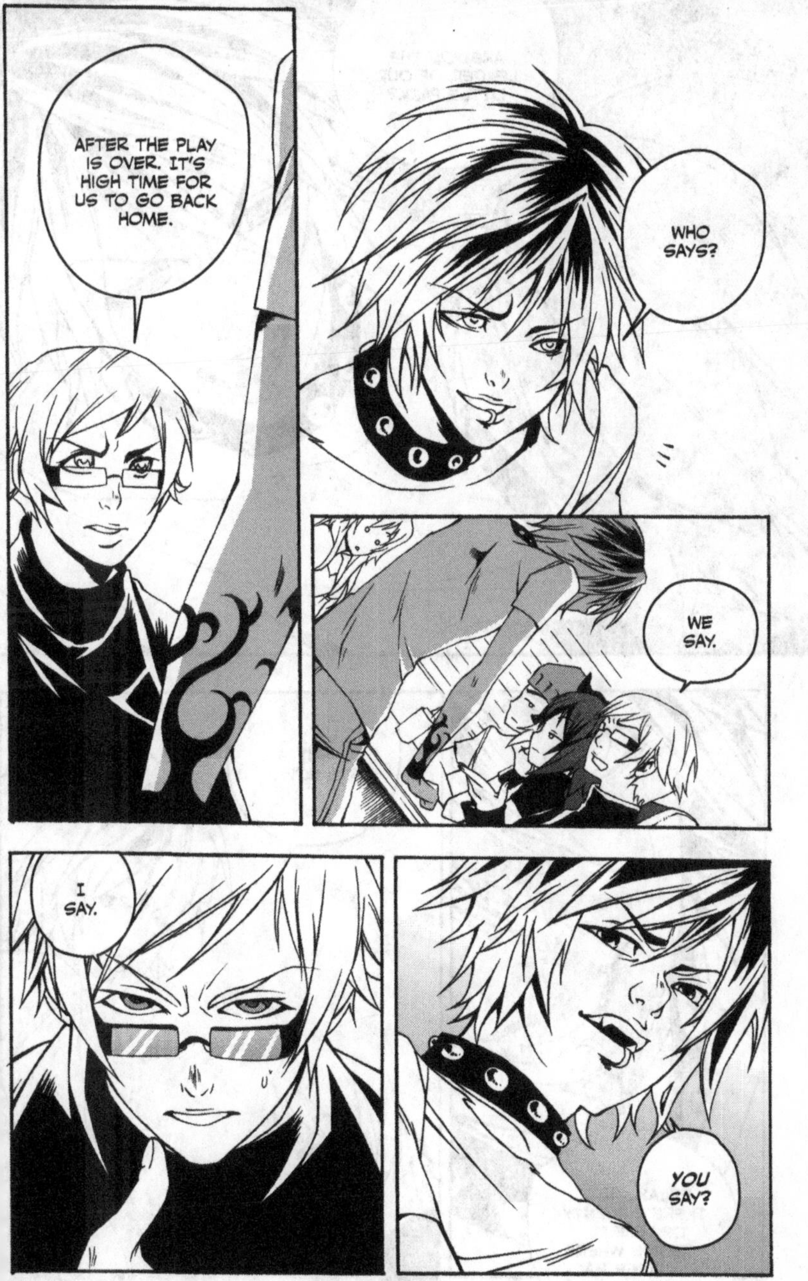
AFTER THE PLAY IS OVER. IT'S HIGH TIME FOR US TO GO BACK HOME.
WHO SAYS?
WE SAY.
I SAY.
YOU SAY?

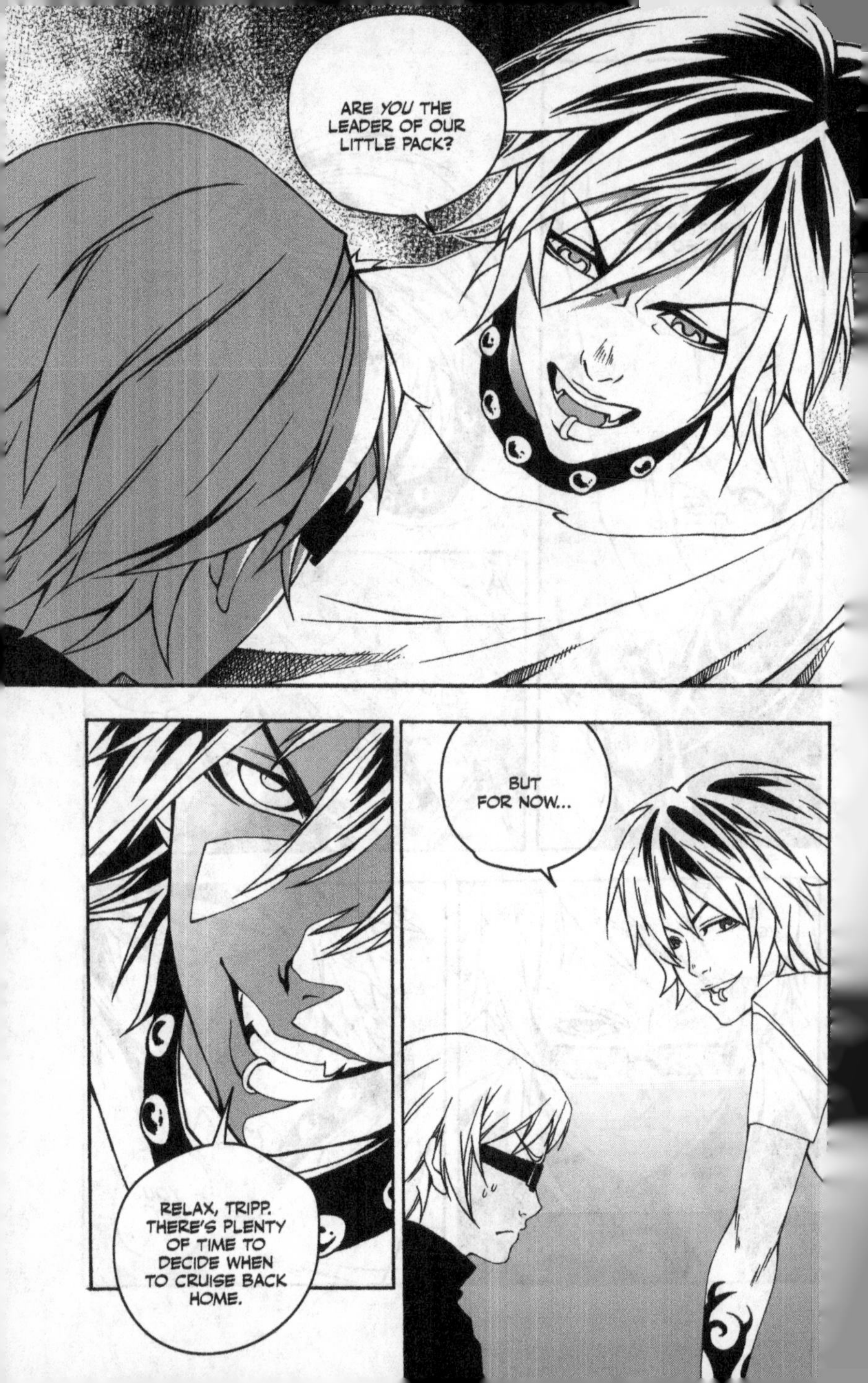
ARE *YOU* THE LEADER OF OUR LITTLE PACK?
RELAX, TRIPP. THERE'S PLENTY OF TIME TO DECIDE WHEN TO CRUISE BACK HOME.
BUT FOR NOW...

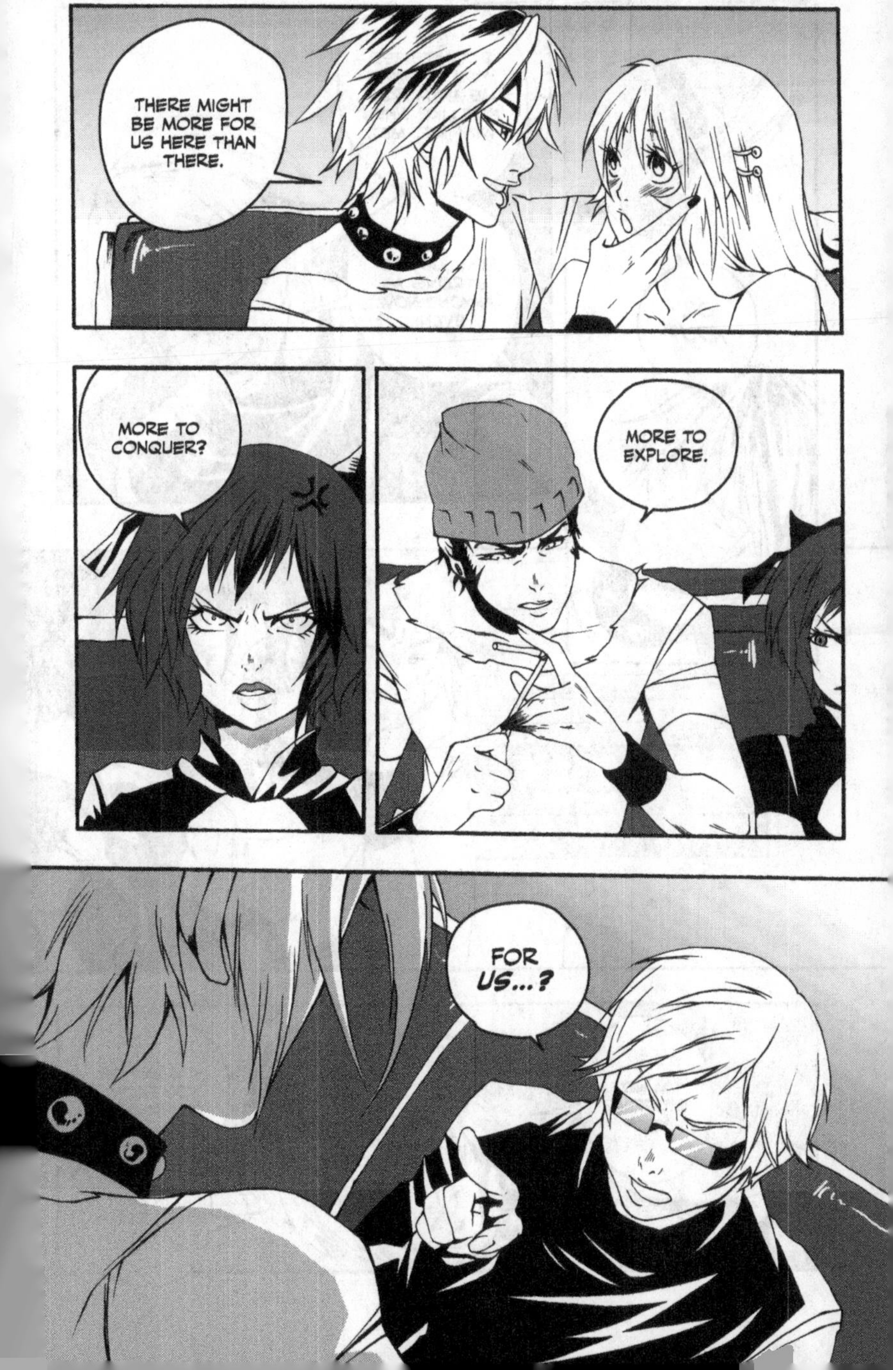
THERE MIGHT BE MORE FOR US HERE THAN THERE.
MORE TO CONQUER?
MORE TO EXPLORE.
FOR US...?

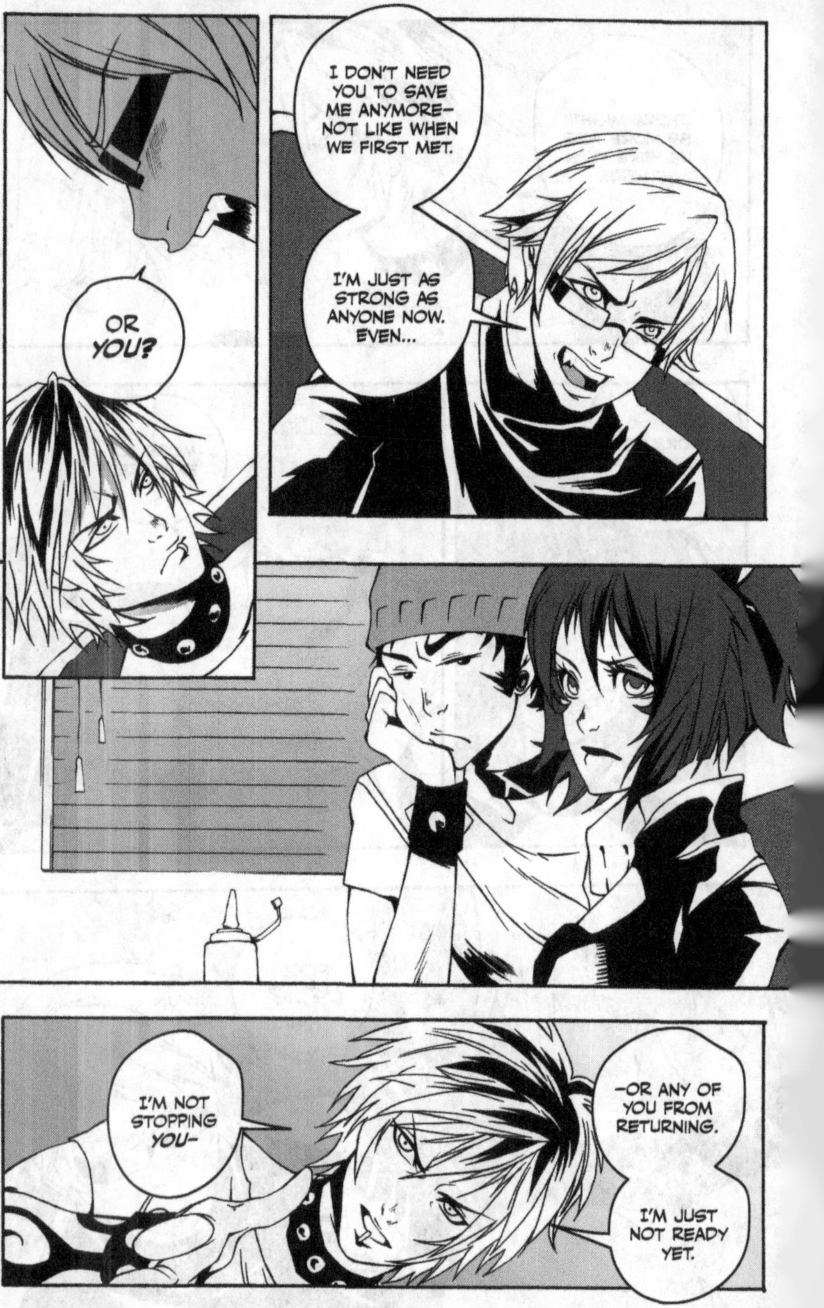
OR YOU?
I DON'T NEED YOU TO SAVE ME ANYMORE– NOT LIKE WHEN WE FIRST MET.
I'M JUST AS STRONG AS ANYONE NOW. EVEN...
I'M NOT STOPPING YOU–
–OR ANY OF YOU FROM RETURNING.
I'M JUST NOT READY YET.

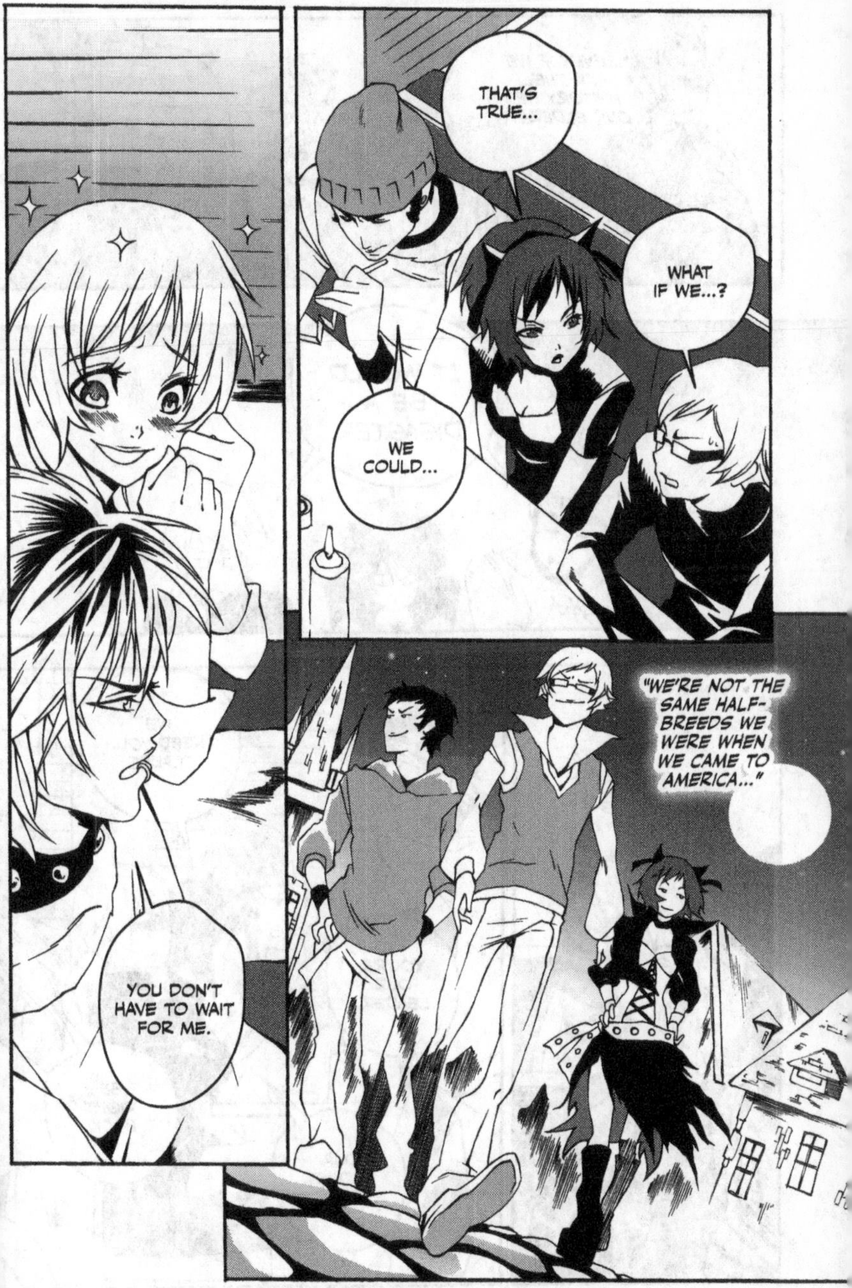
YOU DON'T HAVE TO WAIT FOR ME.
THAT'S TRUE...
WHAT IF WE...?
WE COULD...
"WE'RE NOT THE SAME HALF-BREEDS WE WERE WHEN WE CAME TO AMERICA..."

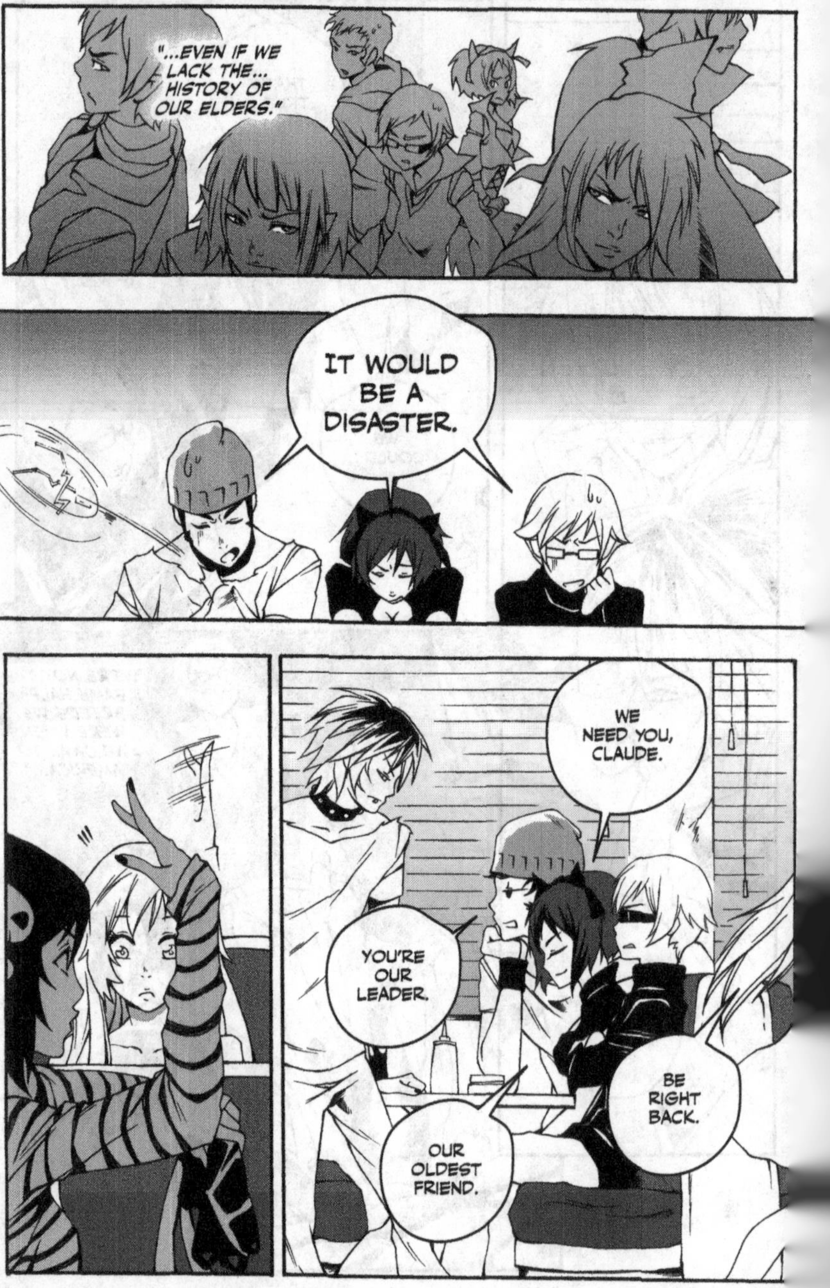
"...EVEN IF WE LACK THE... HISTORY OF OUR ELDERS."
IT WOULD BE A DISASTER.
WE NEED YOU, CLAUDE.
YOU'RE OUR LEADER.
OUR OLDEST FRIEND.
BE RIGHT BACK.

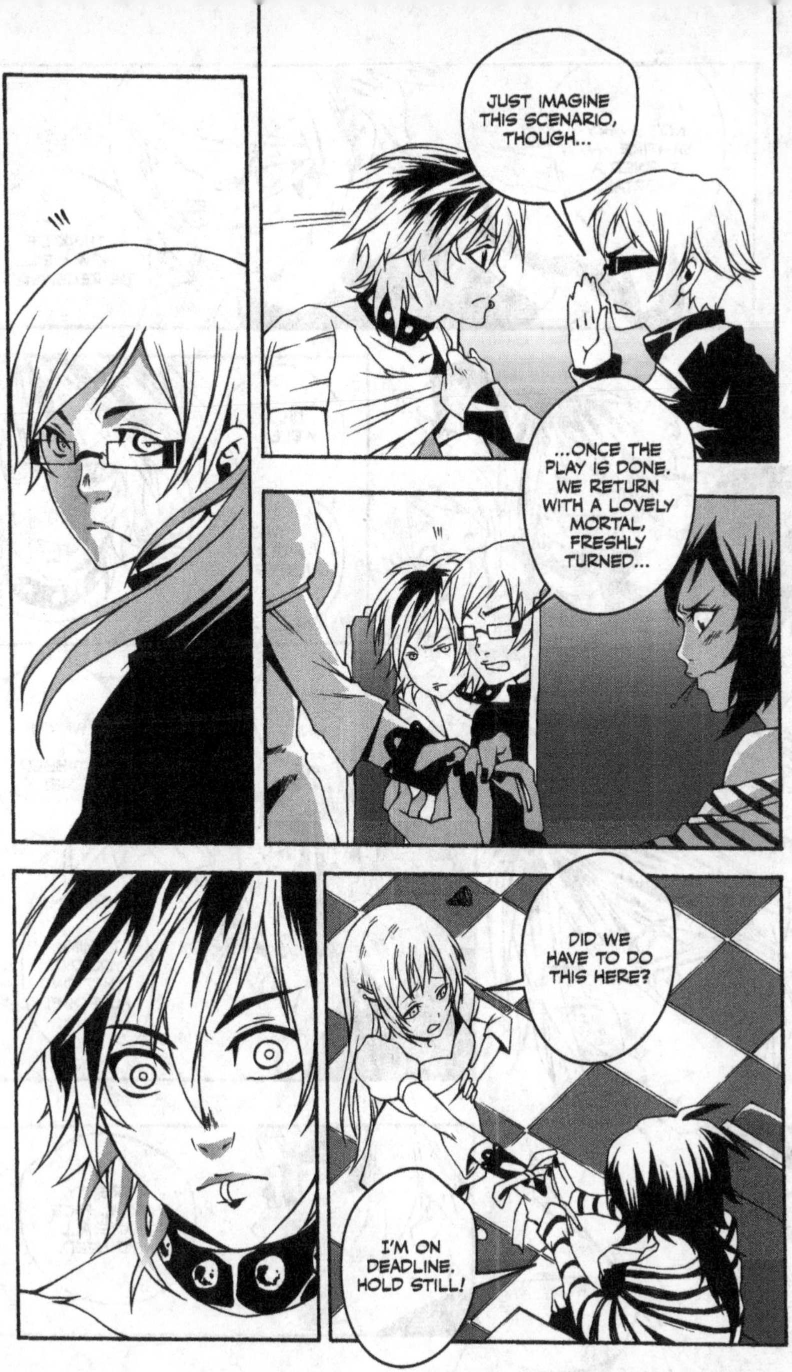
JUST IMAGINE THIS SCENARIO, THOUGH...
...ONCE THE PLAY IS DONE. WE RETURN WITH A LOVELY MORTAL, FRESHLY TURNED...
DID WE HAVE TO DO THIS HERE?
I'M ON DEADLINE. HOLD STILL!

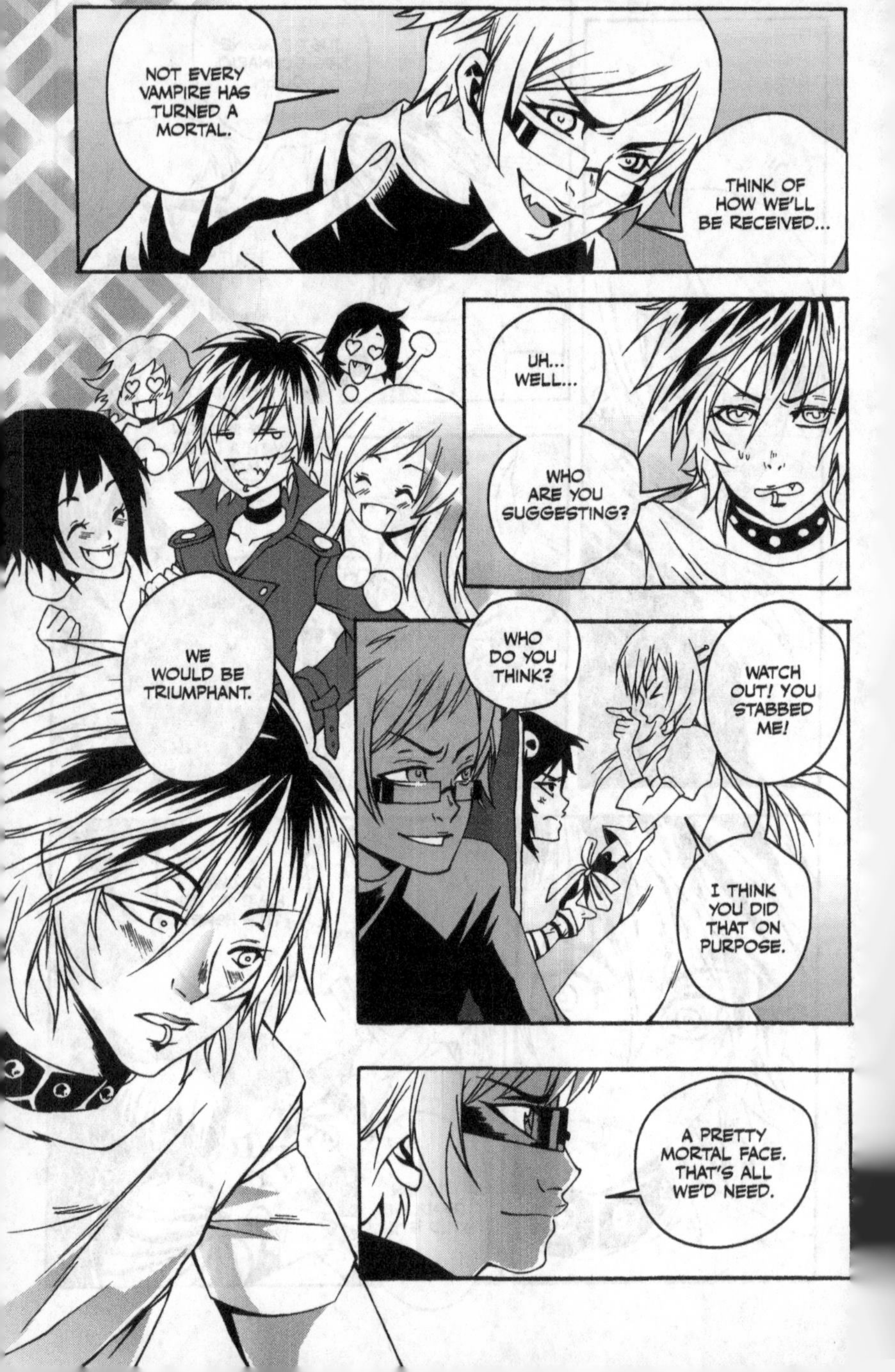
NOT EVERY VAMPIRE HAS TURNED A MORTAL.
THINK OF HOW WE'LL BE RECEIVED...
WE WOULD BE TRIUMPHANT.
UH... WELL...
WHO ARE YOU SUGGESTING?
WHO DO YOU THINK?
WATCH OUT! YOU STABBED ME!
I THINK YOU DID THAT ON PURPOSE.
A PRETTY MORTAL FACE. THAT'S ALL WE'D NEED.

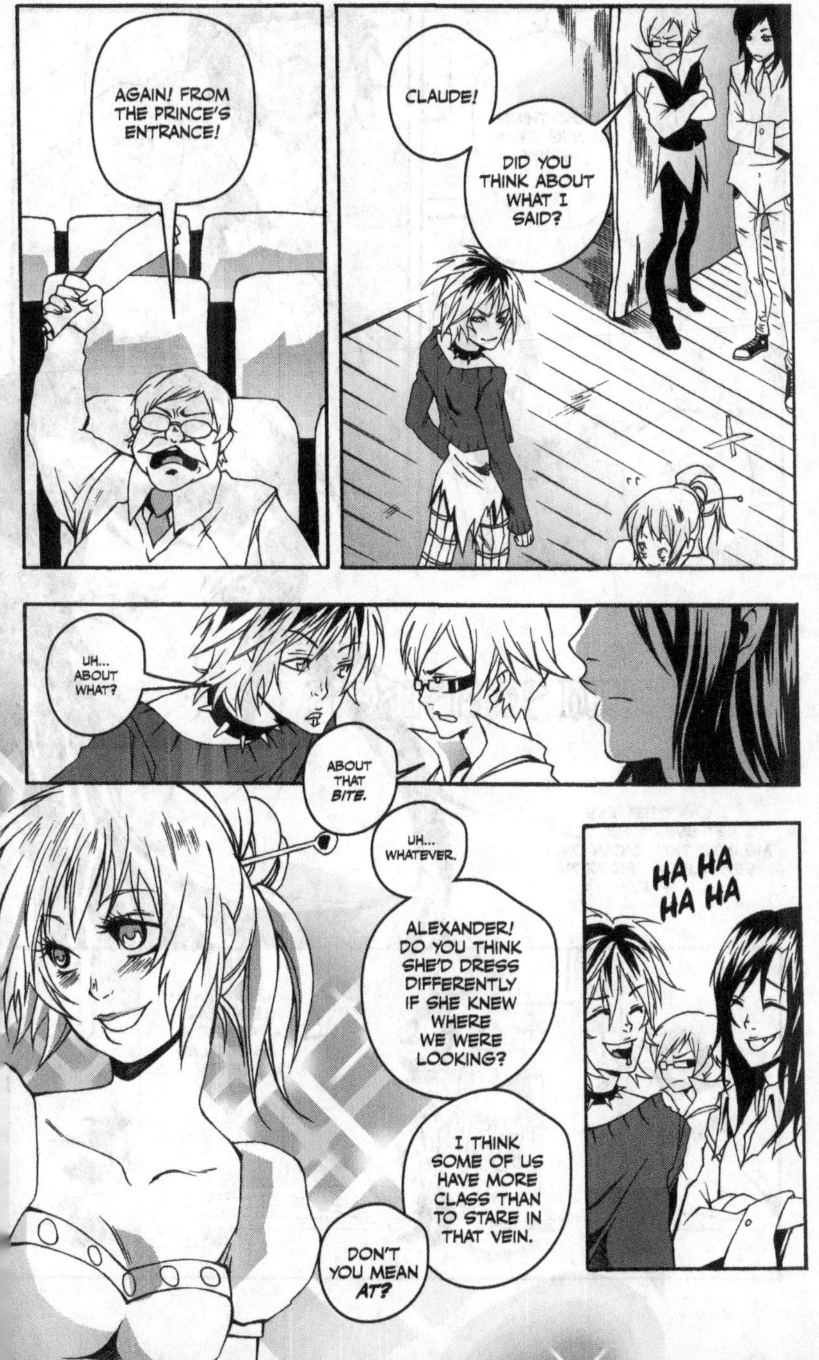
AGAIN! FROM THE PRINCE'S ENTRANCE!
CLAUDE!
DID YOU THINK ABOUT WHAT I SAID?
UH... ABOUT WHAT?
ABOUT THAT *BITE*.
UH... WHATEVER.
ALEXANDER! DO YOU THINK SHE'D DRESS DIFFERENTLY IF SHE KNEW WHERE WE WERE LOOKING?
I THINK SOME OF US HAVE MORE CLASS THAN TO STARE IN THAT VEIN.
DON'T YOU MEAN *AT*?
HA HA HA HA

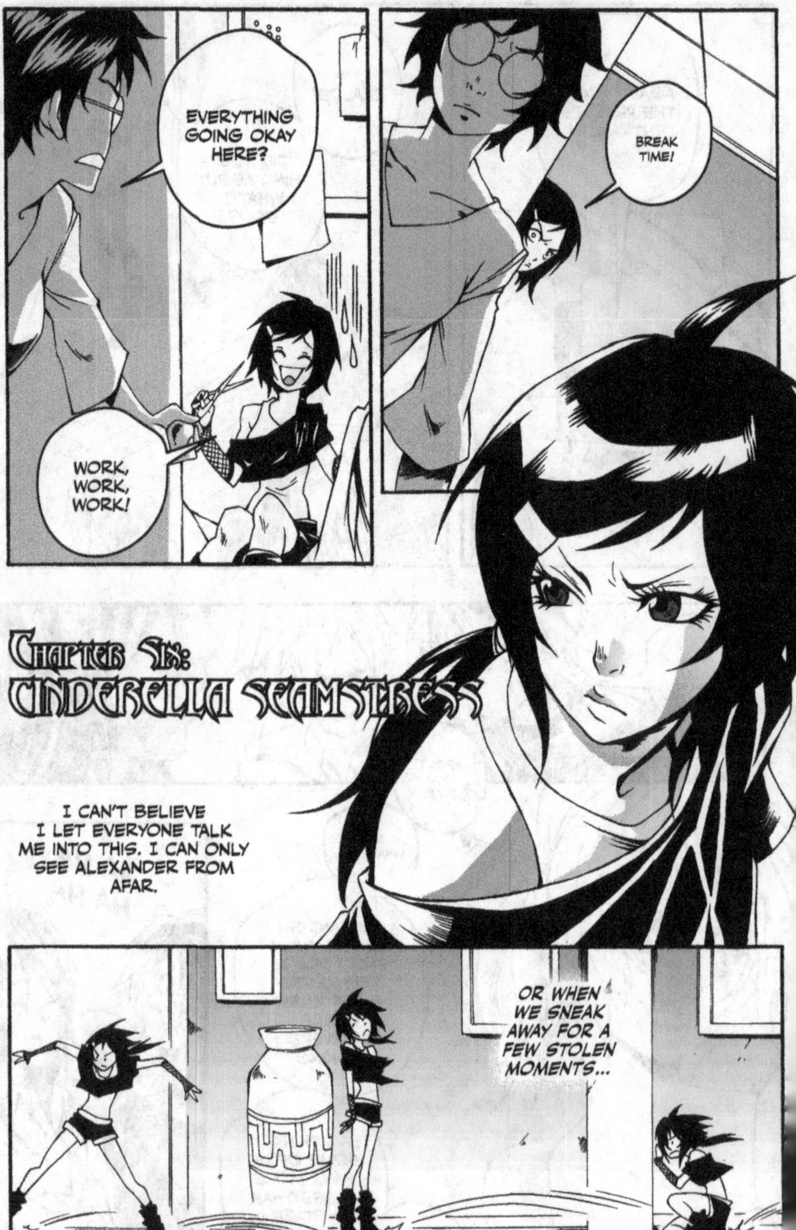
EVERYTHING GOING OKAY HERE?
WORK, WORK, WORK!
BREAK TIME!
CHAPTER SIX: CINDERELLA SEAMSTRESS
I CAN'T BELIEVE I LET EVERYONE TALK ME INTO THIS. I CAN ONLY SEE ALEXANDER FROM AFAR.
OR WHEN WE SNEAK AWAY FOR A FEW STOLEN MOMENTS...

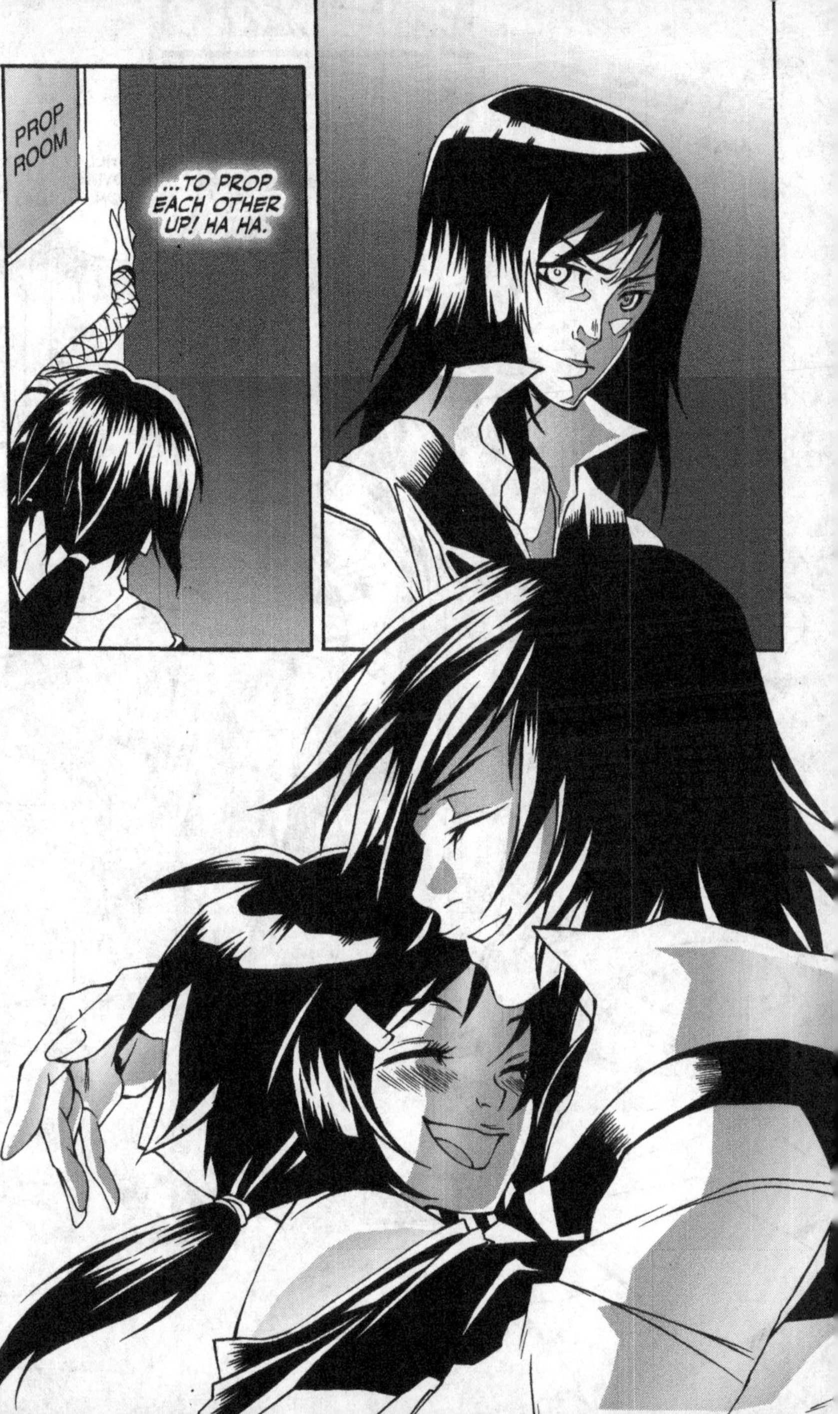
PROP ROOM
...TO PROP EACH OTHER UP! HA HA.

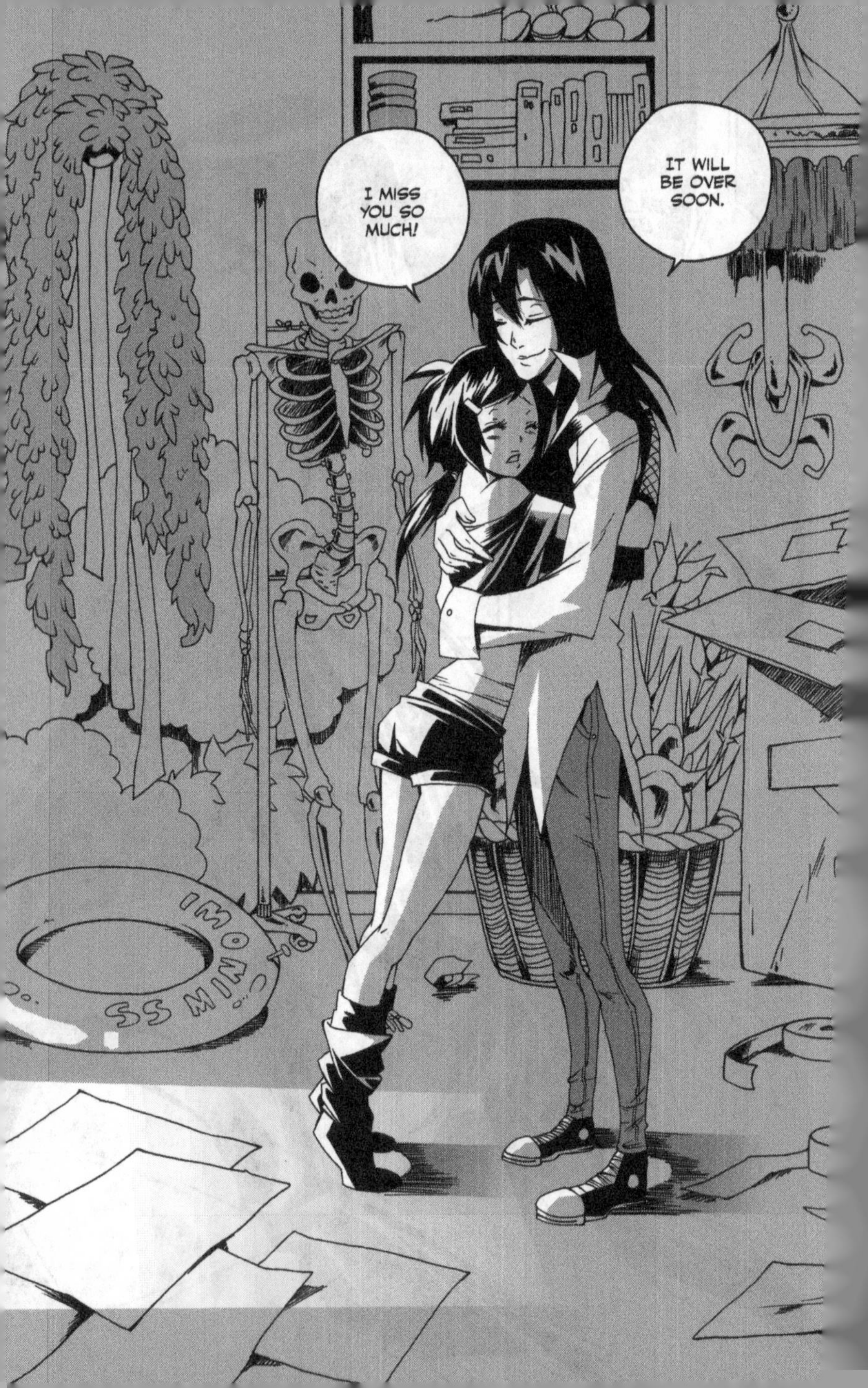
I MISS YOU SO MUCH!
IT WILL BE OVER SOON.

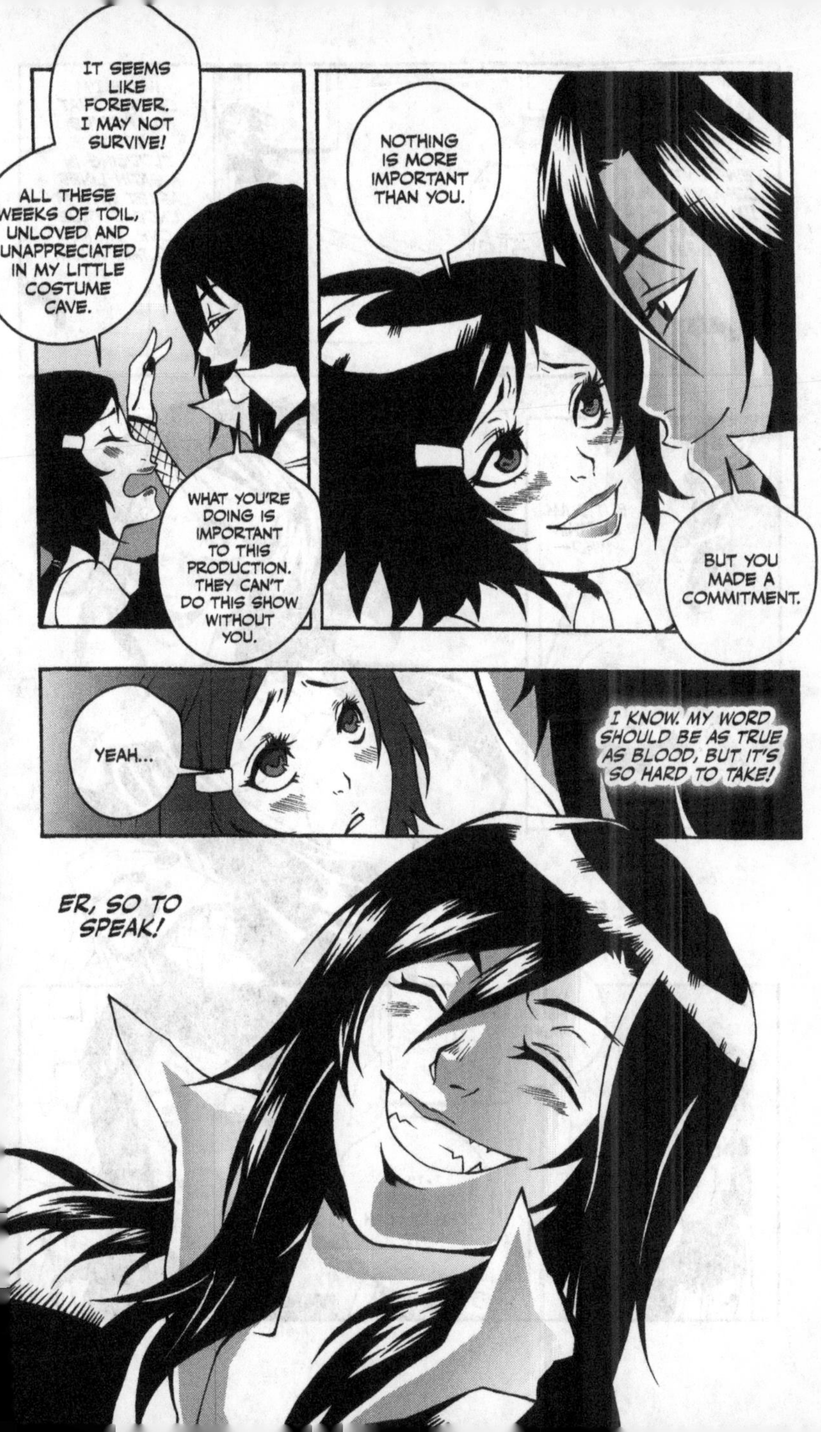
IT SEEMS LIKE FOREVER. I MAY NOT SURVIVE!
ALL THESE WEEKS OF TOIL, UNLOVED AND UNAPPRECIATED IN MY LITTLE COSTUME CAVE.
WHAT YOU'RE DOING IS IMPORTANT TO THIS PRODUCTION. THEY CAN'T DO THIS SHOW WITHOUT YOU.
NOTHING IS MORE IMPORTANT THAN YOU.
BUT YOU MADE A COMMITMENT.
YEAH...
I KNOW. MY WORD SHOULD BE AS TRUE AS BLOOD, BUT IT'S SO HARD TO TAKE!
ER, SO TO SPEAK!

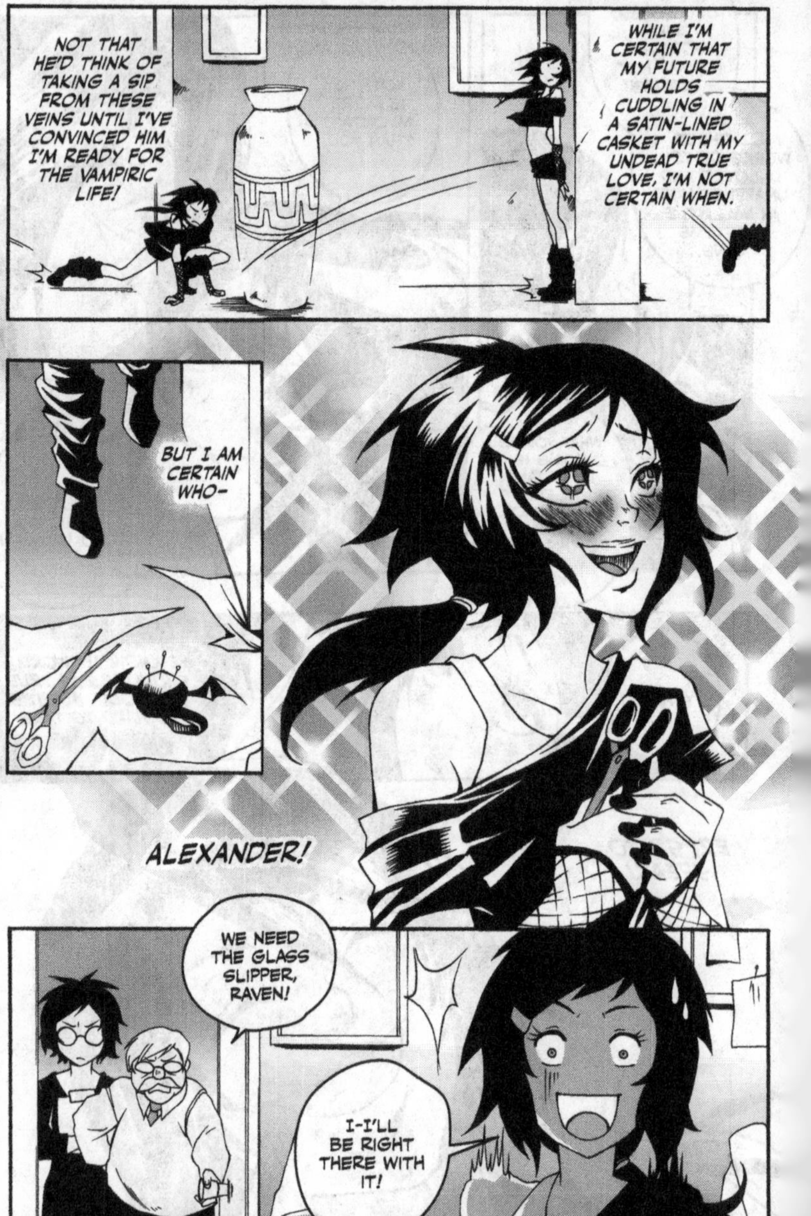
NOT THAT HE'D THINK OF TAKING A SIP FROM THESE VEINS UNTIL I'VE CONVINCED HIM I'M READY FOR THE VAMPIRIC LIFE!
WHILE I'M CERTAIN THAT MY FUTURE HOLDS CUDDLING IN A SATIN-LINED CASKET WITH MY UNDEAD TRUE LOVE, I'M NOT CERTAIN WHEN.
BUT I AM CERTAIN WHO-
ALEXANDER!
WE NEED THE GLASS SLIPPER, RAVEN!
I-I'LL BE RIGHT THERE WITH IT!

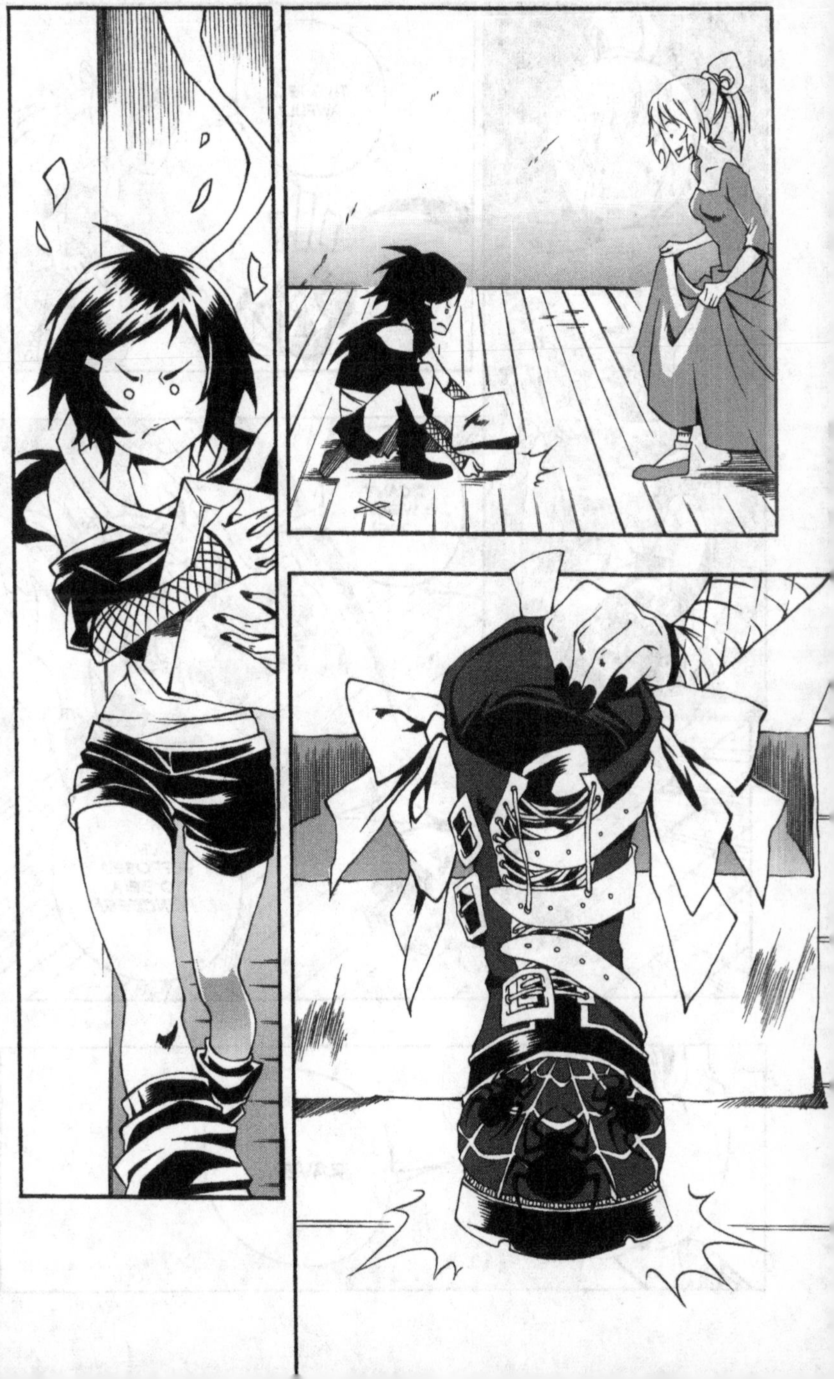

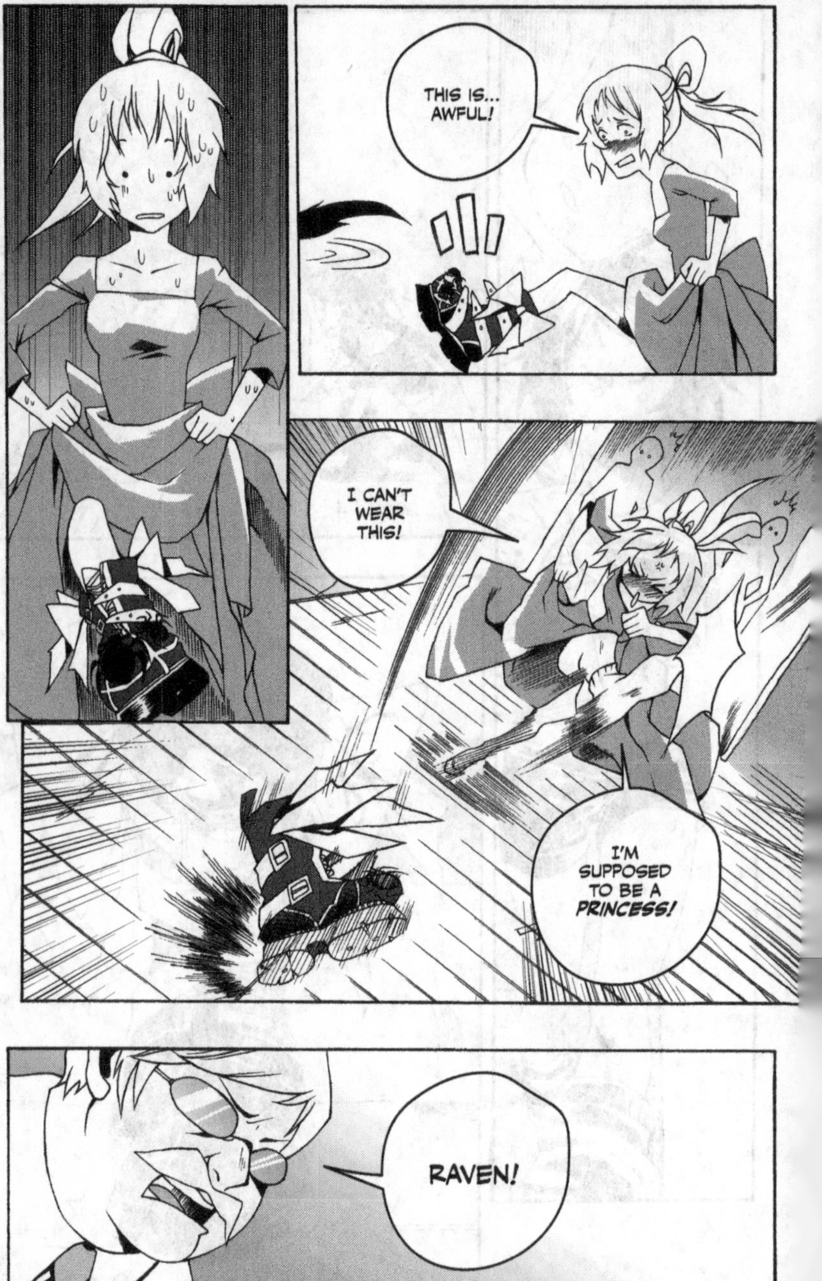
THIS IS... AWFUL!
I CAN'T WEAR THIS!
I'M SUPPOSED TO BE A *PRINCESS!*
RAVEN!

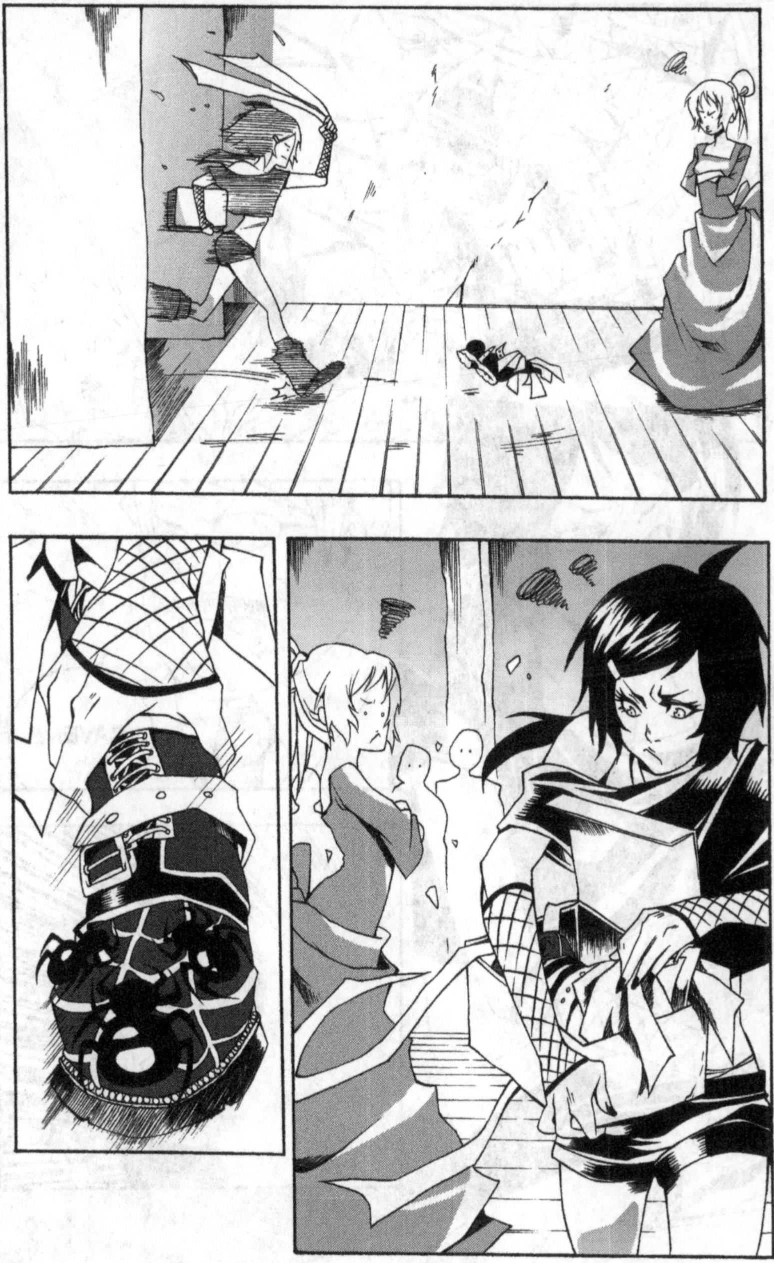

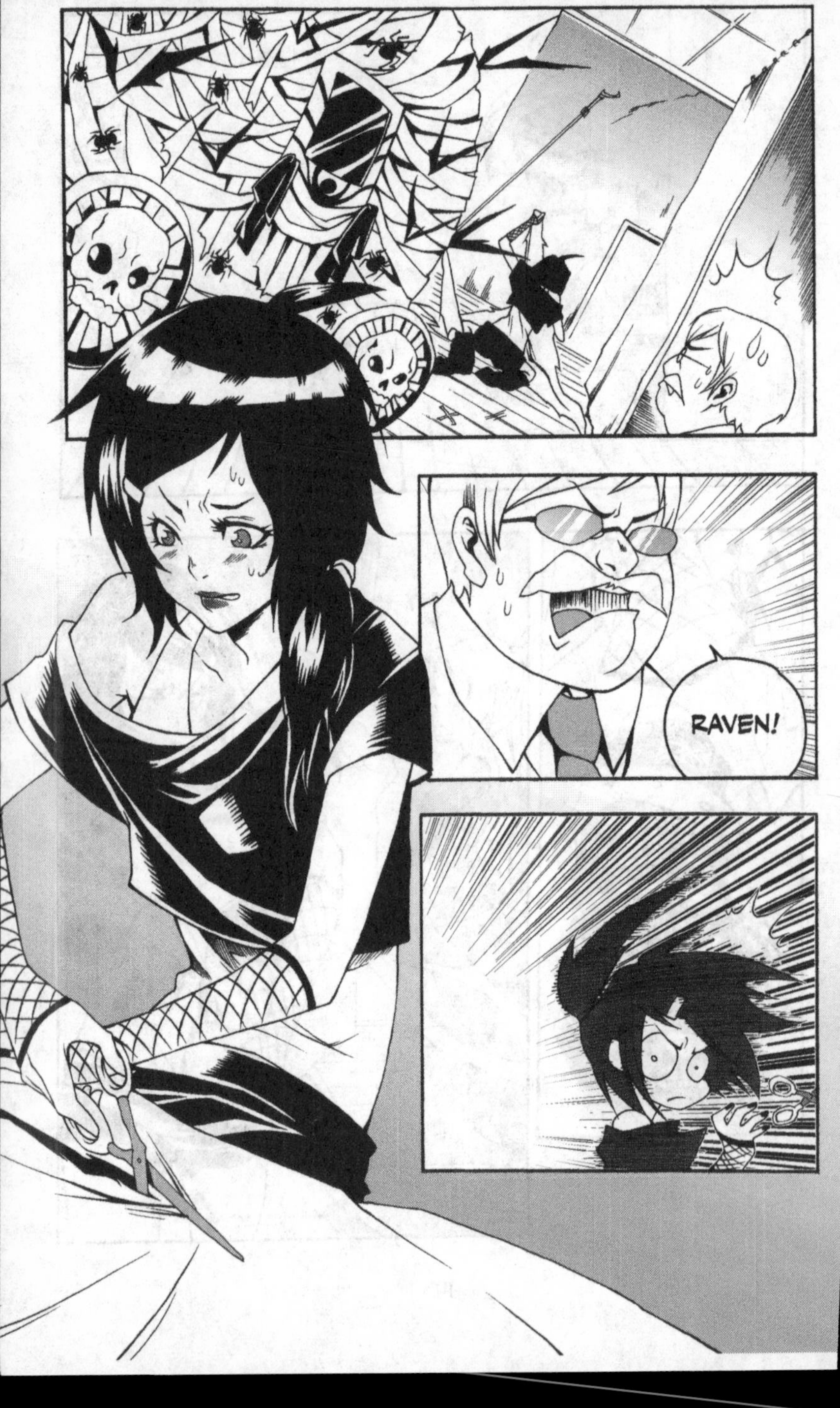
RAVEN!

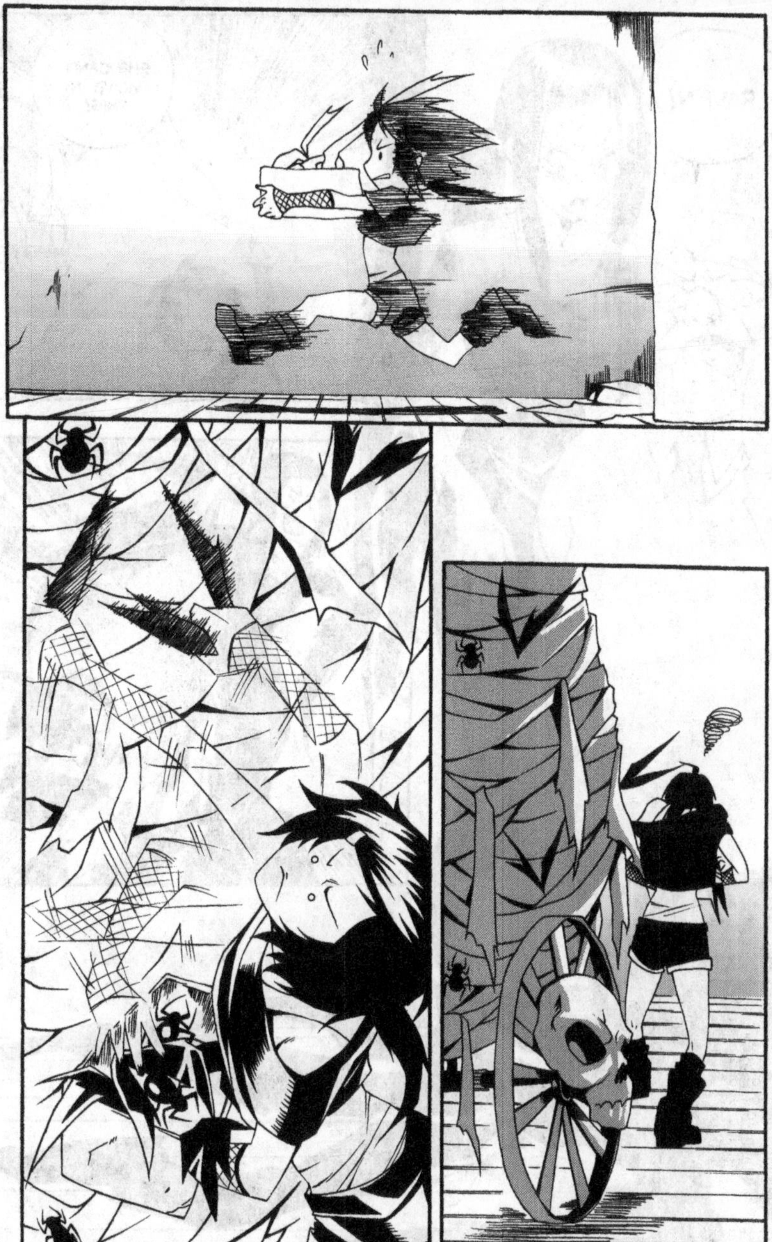

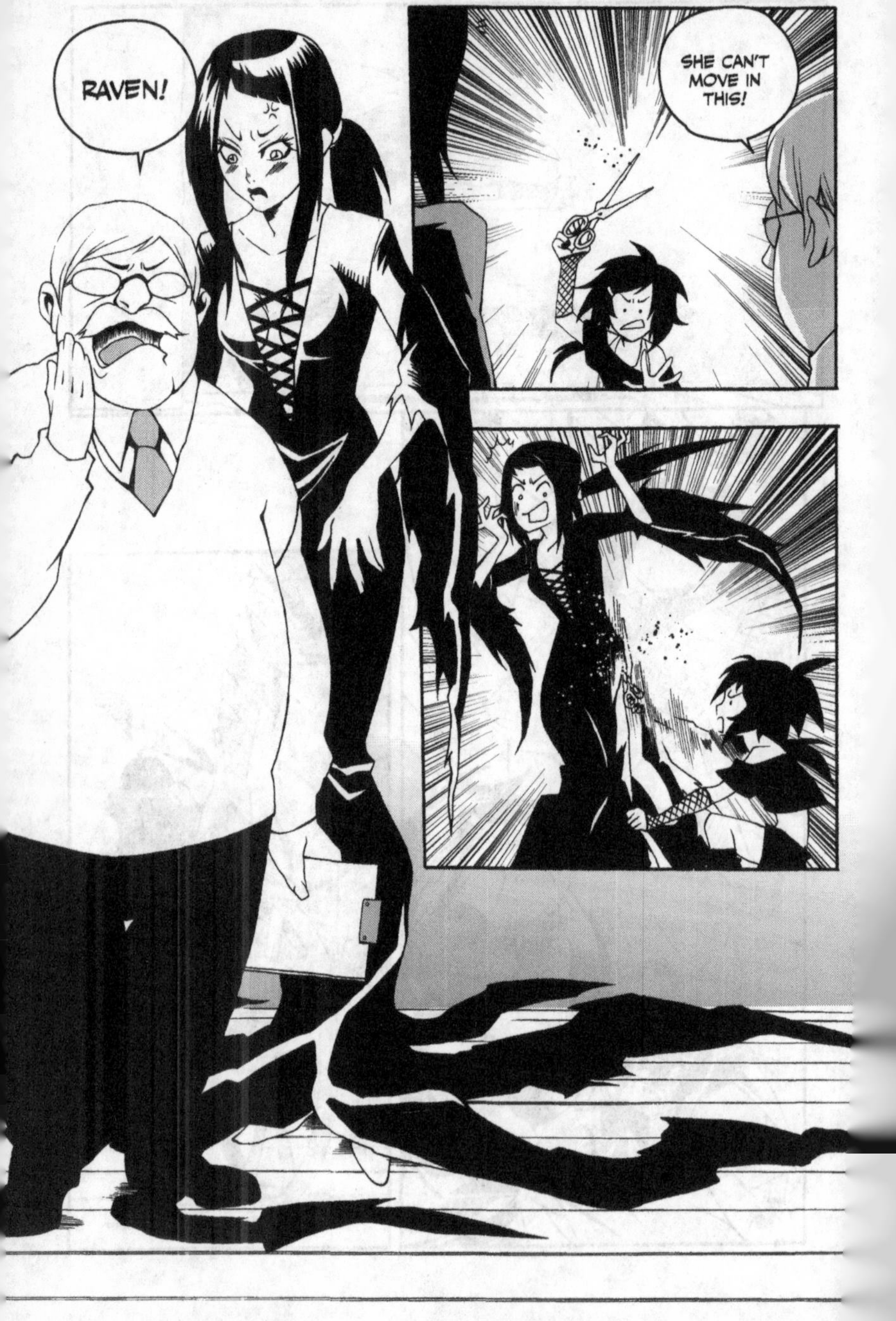
RAVEN!
SHE CAN'T MOVE IN THIS!

HE DOESN'T LIKE ANYTHING! HE OBVIOUSLY DOESN'T HAVE TASTE.

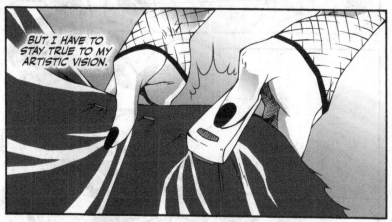

BUT I HAVE TO STAY TRUE TO MY ARTISTIC VISION.

THE PROBLEM WITH STICKING TO YOUR ARTISTIC VISION IS STICKING TO IT WHEN NOBODY SEEMS TO UNDERSTAND OR BELIEVE THAT YOU HAVE ONE.

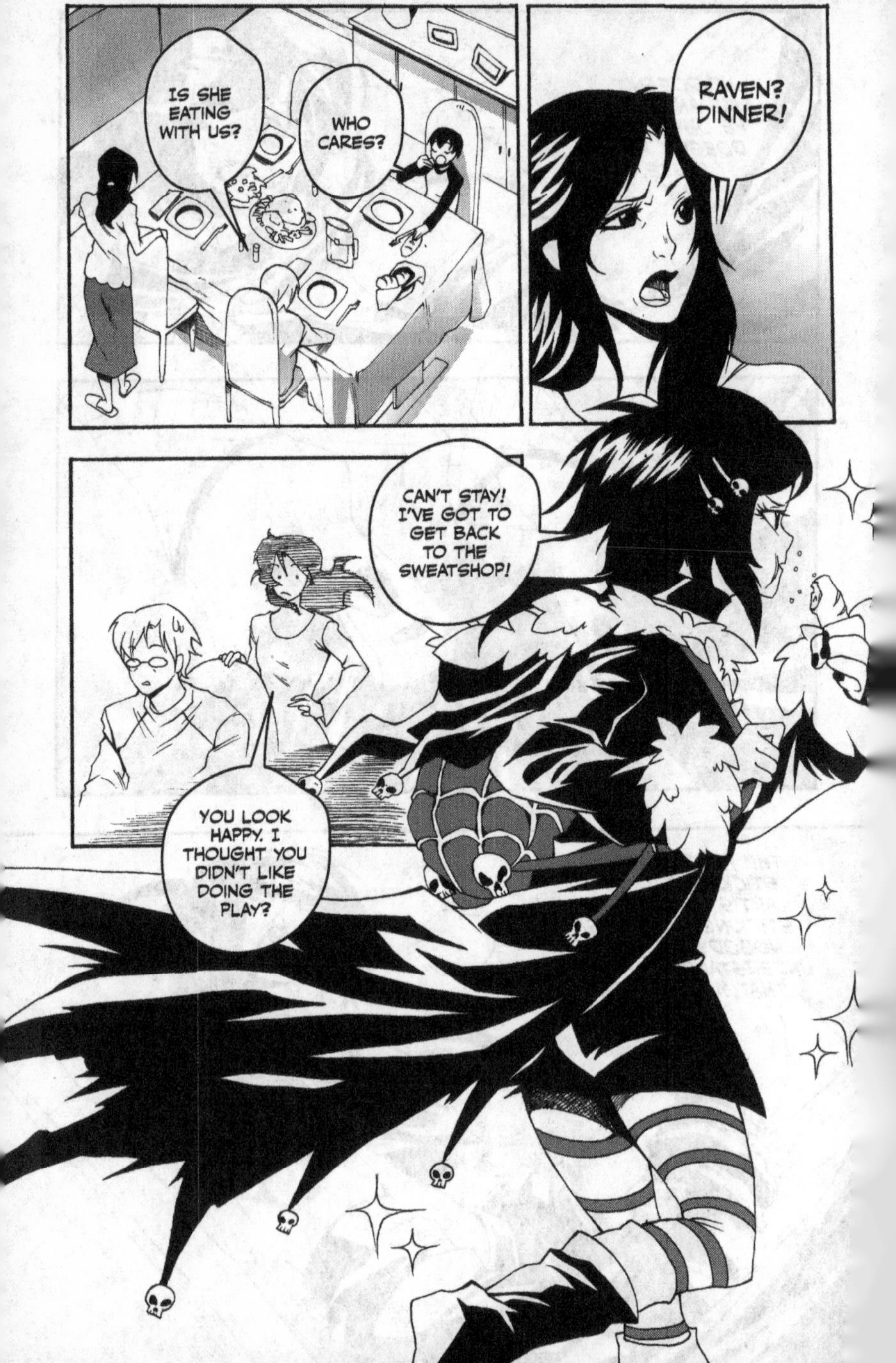
IS SHE EATING WITH US?
WHO CARES?
RAVEN? DINNER!
CAN'T STAY! I'VE GOT TO GET BACK TO THE SWEATSHOP!
YOU LOOK HAPPY. I THOUGHT YOU DIDN'T LIKE DOING THE PLAY?

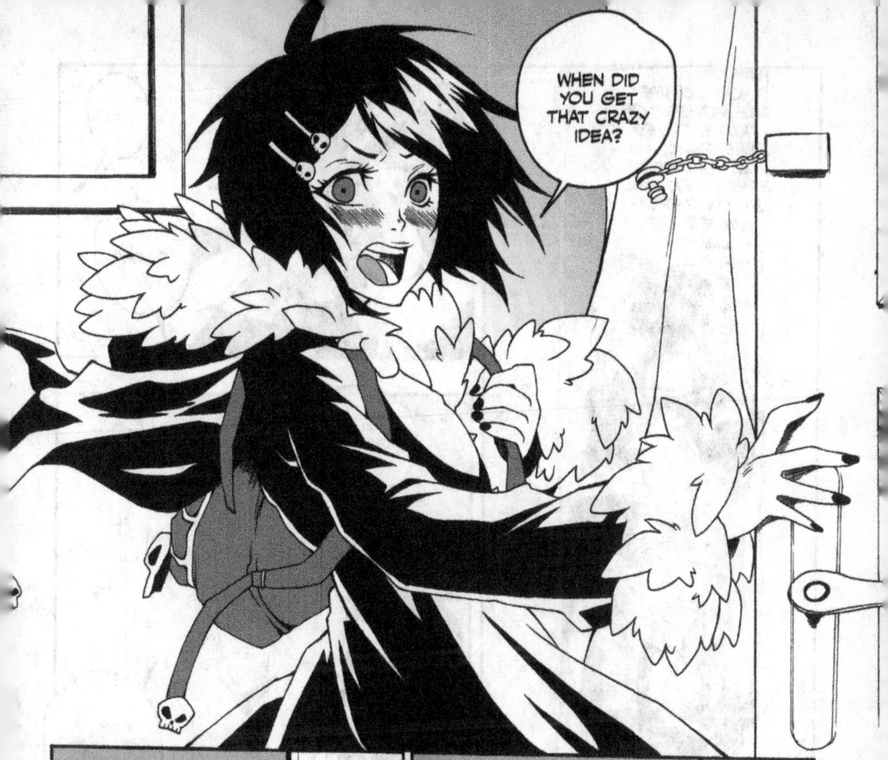
WHEN DID YOU GET THAT CRAZY IDEA?
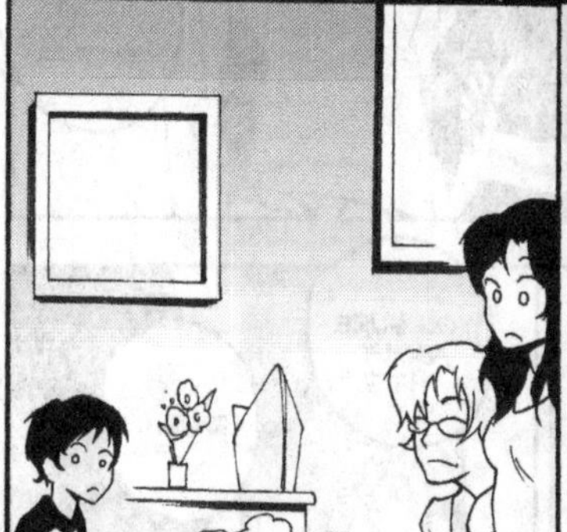
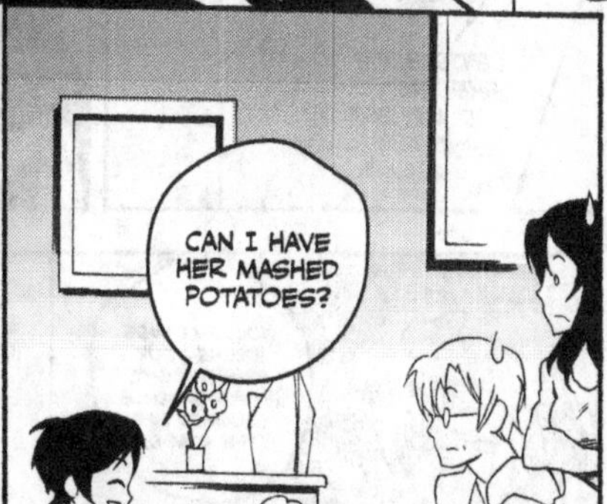
CAN I HAVE HER MASHED POTATOES?

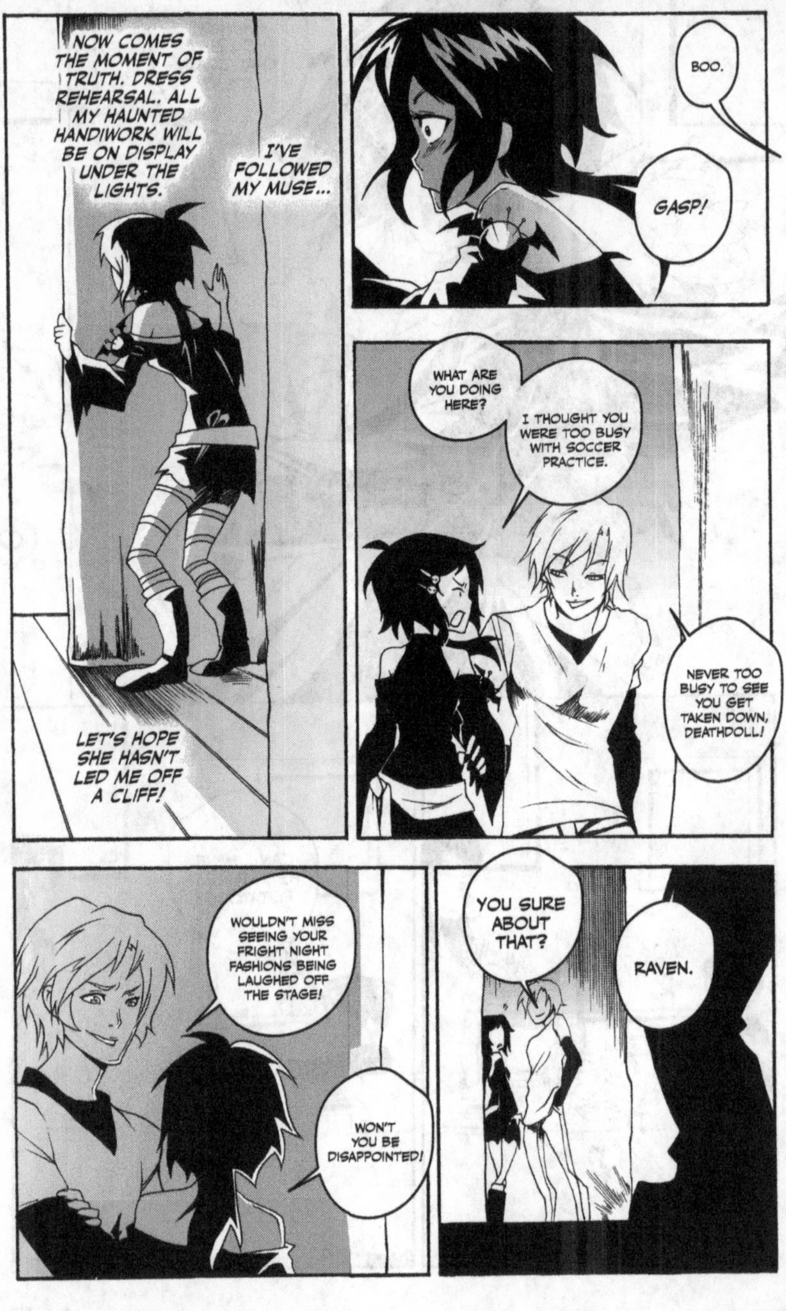
NOW COMES THE MOMENT OF TRUTH. DRESS REHEARSAL. ALL MY HAUNTED HANDIWORK WILL BE ON DISPLAY UNDER THE LIGHTS.
I'VE FOLLOWED MY MUSE...
LET'S HOPE SHE HASN'T LED ME OFF A CLIFF!
BOO.
GASP!
WHAT ARE YOU DOING HERE?
I THOUGHT YOU WERE TOO BUSY WITH SOCCER PRACTICE.
NEVER TOO BUSY TO SEE YOU GET TAKEN DOWN, DEATHDOLL!
WOULDN'T MISS SEEING YOUR FRIGHT NIGHT FASHIONS BEING LAUGHED OFF THE STAGE!
WON'T YOU BE DISAPPOINTED!
YOU SURE ABOUT THAT?
RAVEN.

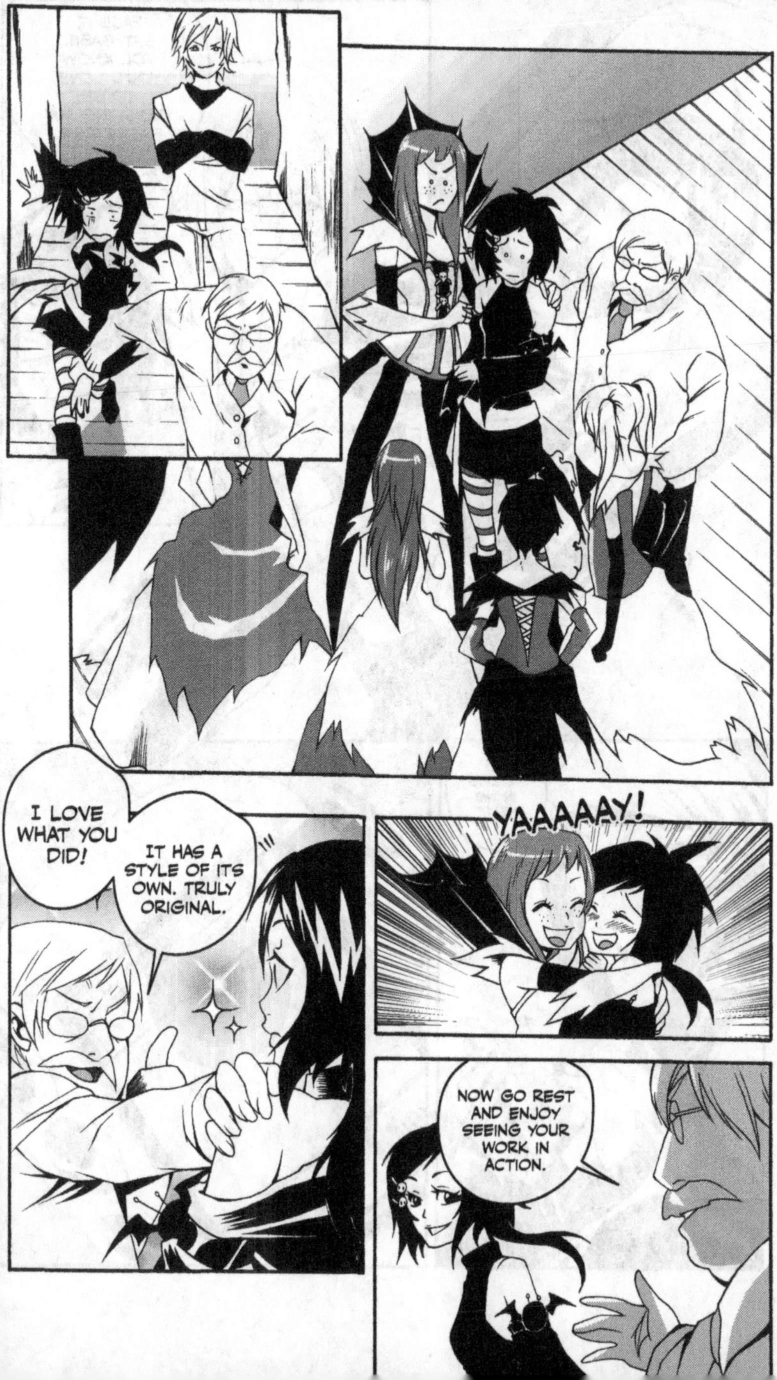
I LOVE WHAT YOU DID!
IT HAS A STYLE OF ITS OWN. TRULY ORIGINAL.
YAAAAAY!
NOW GO REST AND ENJOY SEEING YOUR WORK IN ACTION.

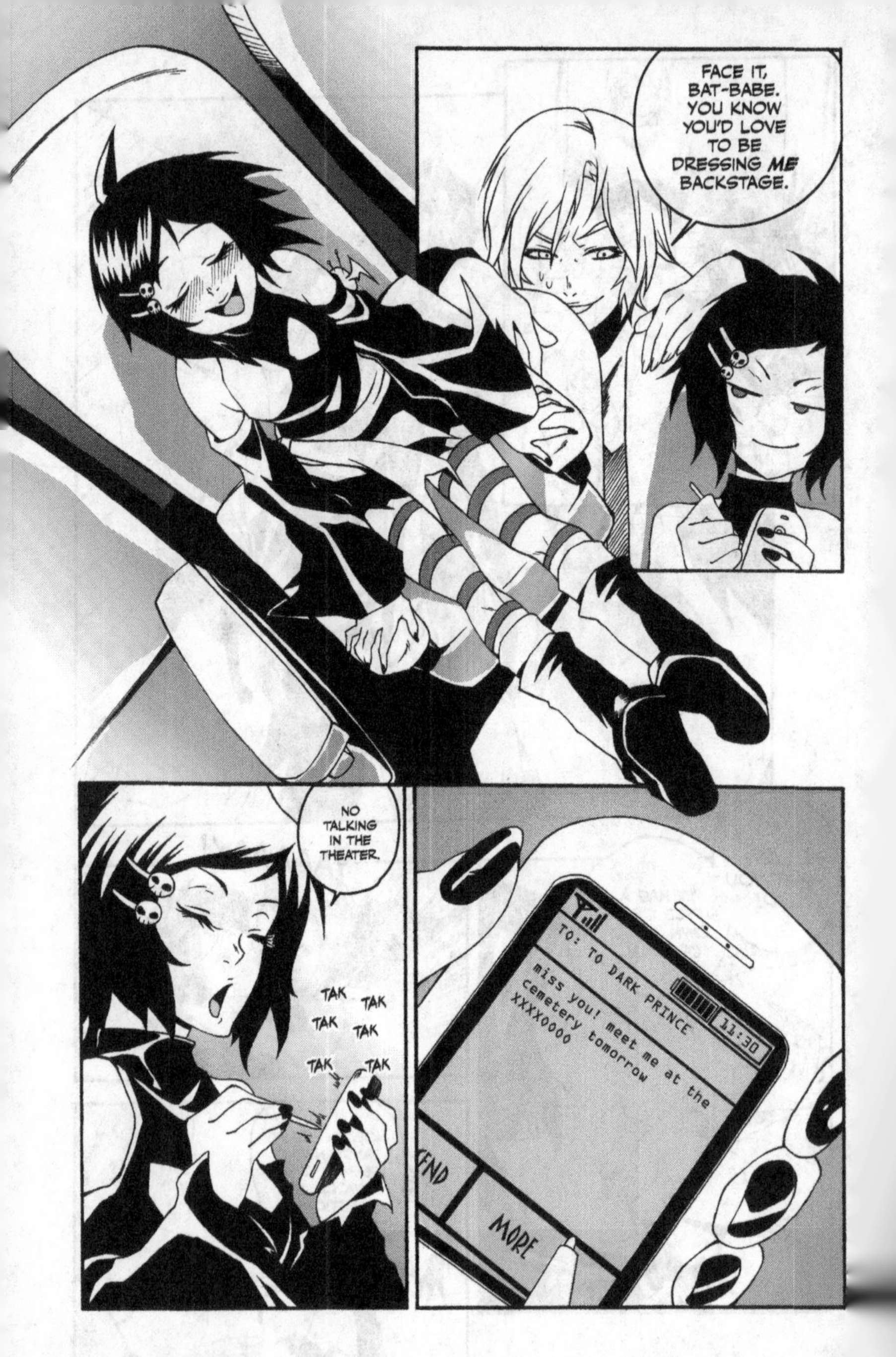
FACE IT, BAT-BABE. YOU KNOW YOU'D LOVE TO BE DRESSING *ME* BACKSTAGE.
NO TALKING IN THE THEATER.
TAK TAK TAK TAK TAK TAK
TO: TO DARK PRINCE
11:30
miss you! meet me at the cemetery tomorrow XXXXOOOO
MORE

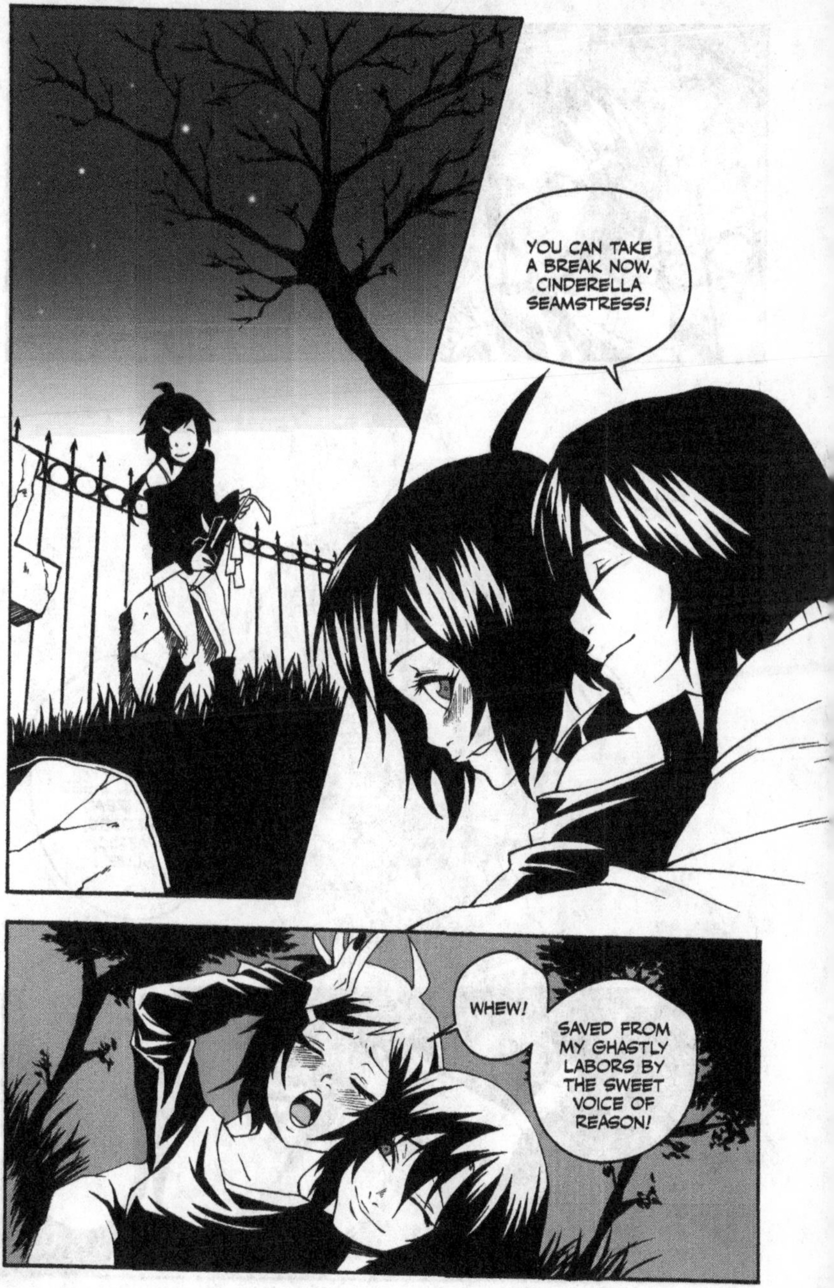
YOU CAN TAKE A BREAK NOW, CINDERELLA SEAMSTRESS!
WHEW!
SAVED FROM MY GHASTLY LABORS BY THE SWEET VOICE OF REASON!

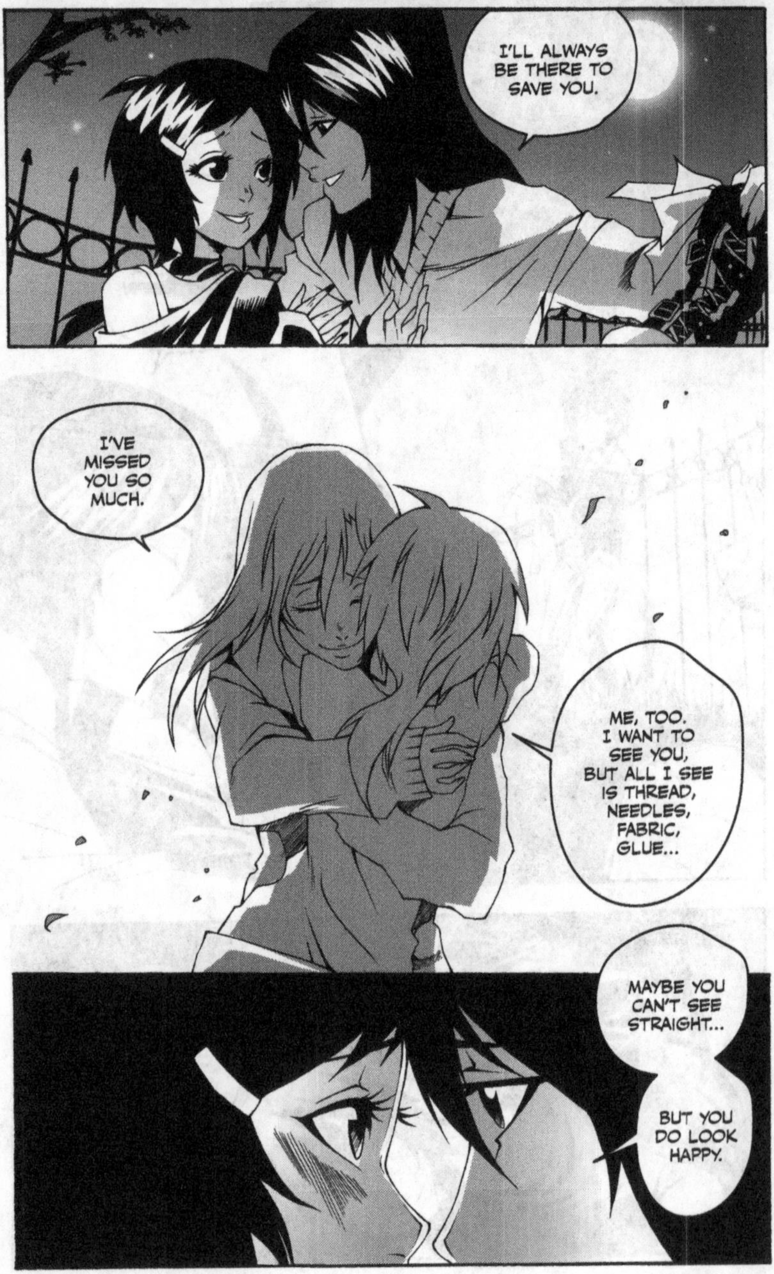
I'LL ALWAYS BE THERE TO SAVE YOU.
I'VE MISSED YOU SO MUCH.
ME, TOO. I WANT TO SEE YOU, BUT ALL I SEE IS THREAD, NEEDLES, FABRIC, GLUE...
MAYBE YOU CAN'T SEE STRAIGHT...
BUT YOU DO LOOK HAPPY.

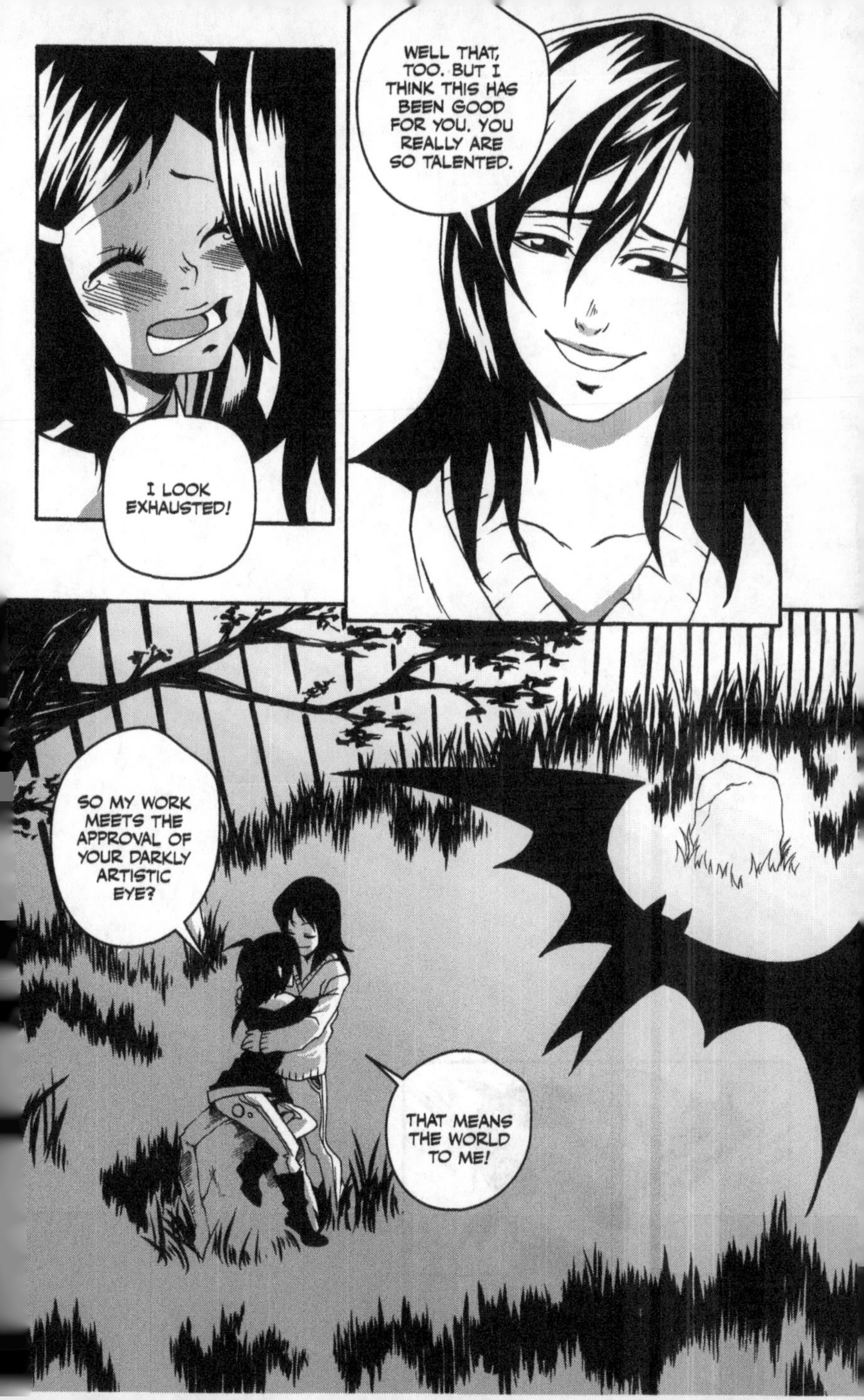
I LOOK EXHAUSTED!
WELL THAT, TOO. BUT I THINK THIS HAS BEEN GOOD FOR YOU. YOU REALLY ARE SO TALENTED.
SO MY WORK MEETS THE APPROVAL OF YOUR DARKLY ARTISTIC EYE?
THAT MEANS THE WORLD TO ME!

Chapter Seven: Picking the Locket

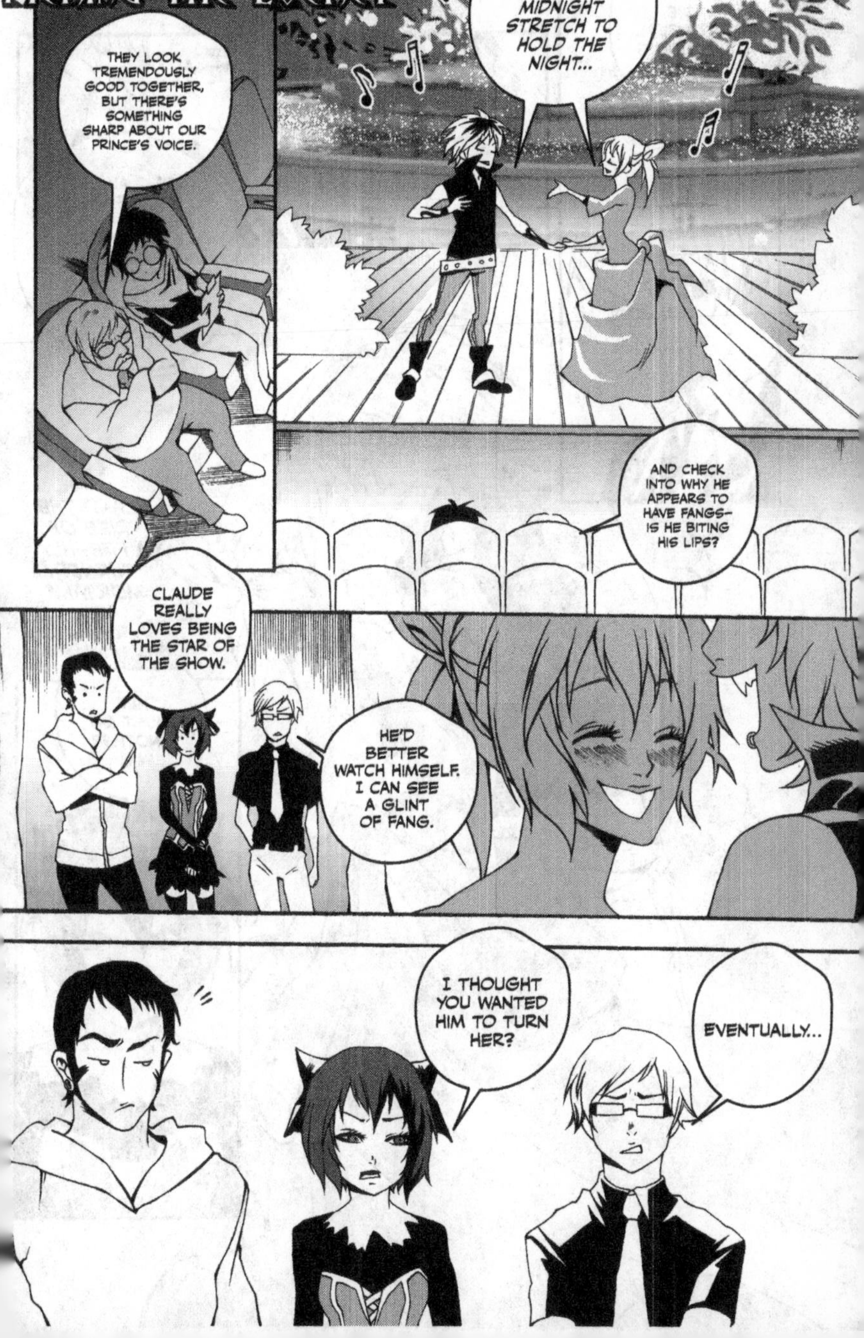
THEY LOOK TREMENDOUSLY GOOD TOGETHER, BUT THERE'S SOMETHING SHARP ABOUT OUR PRINCE'S VOICE.
...LET THE HOUR BEFORE MIDNIGHT STRETCH TO HOLD THE NIGHT...
AND CHECK INTO WHY HE APPEARS TO HAVE FANGS– IS HE BITING HIS LIPS?
CLAUDE REALLY LOVES BEING THE STAR OF THE SHOW.
HE'D BETTER WATCH HIMSELF. I CAN SEE A GLINT OF FANG.
I THOUGHT YOU WANTED HIM TO TURN HER?
EVENTUALLY...

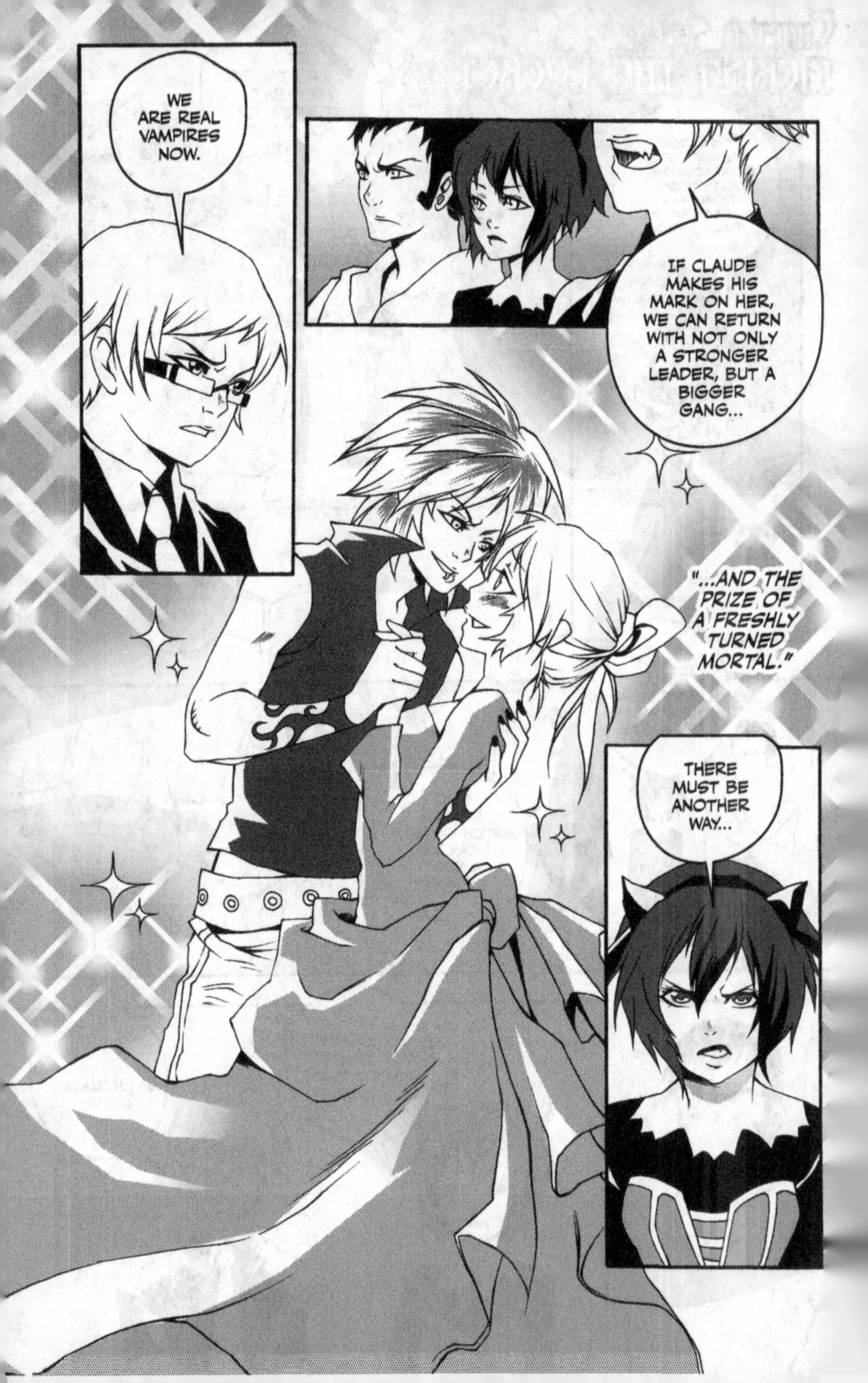
WE ARE REAL VAMPIRES NOW.
IF CLAUDE MAKES HIS MARK ON HER, WE CAN RETURN WITH NOT ONLY A STRONGER LEADER, BUT A BIGGER GANG...
"...AND THE PRIZE OF A FRESHLY TURNED MORTAL."
THERE MUST BE ANOTHER WAY...

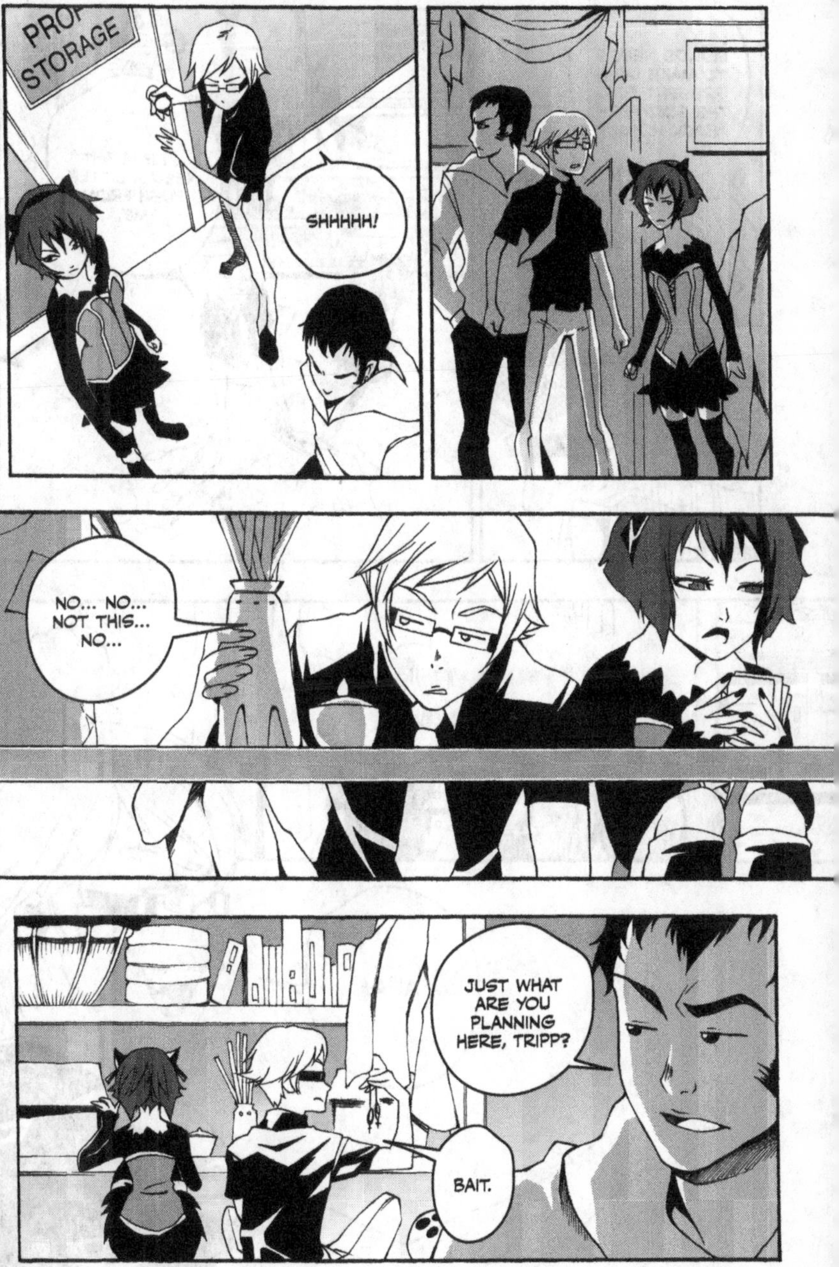
PROP STORAGE
SHHHHH!
NO... NO... NOT THIS... NO...
JUST WHAT ARE YOU PLANNING HERE, TRIPP?
BAIT.

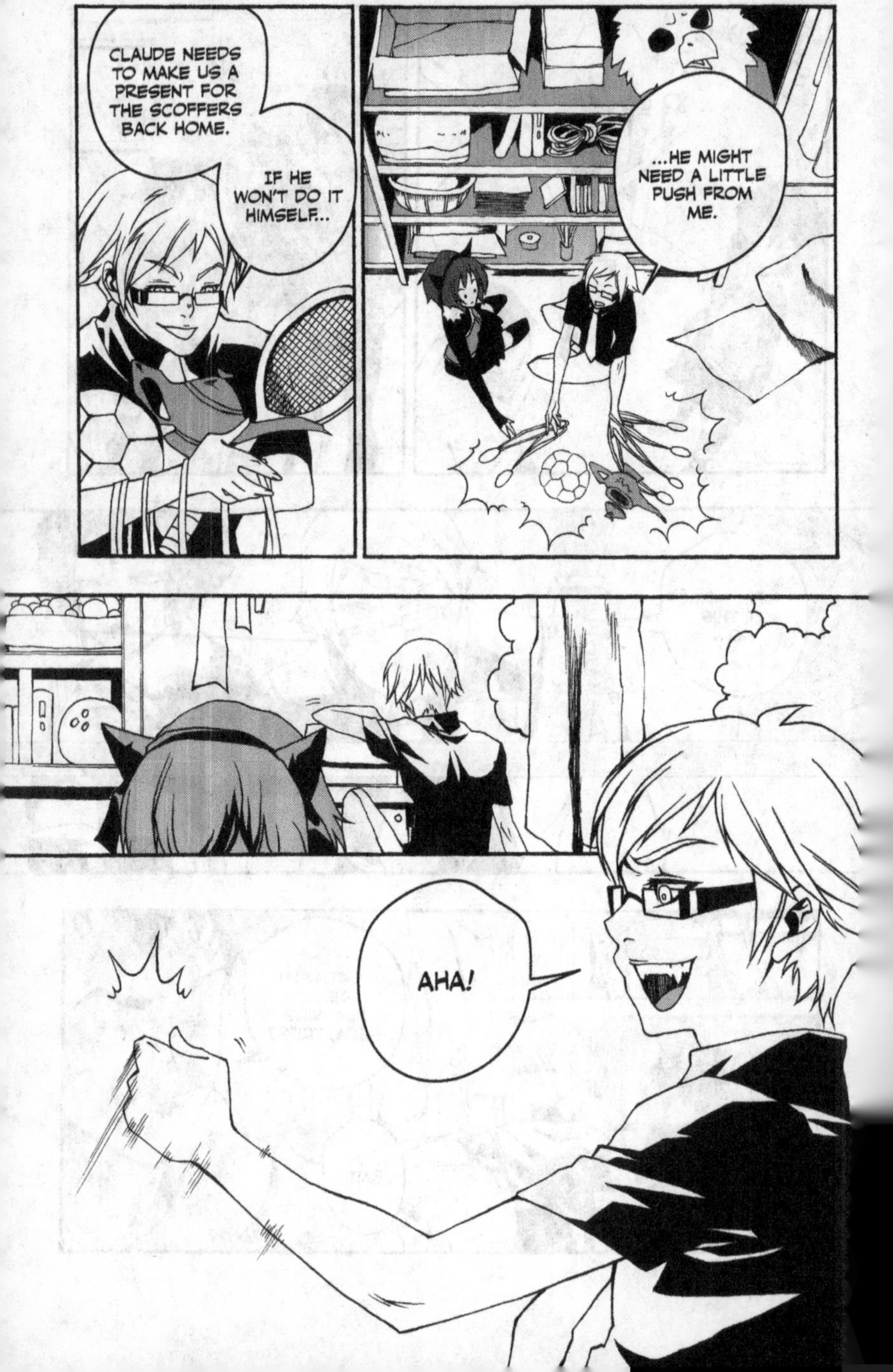
CLAUDE NEEDS TO MAKE US A PRESENT FOR THE SCOFFERS BACK HOME.
IF HE WON'T DO IT HIMSELF...
...HE MIGHT NEED A LITTLE PUSH FROM ME.
AHA!

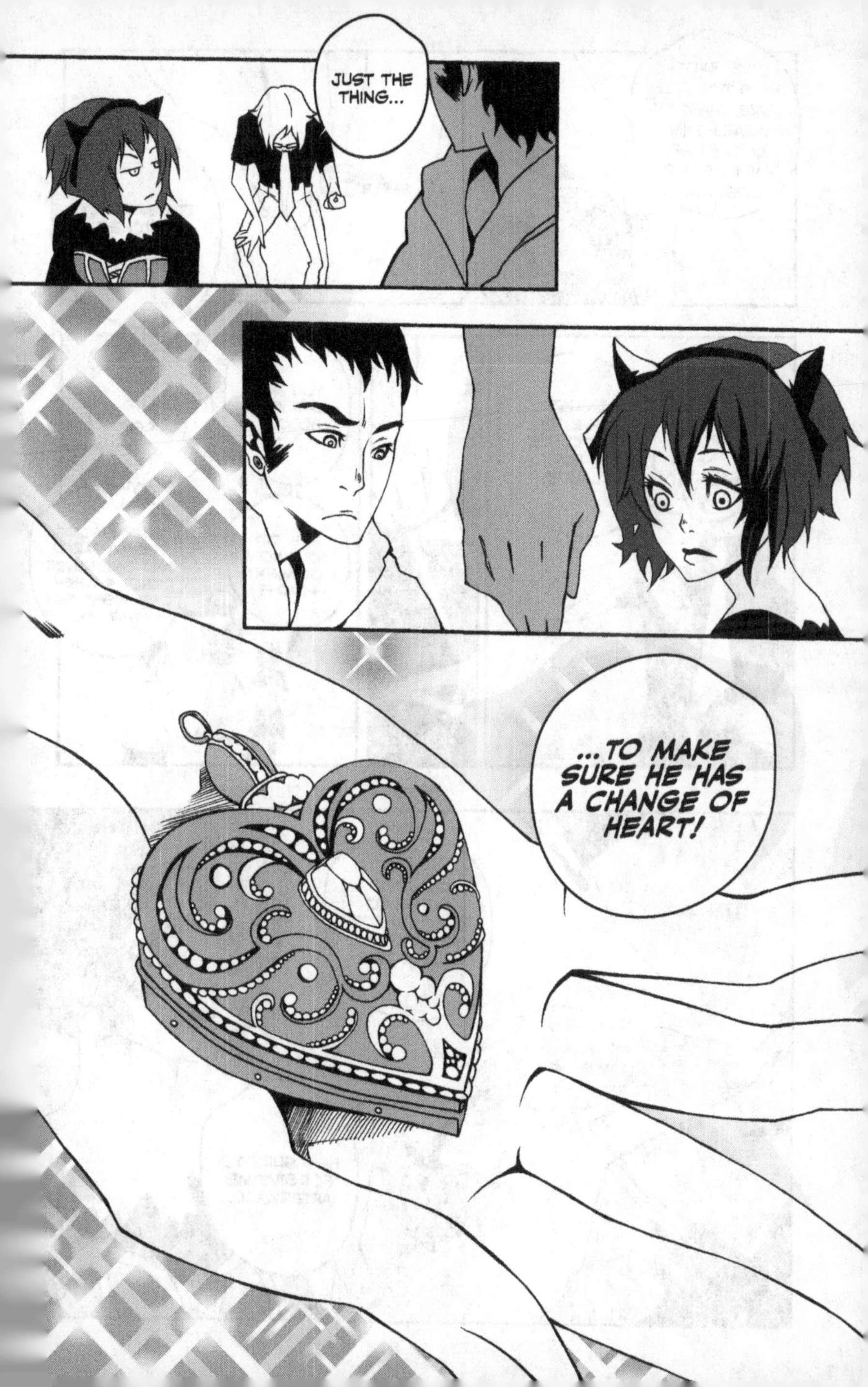
JUST THE THING...
...TO MAKE SURE HE HAS A CHANGE OF HEART!

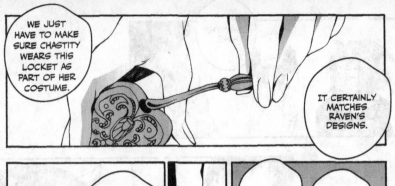

WE JUST HAVE TO MAKE SURE CHASTITY WEARS THIS LOCKET AS PART OF HER COSTUME.

IT CERTAINLY MATCHES RAVEN'S DESIGNS.

I JUST HAVE TO CUSTOMIZE IT FOR CLAUDE.

YOU ARE CARRYING BLOOD?

OF COURSE!

HOW DID YOU KNOW YOU MIGHT NEED—?

LUCK FAVORS THE PREPARED. AND ONE NEVER KNOWS WHEN ONE MIGHT GET THIRSTY!

CLAUDE'S GOING TO KILL YOU FOR SETTING HIM UP LIKE THIS.

HE'S SURE TO FORGIVE ME AFTERWARD.

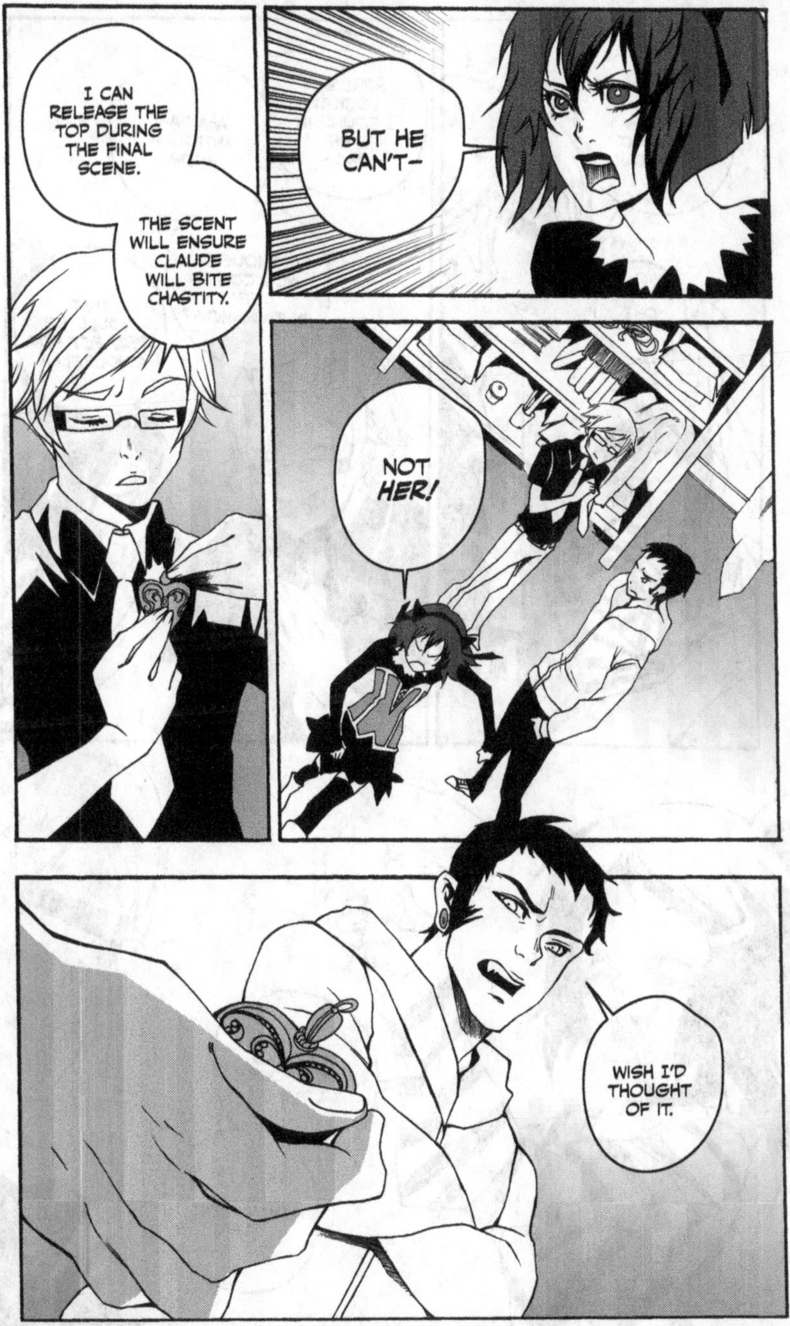
I CAN RELEASE THE TOP DURING THE FINAL SCENE.
THE SCENT WILL ENSURE CLAUDE WILL BITE CHASTITY.
BUT HE CAN'T-
NOT HER!
WISH I'D THOUGHT OF IT.

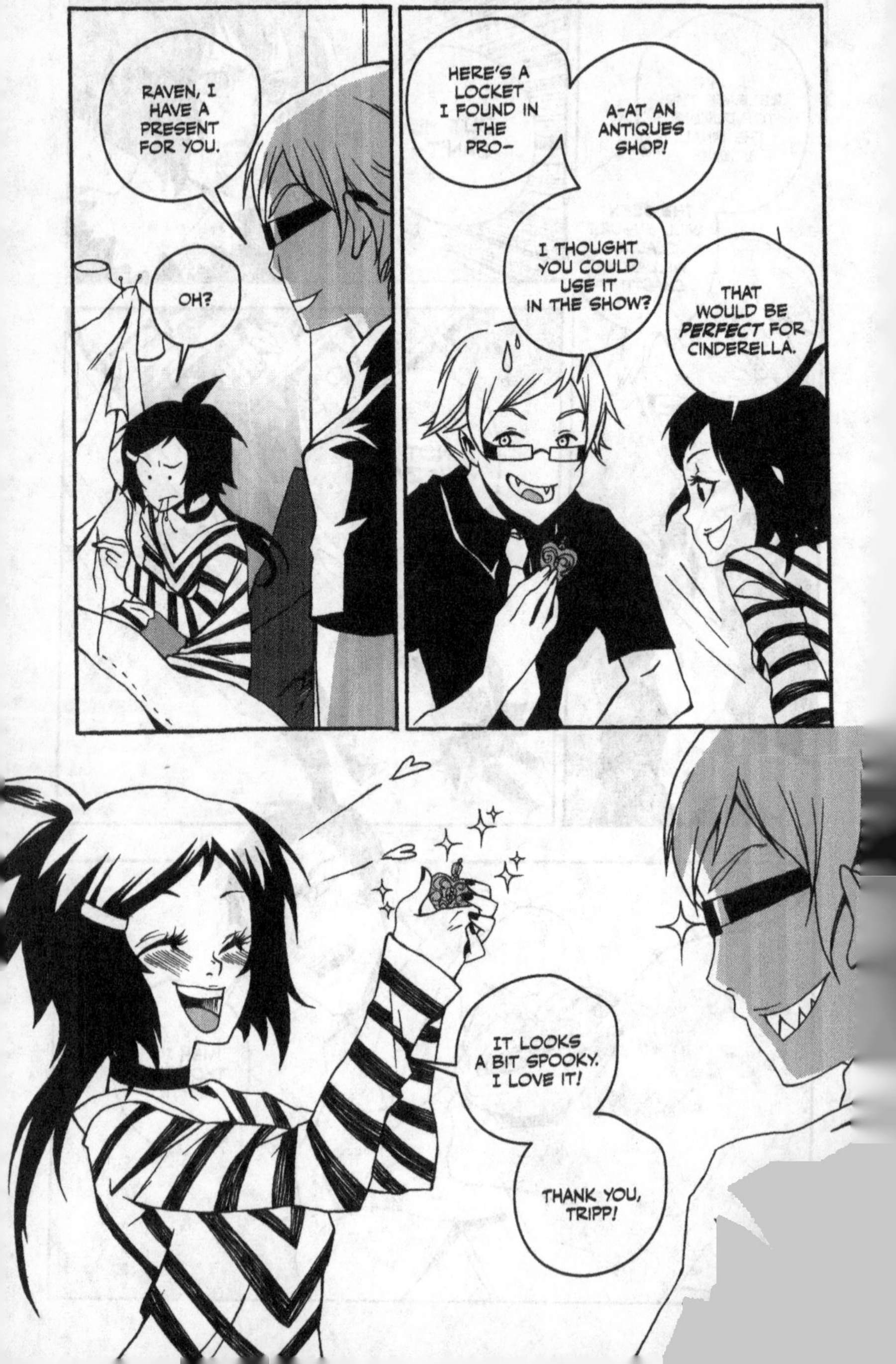
RAVEN, I HAVE A PRESENT FOR YOU.
OH?
HERE'S A LOCKET I FOUND IN THE PRO-
A-AT AN ANTIQUES SHOP!
I THOUGHT YOU COULD USE IT IN THE SHOW?
THAT WOULD BE *PERFECT* FOR CINDERELLA.
IT LOOKS A BIT SPOOKY. I LOVE IT!
THANK YOU, TRIPP!

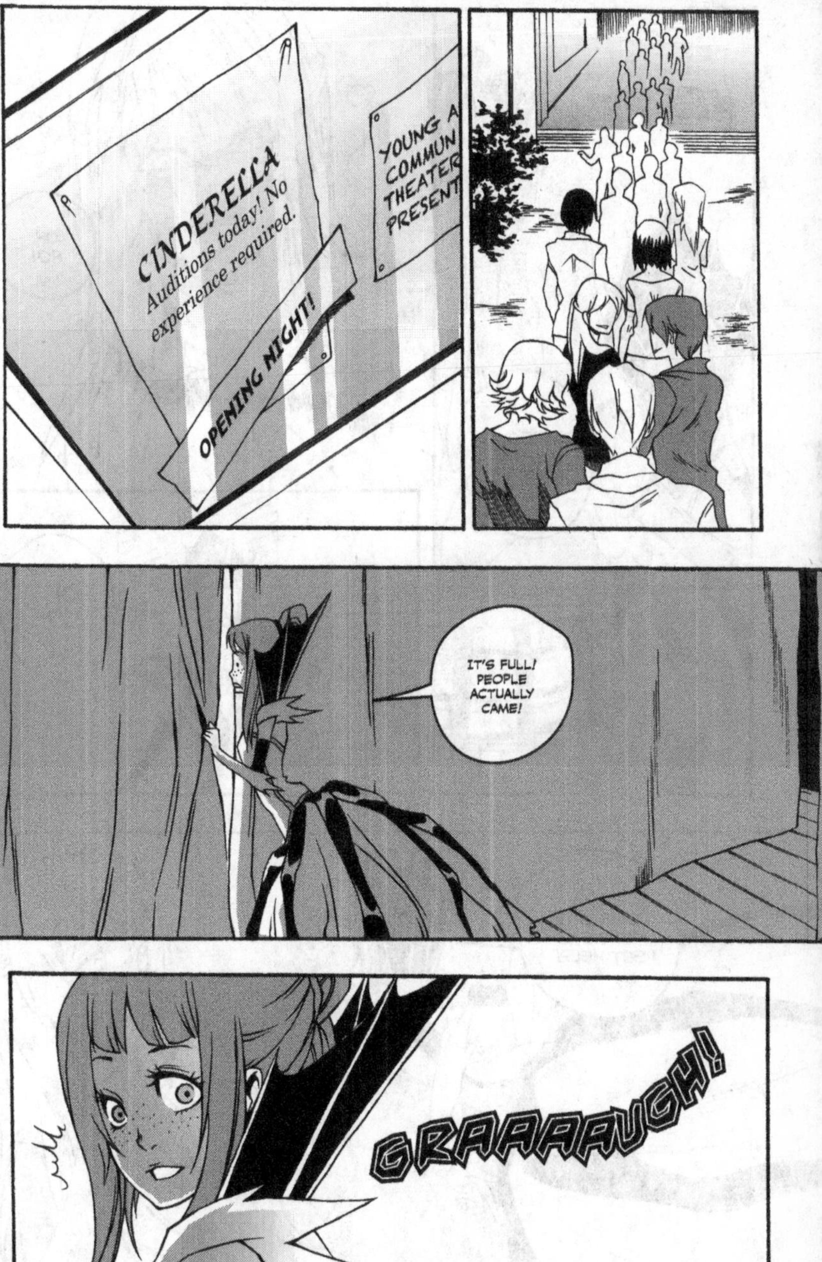
CINDERELLA
Auditions today! No experience required.
OPENING NIGHT!
YOUNG A
COMMUN
THEATER
PRESENT
IT'S FULL! PEOPLE ACTUALLY CAME!
GRAAAAAUGH!

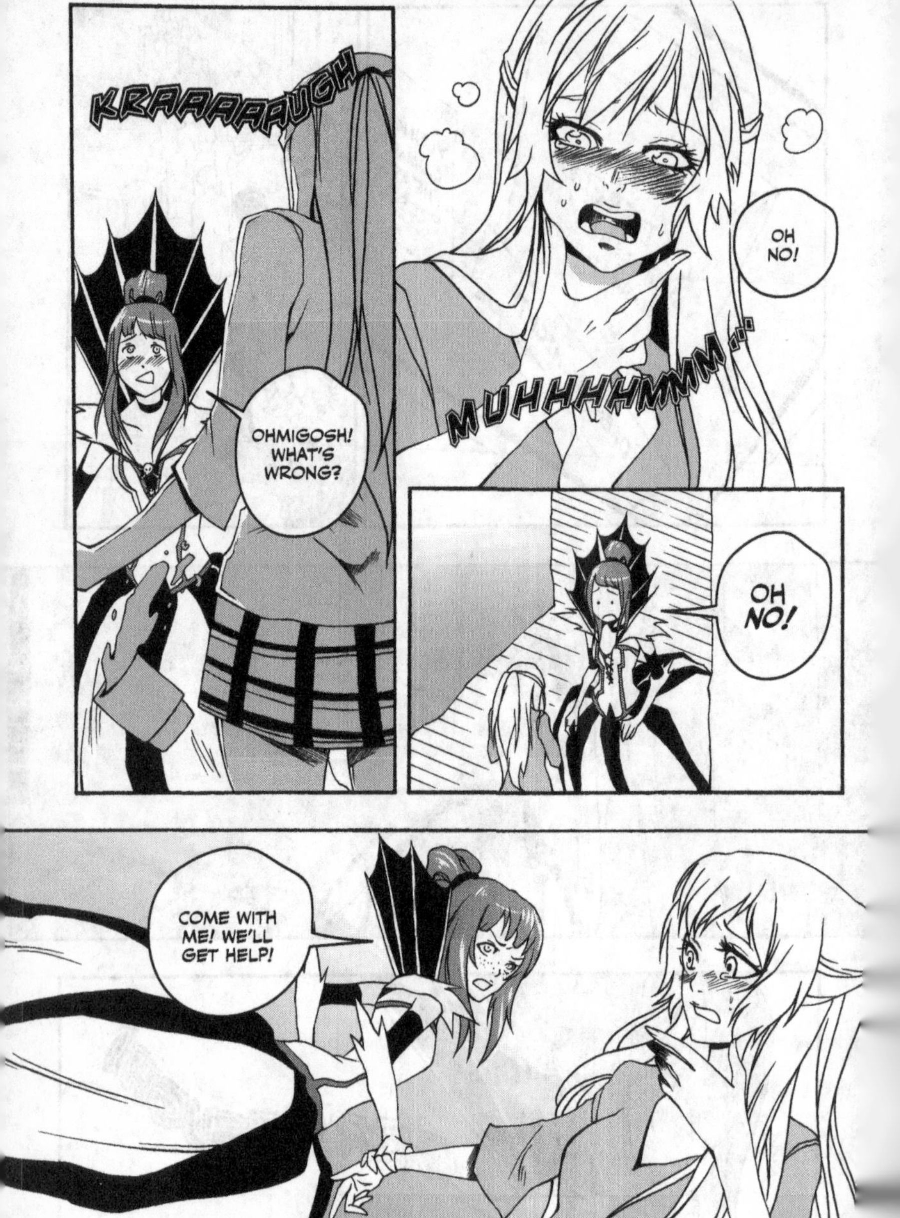
KRAAAAAAUGH
OHMIGOSH! WHAT'S WRONG?
OH NO!
MUHHHHMMM...
OH NO!
COME WITH ME! WE'LL GET HELP!

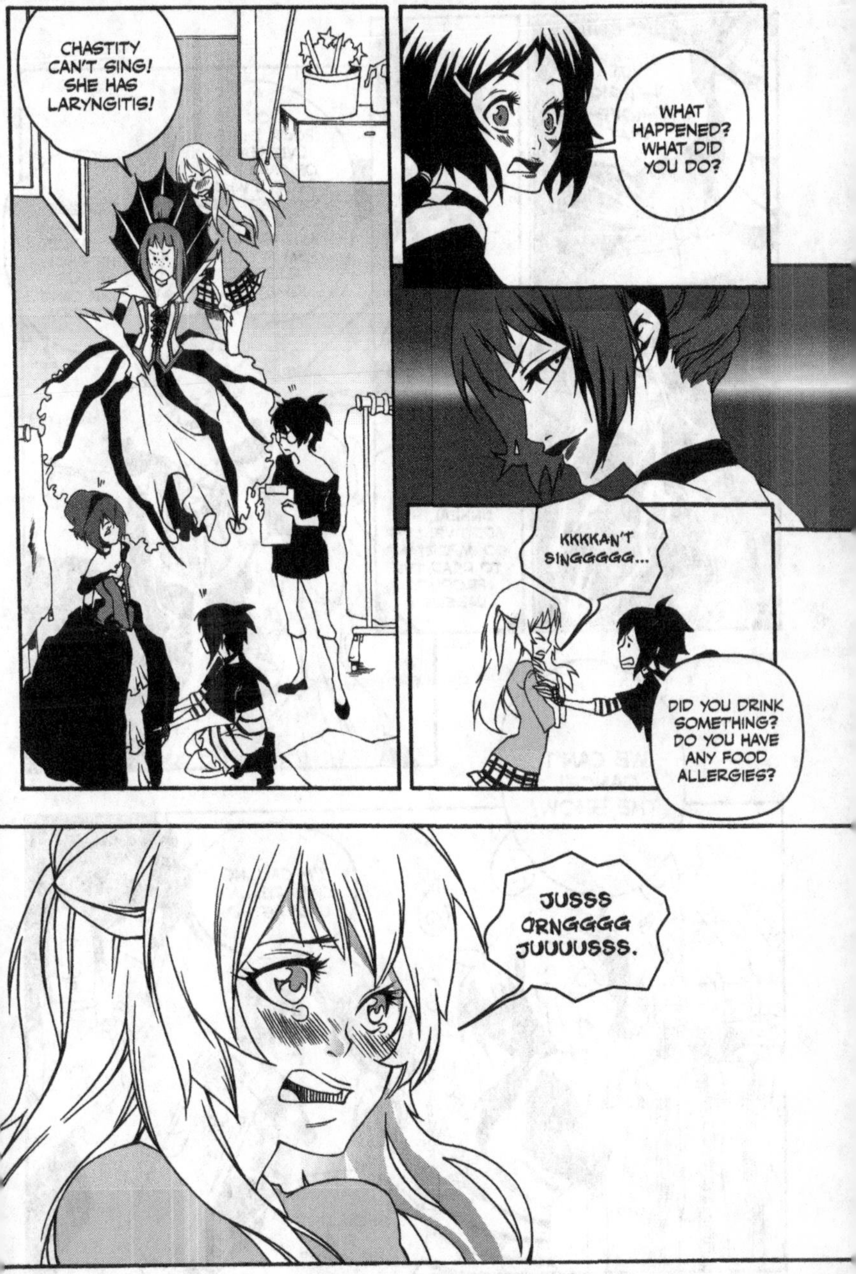
CHASTITY CAN'T SING! SHE HAS LARYNGITIS!
WHAT HAPPENED? WHAT DID YOU DO?
KKKKAN'T SINGGGGG...
DID YOU DRINK SOMETHING? DO YOU HAVE ANY FOOD ALLERGIES?
JUSSS ORNGGGG JUUUUSSS.

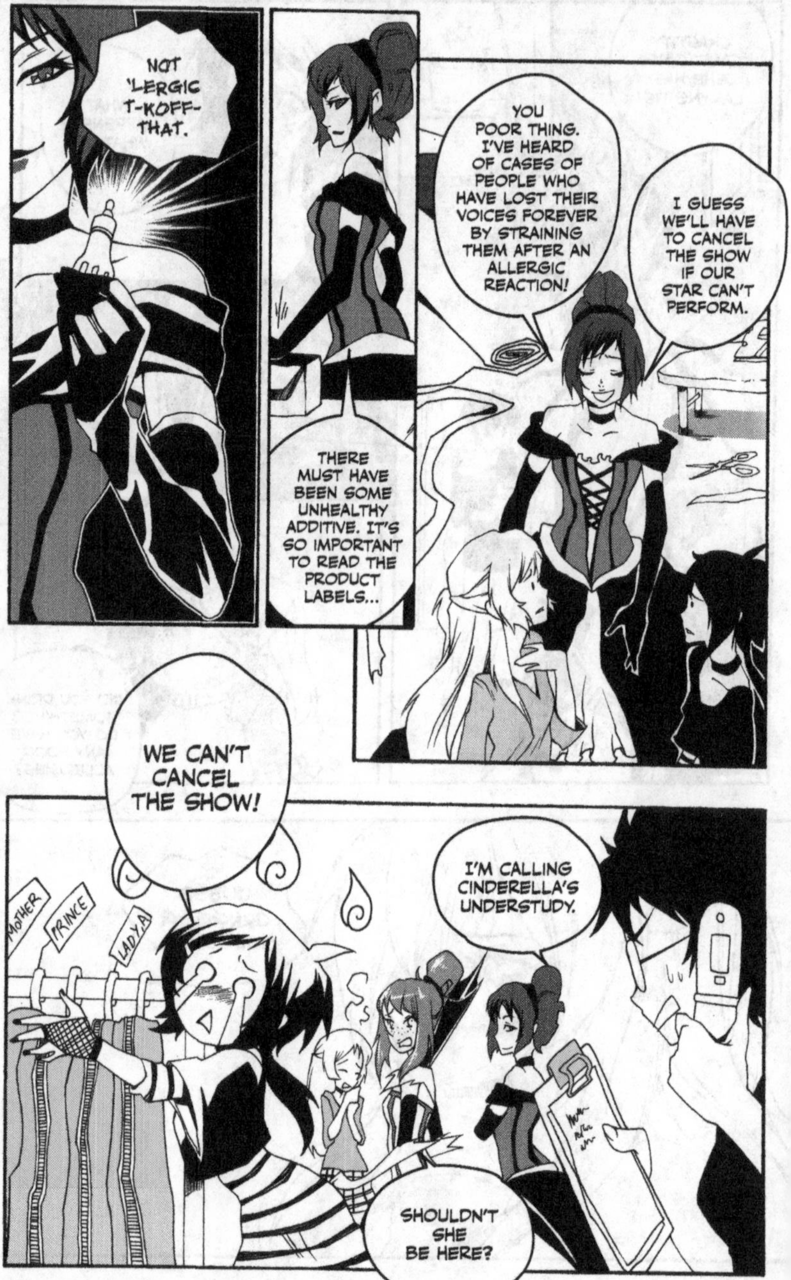
NOT 'LERGIC T-KOFF- THAT.
THERE MUST HAVE BEEN SOME UNHEALTHY ADDITIVE. IT'S SO IMPORTANT TO READ THE PRODUCT LABELS...
YOU POOR THING. I'VE HEARD OF CASES OF PEOPLE WHO HAVE LOST THEIR VOICES FOREVER BY STRAINING THEM AFTER AN ALLERGIC REACTION!
I GUESS WE'LL HAVE TO CANCEL THE SHOW IF OUR STAR CAN'T PERFORM.
MOTHER
PRINCE
LADY A
WE CAN'T CANCEL THE SHOW!
I'M CALLING CINDERELLA'S UNDERSTUDY.
SHOULDN'T SHE BE HERE?

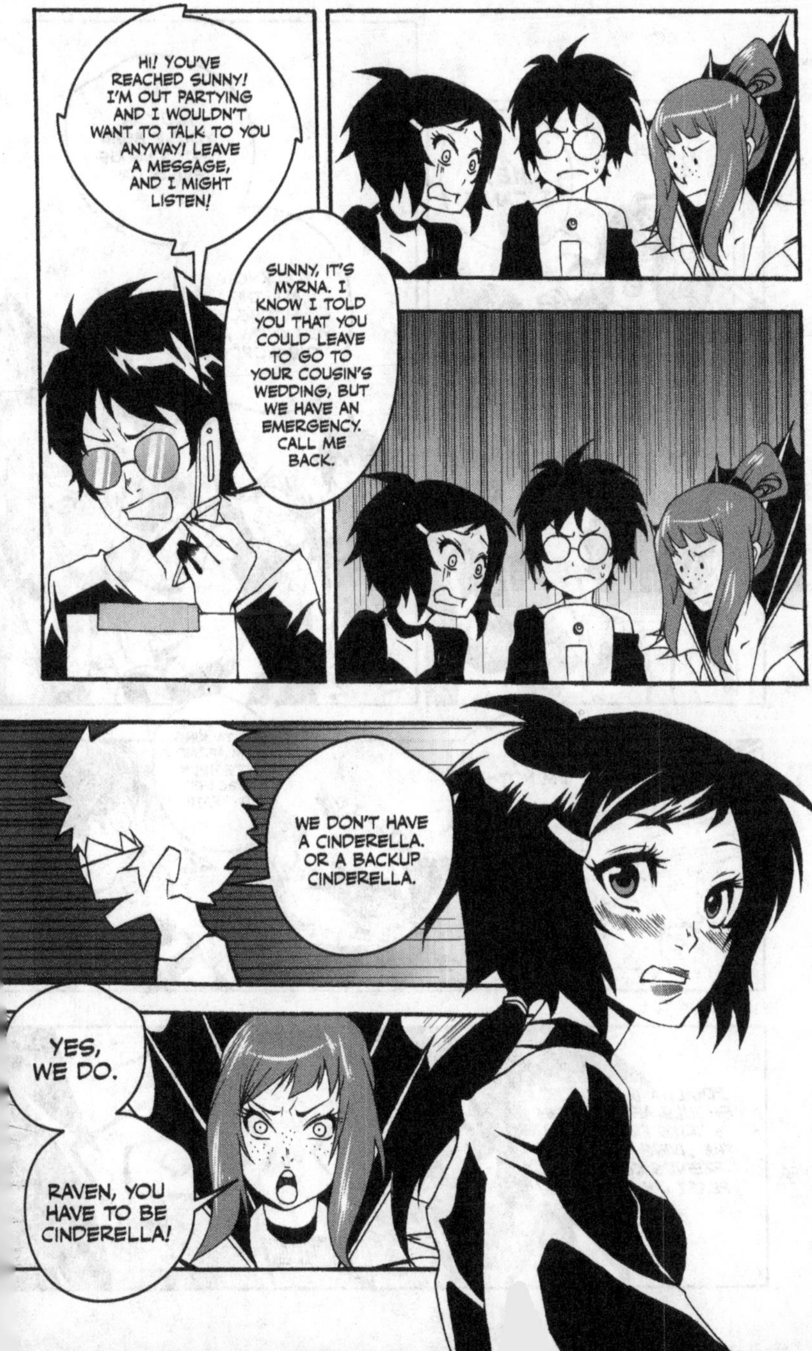
HI! YOU'VE REACHED SUNNY! I'M OUT PARTYING AND I WOULDN'T WANT TO TALK TO YOU ANYWAY! LEAVE A MESSAGE, AND I MIGHT LISTEN!
SUNNY, IT'S MYRNA. I KNOW I TOLD YOU THAT YOU COULD LEAVE TO GO TO YOUR COUSIN'S WEDDING, BUT WE HAVE AN EMERGENCY. CALL ME BACK.
WE DON'T HAVE A CINDERELLA. OR A BACKUP CINDERELLA.
YES, WE DO.
RAVEN, YOU HAVE TO BE CINDERELLA!

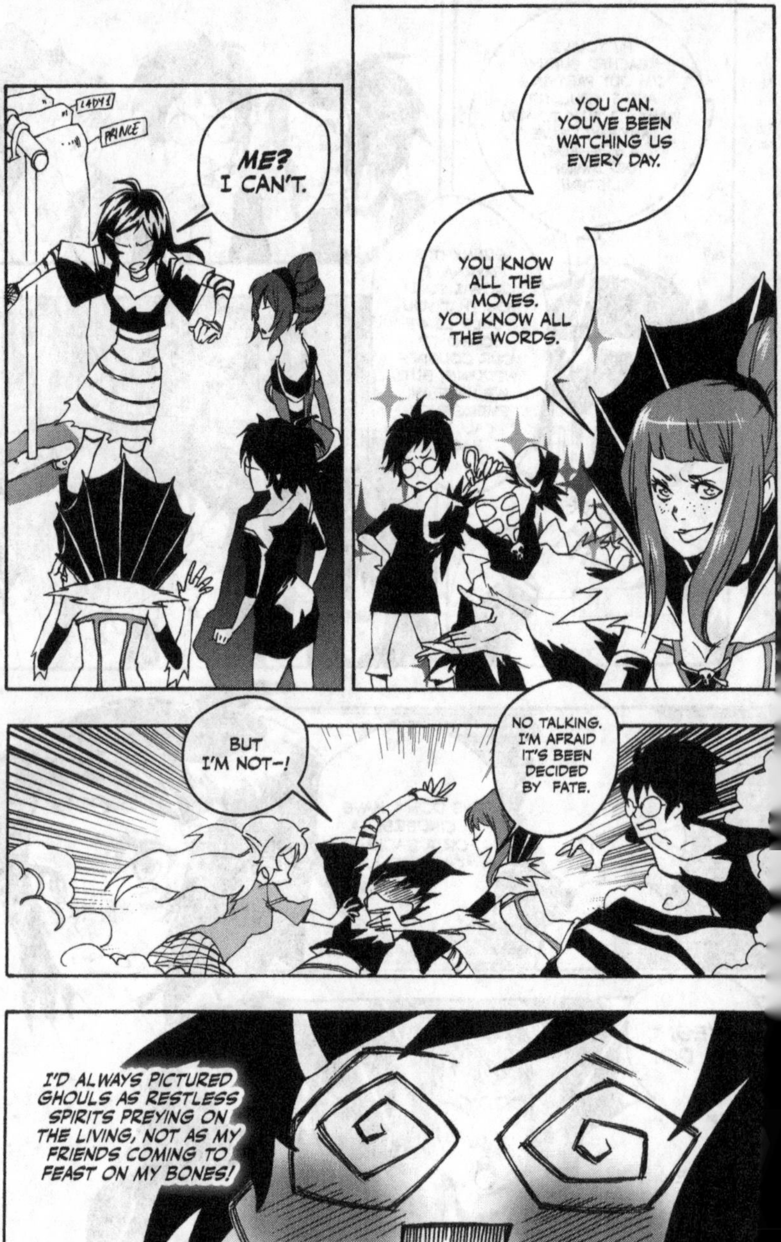
LADY 1
PRINCE
ME? I CAN'T.
YOU CAN. YOU'VE BEEN WATCHING US EVERY DAY.
YOU KNOW ALL THE MOVES. YOU KNOW ALL THE WORDS.
BUT I'M NOT--!
NO TALKING. I'M AFRAID IT'S BEEN DECIDED BY FATE.
I'D ALWAYS PICTURED GHOULS AS RESTLESS SPIRITS PREYING ON THE LIVING, NOT AS MY FRIENDS COMING TO FEAST ON MY BONES!

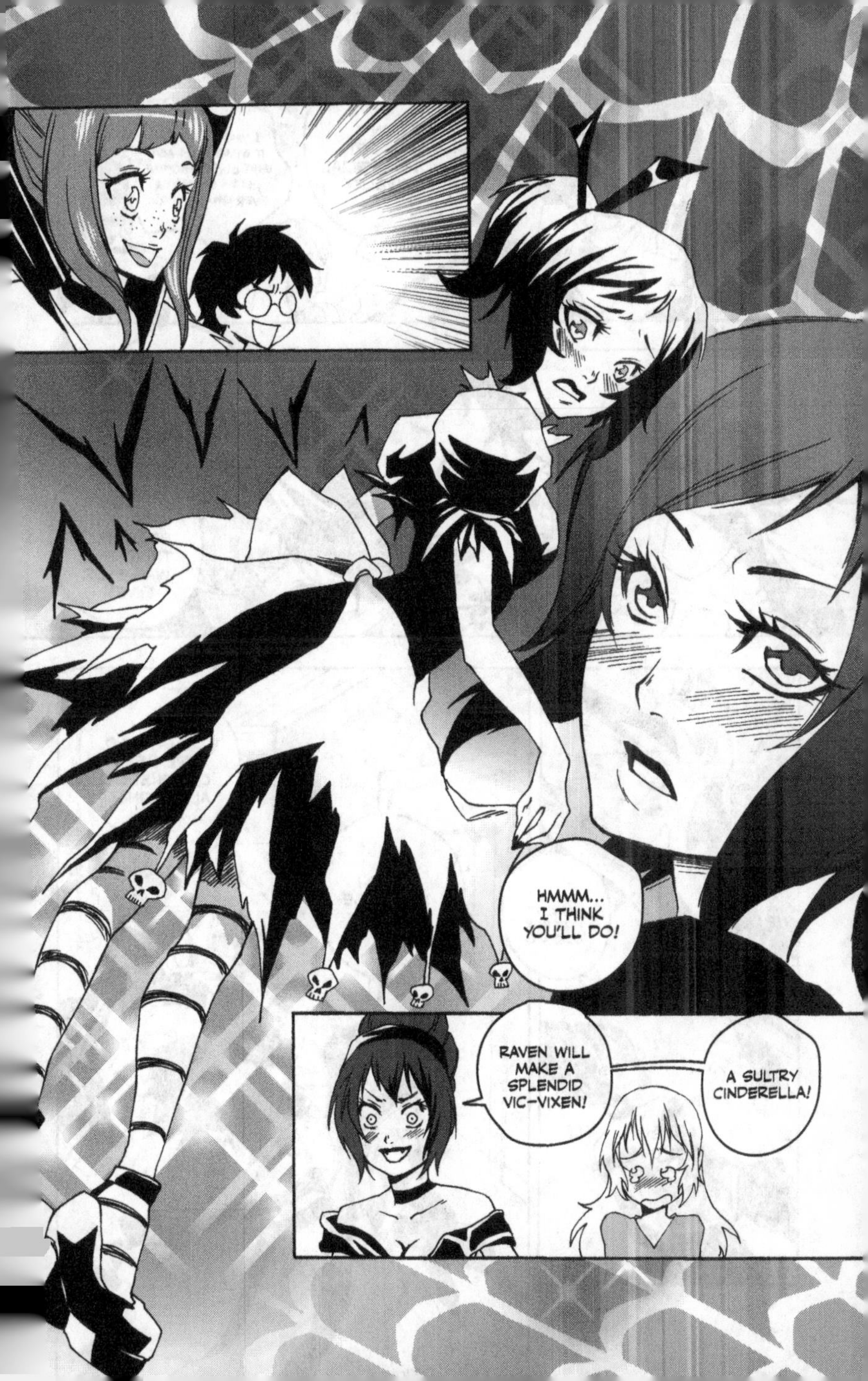
HMMM... I THINK YOU'LL DO!
RAVEN WILL MAKE A SPLENDID VIC-VIXEN!
A SULTRY CINDERELLA!

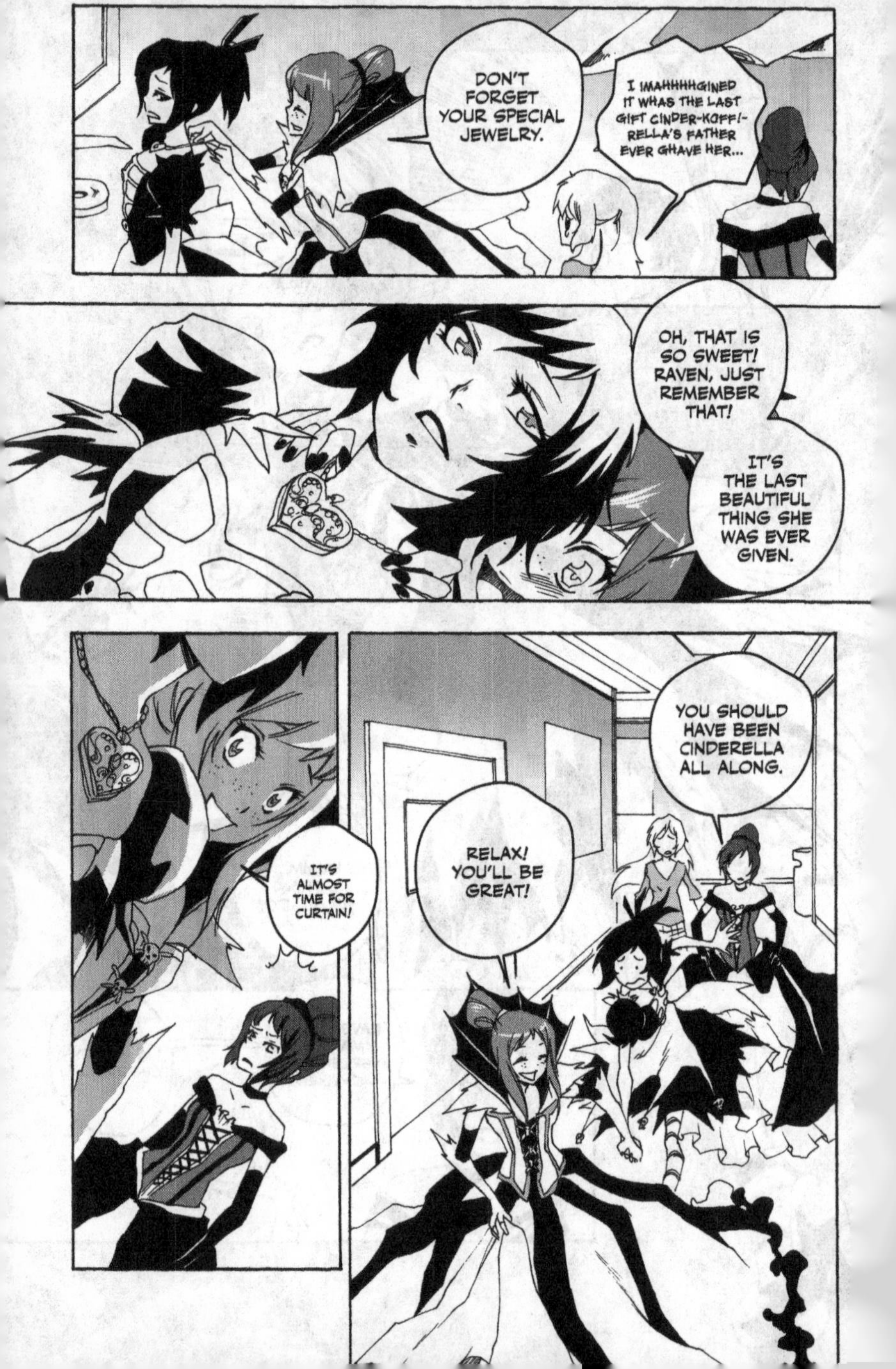
DON'T FORGET YOUR SPECIAL JEWELRY.
I IMAHHHHGINED IT WHAS THE LAST GIFT CINDER-KOFF!-RELLA'S FATHER EVER GHAVE HER...
OH, THAT IS SO SWEET! RAVEN, JUST REMEMBER THAT!
IT'S THE LAST BEAUTIFUL THING SHE WAS EVER GIVEN.
IT'S ALMOST TIME FOR CURTAIN!
RELAX! YOU'LL BE GREAT!
YOU SHOULD HAVE BEEN CINDERELLA ALL ALONG.

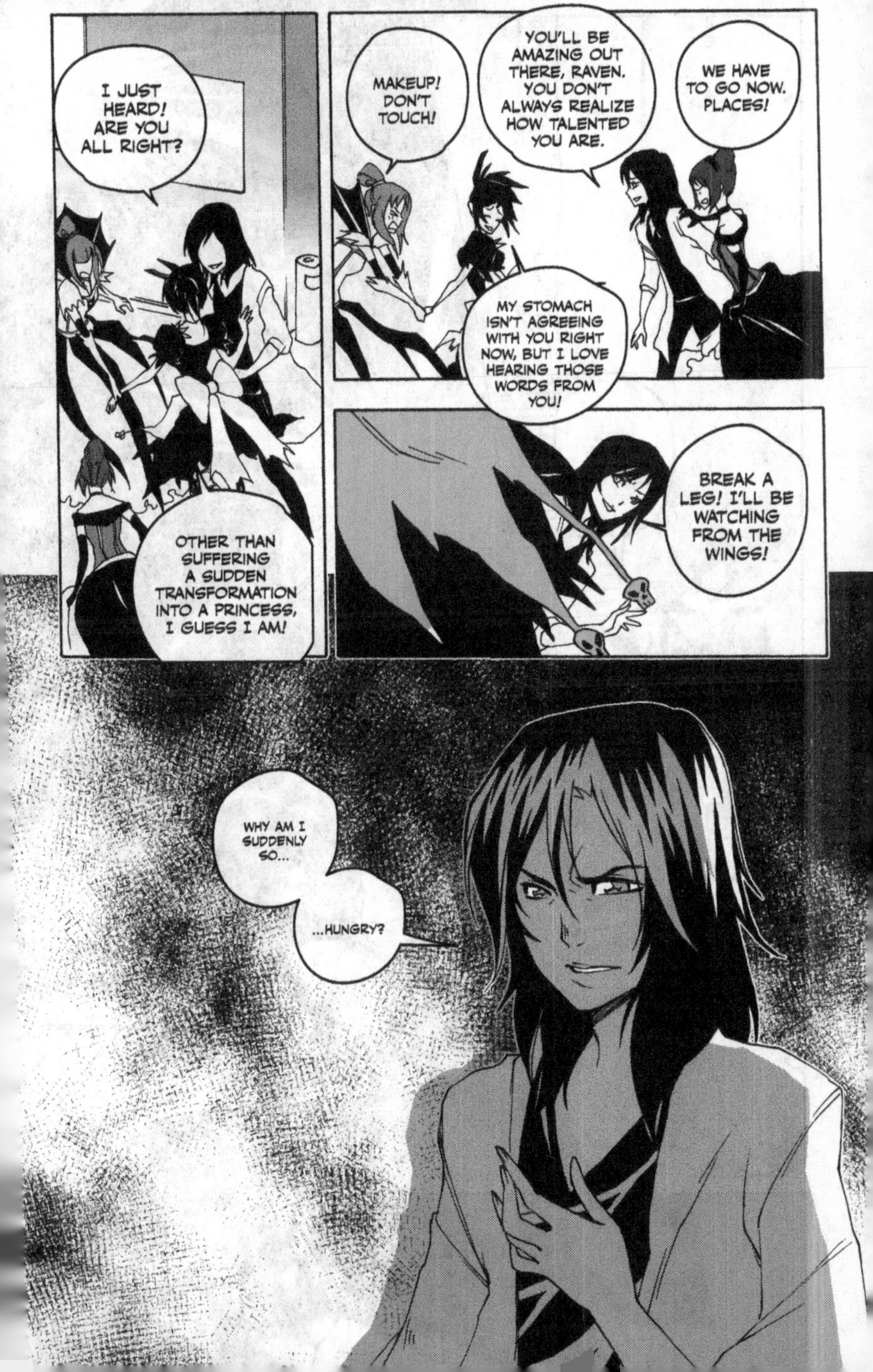
I JUST HEARD! ARE YOU ALL RIGHT?
OTHER THAN SUFFERING A SUDDEN TRANSFORMATION INTO A PRINCESS, I GUESS I AM!
MAKEUP! DON'T TOUCH!
YOU'LL BE AMAZING OUT THERE, RAVEN. YOU DON'T ALWAYS REALIZE HOW TALENTED YOU ARE.
MY STOMACH ISN'T AGREEING WITH YOU RIGHT NOW, BUT I LOVE HEARING THOSE WORDS FROM YOU!
WE HAVE TO GO NOW. PLACES!
BREAK A LEG! I'LL BE WATCHING FROM THE WINGS!
WHY AM I SUDDENLY SO...
...HUNGRY?

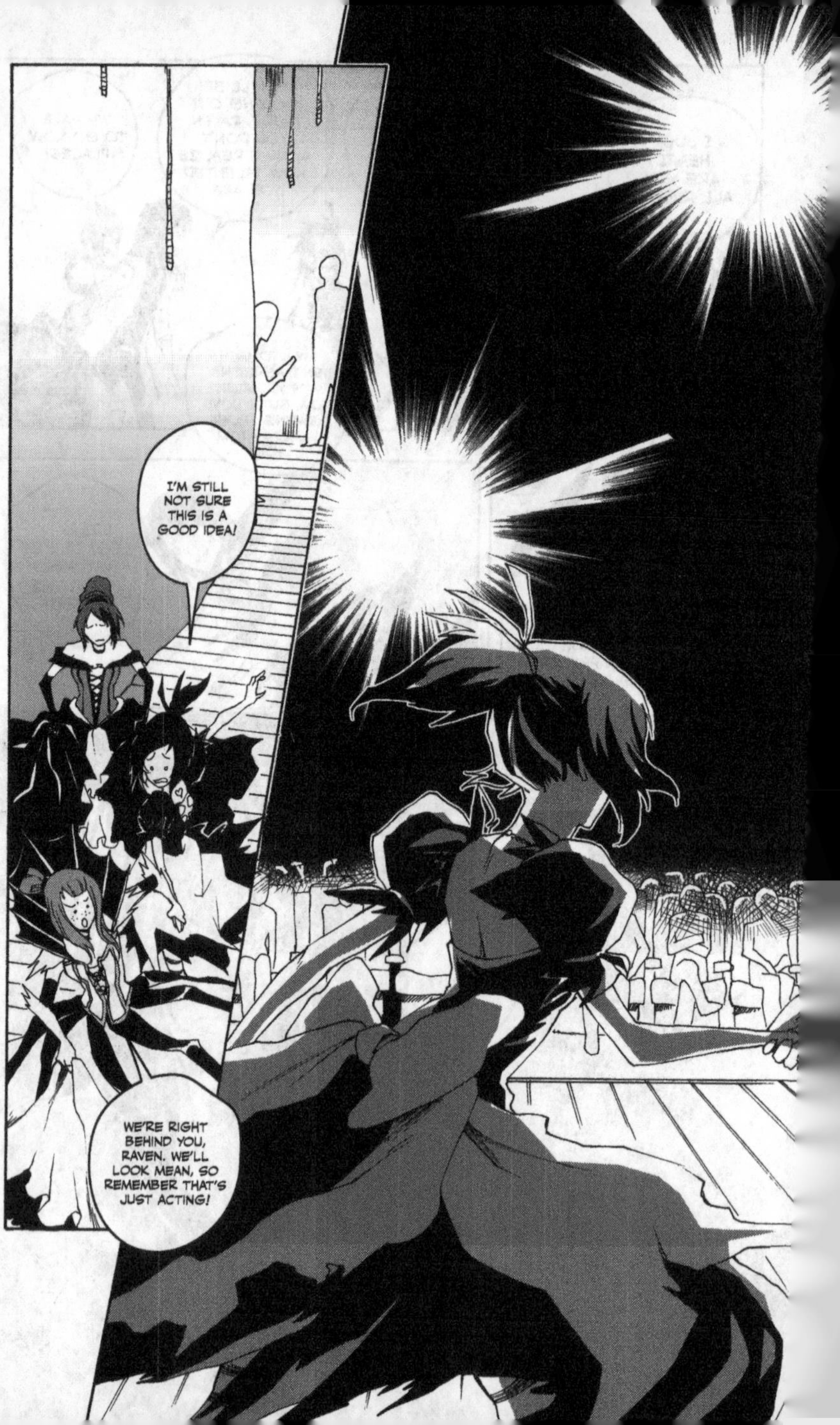
I'M STILL NOT SURE THIS IS A GOOD IDEA!
WE'RE RIGHT BEHIND YOU, RAVEN. WE'LL LOOK MEAN, SO REMEMBER THAT'S JUST ACTING!

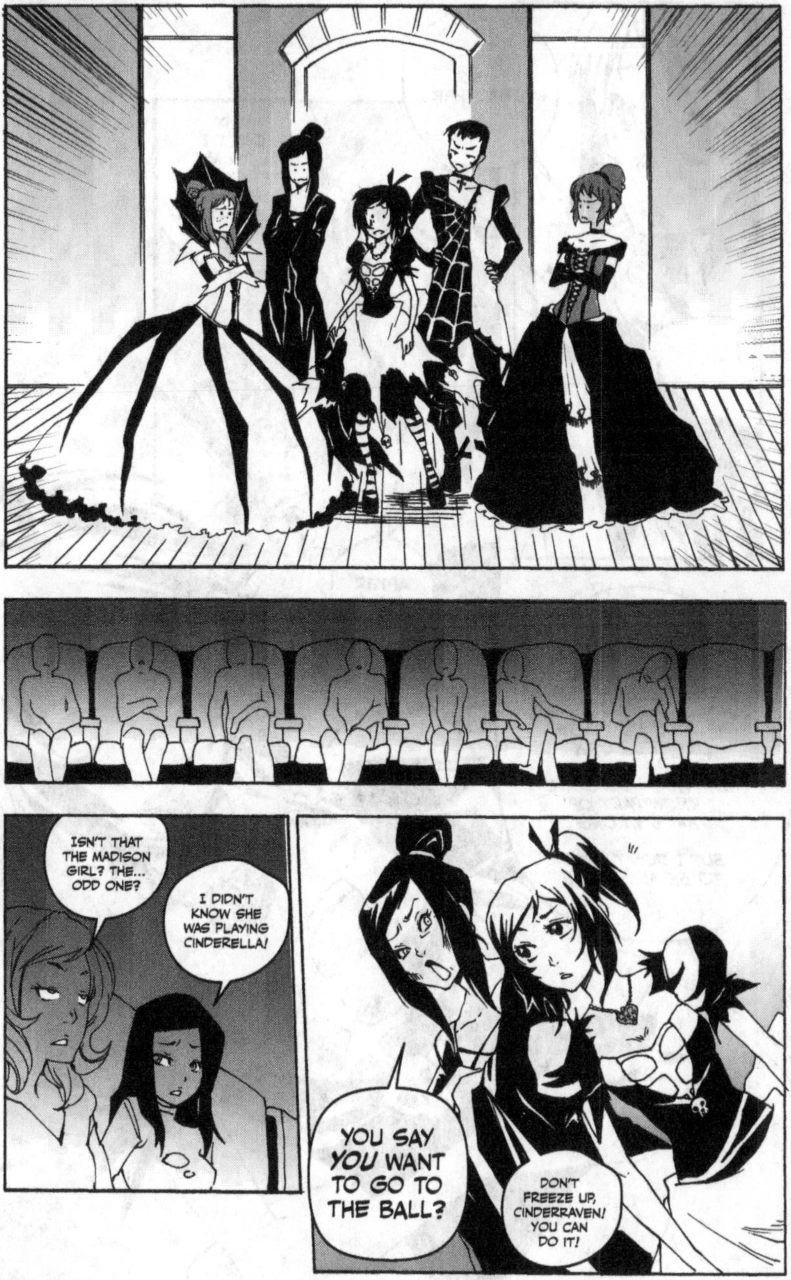
ISN'T THAT THE MADISON GIRL? THE... ODD ONE?
I DIDN'T KNOW SHE WAS PLAYING CINDERELLA!
YOU SAY *YOU* WANT TO GO TO THE BALL?
DON'T FREEZE UP, CINDERRAVEN! YOU CAN DO IT!

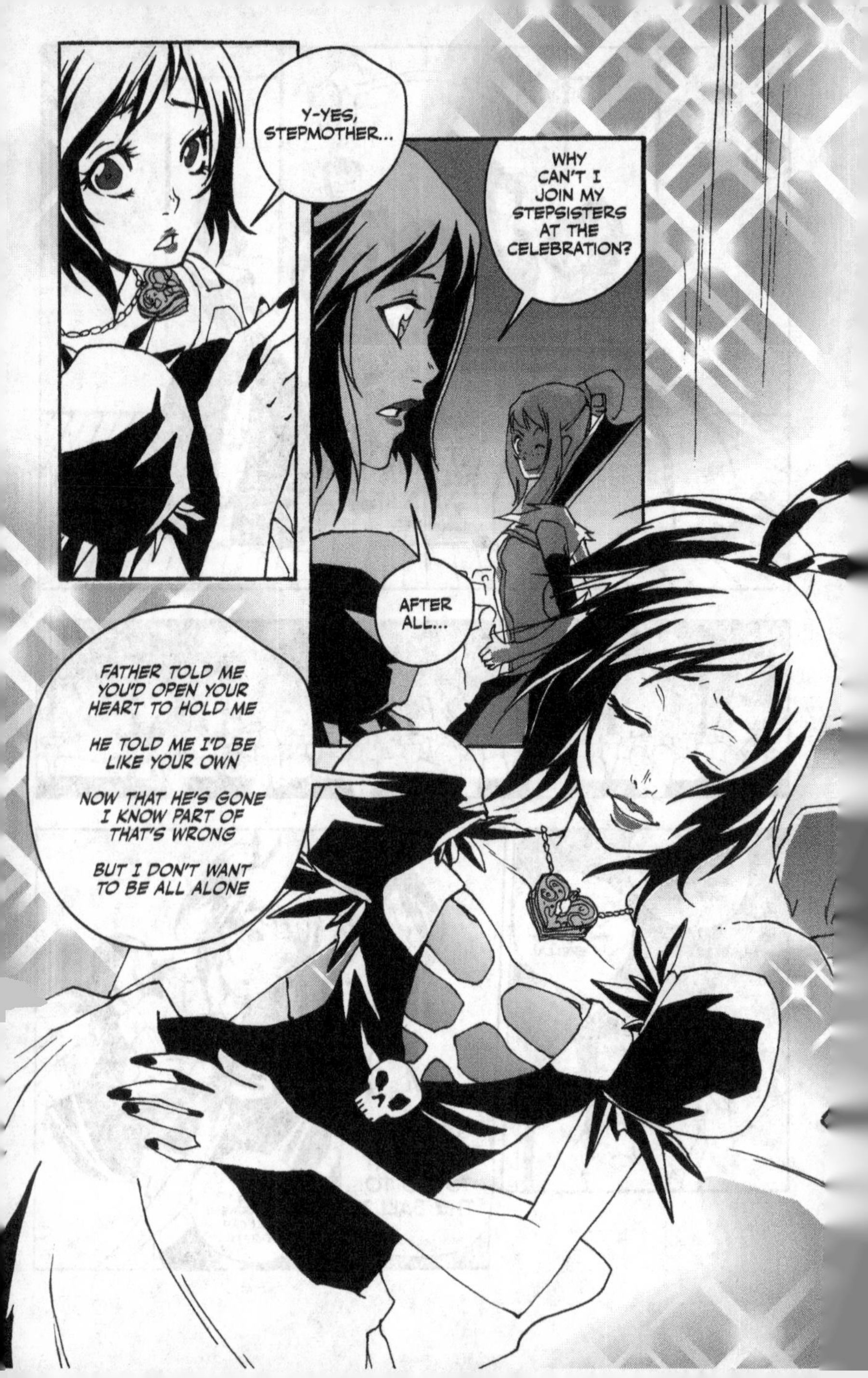
Y-YES, STEPMOTHER...
WHY CAN'T I JOIN MY STEPSISTERS AT THE CELEBRATION?
AFTER ALL...
FATHER TOLD ME YOU'D OPEN YOUR HEART TO HOLD ME
HE TOLD ME I'D BE LIKE YOUR OWN
NOW THAT HE'S GONE I KNOW PART OF THAT'S WRONG
BUT I DON'T WANT TO BE ALL ALONE

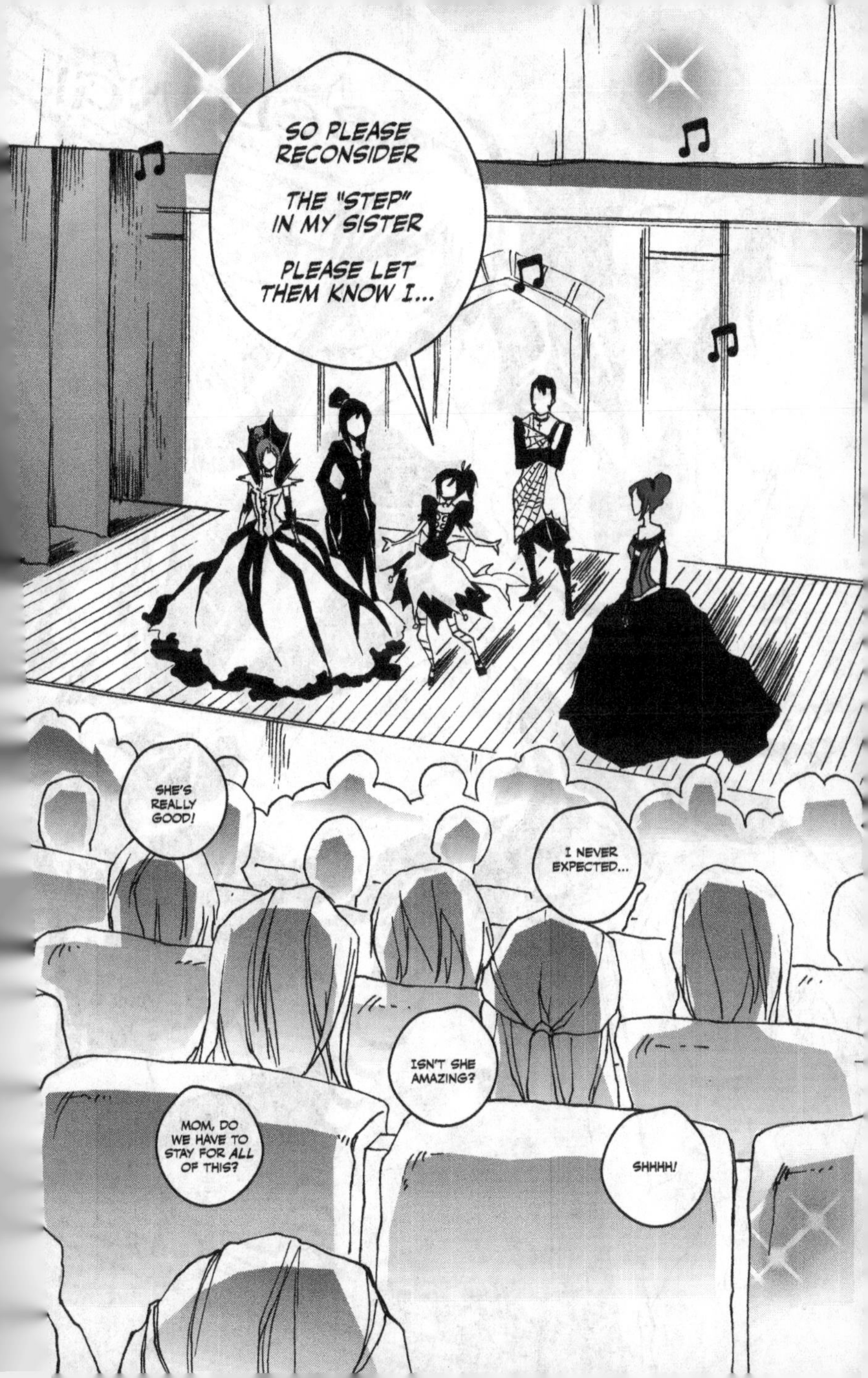
SO PLEASE RECONSIDER
THE "STEP" IN MY SISTER
PLEASE LET THEM KNOW I...
SHE'S REALLY GOOD!
I NEVER EXPECTED...
ISN'T SHE AMAZING?
MOM, DO WE HAVE TO STAY FOR ALL OF THIS?
SHHHH!

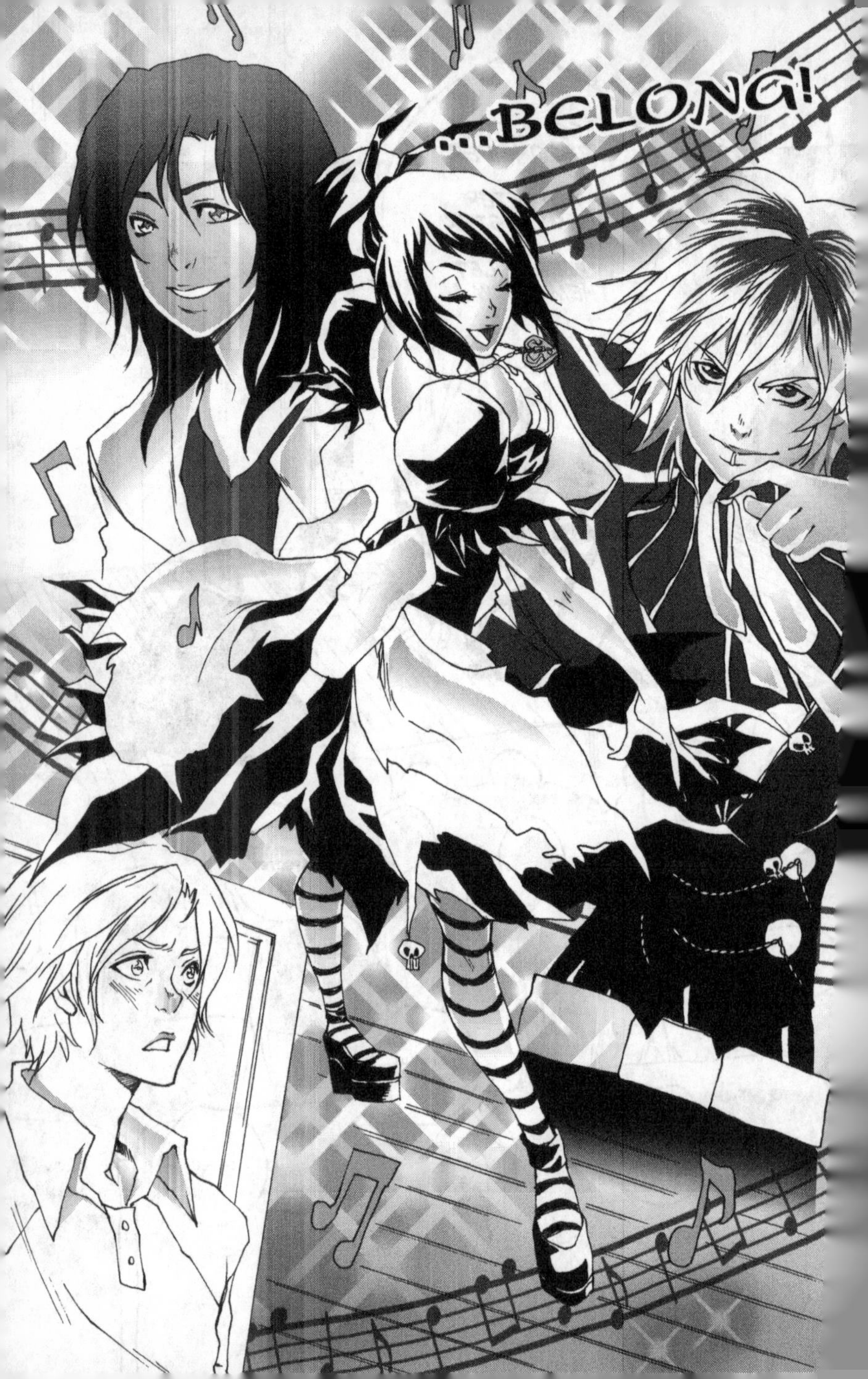
...BELONG!

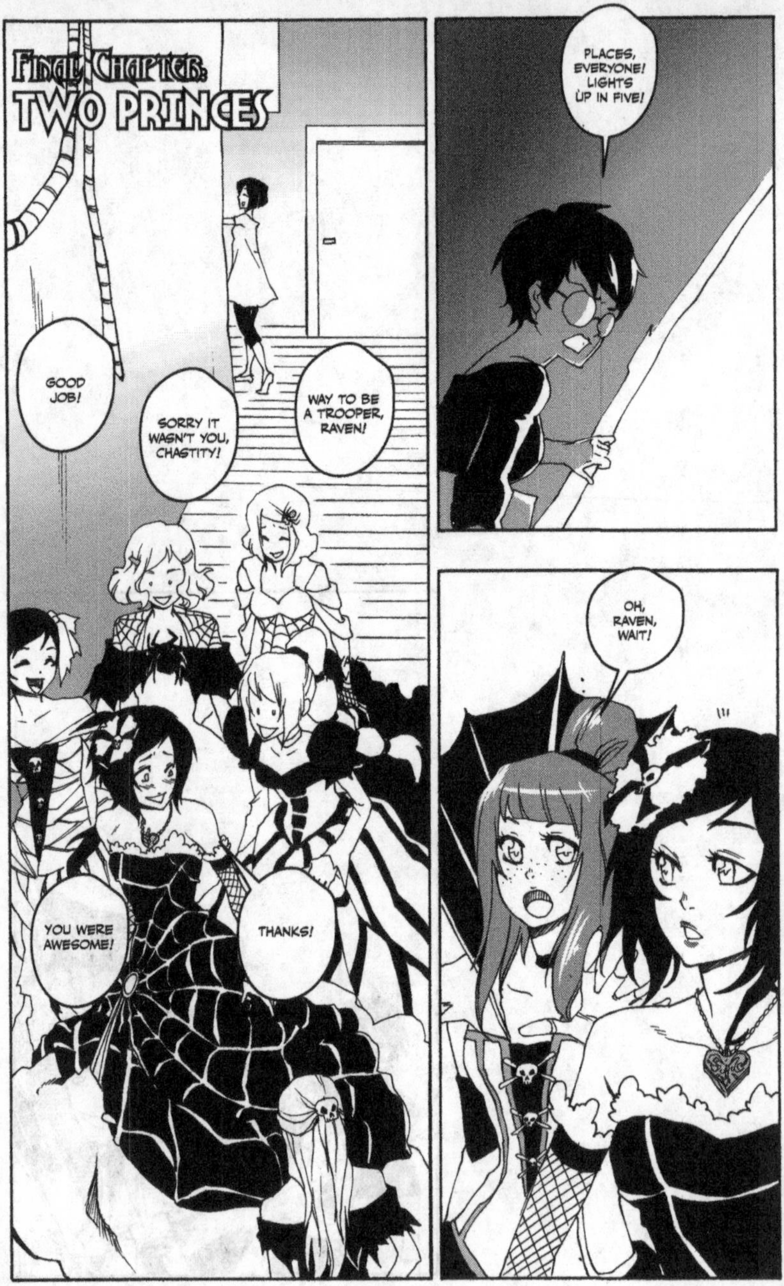
Final Chapter:
TWO PRINCES
GOOD JOB!
SORRY IT WASN'T YOU, CHASTITY!
WAY TO BE A TROOPER, RAVEN!
YOU WERE AWESOME!
THANKS!
PLACES, EVERYONE! LIGHTS UP IN FIVE!
OH, RAVEN, WAIT!

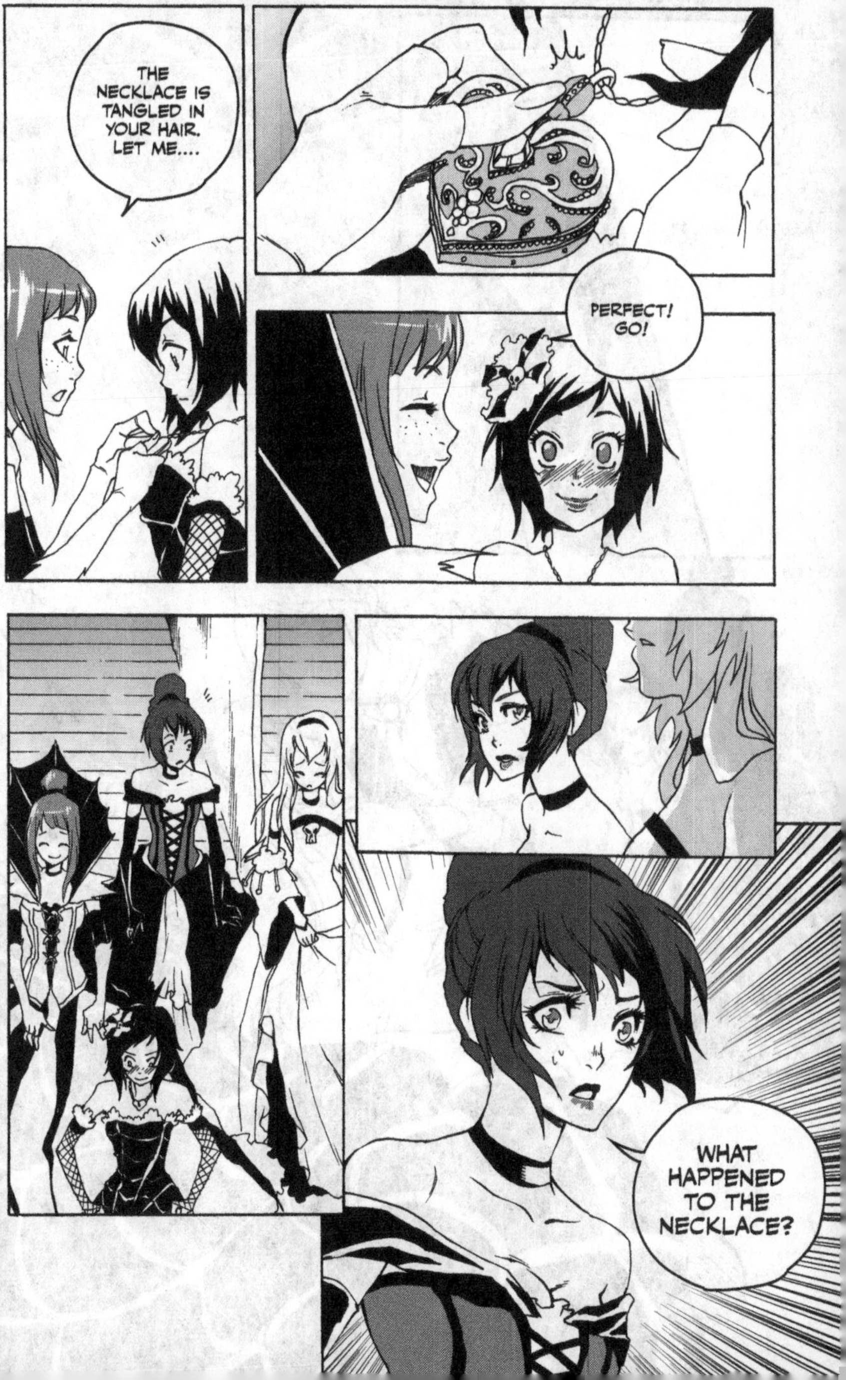
THE NECKLACE IS TANGLED IN YOUR HAIR. LET ME....
PERFECT! GO!
WHAT HAPPENED TO THE NECKLACE?

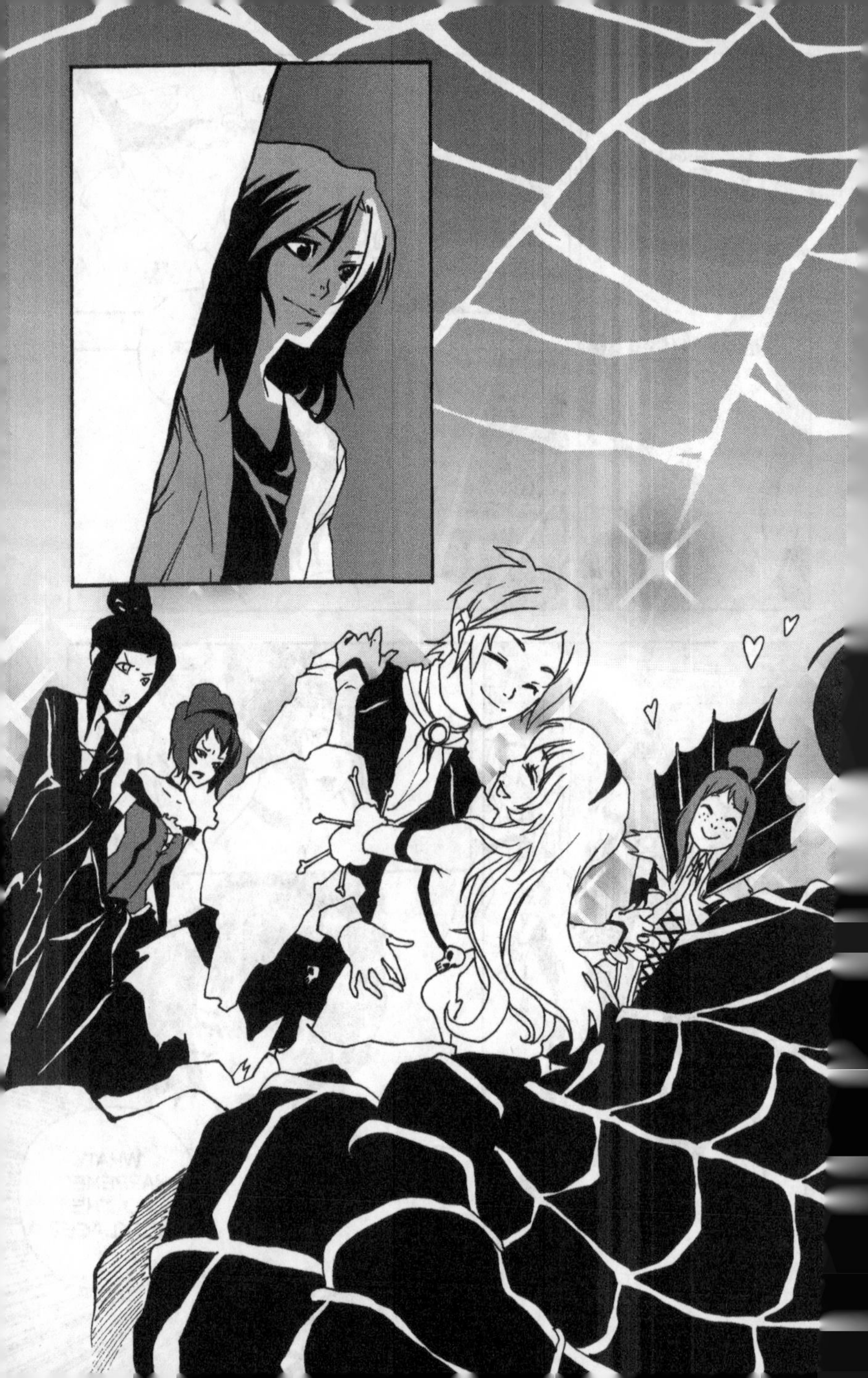

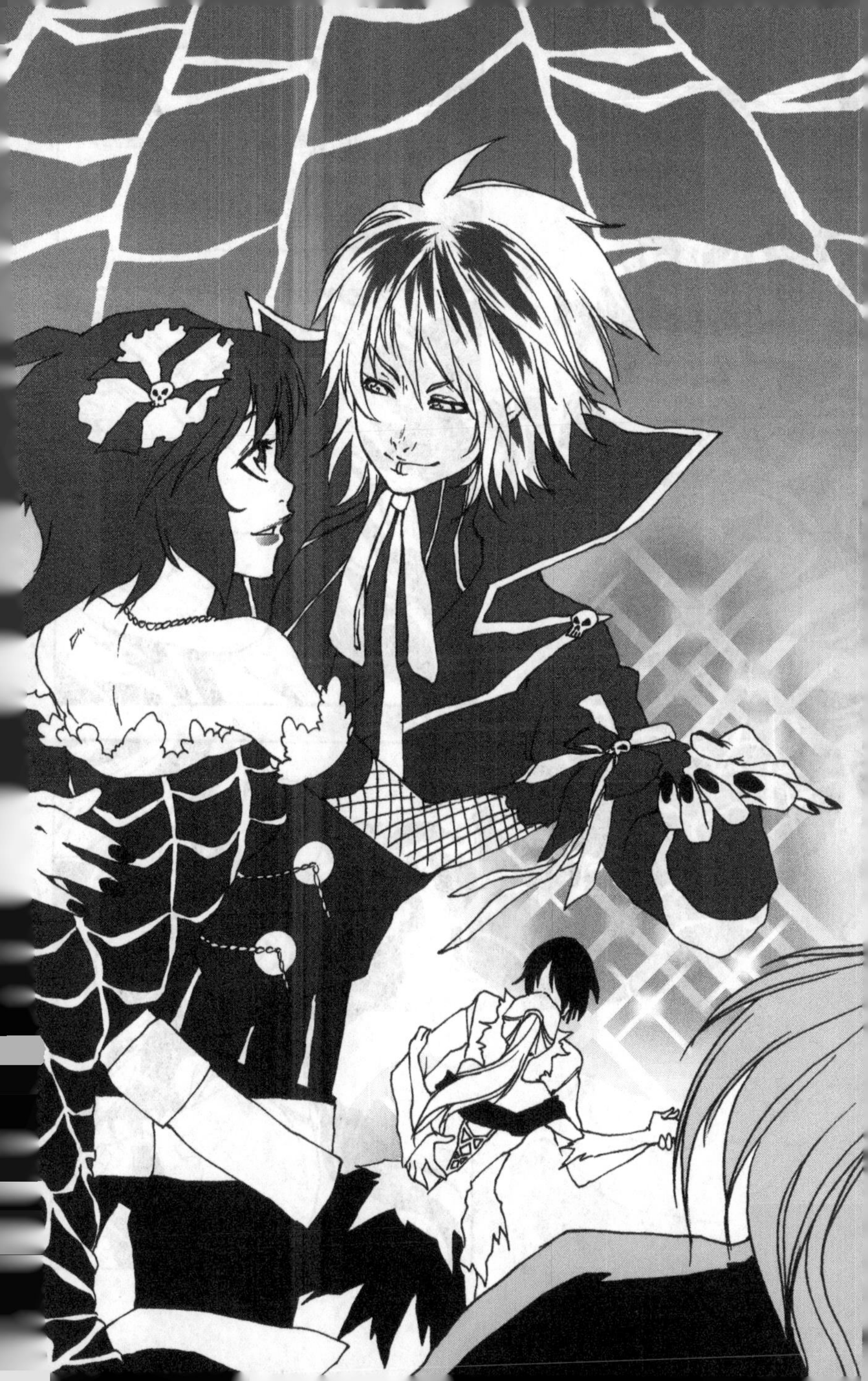

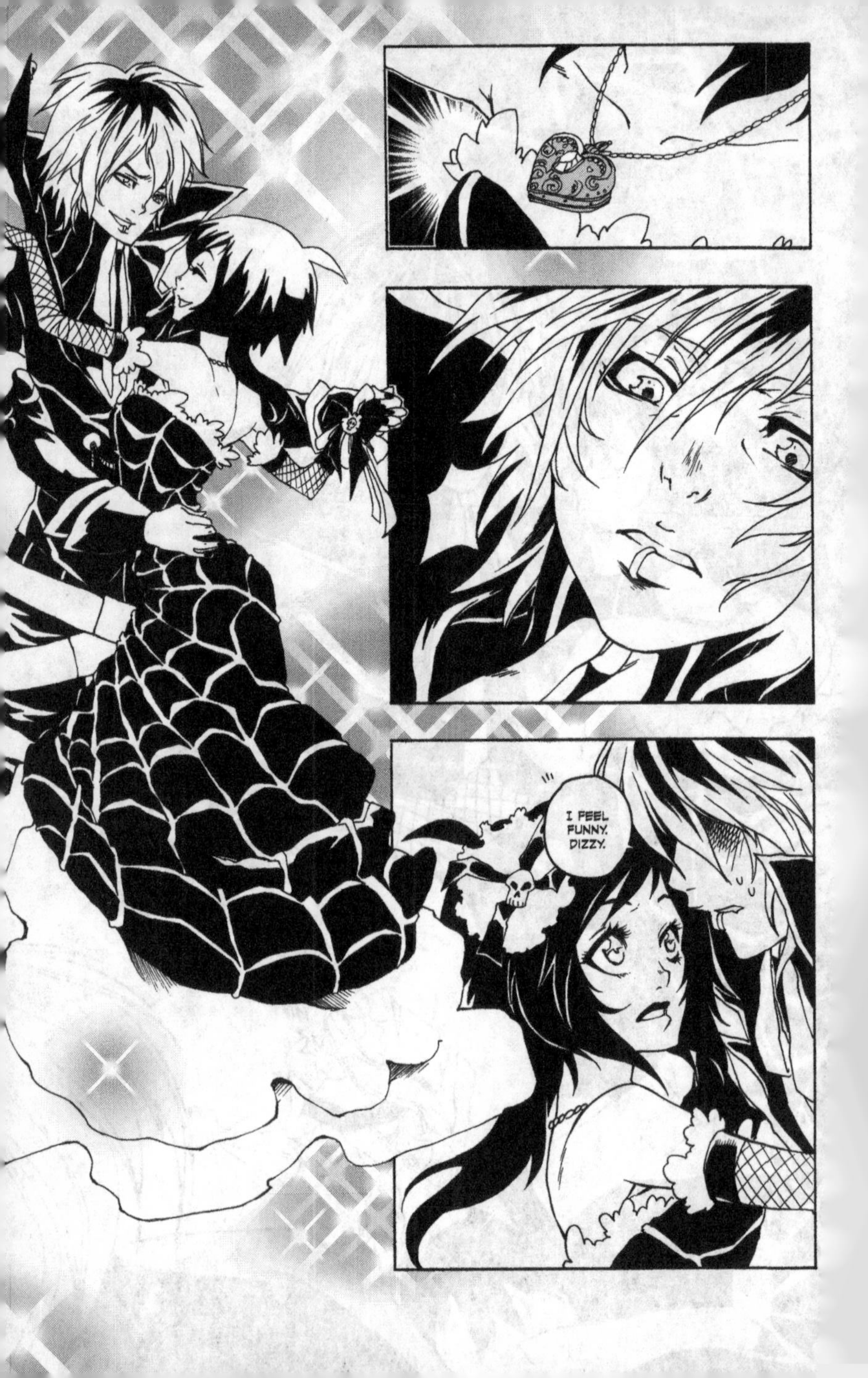
I FEEL FUNNY. DIZZY.

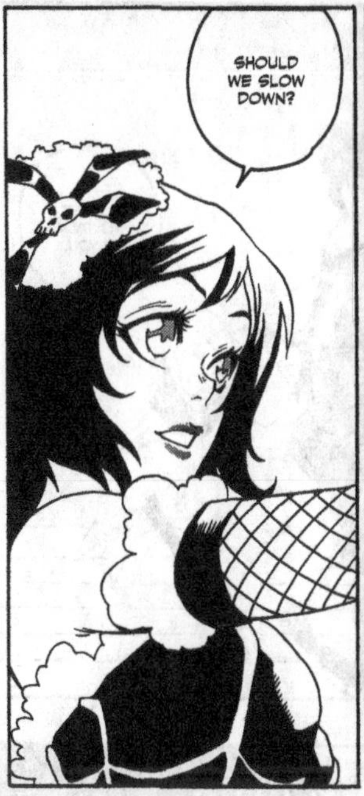
SHOULD WE SLOW DOWN?
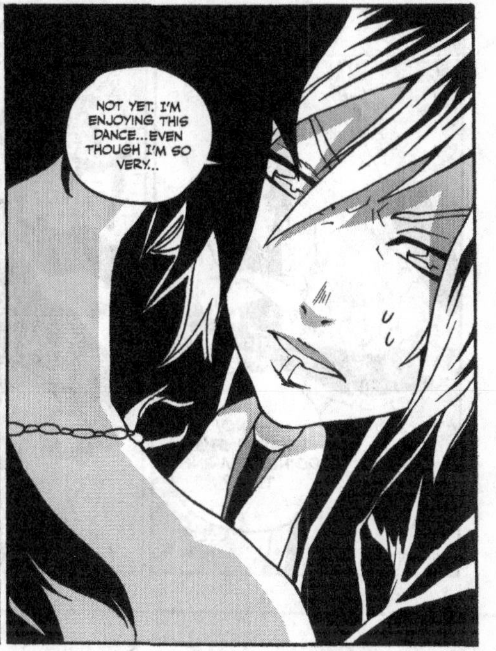
NOT YET. I'M ENJOYING THIS DANCE...EVEN THOUGH I'M SO VERY...
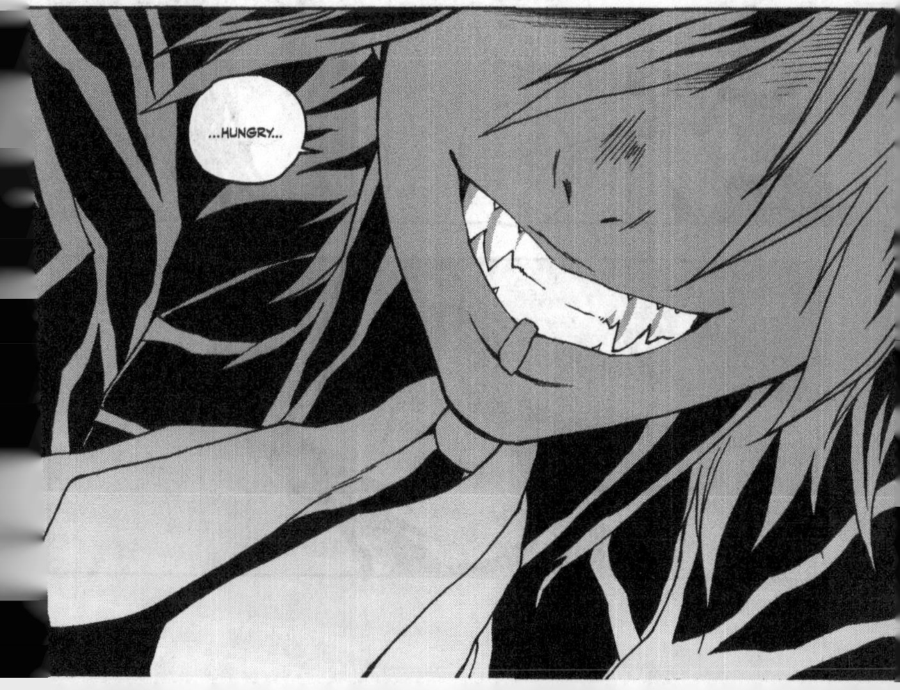
...HUNGRY...

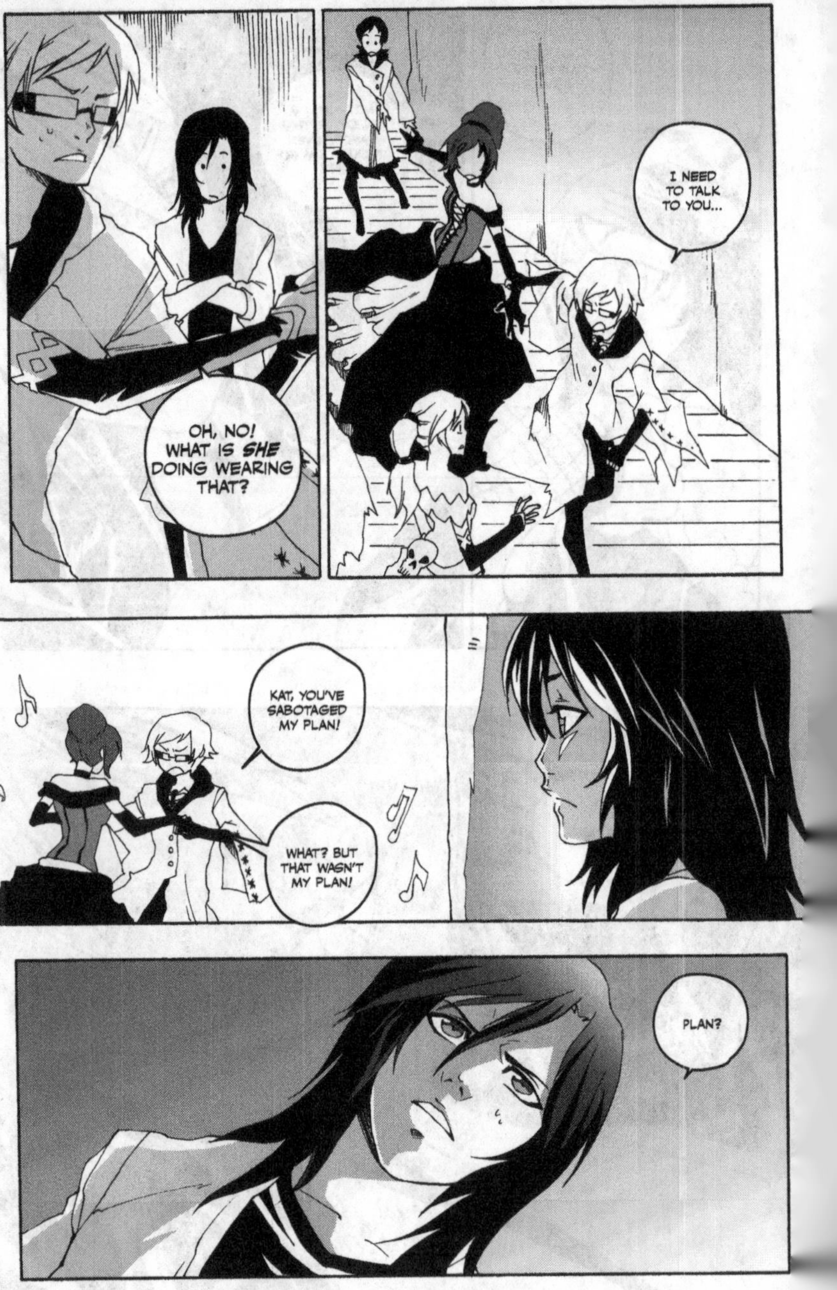
OH, NO! WHAT IS *SHE* DOING WEARING THAT?
I NEED TO TALK TO YOU...
KAT, YOU'VE SABOTAGED MY PLAN!
WHAT? BUT THAT WASN'T MY PLAN!
PLAN?

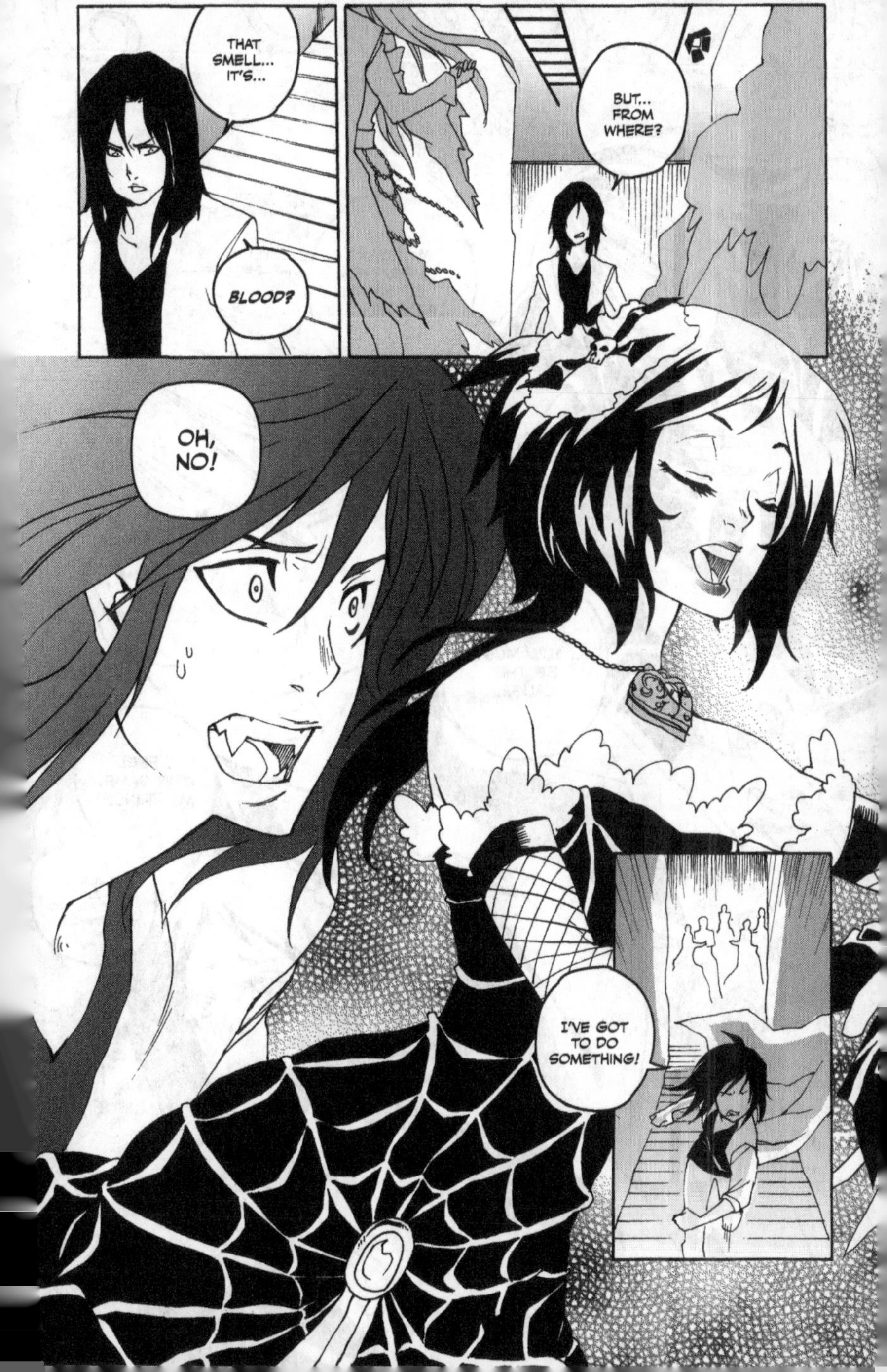
THAT SMELL... IT'S...
BLOOD?
BUT... FROM WHERE?
OH, NO!
I'VE GOT TO DO SOMETHING!

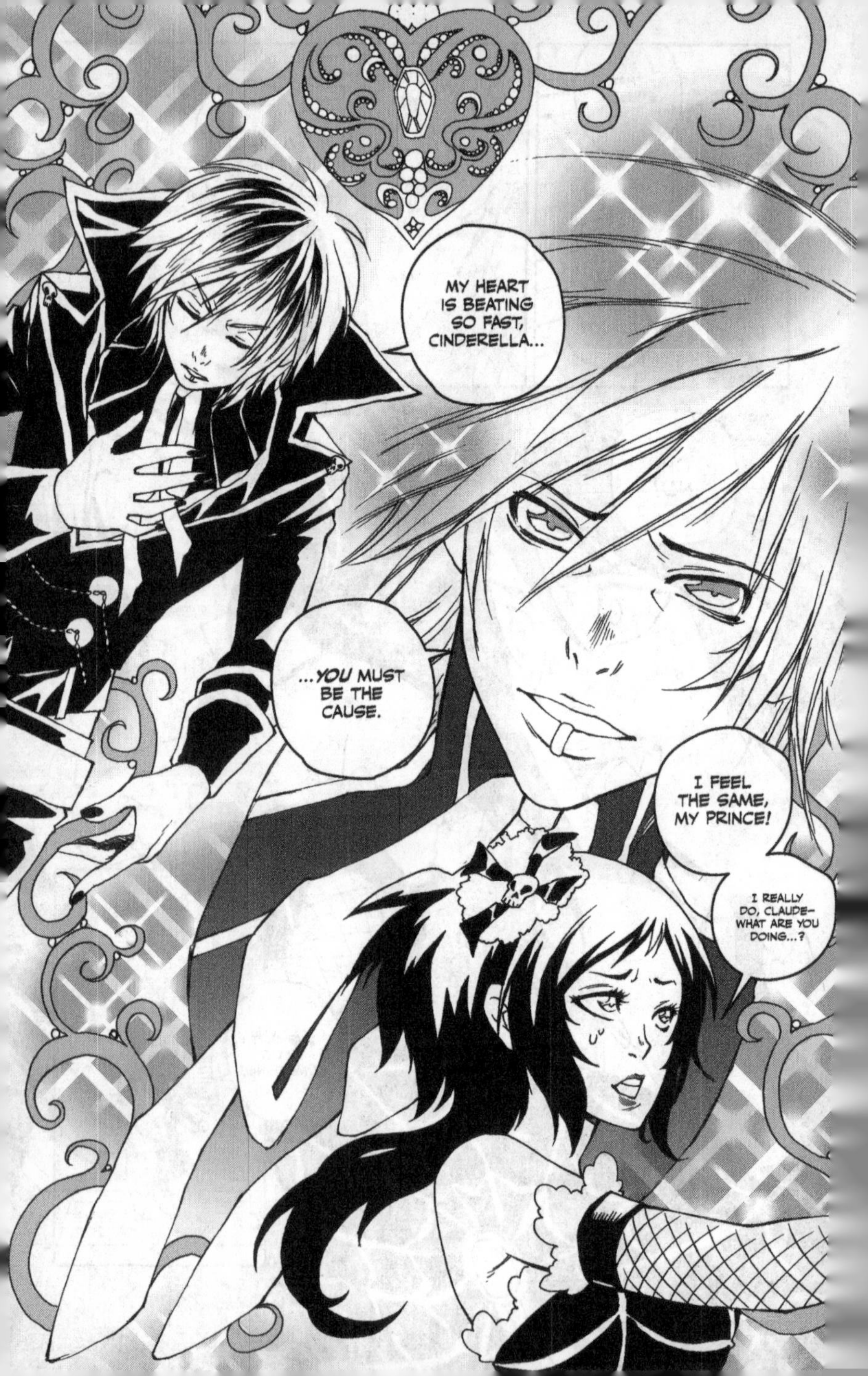
MY HEART IS BEATING SO FAST, CINDERELLA...
...YOU MUST BE THE CAUSE.
I FEEL THE SAME, MY PRINCE!
I REALLY DO, CLAUDE–WHAT ARE YOU DOING...?

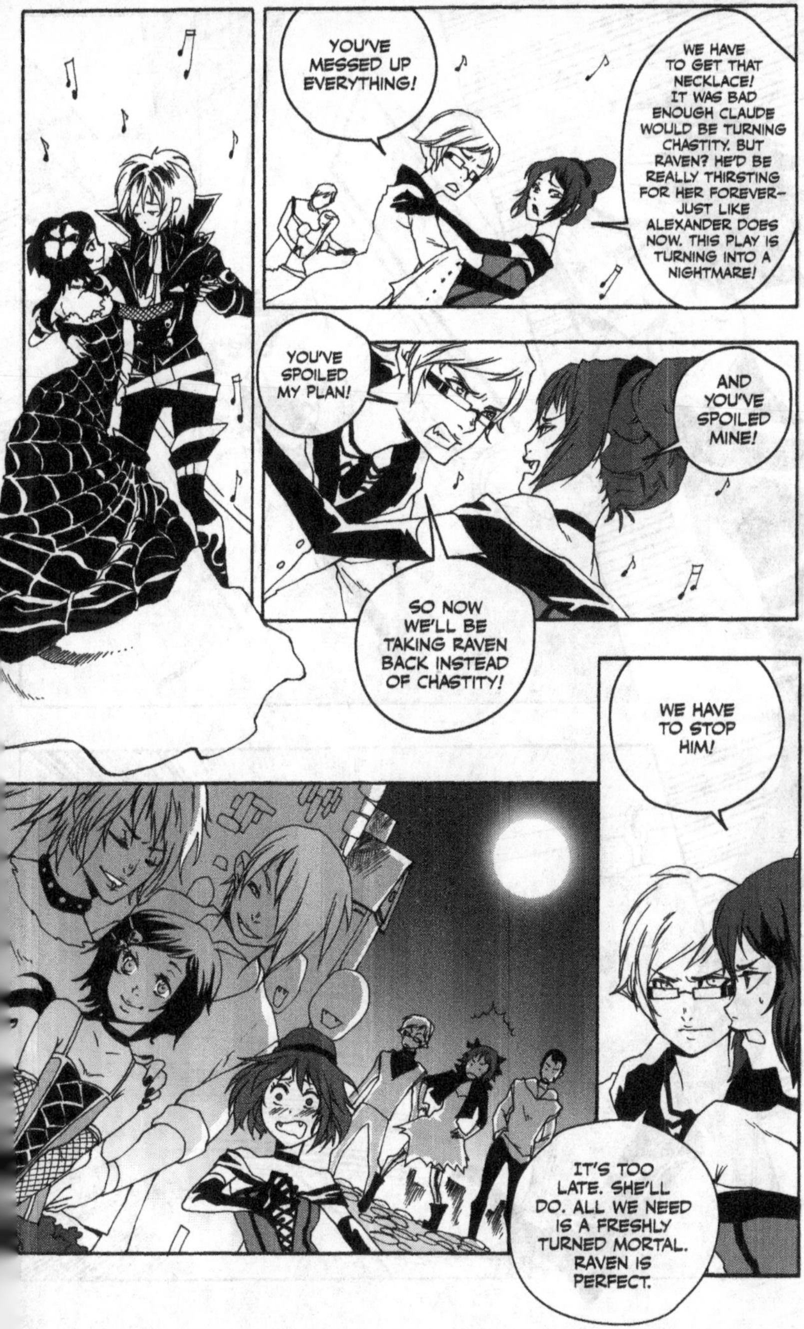
YOU'VE MESSED UP EVERYTHING!
WE HAVE TO GET THAT NECKLACE! IT WAS BAD ENOUGH CLAUDE WOULD BE TURNING CHASTITY. BUT RAVEN? HE'D BE REALLY THIRSTING FOR HER FOREVER-JUST LIKE ALEXANDER DOES NOW. THIS PLAY IS TURNING INTO A NIGHTMARE!
YOU'VE SPOILED MY PLAN!
AND YOU'VE SPOILED MINE!
SO NOW WE'LL BE TAKING RAVEN BACK INSTEAD OF CHASTITY!
WE HAVE TO STOP HIM!
IT'S TOO LATE. SHE'LL DO. ALL WE NEED IS A FRESHLY TURNED MORTAL. RAVEN IS PERFECT.

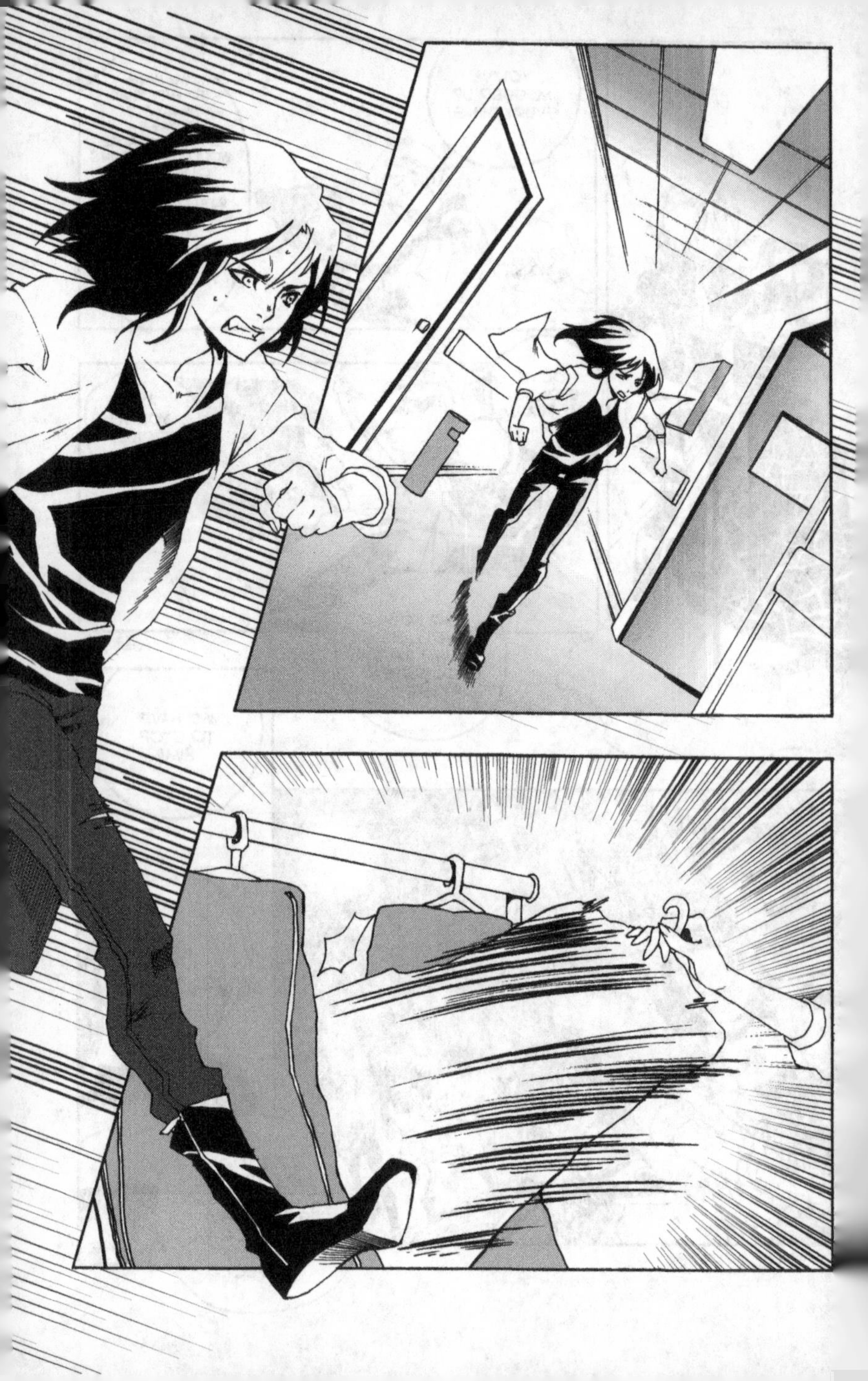

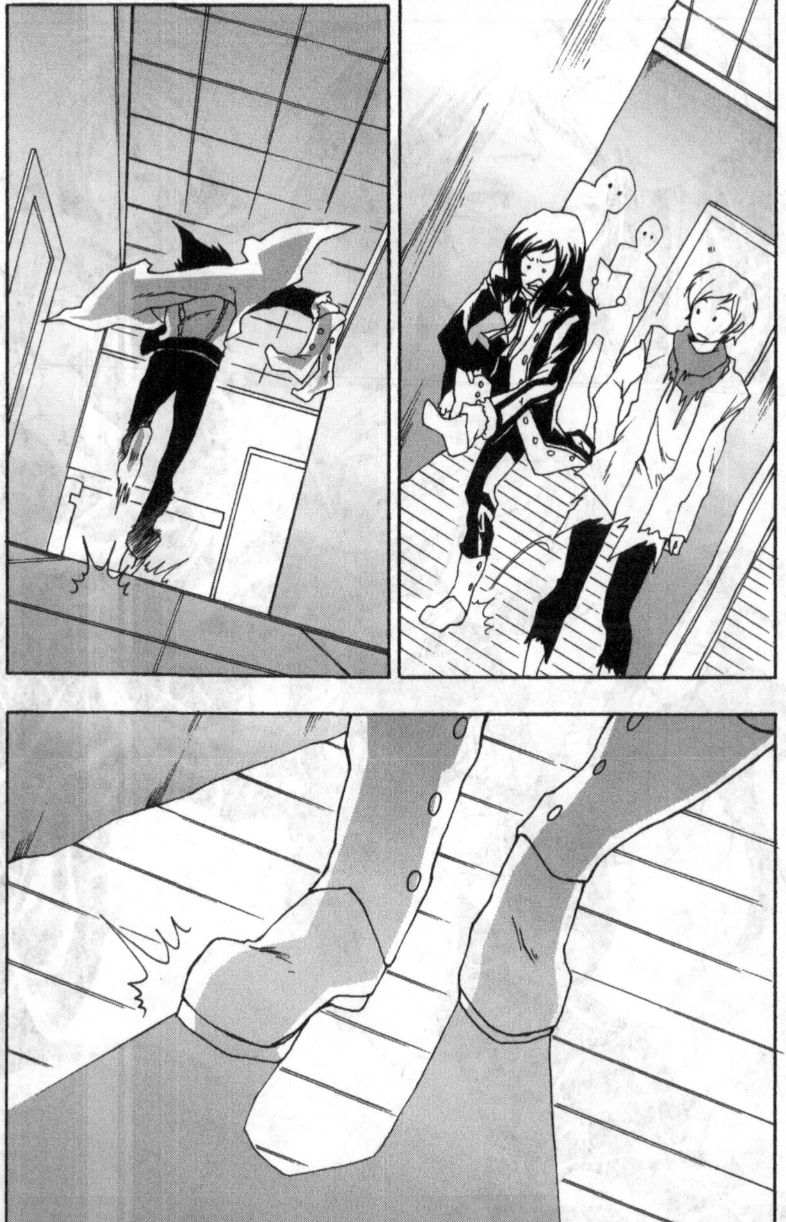

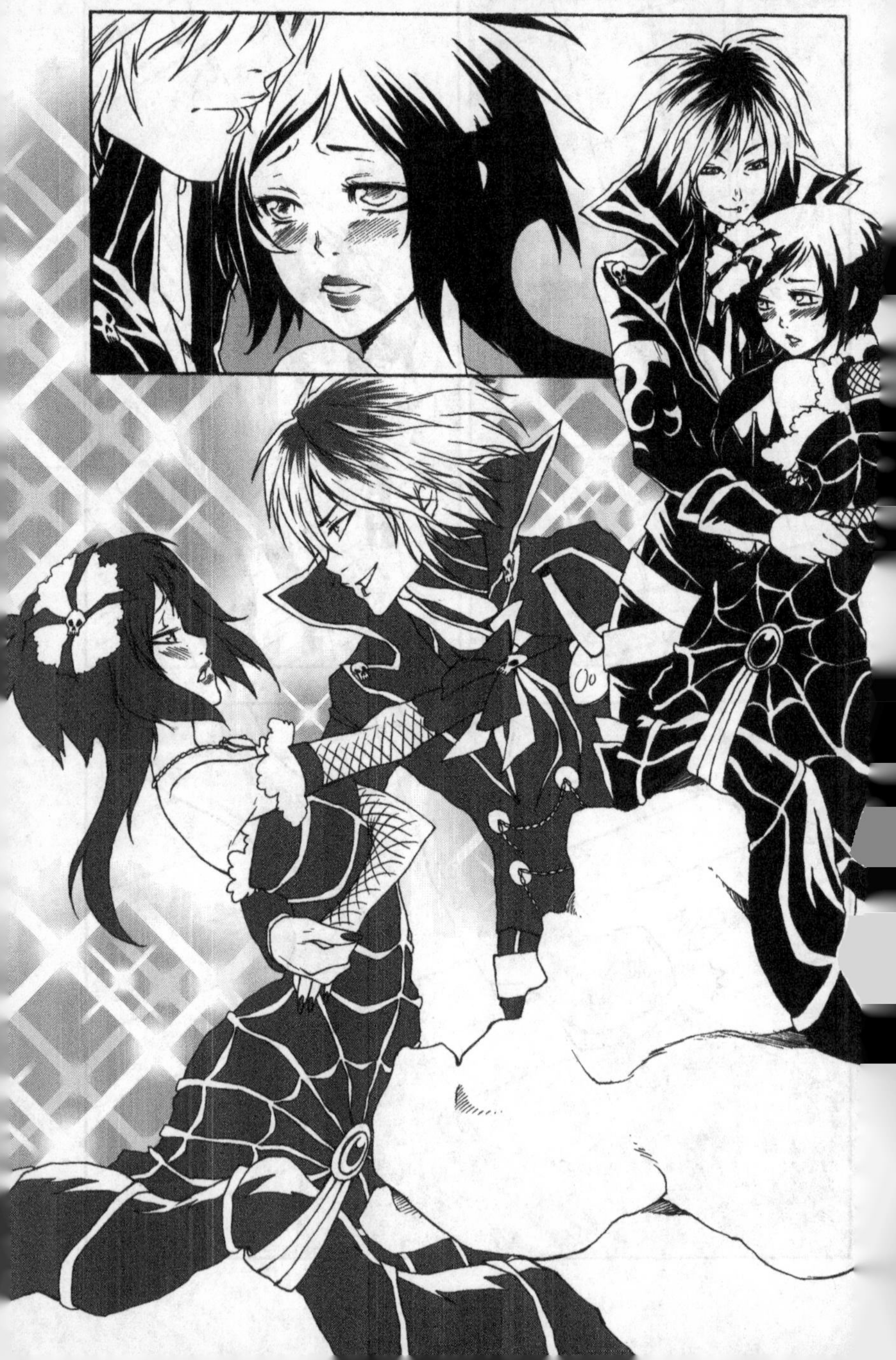

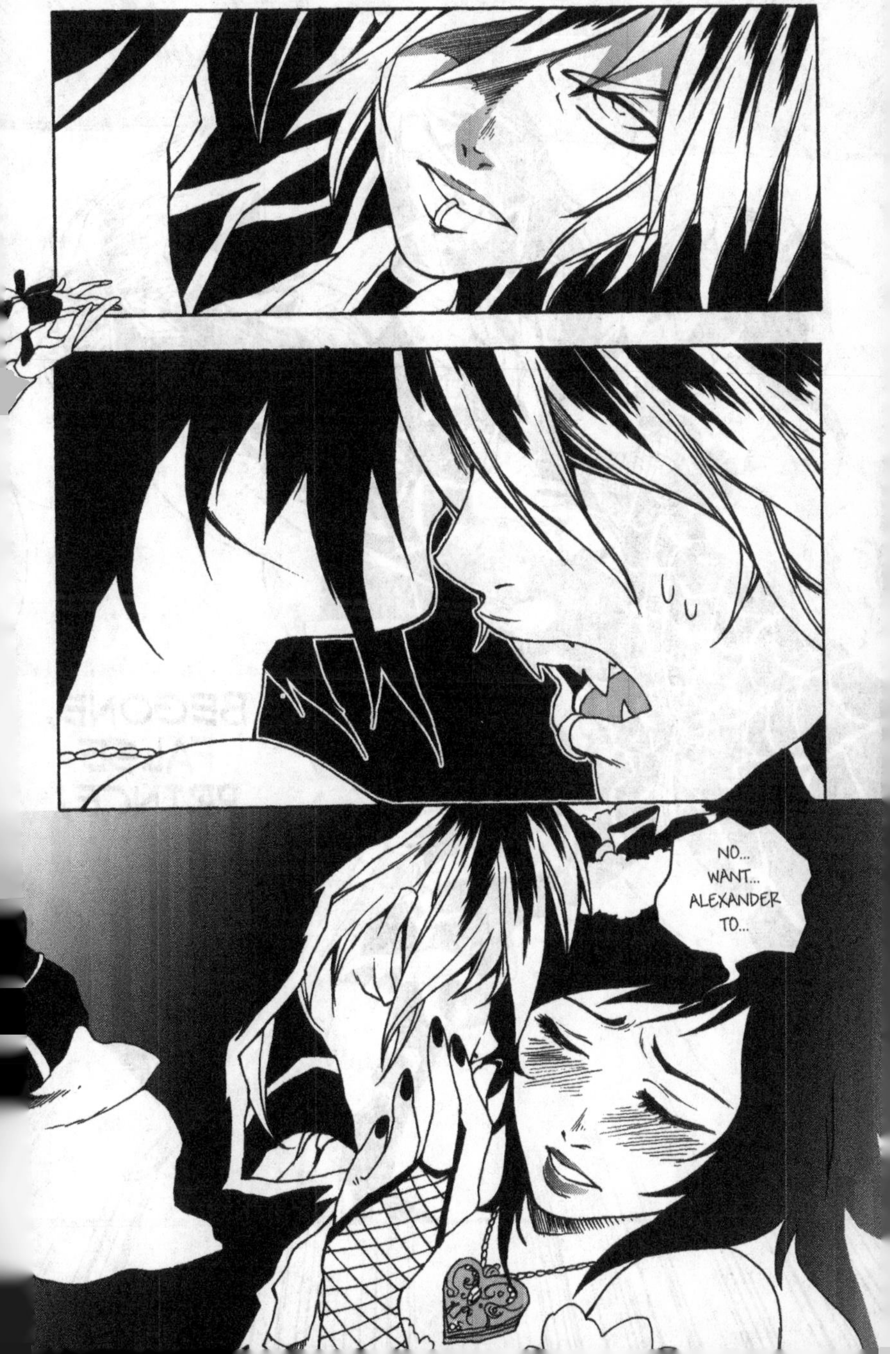
NO... WANT... ALEXANDER TO...

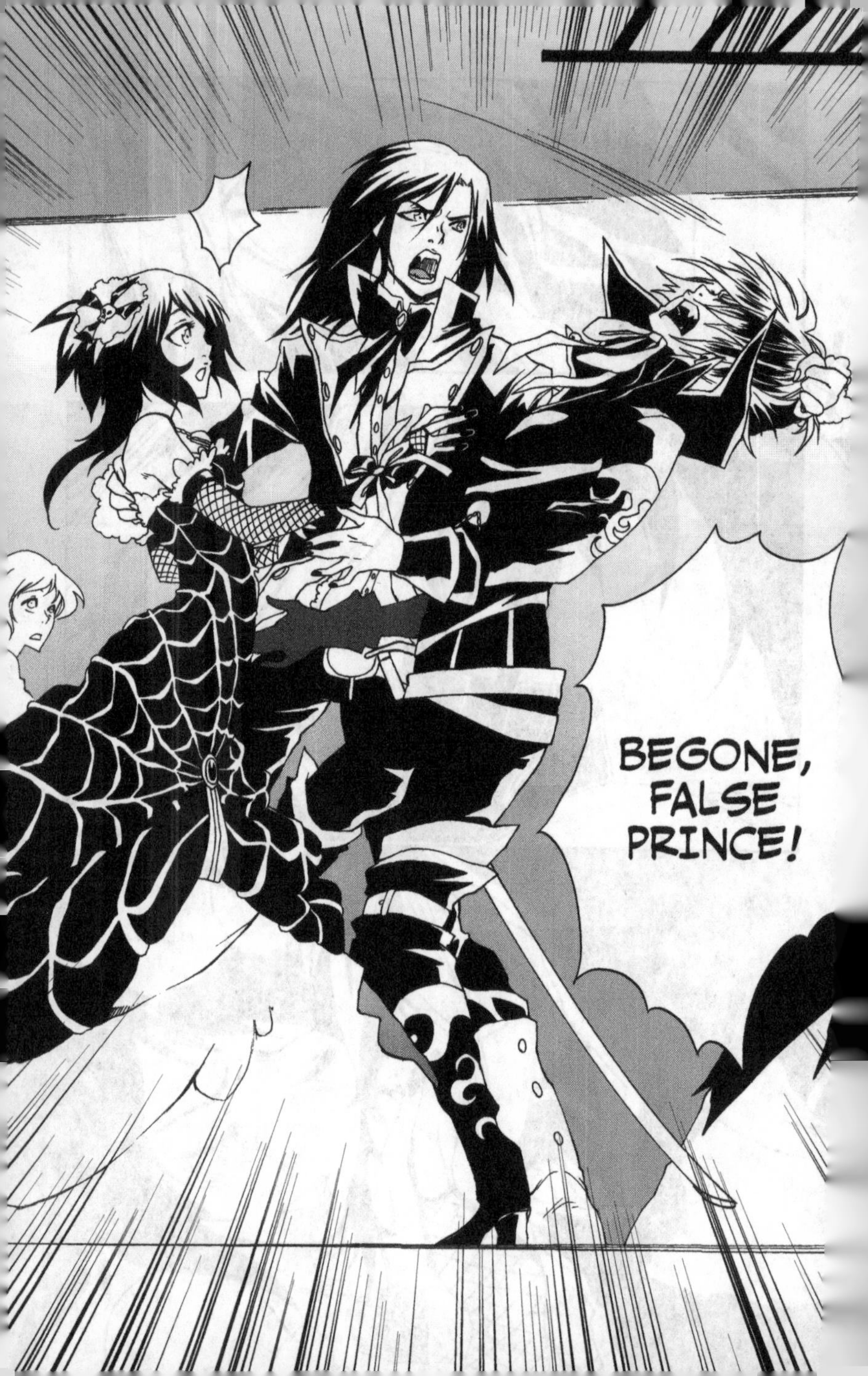
BEGONE, FALSE PRINCE!

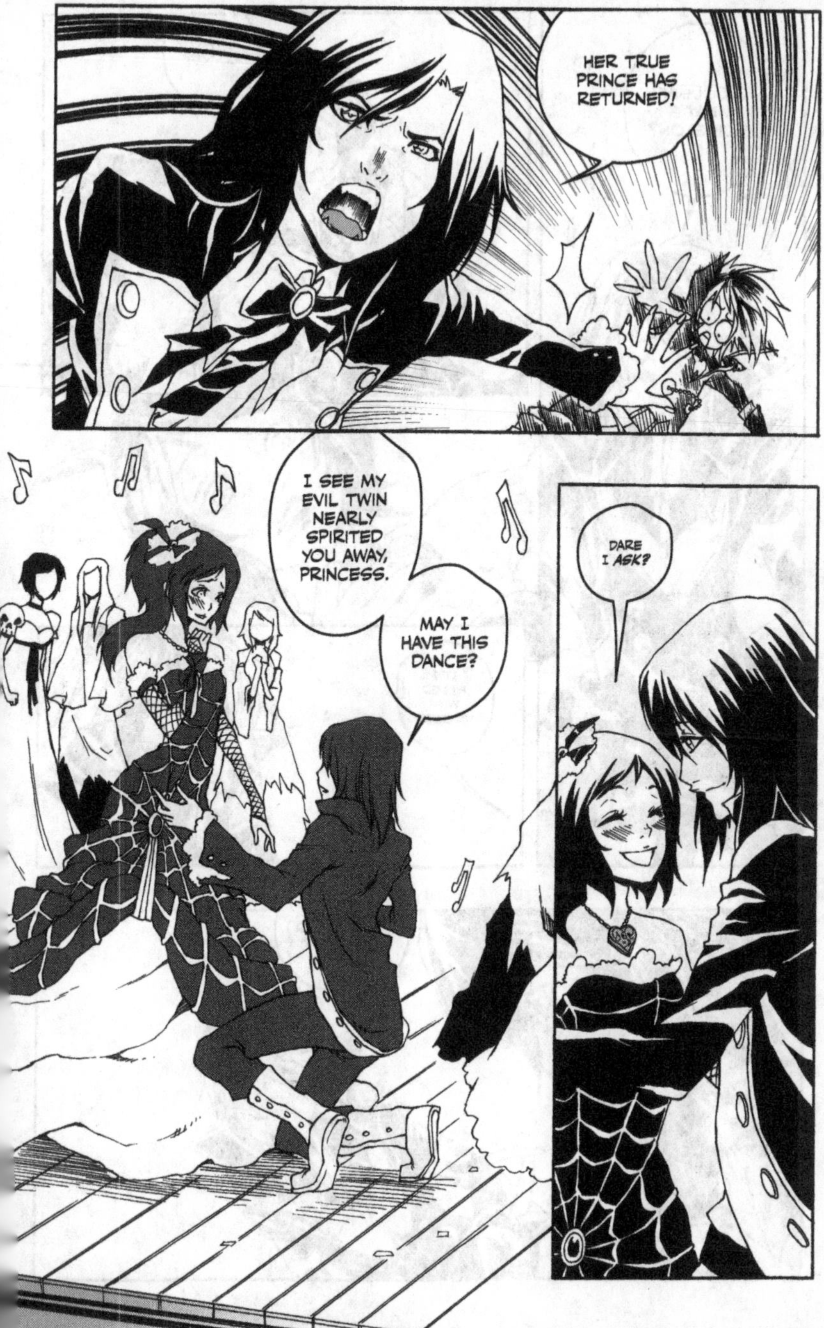
HER TRUE PRINCE HAS RETURNED!
I SEE MY EVIL TWIN NEARLY SPIRITED YOU AWAY, PRINCESS.
MAY I HAVE THIS DANCE?
DARE I *ASK?*

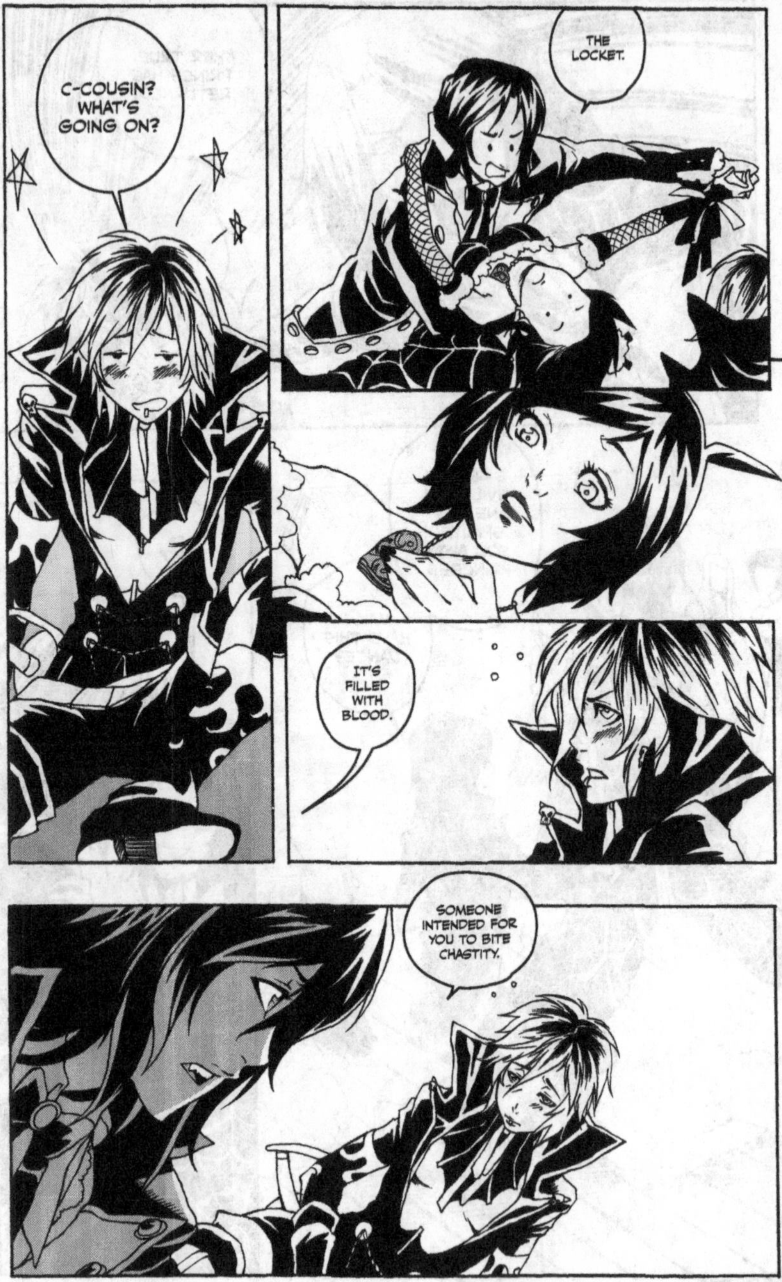
C-COUSIN? WHAT'S GOING ON?
THE LOCKET.
IT'S FILLED WITH BLOOD.
SOMEONE INTENDED FOR YOU TO BITE CHASTITY.

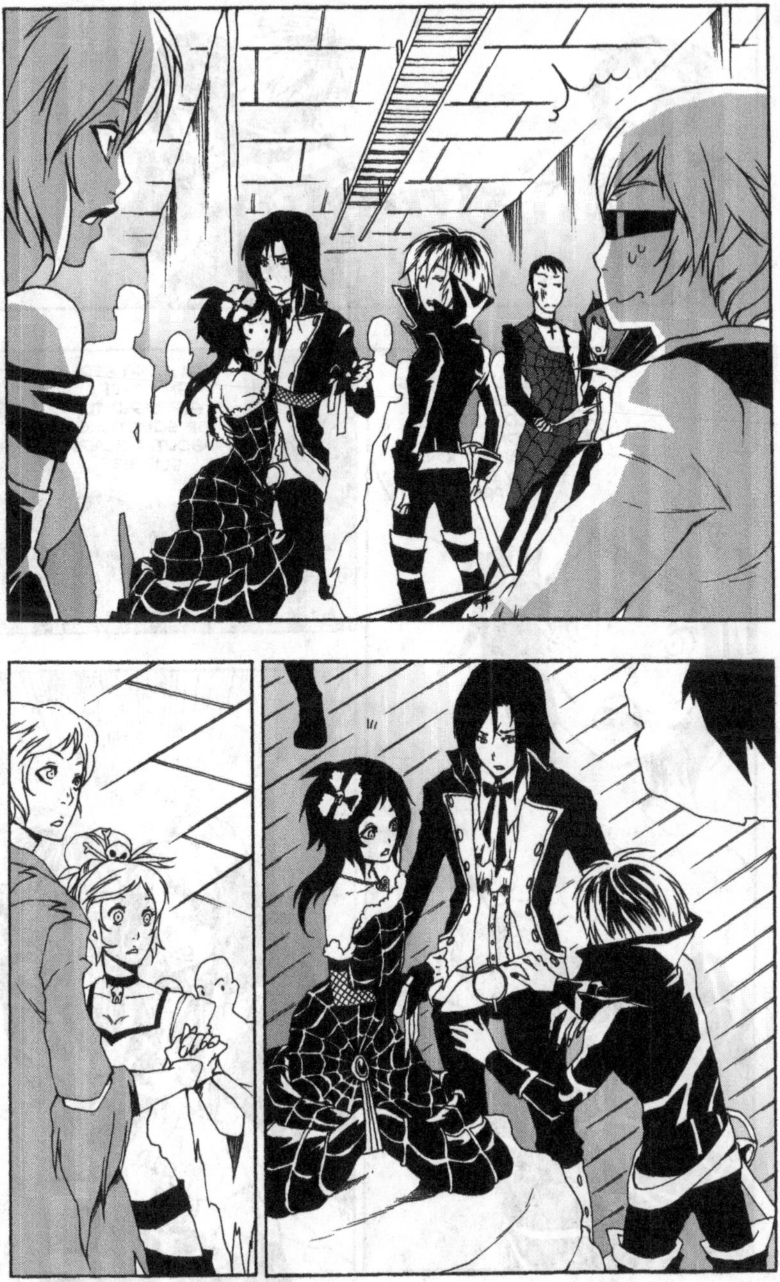

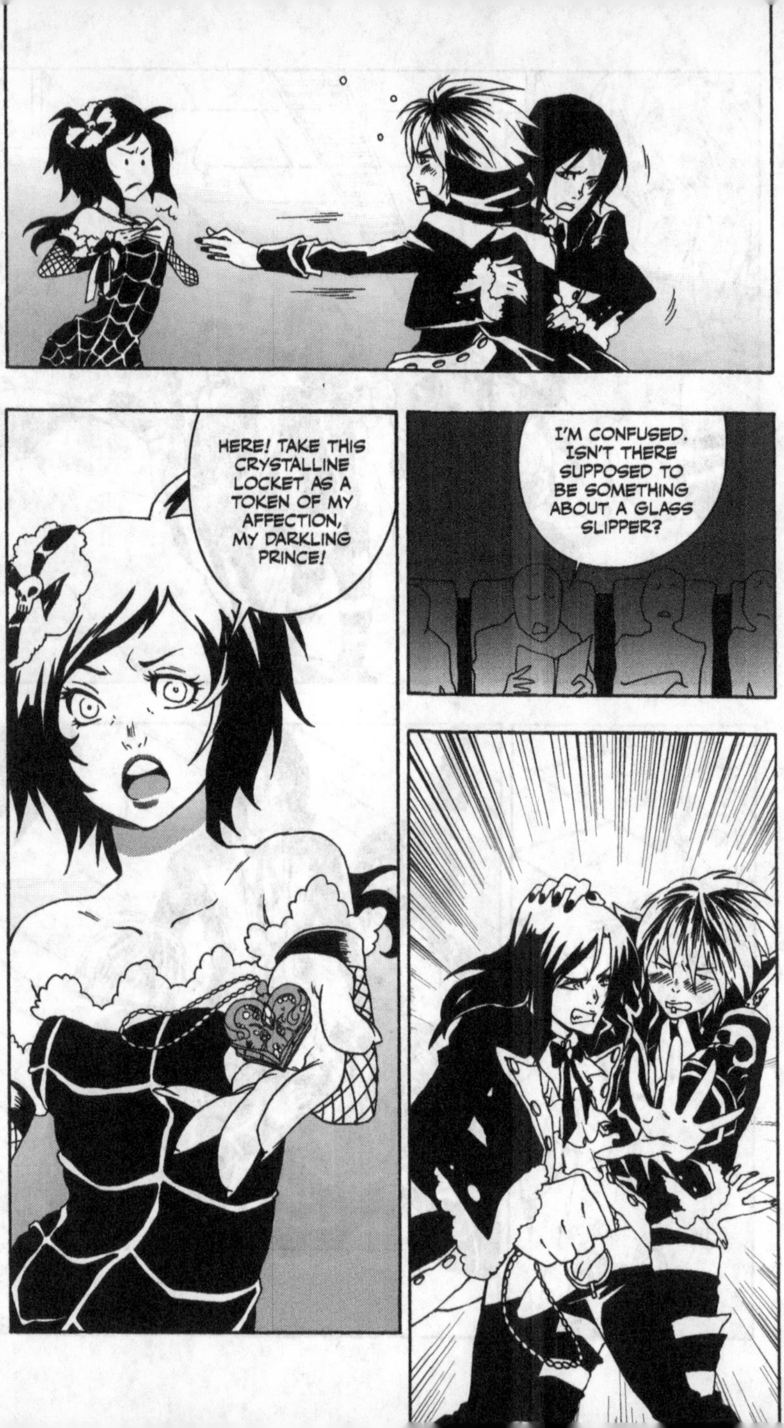
HERE! TAKE THIS CRYSTALLINE LOCKET AS A TOKEN OF MY AFFECTION, MY DARKLING PRINCE!
I'M CONFUSED. ISN'T THERE SUPPOSED TO BE SOMETHING ABOUT A GLASS SLIPPER?

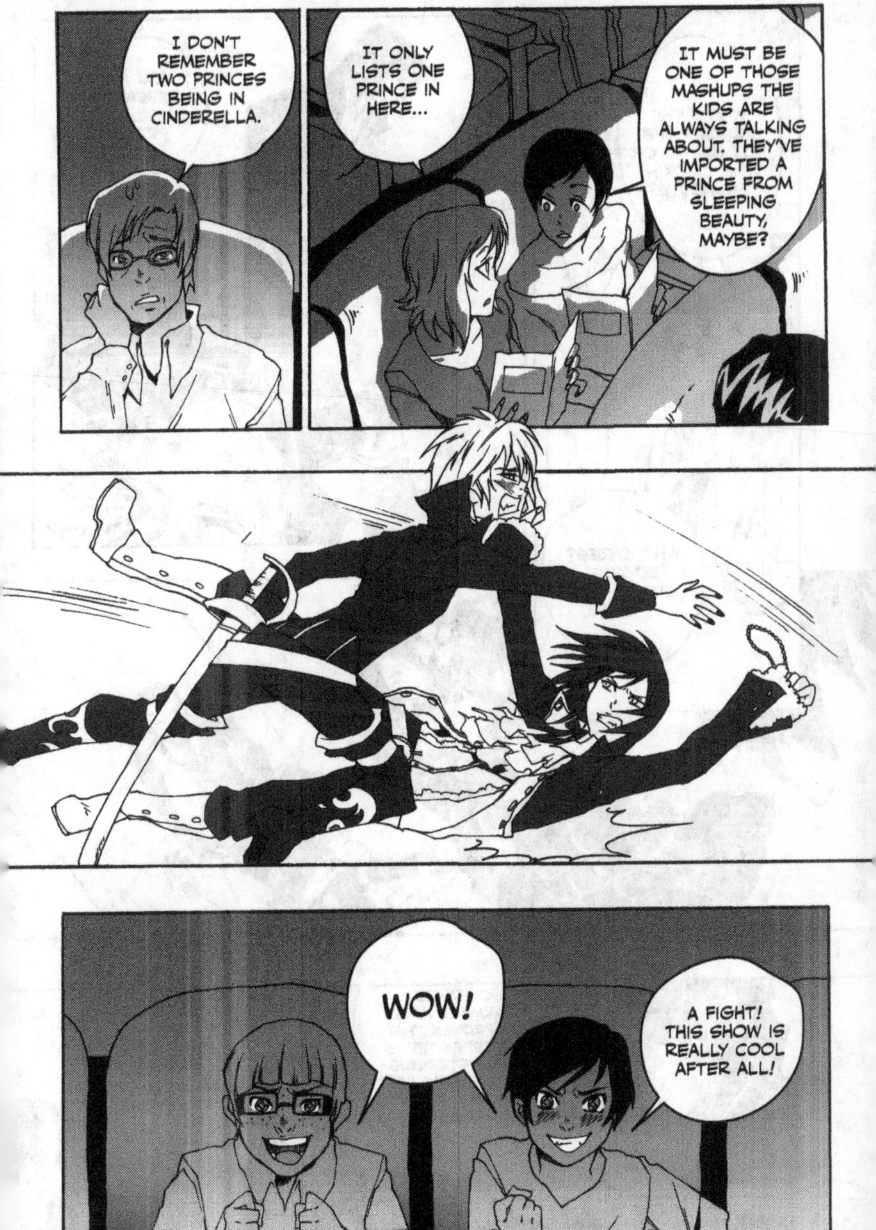
I DON'T REMEMBER TWO PRINCES BEING IN CINDERELLA.
IT ONLY LISTS ONE PRINCE IN HERE...
IT MUST BE ONE OF THOSE MASHUPS THE KIDS ARE ALWAYS TALKING ABOUT. THEY'VE IMPORTED A PRINCE FROM SLEEPING BEAUTY, MAYBE?
WOW!
A FIGHT! THIS SHOW IS REALLY COOL AFTER ALL!

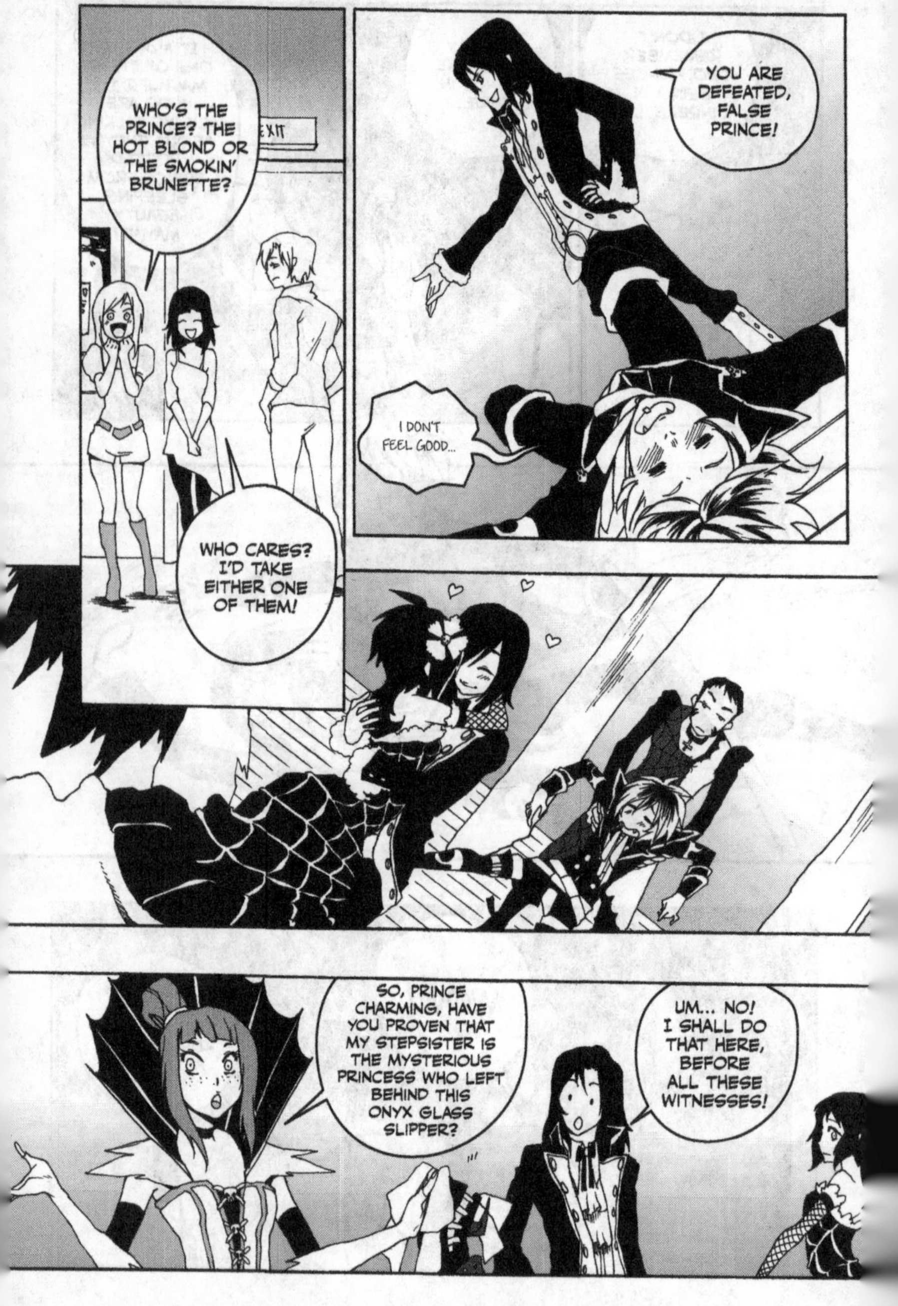
WHO'S THE PRINCE? THE HOT BLOND OR THE SMOKIN' BRUNETTE?
EXIT
WHO CARES? I'D TAKE EITHER ONE OF THEM!
YOU ARE DEFEATED, FALSE PRINCE!
I DON'T FEEL GOOD...
SO, PRINCE CHARMING, HAVE YOU PROVEN THAT MY STEPSISTER IS THE MYSTERIOUS PRINCESS WHO LEFT BEHIND THIS ONYX GLASS SLIPPER?
UM... NO! I SHALL DO THAT HERE, BEFORE ALL THESE WITNESSES!

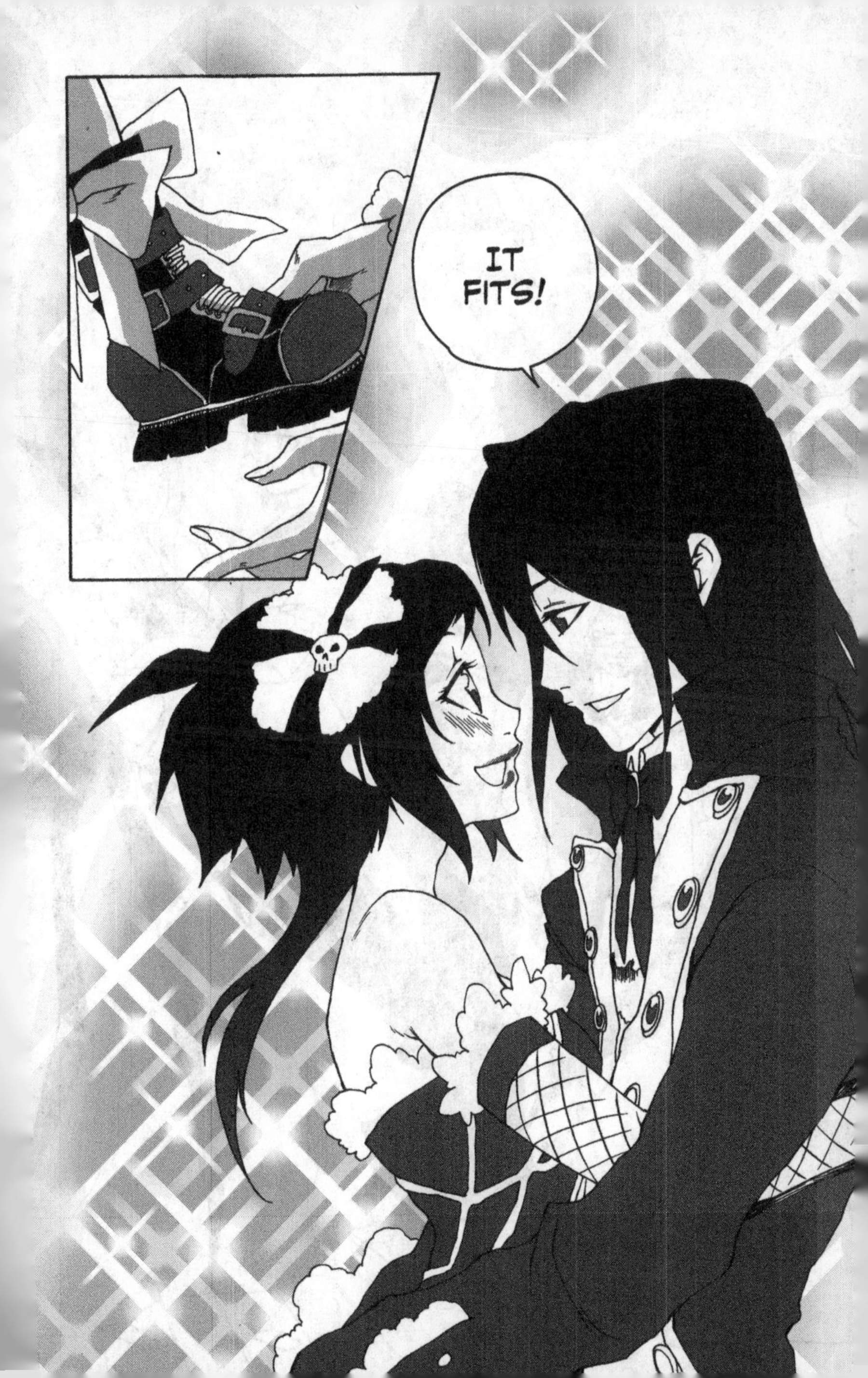
IT FITS!

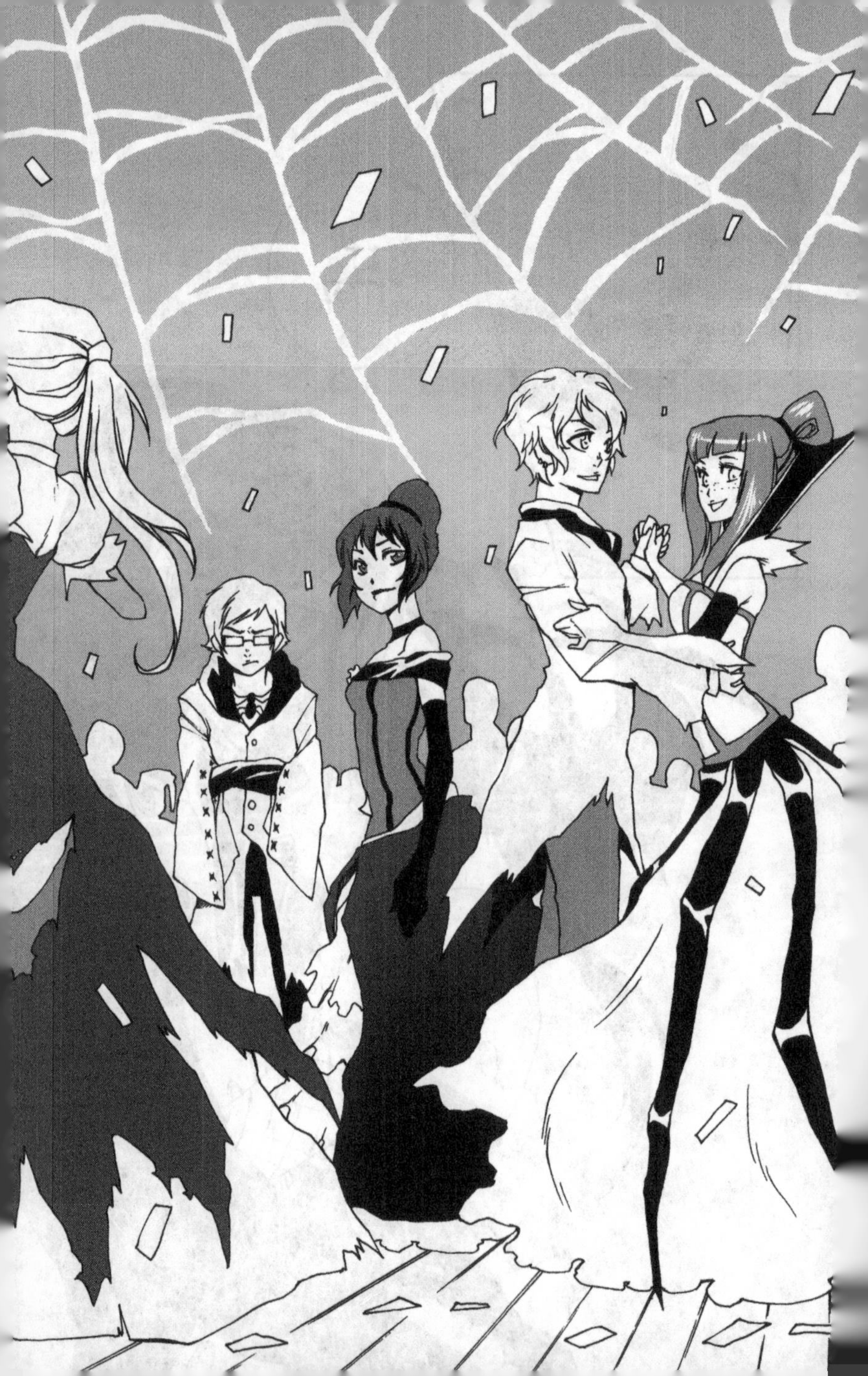

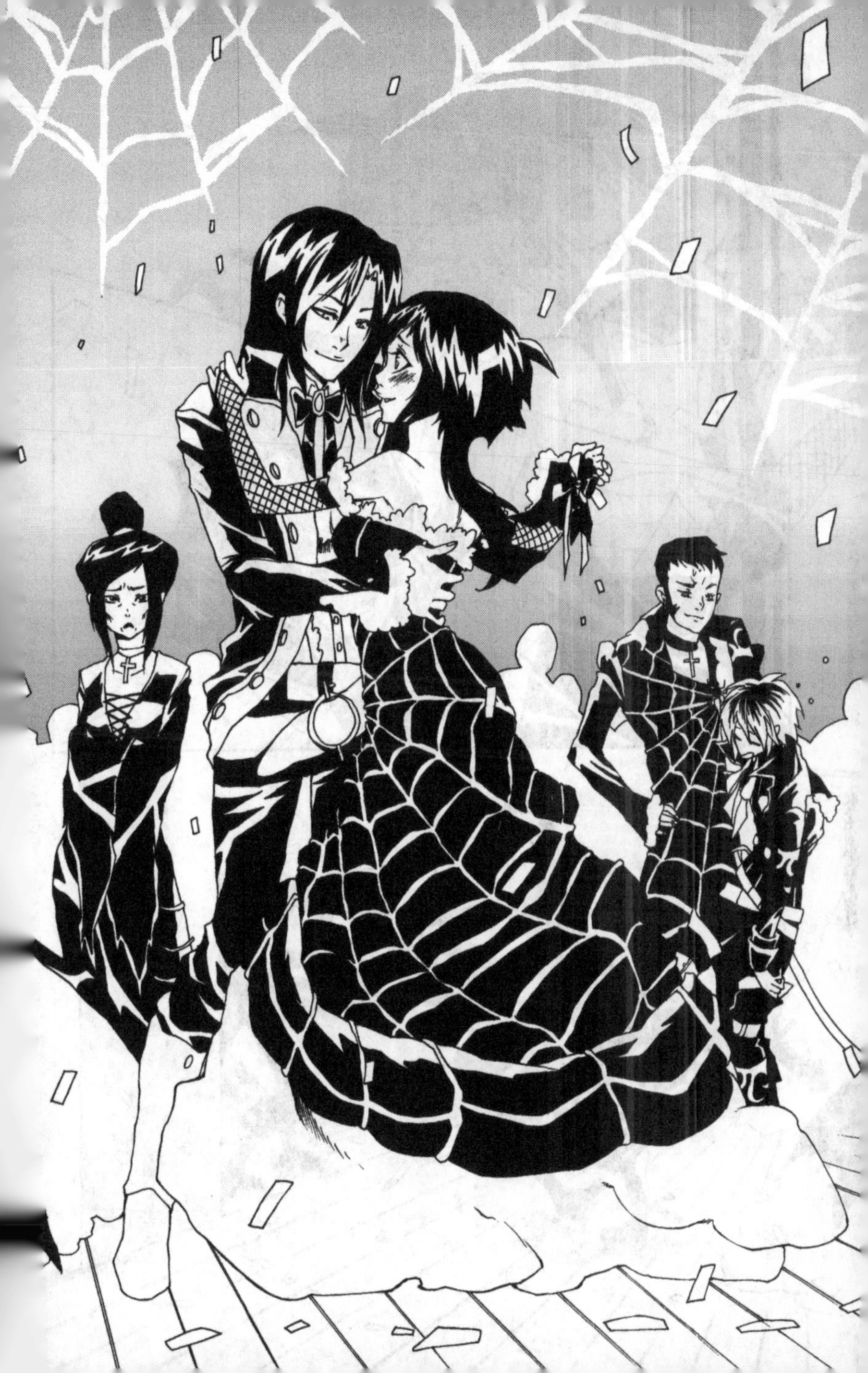

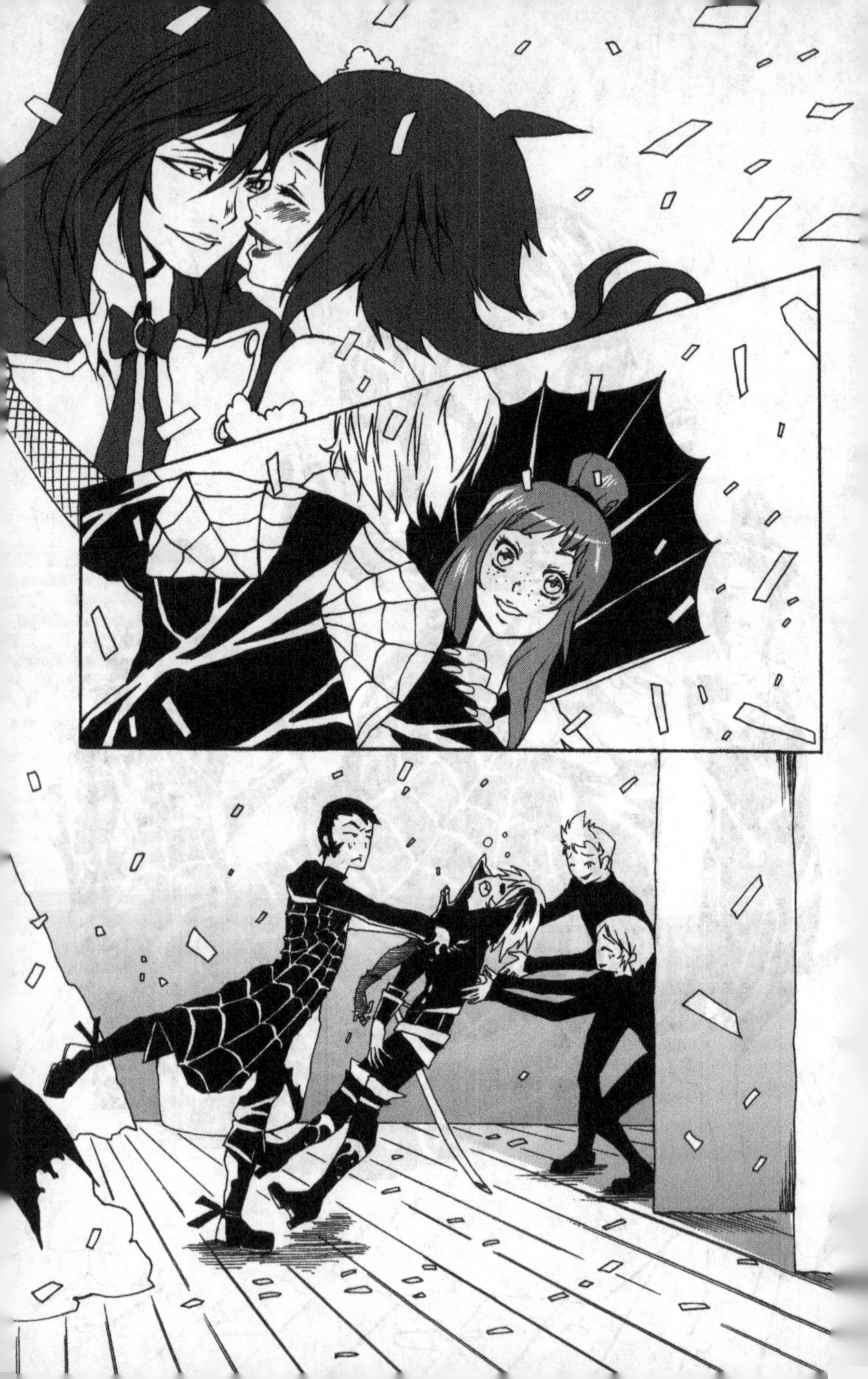

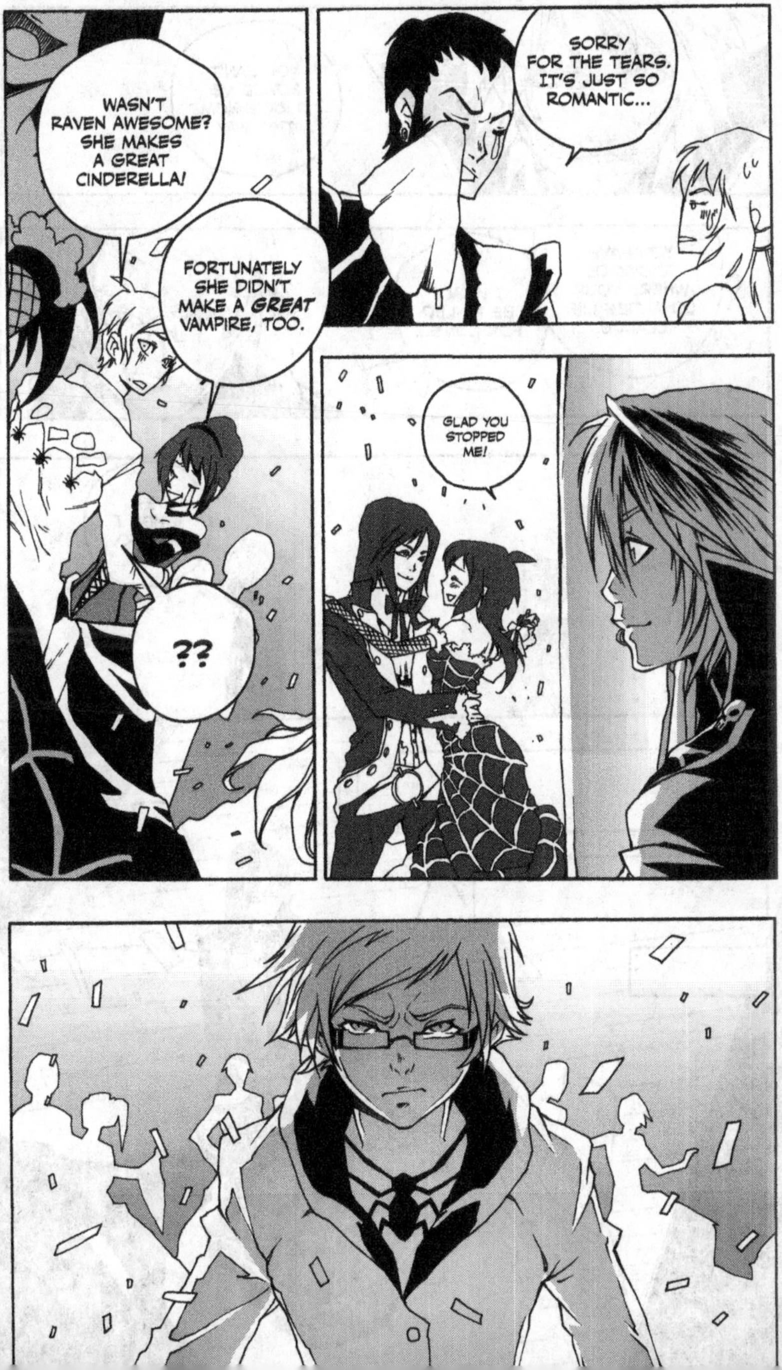
WASN'T RAVEN AWESOME? SHE MAKES A GREAT CINDERELLA!
FORTUNATELY SHE DIDN'T MAKE A *GREAT* VAMPIRE, TOO.
??
SORRY FOR THE TEARS. IT'S JUST SO ROMANTIC...
GLAD YOU STOPPED ME!

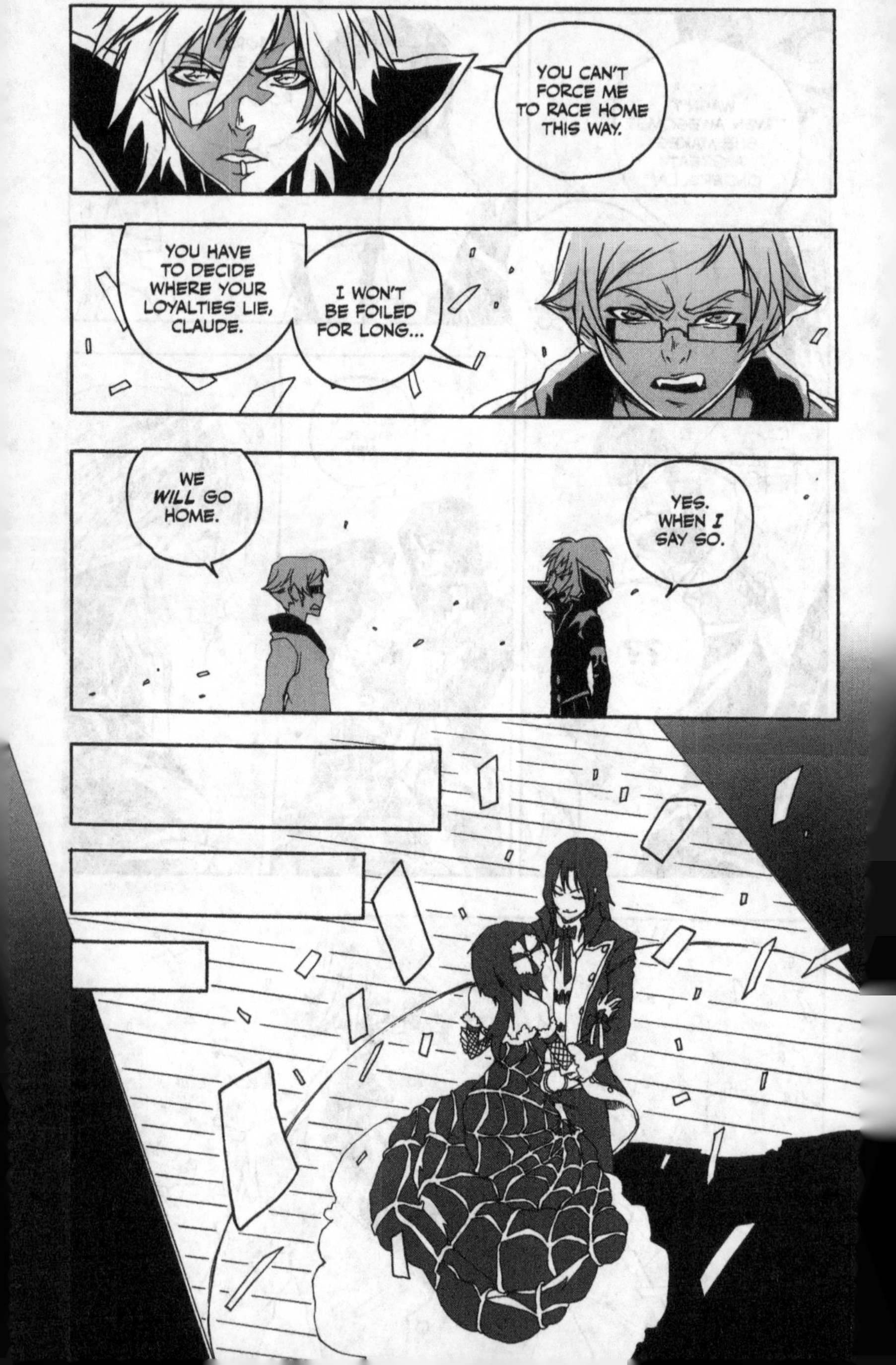
YOU CAN'T FORCE ME TO RACE HOME THIS WAY.
YOU HAVE TO DECIDE WHERE YOUR LOYALTIES LIE, CLAUDE.
I WON'T BE FOILED FOR LONG...
WE WILL GO HOME.
YES. WHEN I SAY SO.

OKAY, SO MAYBE THE PLAY DIDN'T GO EXACTLY AS PLANNED...
...BUT THEY LIVED HAPPILY EVER AFTER.
AND SOMEDAY...
...MY VAMPIRE PRINCE AND I WILL LIVE HAPPILY ETERNALLY AFTER!
CLAP
CLAP
CLAP
CLAP
THE END

Dear Guys and Ghouls,

I had the best time writing and publishing *Vampire Kisses: Graveyard Games*. It was so much fun to see the whole process from the early sketches to the final art. Raven's unique style comes to life once again and Alexander and Claude are as hot as ever. Claude's now full-vampire gang practically springs off the page as they pursue trouble.

I know many of you are fangtastic artists. I love what you have sent me, and I keep all the art in my fan art collection.

In the following pages I want to present some new fan art by a selection of the talented young artists who submitted. I'm excited to share these pieces with you.

Enjoy, and keep reading!

Many fangs,

Ellen :)

Fan Art

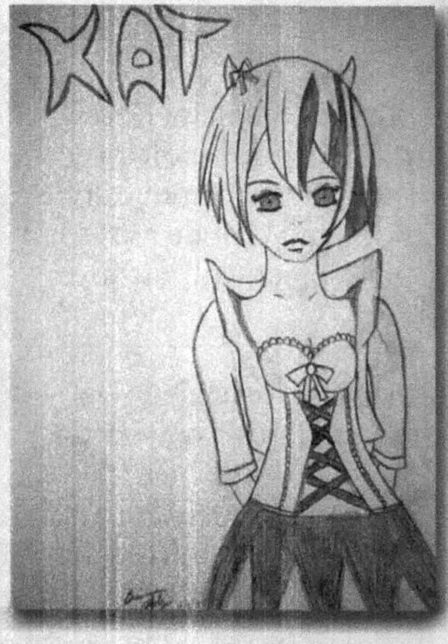
KAT

By Brianna Holguin

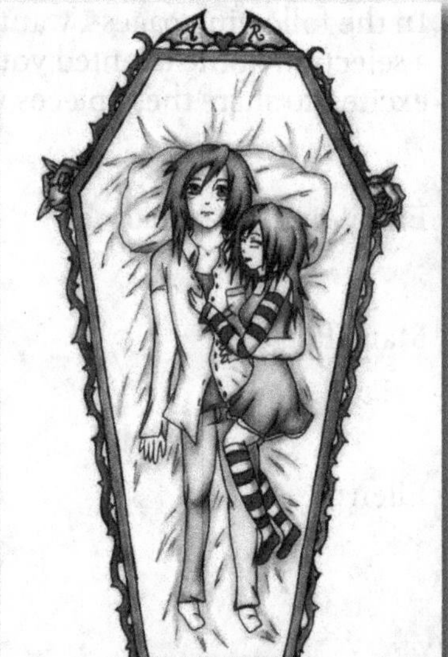

By Vampy Grave

Fan Art

By Catie Ann

By Aj Ureta

FAN ART

By Genesis Pena

FAN ART

By Jessica Morgan

By Haley Trice

Fan Art

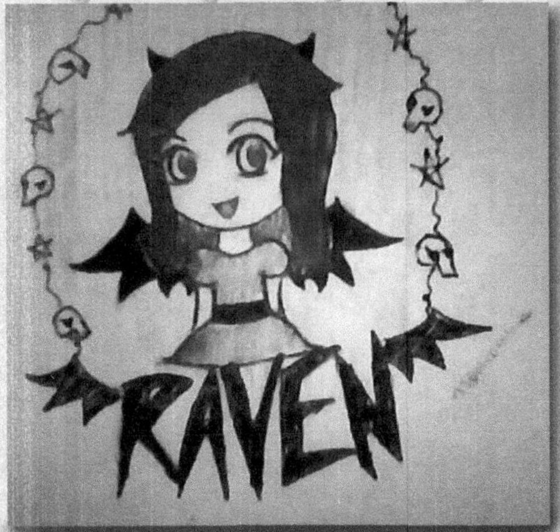
RAVEN

By Monica Smith

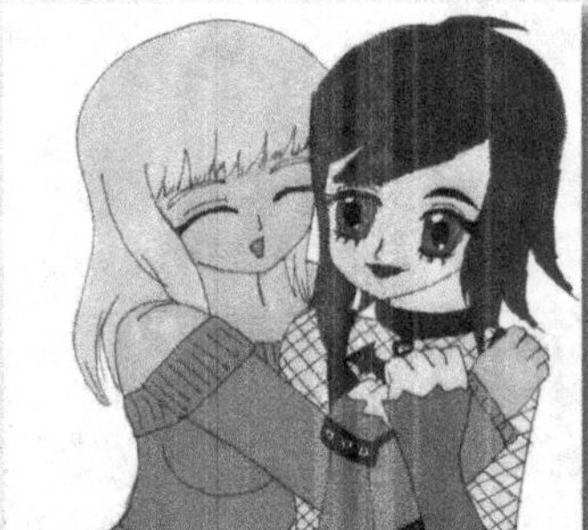

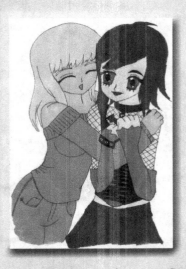

By Jessica Alonso

FAN ART

By Sharmaine Encabo

Fan Art

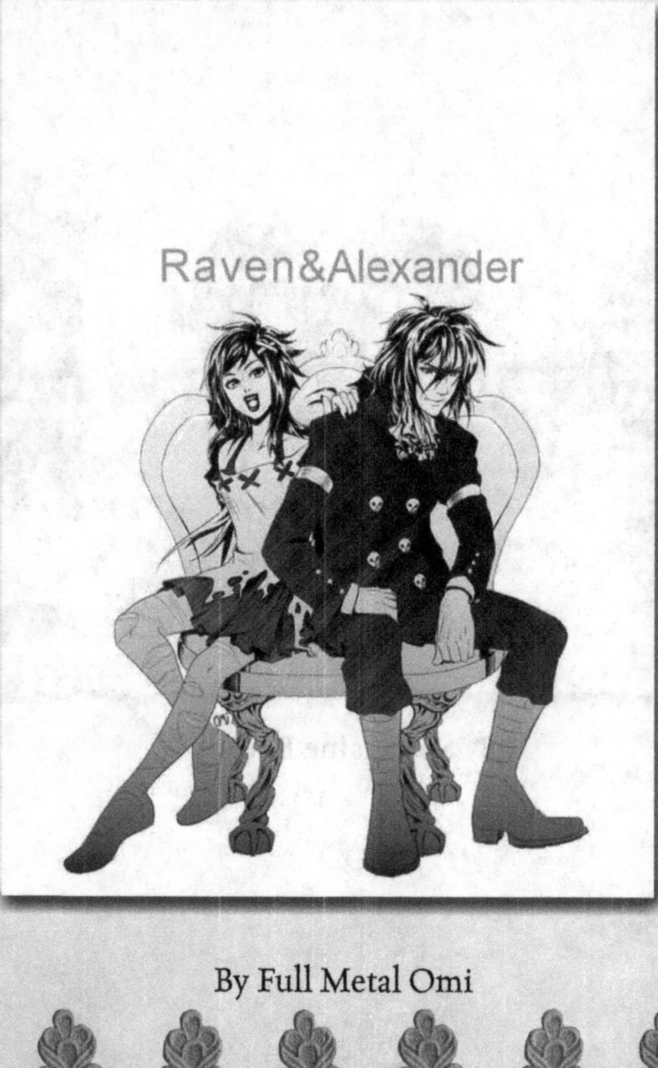
Raven&Alexander

By Full Metal Omi

Fan Art

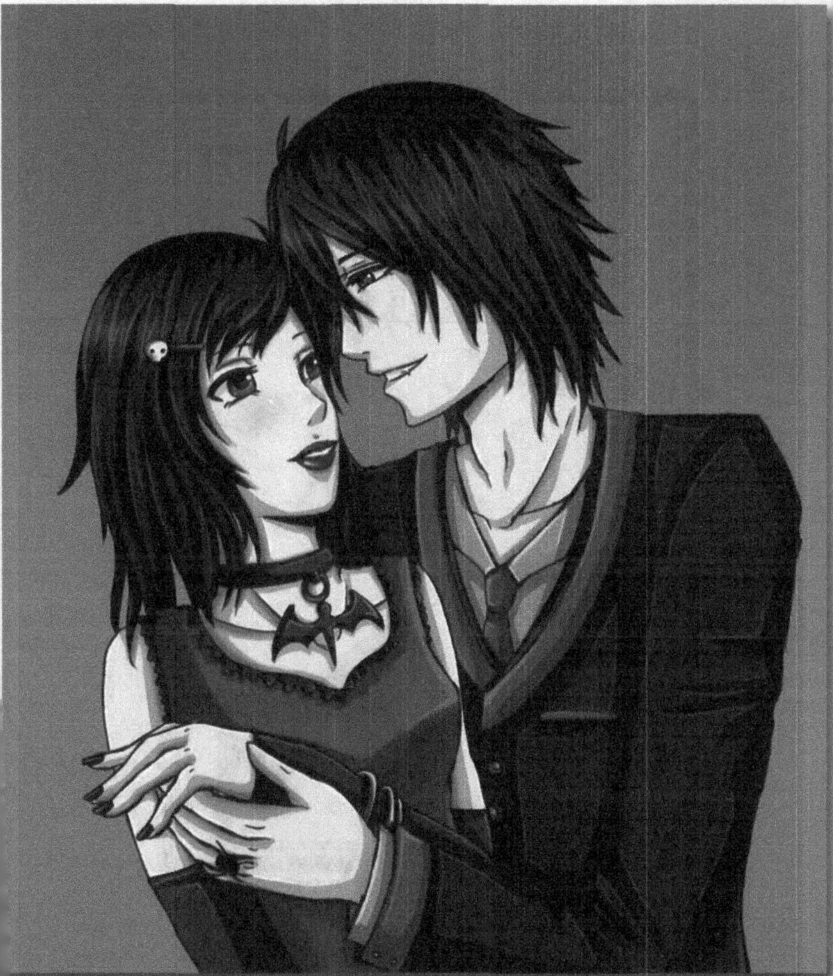

By Sami Arrington

FAN ART

TRIPP & KAT

By Karen Vasquez

FAN ART

By Homura Kuchiki

By Kitana Takano

Claude

KEEP READING FOR MORE
OF RAVEN AND ALEXANDER'S
ELECTRIFYING ROMANCE IN:

VAMPIRE KISSES 8

CRYPTIC CRAVINGS

1

Blood Exchange

I had to admit it, Dullsville was no longer dull.

In fact, for me, Raven Madison, the morbidly monotonous town I'd grown up in had finally become the most exciting place on earth.

Not only was I madly in love with my vampire boyfriend, Alexander Sterling, but I'd witnessed for the first time in my vampire-obsessed existence an actual vampire bite. The only problem was that it wasn't my neck being bitten.

This wouldn't have been such a tragedy for me if the recipient of the bite had been Onyx or Scarlet, the superfabulous Underworldy friends I'd met at the Coffin Club, but the bite was given to my own vampire adversary, a real vampire and gothic beauty, Luna Maxwell.

I'd been waiting almost a year to be bitten, since I'd met Alexander, not to mention my entire life of immortal dreaming, but for Luna it happened within hours of meeting another vampire. That night, on Alexander's lawn, there had been an amazing group of partygoers—a handful of vampires mixing with the mortal local students. It was something I'd never thought would happen. While playing spin the bloody bottle, Luna and Sebastian, Alexander's handsome and hapless best friend, had locked eyes and gone in for more than a juicy lip-lock. His fangs pierced the soft flesh of her swanlike neck. Luna had stared up at me, her eyes dreamy, as if she were some hippie tripping at Woodstock. She glowed even more radiantly than she normally did as a morbid fairy girl fashionista. Most of the partyers missed the action, but those who saw the bite passed it off as a macabre prank.

Sebastian had since moved out of the Mansion, and the rest of the vampires were perhaps back in Romania, or haunting the Coffin Club several towns away in Hipsterville. We hadn't gotten word of their whereabouts, and I hadn't seen any signs of them at Dullsville's cemetery.

For the week following the love bite, I tried my best to get Alexander's mind off his disappointment. He was suffering because his best friend's impulsive behavior had put not only himself and Luna but even Alexander's secret in possible jeopardy. Happily, tonight Alexander was finally obliging.

We were lying in the grass on a hilltop that overlooked Dullsville. From there we were able to see the glamorous sites of Hipsterville, such as the graveyard, but I didn't notice them because I was lost in Alexander's lips.

I hadn't broached the tender subject of receiving my own love bite with Alexander in a while. But I saw this evening, alone with him and without distractions, as my chance for another try.

Fiddling with a link chain hanging from his black leather belt, I asked, "Do you think it's easier for Sebastian to fall for a girl and to take her blood?"

Alexander furrowed his brow.

"Or was it easy to do what he did at the party," I continued, "because Luna is already a vampire?"

"I can't speak for someone else."

"But I want to know what you think."

Alexander paused. "Then yes, I think it's easier for him. He is very impulsive." His tone was clear and matter-of-fact.

I sighed.

Alexander reached for me and guided my hair back from my face with his fingers. "It means more to me than that," he said directly.

"Me too," I said, touching his shoulder. "But what if I were already a vampire?" I asked thoughtfully. "What if someone else turns me—not on sacred ground—so I won't be bonded to them forever. But—"

Alexander withdrew his arm. "That's what you want?" he asked, his voice almost cracking. "To be turned—by anyone? Sebastian? Or Jagger?"

"I was just thinking out loud," I quickly refuted. I didn't

realize I'd hurt him.

"It would be that easy to have someone turn you? Just like that?"

When Alexander posed it to me like that, my fantastical solution didn't seem so romantic or practical in its reality.

"That's not what I meant."

"Are you so sure? You'd have my best friend bite you? Or worse, my longtime enemy?"

"But now you are friends with Jagger," I said, trying to lighten the mood.

"That's not the point."

"Of course not—I only want you. . . . I was just trying to take the pressure off of you. I was just thinking out loud."

Alexander didn't seem pleased with my response and continued to stare off into the distance.

"Let's be clear," I said, turning his face toward me. "I want to be a vampire. But I want to be one with you."

He barely broke a smile.

"I'm turning eighteen soon and you'll be seventeen," he finally said. "It's something I think about, Raven. You. Me. Our future. I want you to know that. But this is something that is life changing—especially for you."

"I know." I gazed up at my dreamy boyfriend's eyes. His face was so handsome in the moonlight. "But will you really be eighteen? Or something else, in vampire years?"

"I will really be eighteen," he said.

"And then the next year?"

"Uh . . . nineteen," he said as if I should have known.

"But you are immortal."

"The aging process will slow down. But that's many, many years from now. Is that what you are worried about? Us not being able to be together unless you are immortal, too?"

"I've always wanted to be a vampire, since I was born," I said to him urgently. "But then when I met you, I wanted to be one—to be turned by you. To have the covenant ceremony that you didn't have with Luna in Romania. A beautiful wrought-iron lace trellis with a coffin and two goblets, on sacred ground. I'd be dressed in a black corset dress and hold black roses. You'd be wearing a black suit and have a black rose in your jacket lapel. We'd say a few Romanian words and drink from each other's glasses. Then, you'd turn me."

"Wow!" he said with a laugh. "I guess you have thought about it, too."

"But it's not about me living forever. It's about me being romantically bonded with you and experiencing the world as a vampire." I stared up at him, the stars shining above him.

I waited for him to laugh, to think my ideas were childish and naive.

Instead he leaned into me and stared straight into my eyes, his chocolate ones dreamy and seductive. "There is a yearning that I have for you—that goes deeper than love,"